I0577164

Thornton Kirkland Lothrop

William Henry Seward

Thornton Kirkland Lothrop

William Henry Seward

ISBN/EAN: 9783337011543

Printed in Europe, USA, Canada, Australia, Japan

Cover: Foto ©Raphael Reischuk / pixelio.de

More available books at **www.hansebooks.com**

American Statesmen

WILLIAM HENRY SEWARD

BY

THORNTON KIRKLAND LOTHROP

BOSTON AND NEW YORK
HOUGHTON, MIFFLIN AND COMPANY
The Riverside Press, Cambridge
1899

Copyright, 1896 and 1899,
By THORNTON KIRKLAND LOTHROP.

Copyright, 1899,
By HOUGHTON, MIFFLIN & CO.

All rights reserved.

PREFACE

THE obvious difficulty of giving within the limits of a single volume an adequate account of a statesman whose public career extended over a period of forty years, is increased in the case of Seward by the fact that the period of his political life was substantially coincident with that of the great contest for supremacy between the free and slave States, from the time of the passage of the Missouri Compromise to the close of the civil war, and with that of the subsequent struggle as to reconstruction. His first vote was cast in the year after the admission of Missouri as a slave State; he took his seat in the New York Senate in January, 1831; he resigned the office of secretary of state of the United States in March, 1869; for twenty-eight of the intervening years he was in the public service, — for four years in the Senate of New York, and for four years the governor of that State. He was a senator of the United States during the twelve years in which the contest between freedom and slavery was carried on in Congress with the utmost bitterness of language and feeling; and then, entering Lincoln's cabinet as secretary of state, he held that office until the inauguration of General Grant as president.

In the half century between the time when he came of age and his withdrawal from public life, there were many revolutions in political issues and parties, in most of which, if not in all, Seward played a leading part. His earliest published political speech predicted that in this country no "parties upon cardinal principles would again arise," but only those formed as to "questions of limited extent, or out of regard to men of differently estimated merit;" yet he himself, contradicting his own prophecy, spent many of the best years of his life in endeavoring to induce the voters of the North, either to support an existing party on account of its fidelity to the cardinal principle of freedom, or to unite in building up a new one, of which this principle should be the corner stone; and, circumstances and the mistaken passion and labors of his political opponents working with him, his efforts were at last crowned with success.

It was a long way, however, from the purely personal question between Clay, Adams, and Crawford in the presidential election of 1824, through the economic issues of the United States Bank, of internal improvements at the public expense, of the protection of American industry or a tariff for revenue only, to such fundamental political and moral problems as those connected with the extension or limitation of slavery, the nature and degree of our constitutional obligation as to the rendition of fugitive slaves, and other similar questions which convulsed the country in the decade from 1851 to 1860.

The mass of the people, both North and South, was averse to making party issues upon matters so closely connected with the whole frame of our government and with our national life, and it was only gradually and by slow degrees that these forced themselves to the front, and at last dominated and absorbed all our politics.

As to all these various political issues, Seward held decided opinions, he took a keen interest in them, and he became early a recognized party leader. It is of course impossible, in a work of this size, to give a detailed account of his public life; it is hoped, however, that enough has been said to enable the reader to see how he acquired his great hold upon the people, and earned the high place which he must always have in the history of our country.

No attempt has been made to describe his by no means undistinguished professional labors, or his personal, domestic, and social life, except so far as these may throw light on his public career; but while these omissions may affect the claim of the work as a complete biography, they will not, it is hoped, substantially diminish its value as a volume in the series of American Statesmen. In preparing this edition for publication the book has been carefully revised, some new matter has been added, and facts, never before published, giving a different character to Mr. Seward's letter to Mr. Lincoln of April 1, 1861, having come to my knowledge, parts of the fifteenth chapter have been materially modified.

T. K. L.

November, 1898.

CONTENTS

CONTENTS

ILLUSTRATIONS

WILLIAM HENRY SEWARD

CHAPTER I

YOUTH. — ADMISSION TO THE BAR. — FIRST STEPS
IN POLITICS

WILLIAM HENRY SEWARD was born on the
16th of May, 1801, in Florida, a village in the
town of Warwick, in the county of Orange, and
State of New York. His father, Dr. Samuel S.
Seward, was a physician of good standing, and
the first vice-president of the county medical society. Dr. Seward was a farmer as well as physician, and also the magistrate, storekeeper, banker,
and money-lender of the little place. He lived to
a good old age, dying after his son's election to
the Senate of the United States, in 1849.

The family was of New Jersey origin. John
Seward, the grandfather of William Henry, served
in the Revolution, beginning as captain, and ending his campaigns as colonel of the First Sussex
Regiment. Sussex is the northernmost county of
New Jersey, and Orange County lies on the southern border of New York, so that the migration of

Dr. Seward did not carry him far from his original home. He married a Miss Jennings from the neighborhood of Florida, and Seward speaks of his mother as a "person of excellent sense, gentleness, truthfulness and candor." William Henry was the fourth of six children, and, after the fashion of those days, was selected, as the least physically robust, to receive a college education. The village school, the academy at Goshen, and a term or two in a short-lived academy in Florida, gave him his preparatory training, and at the age of fifteen he passed the examination for the junior class at Union College, Schenectady; though the rules as to age at that institution compelled him to enter as sophomore.

Before going to college, Seward had taken his share of the household duties and labors at home. His father had three domestic servants (slaves, some of whom lived to a good old age and were Seward's pensioners to the end of their days); but William Henry drove the cows to pasture in the early morning and back again at night; he had the wood to chop and bring in, and other daily chores to do. He began his labors at dawn, and finished them at bedtime, about nine o'clock. At school he was a bright and studious boy, perhaps a bit of a prig. His first composition, an essay on Virtue, began: "Virtue is the best of all the vices." He refused, when at the academy, to join in a lock-out; at college he sought his tutor's aid that he might really get hold of his Latin, and was evidently desirous to make the most of his opportunities. He was not wanting, however, in the hasty temper or the audacity of youth; and when an instructor had, as Seward thought, treated him unfairly, he remonstrated, refused to recite, marched out of the class-room, left the college buildings and established himself in a hotel, declining to return until he had received an apology. The judicious intervention of Dr. Nott, then and for nearly half a century president of Union College, quickly settled the matter, and Seward went back to his work. This seems to have been his only collision with the authorities; but a little later in his college career troubles of another sort came upon him.

On his arrival in Schenectady he had been dissatisfied with the work of the traveling tailor who had furnished his wardrobe; and, that he might be dressed in a less rustic fashion, he had gone to the shops patronized by the students. His scanty allowance did not enable him to pay for this extravagance, his father would not help him, and his creditors became clamorous; so without consulting or even informing his family, he resolved to abandon his college career, and begin at once to make his own way in the world. He quietly left Schenectady, joined a friend who was engaged to teach at the South, and sailed with him for Savannah. His father, learning of his departure, started in pursuit, and endeavored unsuccessfully to intercept him in New York. Seward arrived

safely in Georgia, and obtained a position there as
the teacher of a newly established academy. His
father learned his whereabouts and wrote in a
rage to the trustees, threatening them with all the
terrors of the law if they continued to harbor the
delinquent, whom he described as "a much-in-
dulged son, who, without any just provocation,
had absconded from Union College, thereby dis-
gracing a well-acquired position, and plunging his
parents into profound shame and grief." Seward,
however, remained at his post as teacher until the
appointment and arrival of his successor, and then
returned home to pass six months studying law in
an attorney's office at Goshen. At the end of this
time he rejoined the senior class at Union College,
graduating with honor in 1820. His father upon
his return was far from killing the fatted calf for
this wandering son; he still declined to assist him
in paying the tailor's bills, and they were finally
discharged by installments from Seward's own
hard earnings. Writing of this after the lapse
of half a century, Seward says: "I would by no
means imply a present conviction that the fault
was altogether with my father. On the other
hand, I think now the fault was not altogether
mine." As, before his own exodus, two of his
brothers had already left home on account of
money difficulties with their father, there was
probably some justification for these conclusions.

On leaving college, Seward resumed the study
of the law, and occupied himself also with office

work and such other professional employment as
he could obtain in the inferior courts. He was
admitted to the bar at Utica in October, 1822.
His earnings while a student had not only enabled
him to cancel his college debts and to pay his way,
but left him sixty dollars with which to begin life.
He started at once for western New York, and at
Auburn accepted an offer of a partnership with
Elijah Miller, a leading lawyer of that town.
How far Mr. Miller was induced to make this proposal by his good opinion of Seward's abilities,
and how much he was influenced by his knowledge
of the mutual interest in each other of his daughter
Frances and the young lawyer, one cannot tell,
but the legal partnership was speedily followed by
a closer relation between them, Seward marrying
Frances Miller on the 20th of October, 1824.
His marriage was a satisfaction, and his professional success was an agreeable disappointment to
his father, who had dismissed him, when he left
home to begin his practice, with a present of fifty
dollars, and "the assurance of his constant expectation that he would come back too soon."

Seward's first appearance in court, after his
admission to the bar, was in defense of a convict
just discharged from the state prison at Auburn,
who had been warned to leave town at once. The
temptation of an open house-door was too much
for him. He went in and began to steal, but was
disturbed in his operations and only got a few
trifles. He was indicted for the larceny of a

quilted holder and a piece of calico. Seward
proved that the holder was *sewed*, not *quilted*, and
that the bit of cloth was *jean*, not *calico*. The
variance caused his client's acquittal, and his success in this case was followed by a considerable
amount of criminal business. Seward was a careful draughtsman, taking pains, not merely with
the substance but with the clerkly appearance of
every instrument that left his office, so that he
was much employed in this way also, and in his
first year his professional income exceeded the five
hundred dollars guaranteed him by Mr. Miller.

In 1828, he was nominated by Governor Clinton for surrogate of Cayuga County; but while
he was in Albany, awaiting the confirmation of
his appointment by the Senate, a meeting in favor
of the renomination of President John Quincy
Adams was held there. Clinton had just come
out for Jackson, and a decided majority of the
New York senators were Jackson men. Seward
was for Adams. He went to the Adams meeting,
and in consequence of this his nomination was rejected. His name was never again submitted to a
senate for its action until more than thirty years
afterward, when Lincoln nominated him as secretary of state.

In these early years of his professional life, he
took a lively interest in the militia of the State
of New York. He was the adjutant of the troop
which met Lafayette on his arrival at Auburn in
1825, and accompanied him on his night journey

eastward to Syracuse. A few years later he organized a company of artillery, contributed largely to its equipment, and was chosen its captain. By successive promotions he attained the rank of brigadier-general, but declined the major-general's commission which was subsequently offered him.

Seward's family were Jeffersonian Republicans, and in the divisions which rent that party in the State of New York into personal factions, — on the one side the Tammany men, or "Buck-tails," as they were called, supporting Vice-President Tompkins; and on the other the followers of Governor Clinton, "the Clintonians," — Seward at first remained with his father on the side of Tammany. When Vice-President Tompkins visited Schenectady, Seward, then in the senior class, delivered an address of welcome on behalf of the students who were of the Vice-President's party; and in his last college term he wrote an essay to prove that the Erie Canal, then in process of construction under Clinton's auspices, was an impossibility; and that, even if it could be completed, it would be the financial ruin of the State. But he had never been quite satisfied with his father's explanation of Washington's dissent from, and Hamilton's opposition to, the Republican party, which Dr. Seward attributed to an alleged failure in Washington's intellectual power and independence, and to Hamilton's desire for a monarchy. Moreover, his original journey to Auburn had opened his eyes to the importance as well as to the practi-

cability of the Erie Canal; and so it happened by
a gradual process of change and development, that
in 1824 he cast his vote for De Witt Clinton as
governor, and definitively abandoned the party he
had been educated to support.

In the summer of 1824, before his marriage,
Seward, with his father and mother and Mr. Miller's family, made a journey to Niagara. As they
were driving through Rochester on their way home,
a wheel came off the coach, and most of the party
were thrown out. Among the passers-by attracted
by the accident was Thurlow Weed, then a resident of Rochester, "the editor of a dingy weekly
Clintonian newspaper, called the ' Monroe Telegram,' — one of the poorest and worst dressed men
in the town, living in a cheap house in an obscure
part of the village;" but even then wielding a
very decisive power in the politics of western New
York. Weed was helpful to them in their misfor-
tune; and this was Seward's first meeting with
the man whose friendship and influence played so
important a part in his whole political career.

Not long after his return from this journey,
Seward wrote his first published political paper,
an Address of the county convention at Auburn,
in October, 1824. This address was a bold on-
slaught on the "Albany Regency," a combination
of a dozen politicians, who, under the direction of
Martin Van Buren, dictated for many years the
nominations and policy of the Democratic party
of the State of New York. On the fourth of

July, 1825, Seward spoke at Auburn, and something of what he said is interesting as a summary of his own convictions at that time and his forecast of the political future: —

"The Missouri question is settled and almost forgotten; the tariff bill has become a law; the sceptre has passed from the Ancient Dominion, and the union of these States is still unshaken. Believe me, fellow citizens, those men's wishes for confusion far outrun their wisdom, who believe, or profess to believe, that parties upon cardinal principles will again arise. The time and the occasion for these parties have alike gone by, and the attempt to rouse the vindictive feelings which once existed is as idle as the hope to call spirits from the vasty deep. New parties are yearly formed and as often dissolved, because they arise upon questions of limited extent, or out of regard to men of differently estimated merit. And such parties will succeed each other, as in rolling seas wave succeeds wave; but there will at times be a calm, and such light and transitory excitement will only serve to keep the political waters in healthful motion.

"Those, too, misapprehend the true interests of the people of these States, or their intelligence, who believe, or profess to believe, that a separation will ever take place between the North and South. The people of the North have been seldom suspected of a want of attachment to the Union, and those of the South have been much misrepresented by a few politicians of a stormy character, who have ever been unsupported by the people there. The North will not willingly give up the power they now have in the national councils, of gradually completing a work in which, whether united or separate, from proximity of territory, we shall ever be interested — the emancipation of slaves. And the South will never, even in a moment of resentment, expose themselves to a war with the North, while they have such a great domestic population of slaves, ready to embrace any opportunity to assert their freedom and inflict their revenge. . . . If, indeed, these States were to be divided by a geographical line, that line would be drawn along the Alleghany Mountains or the Mississippi River."

The sphere of Seward's political activity for the next few years did not extend beyond the limits of his town and county, and it is not till 1828 that we find him appearing on a larger field of public affairs. In August of that year he presided over a convention of the young men of the State favorable to the reëlection of John Quincy Adams to the presidency. The convention numbered more than three hundred and fifty members, a body of earnest, active workers with strong political convictions. It was one of the last of the state assemblages of the National Republican party, which was utterly routed and dispersed by the Democrats under Jackson in the presidential election of that year. Upon its disappearance Seward joined, and

soon became active in, the anti-Masonic party in
western New York, of which Thurlow Weed was
a moving spirit. The rise and progress of this
party is one of the most curious episodes in our
state and national politics.

In 1826 there lived in Batavia, in the State of
New York, one William Morgan, a most humble
and insignificant person, a Freemason, whose extreme poverty tempted him to publish a book, announced as a revelation of the secrets of the order,
by the sale of which he expected to make a good
deal of money. Some over-zealous and misguided
fanatics among the Masons, learning of his proposed publication, arrested him on a frivolous pretext, hurried him from place to place, and at last
procured his confinement in a deserted fort at
Niagara. Here he utterly disappeared, having
been, if one may trust the evidence, taken off in
a boat and drowned in the waters of Lake Ontario.
All attempts to detect and convict the authors of
this crime were baffled by the powerful association
of which they were members; but there was no
anti-Masonic party before the summer of 1827,
when a gentleman who had been the treasurer of
the town of Rochester ever since its incorporation,
and to whose reëlection there was no open opposition, was beaten at the polls by a candidate whose
nomination even had been previously unknown.
For this political overturn the Freemasons claimed
the credit. The defeated officer was not a Mason;
he had by chance been an eye-witness of something

subsequently shown to have been connected with
Morgan's disappearance; and he had also taken a
prominent part in the investigations set on foot to
discover the criminals. The result of this petty
local election, and the consequent exultation of the
Masons, angered the people of the village and
county, and in the autumn anti-Masonic candidates were nominated and elected to the state
Assembly. The next year (1828) the anti-Masons
extended and perfected their political organization;
they obtained control of the western counties of
New York; they captured some isolated towns
elsewhere, and attracted the attention of the public throughout the State. They held a convention,
nominated a candidate for governor, and succeeded
in choosing five out of the thirty-two state senators,
and seventeen members of the Assembly. The
"Anti-Masonic Enquirer," Thurlow Weed's paper,
had a circulation not merely in the western, middle and northern counties of New York, but in
some parts of Pennsylvania and Ohio. There was
no general state election in 1829. In March,
1830, the "Albany Evening Journal" was established as an anti-Masonic paper under Weed's
editorship; and a national convention of the party,
which Seward attended, was held at Philadelphia
in September.

In the following year Seward came to New England for the first time in his life. Arriving in
Boston on the anniversary of Morgan's abduction,
he went to the anti-Masonic committee room, where

he was called upon to speak, and found himself
to his surprise "preaching politics" in that city.
He visited John Quincy Adams at Quincy, and
the acquaintance thus begun ripened into a warm
and enduring friendship. He found Mr. Adams
an anti-Masonic candidate for Congress, "in-
tensely engaged in writing a bitter polemic against
Freemasonry." A little later there was a second
national anti-Masonic convention at Baltimore, to
which Seward was also a delegate. Here Chief
Justice Marshall occupied a seat on the platform,
and William Wirt (who had been Monroe's attorney-general) was nominated as a candidate for
president. It was known, when this was done,
that Henry Clay intended to be a presidential candidate; but he had already expressed himself so
strongly against the anti-Masons, that his nomination by them was impossible. It was certain,
therefore, that the opposition in New York to
General Jackson's reëlection would be divided,
and it was feared that it would therefore be impossible to carry the State against him. The result
justified this apprehension. Jackson had a decisive majority in New York, and both in the electoral college and in the country made considerable
gains over his vote of four years before. Clay
sustained an overwhelming defeat. Wirt received
only the four electoral votes of Vermont. The
two parties representing the opposition to Jackson
were utterly crushed, and his removal of the government deposits from the United States Bank in

the following year failed to reanimate either of
them in New York. The anti-Masons sent only
nine members to the Assembly, as against thirty-
five the year before, and at a conference of the
leaders in December, 1833, it was unanimously
agreed that the party was at an end.

The anti-Masonic party owed its origin and its
strength to the conviction of the leading young
men of western New York that the existence of a
secret society, whose members were bound to one
another by an obligation which had been able to
paralyze the exertions of counsel, to shut the
mouths of witnesses or compel them to perjure
themselves, to unnerve the arm of justice and to
override and corrupt all departments of the government, was inconsistent with the safety, and even
threatened the existence, of a popular government.
Many men of distinction, ability, and experience
shared these views, and supported the party; among
them were Chief Justice Marshall and Judge
Story, John Quincy Adams, John C. Calhoun,
William Henry Harrison, Richard Rush, and Edward Everett. The extent of their feeling about
the matter may be judged from the fact that ex-
President Adams and Judge Story seriously considered whether such secrecy as there is about the
college Greek-letter societies ought not, on public
grounds, to be prohibited.

A national party, however, could not be built
up on a solitary instance either of the open defi-
ance or secret evasion of the law in one section of

a single State. Though the popular excitement
in New York and the neighboring States, caused
by the Morgan affair, was natural, yet in their attacks upon the Masonic orders the anti-Masons
overlooked for the time the benevolent purposes of
the organization, and applied to it a general proposition, that, "Secret societies, composed of members bound together by unlawful oaths, and extended over the whole land, are opposed to the
genius of our government, subversive of the laws,
and inconsistent with private rights and the public welfare."

Seward joined the anti-Masons, as he himself
says, because he thought them the only political
organization, having any life, which was opposed
to Jackson, Calhoun, and Van Buren, three political leaders whose policy seemed to him to involve
"not only the loss of our national system of revenue, and of enterprises of state and national improvement, but also the future disunion of the
States, and ultimately the universal prevalence of
slavery." It was as the representative of this
short-lived but vigorous party that he made his
entrance into public office, being elected in the
autumn of 1830 to the Senate of the State.

The New York Senate at that time consisted of
only thirty-two members, each chosen for four
years, their terms expiring in rotation, so that
neither the whole Senate nor more than one member from a district was changed in any one year.
Seward, when he took his seat there in January,

1831, was only twenty-nine years old, small and slender, with blue eyes, light sandy hair, a smooth face, and a youthful air and expression which made him appear even younger than he was. He was one of a very small minority, the majority being all members of, or dependent on, the Albany Regency, the all-powerful central force of the New York Democracy. He had had no previous experience in public affairs, while nearly all his fellow senators were not only older and more mature, but were familiar with their position and its labors; and he was for a time diffident, embarrassed and silent. His first set speech was an argument for a reform in the militia system; the changes he then advocated were afterwards substantially adopted, and their value was shown in the prompt response of New York to President Lincoln's call for troops in April, 1861. The closing passage of this maiden speech of Seward's, though it may have been a mere rhetorical flight, has about it, in view of later events, a curious, prophetic ring, when he speaks of "the military spirit which brought the nation into existence, and will be able to carry us through the dark and perilous ways of national calamity yet unknown to us, but which must at some time be trodden by all nations."

During his term in the Senate, he was an earnest supporter of the first law passed in New York abolishing imprisonment for debt except in cases of fraud; and an early and strenuous advocate for the enactment of general laws, — such as are now

found in the statute books of most States, — giving to all citizens the right to form business corpo-
rations, instead of creating such companies as a
favor by special charter.

At this time, and down to the adoption of the
Constitution of 1846, the Senate of New York was
not merely a branch of the legislative department;
it had also judicial functions. Like the English
House of Lords, it was the court of last resort;
and a considerable portion of Seward's time was
taken up by his judicial labors. The work was
excellent professional training; he was interested
in it, and discharged its duties conscientiously, and
with distinct ability and independence.

In the summer of 1833, Seward, at his father's
invitation, accompanied him to Europe. The account of his travels has no especial interest to-day,
aside from a visit which he made to Lafayette at
La Grange. He returned in season for his last
winter's work as senator.

The presidential election of 1824 had been purely
a personal contest. No one of the series of resolutions recommending the various candidates suggested any difference in their political opinions;
and though in the campaign of 1828 the friends of
Jackson attacked President Adams's position on
the tariff, and on questions of internal improvements, no distinction could be drawn between
Jackson and the President on these points, since
Jackson had voted for all the measures of the kind
that Adams supported. Jackson's first term was

characterized by discussions and divisions as to the tariff and internal improvements, and by the opening of his attack on the United States Bank. Before his second election a convention of the young men of the National Republican party had adopted a series of resolutions, declaring adequate protection to American industry to be indispensable to the prosperity of the country, and that a uniform system of internal improvements, sustained and supported by the general government, was an important security for the harmony, strength and permanency of the republic. Yet it may fairly be said, taking the whole country together, that the question of personal loyalty to Jackson entered into the campaign of 1832 at least as largely as any matter of public policy. The union of the opposition, which was divided into National Republicans and anti-Masons, would not have changed the result.

Jackson's decisive majority authorized him, as he thought, to carry on a personal government for the next four years and to make war in such a way as seemed to him effectual, without regard to constitutional or legal limitations, upon any policy or institution in which he disbelieved, or which was supported by men who withstood his imperious will. The opposition, demoralized and disheartened by its overwhelming defeat in 1832, so far rallied two years later as to unite in the formation of the Whig party, the fundamental articles of whose political creed were the support of a policy of internal improvements, protection to American industry, and a national bank.

Of this new party Seward was the candidate for governor in 1834. He failed of an election, and returning to Auburn resumed the practice of the law. His four years in the state Senate had strengthened him in every way; the life had enlarged his horizon; the constant intercourse with men of more experience than himself, and discussions in public and private, had developed him; his position as a judge not merely gave him the opportunity to hear, but required him to listen to and to weigh the arguments of all the leading lawyers of the State; and this legal work was on a higher plane than his previous practice at the bar. His absence had rather improved than injured his standing as a lawyer; he was at once full of business, and was soon overworked. The summer of 1835 he spent in traveling for the benefit of his wife's health.

In June, 1836, he became the agent of some gentlemen who had purchased of the Holland Company its lands in Chautauqua County, in the extreme southwest of the State of New York. The settlers on these lands were to pay for them by installments, and only received their deeds when the final payments were made. The gentlemen for whom Seward was acting bought the rights of the Holland Company in these lands, and then got into difficulties with the settlers, who were refusing to pay and were fast becoming disorderly and dangerous. To deal with them required both firmness and forbearance, good sense, tact, kindness of heart and manner, and an evident disposition to do exact justice. The work necessitated a more or less prolonged residence in the county, and was Seward's most engrossing occupation until his nomination and election as governor by the Whigs of New York, in the autumn of 1838.

CHAPTER II

THE Chautauqua affairs had been so far settled in the previous year that the financial crisis of 1837 had not seriously affected them, and when he entered upon his duties as governor, Seward thought himself free from all personal and business anxieties.

His election meant a revolution in New York politics. For forty years there had been no governor who was not a Democrat; but though the Whigs had now carried the State, the Senate was still Democratic, and could control both the legislation and appointments to office. It was not till 1840 that Seward's own party had command, and in the last year of his second term (1842) he was again confronted by a hostile, not to say vindictive, majority in both branches of the legislature.

During his four years as governor, the State spent many millions in public improvements. The Erie Canal was enlarged, new canals were built, and state aid was given to railways and other similar enterprises. For only a small part of this legislation were the Whigs really responsible.

Most of it they received as an inheritance from their Democratic predecessors.[1]   .

The Erie Canal was De Witt Clinton's scheme, and its success, from the outset, was so overwhelming that it is not strange that it gave rise to all sorts of similar schemes, of varying merit and demerit. Seward was an ardent, perhaps an indiscriminate advocate of all these. He believed in internal improvements, in constructing either by the State itself, or with the aid of the State, all manner of ways of communication by land and by water, railways and canals, from north to south, from east to west, between tide-water and the lakes, through the great valleys of central New York, to the coal and iron fields within and on her borders. Some of the works which he favored

---

[1] Seward says that of the state debt of $30,000,000, in 1844, all but about $4,000,000 originated under Democratic administrations (*Works*, iii. p. 365); and Hammond, the historian of New York, and a Democrat, admits that most of the debt was contracted and sanctioned by Democratic legislatures and governors; though he explains that they were forced to do this in order to keep their power, as the people were so eager for public works that they would have brought in the Whigs, had the Democracy shown any faltering in promoting them. In a letter of January 30, 1844, Seward writes: "With unimportant exceptions every one of these contracts was made by the statesmen who now disavow and disown them. . . . The same statesmen who now denounce these works (the enlargement of the Erie Canal and the New York and Erie Railroad) are the same persons who called the latter enterprise into existence by a loan of $3,000,000. An intervening administration [his own] added no new enterprise, and only executed the contracts which it found in existence." — *Works*, iii. pp. 392, 393.

may have been premature; he may have crowded and hurried them more than the finances of the State would warrant; some may not have been in themselves good paying investments; but the policy which inaugurated and fostered them was broad and far-sighted, and they one and all have enabled the State to reap the full benefit of its admirable geographical situation, and have helped to make the city of New York the seaboard metropolis of the New World.

The necessity of public education in a community governed by universal suffrage was a cardinal article of Seward's political faith, and he was earnest in season and out of season in his endeavors to extend and develop the school system of New York. He saw the reluctance of the Roman Catholics to send their children to public schools not under their own control and where the peculiar tenets of their faith were not taught. For this and other reasons, he advocated the substitution of new school boards in the city of New York in the place of the close corporation, the "Committee of Public Instruction," a body exclusively Protestant, which had the entire control of its schools and school funds. He also earnestly recommended that sectarian or parochial schools should receive a share of the public money devoted to educational purposes. His support of the first of these measures drew upon him the hostility of many of his party in New York city; while his repeated recommendations of the latter policy alienated large bodies of Protestant voters. His suggestions of changes in legal procedure and practice, to lessen the delays and diminish the expense of litigation, were not favorably received by the bench or bar; and the opposition to him upon these various grounds, to say nothing of the hostility of the disappointed office-holders and their friends, caused the reduction of his personal majority in 1840, and contributed, with other national and more general causes, to the total overthrow of the Whig party in New York in the autumn of 1842.

During his public service as governor, the charities of the State found in him a warm friend; and its first lunatic asylum almost owed to him its existence. The records of his pardon papers, so far as they have been printed, are a most honorable testimony, not merely to the humanity and good sense which he brought to bear on each particular case, but to the sound principles which governed him in the exercise of this high prerogative, and which are so often neglected for the less creditable reasons of importunity and influence.

In the distribution of offices he simply followed the then well-established New York custom. From the beginning of the century, "the cohesive power of public plunder" had been the strongest bond of union among the members of the different factions who followed the banner of one or the other of the political leaders; and long before it was formulated as a political axiom, it was the well-settled rule of every party and faction in the State, that

"to the victors belong the spoils." Fifty years of
added experience may enable us to criticise and
repudiate this doctrine, from whose disastrous
consequences we suffer daily in nearly every department of our administration, from that of the
humblest messenger in our smallest municipalities
to the most important posts in our national government. But a half century ago "civil service reform" would have been an incomprehensible
phrase, not merely to the politicians but to the
people, and Seward was in this respect no wiser
than his generation. He expected from those
whom he appointed to office absolute and unques-
tioning support. When a lawyer, whom he had
nominated as judge, appeared before a legislative
committee to oppose a change in the management
of the public schools, recommended by the state
superintendent of education, Seward withdrew the
nomination. The unsatisfactory nature of the
spoils system did not fail, however, to impress itself upon him. He says in a letter: "The list of
appointments made this winter is fourteen hundred, for all of which I am of course responsible,
while in many, if not most, instances the circumstances under which the nominations were made
left me without freedom of election. . . . I am
not surprised by any manifestation of disappointment or dissatisfaction. This only I claim, that
no interest, passion, prejudice or partiality of
my own has controlled any decision that I have
made."

His courage and good temper in the trying years when he was confronted with a legislature where his political opponents were in a majority in either one or both branches were admirable. He never flinched or lost his self-control before their petty insults or their grosser provocations, but bore them with perfect apparent equanimity, repelling with vigor, when necessary, the attacks made on him, but never forgetting his personal self-respect or the dignity of his position.

His official action in two matters, which came before him as governor, excited a good deal of public feeling and discussion. The first of these had its origin in the Canadian rebellion of 1837. There was in that year an insurrection in Upper Canada, in which the Canadian ringleaders were largely assisted by reckless adventurers from northern New York, a party of whom seized Navy Island, in the Niagara River, intrenched themselves there, and manned their works with cannon stolen from the New York state arsenals. A little steamboat, the Caroline, had been engaged to bring them supplies. At the end of her first day's employment she was made fast to a wharf on the American side of the river, and within the limits of the State of New York. Here about midnight she was boarded by a band of loyal Canadians, set on fire, cut loose and left to drift over the falls. There was no resistance. The men on the steamer were asleep and unarmed. Some of them, awakened by the attack, jumped ashore; others were drowned.   One of the crew, Durfee, an American, was shot and killed as he was running away.

When the news of this affair reached Washington, the secretary of state, Mr. Forsyth, wrote to the British minister, complaining of the violation of our territory, and saying that it would form the subject of a demand for redress.   In his reply the British minister offered as an excuse for the attack the "piratical character of the Caroline, and the necessity of self-defense and self-preservation under which Her Majesty's subjects acted in destroying her; the temporary overthrow of the ordinary laws by piratical violence on the New York frontier; and the fact that Her Majesty's subjects in Upper Canada, having already severely suffered from this cause and being threatened with still farther injury, . . . were necessarily impelled to consult their own security by pursuing and destroying the vessel wherever they might find her."

After this dispatch, which treated the matter as an act of private violence with extenuating circumstances, nothing more was heard on the subject from the British government for three years, except the acknowledgment of our formal demand for an apology and redress.   "British interests," says an English historian, "had apparently been secured by the burning of the Caroline, and the natural susceptibilities of the inhabitants of the United States seemed hardly worth consideration."

In November, 1840, Alexander McLeod, a Canadian, while at Lockport in New York, boasted that

he had been one of the party attacking the Caroline, and had himself shot Durfee. He was thereupon arrested on a charge of murder and arson.

On learning of his arrest, the British minister,
Mr. Fox, who had previously treated the affair as
the unauthorized act of private individuals, and
rested his justification of it upon the necessity of
self-preservation, which had impelled the Canadians for their own security to pursue and destroy
the steamer wherever she might be, at once took
the opposite ground, and demanded McLeod's immediate release; because the "destruction of this
steamboat was a public act of persons in Her Majesty's service, obeying the orders of their superior
authorities." This was the first official suggestion
that the attack on the steamer was the act of the
government; and in making it, Mr. Fox was speaking without authority. Forsyth replied that the
matter was now in the hands of the judiciary of
New York, and beyond the President's control.
In February, 1841, Lord Palmerston, then secretary of state for foreign affairs, wrote to Mr. Fox,
approving his course, and saying: "There was
never a matter upon which all parties, Tory, Whig
and Radical, more entirely agreed. If any harm
should be done to McLeod, the indignation and
resentment of all England will be extreme; the
British nation will never permit a British subject
to be dealt with as the people of New York propose to deal with McLeod, without taking signal
revenge upon the offenders; McLeod's execution

would produce war, war immediate and frightful
in its character, because it would be a war of retaliation and vengeance." In this dispatch Lord
Palmerston assumed on behalf of Great Britain
full responsibility for the original attack. On the
12th of March, 1841, the British minister communicated the substance of this letter to Mr. Webster, who, on the change of administration, had
become secretary of state under President Harrison; and our government then had for the first
time an authoritative declaration that the violation
of our territory, the killing of Durfee, and the
destruction of the steamer, with the incidental loss
of life, were acts done under orders of the Canadian authorities, which England justified and
assumed as her own. In the opinion of the administration this declaration entirely changed the
situation, and the transaction became a national
affair. Webster's reply to Fox was delayed in
consequence of Harrison's death.[1] Before sending
it he had learned from Cass, who was in Paris,
that while McLeod's execution would be considered a *casus belli*, any sentence short of this would
not have that effect. This information, however,
did not diminish his eagerness to dispose of the
matter at once, and he advised the President to
send the attorney-general to confer with Governor
Seward upon the new aspect given to the affair by
this letter, and to urge him to direct the prosecution to be discontinued, and McLeod discharged.

[1] He died April 4, 1841, after ten days' illness.

Seward doubted his authority to interfere with the
case as suggested; and in view of the popular excitement thought that such interference, if lawful,
would be extremely injudicious. He was confident
that the people would acquiesce in McLeod's acquittal, or in his pardon, if convicted, but would
be very much stirred up if he were released in the
exceptional manner proposed. For these reasons
he declined to accede to the President's suggestions; though he assured the attorney-general that
he would pardon McLeod if he were convicted, and
that there should be no execution and no war.
This did not satisfy Mr. Webster, and in reply to
Palmerston's dispatch he suggested that McLeod
should apply to the court for a discharge on *habeas
corpus*. This was done. The federal administration, against Seward's earnest remonstrances, permitted the United States attorney, who before his
appointment had been McLeod's counsel, to continue to act for him; the attorney-general of New
York appeared officially on the other side, and the
proceedings in court assumed in this way the aspect of a controversy between the federal government on one side, and the state government on the
other, and were generally so regarded.

As McLeod's application for his discharge was
to be heard in the city of New York, he was
taken there in custody. The legislature was in
session when he passed through Albany. There
was much excitement, and an outcry that, by collusion between the governor and the United States

authorities, McLeod was to be discharged without
a trial. A resolve was passed calling for all the
documents and correspondence relating to the case.
The production of the papers and Seward's accompanying message showed the charge of collusion
to be absolutely groundless. The discharge was
refused by the court. McLeod was tried in October, and acquitted on proof of an alibi.[1]

Seward in this matter was upholding, as was his
official duty, the sovereignty of the State of New
York. Webster's contention was that, after Great
Britain's admission of her responsibility, the case
should be at once ended and McLeod released,
either by an order of the executive discontinuing
the prosecution, or by a judgment of the court,
discharging him.

[1] The comments of the newspaper press on the court's refusal
to discharge McLeod disclosed a distinct difference between the
Whigs of the city of New York and those beyond the Harlem
River. Out of the city opinion was unanimously with the court;
but in New York itself nearly as unanimously against it. The
question was treated as an issue between the State of New York,
her courts and governor on the one side, and on the other the
federal administration, represented by Mr. Webster with his dominating personality, and supported by the whole weight and authority of the United States.

The public questions raised in this case were novel; and though
later writers on international law have supported Mr. Webster's
positions, yet at the time so eminent a jurist as Lord Lyndhurst
was of opinion that " it was very questionable if the Americans
had not right on their side," and that "in a similar case in England they would be obliged to try the man, and, if convicted, nothing but a pardon could save him." — Dana's *Wheaton*, p. 371;
Greville's *Journal*, Part II. vol. i. p. 383.

The New York court decided that, as peace existed between Great Britain and the United States, at the time of the burning of the Caroline, and McLeod was merely a private citizen, holding no commission and acting under no previous authority, and as no responsibility for his act was assumed by his government until after he had been arrested and the court had acquired jurisdiction of the case, its jurisdiction was not ousted by the subsequent admission of his government, and that the case must therefore proceed in the regular way.

What had been done in New York after McLeod's arrest had been originally approved by Van Buren's administration, and Seward felt keenly the treatment he received at the hands of its successors, the representatives of his own party. Writing to a friend before the trial, he says: "Nothing could have been more unkind or unwise than the course pursued towards me by the general government in the McLeod affair. It was not merely unkind, it was ungenerous. They enjoyed my full confidence, they showed me none. I was left to learn the ground taken by the administration from the published documents accompanying the President's message. . . . It has been somewhat oppressive upon me personally to have Mr. Webster roll over upon us the weight of his great name and fame to smother me."

The matter created a good deal of feeling on both sides. If Seward was offended at his treatment by the administration, the President and Mr.

Webster were personally irritated both by his refusal to intervene, and by the failure of the attempt
to obtain McLeod's immediate discharge by the
court. There were also public grounds on which
Mr. Webster wished to dispose of the affair of the
Caroline as speedily and quietly as possible, and
it annoyed him that the governor of New York
would not yield to his judgment and coöperate in
carrying out his wishes.

Before the case was finally disposed of, there
was a change of government in England, and
shortly afterwards Lord Ashburton was dispatched
as a special envoy to this country to settle various
matters in dispute. Among these was the affair of
the Caroline. But with the discharge of McLeod,
Great Britain relapsed into the same indifference
as before his arrest, and it was with difficulty that
Mr. Webster obtained from Lord Ashburton a
statement that "it was perhaps most to be regretted
that some explanation and apology for this occur-
rence was not immediately made." This doubtful
expression of regret, and careful avoidance of an
apology, our government accepted as sufficient
amends for the invasion of our territory and the
killing of our citizens. It was not a triumph of
American diplomacy, and the result quite justified
Lord Palmerston's boast, that "there was no apology for the Caroline and should be none."

It is uncertain whether Seward had at any time
an expectation of going into Harrison's cabinet,
or any reason for such an expectation. A letter

from Harrison to Webster, printed in "Webster's Life and Correspondence," perhaps indicates that Webster had dissuaded Harrison from considering Seward for any cabinet appointment, and that Harrison had listened to his advice. After thanking him for suggestions upon this matter, Harrison writes: "I tell you, however, in confidence, that I have positively determined against S. There is no consideration which would induce me to bring him into the cabinet. We should have no peace with his intriguing, restless disposition." It would have been more useful, as well as more interesting, if Mr. Webster's biographer had either suppressed both letters, or published the one to which this is a reply. It is difficult to see who the mysterious "S" could have been except Seward. If he were the person named, it is evident that Webster had, before he went into Harrison's cabinet, an opinion of Seward by no means favorable, which may partly account for the tone assumed by him in the matter of McLeod. If one considers also that the McLeod matter came up after a controversy with Virginia, to be spoken of presently, had been going on for two years, that President Tyler was first and always a Virginian, and that his personal animosity to Seward at that time and down to the day of his death appears everywhere in his biography, it is possible that there is to be found here an additional explanation of the arrogant and offensive treatment which Seward received at this time at the hands of the administration, and how

it happened that, while he gave them his entire
confidence, he was left to learn their plans and
policy from the newspapers and public documents.

A controversy with Virginia, growing out of a
demand for the surrender of persons charged with
aiding in the escape of a fugitive slave, involved
Seward in a long and unpleasant correspondence
with the governor of that State, gained him noto-
riety and odium in the South, a prominent position
among the advanced anti-slavery Whigs at the
North, and induced the Abolitionists to endeavor
to persuade him to join their ranks and accept
their nomination for president. He preferred,
however, to remain a Whig, believing, as he always insisted, that there could be only two great
parties in the country, and that a third party
could never accomplish, except indirectly, any
important end.

The facts of the case were simple enough, and
the statement of them is all that is needed for
Seward's justification. As he was leaving Albany
for a few days' absence an agent of Virginia appeared with a requisition for two colored men,
charged with stealing a slave. They had been
already arrested and were in jail in New York.
Seward examined the affidavit on which the application was founded, pointed out to the agent what
he considered its fatal defects, informed him that
he should hear the men before answering the requisition, and that he would attend to the matter
on his return. Nothing more was heard from the

agent; but a month later, on receiving a letter on
the subject from the acting governor of Virginia,
Seward ascertained by an official report that the
men had been discharged on *habeas corpus*, because the judge before whom they were brought
was satisfied upon the evidence that "neither of
them had committed an offense against the laws of
Virginia." A courteous note inclosing this report
would seem to have been the dignified and proper
reply to the letter from Virginia; but instead of
confining himself to this, Seward voluntarily embarked in a discussion of the proper construction
of the constitutional provision for the surrender of
fugitives from justice, insisting that it applied
only to offenses recognized as crimes by the jurisprudence of all civilized nations, or to acts made
criminal by the laws both of the State demanding
and of that assenting to the surrender, and did not
apply to acts which any one State chose to make
highly penal, but which had no criminal significance in the other, such as assisting in the escape
of a slave, — an act inspired by the spirit of humanity and of the Christian religion.

This letter gave great offense to the authorities
and people of Virginia; it was considered an insult to the State, a wanton attack on the peculiar
institution upon which its whole social fabric rested.
The correspondence was continued through more
than two years, Seward's letters alone covering seventy printed octavo pages. Virginia sent copies
of the correspondence to the other slave States

and asked their support; the matter was laid before her legislature, and a committee of that body
made an elaborate report upon it.   Her governor
refused to surrender to New York a fugitive
charged with forgery; and when the legislature
disapproved his action, he resigned.   The lieutenant-governor returned the alleged forger; but the
Virginia legislature, by way of retaliation for
Seward's conduct, passed a law imposing special
burdens upon vessels coming from or bound to New
York; authorizing the governor, however, to sus-
pend its operation, whenever New York should
repeal its statute giving alleged fugitive slaves the
right of trial by jury, and should either return
the colored seamen originally demanded, or show
a proper penitence and recant its constitutional
heresies.

The friends of each governor approved his course,
and praised his superior skill in the discussion.
All Virginians, of whatever party, thought the
"attitude, conduct and ability of Governor Gilmer
was in every way a match for the wily arts of
Seward."   But New York was by no means so
unanimous in its support of its chief magistrate.
"The controversy has hitherto been much more
ably managed by Seward than by the Virginians,"
writes John Quincy Adams, in his diary, "but
there have been symptoms of the basest defection
to the cause of freedom among the New York
Whigs, and a disposition to sacrifice Seward to
the South."   There is no question that, at the

time, this correspondence injured Seward with his own party. The Democratic opinion of his position was expressed in a joint resolution of the New York legislature, declaring that "stealing a slave, contrary to the laws of Virginia, is a crime, within the meaning of the constitution," and requesting the governor to transmit to the executive of Virginia a copy of this resolve. Seward returned the resolution with a message in which he said: —

"I could not transmit the resolution in the present case, without silently acquiescing therein, and thus waiving a decision to which I adhere, or accompanying the communication to Virginia with a protest of my dissent. The Senate and Assembly will, therefore, excuse me from assuming the duty which an assent to their request would impose, and will, if it be proper, select some other organ of communication with the executive authorities of our sister commonwealth."

This message was his last important communication to the legislature, his official career in New York ending with the year.

CHAPTER III

PROFESSIONAL LIFE — SIX YEARS A PRIVATE CITIZEN

WHEN Seward returned to Auburn in January, 1843, he had some reason for thinking that his public career was closed. The political condition and outlook of the Whig party in the country were most unpromising. They had elected their president and vice-president, but the former had died, and the latter vetoed every measure intended to carry out their policy. In New York the Democrats had again obtained entire control of the state government, and for this many Whigs held Seward's administration responsible. He was blamed for the state debt, though Democratic legislation had created it; his Virginia correspondence had alienated conservatives; his course in the McLeod matter had incurred the hostility of Webster's friends; and his views about the distribution of the school funds had given much dissatisfaction to Protestants. It seemed, therefore, not only that there was no prospect of success for his party, but that, even should they unexpectedly carry an election, there was no probability that any public service would be required of him. It was perhaps

best for him that he felt that his public career
was closed, for the condition of his own affairs was
such as to require all his attention, and he was
glad to think that he was still young enough to
"repair all the waste of his private fortune."
During his term as governor he had entirely neglected his own business matters, and had spent
more than his income; his moderate personal estate
had been nearly consumed, and he now found himself so embarrassed that he was advised to seek the
benefit of the bankrupt act. But this he refused
even to consider, and opening his old office set himself to work to earn his living and pay his debts.

Resuming his practice with a local action of the
most trifling character, the circle of his clients
continually widened and his cases increased both
in number and importance; he became counsel for
the owners of several valuable patents, and in a
few years was able to write to his wife: "Every
day since my retreat from public life, the profes-
sion which I once so ungratefully despised has
been increasing its rewards, until we are no longer
pressed by fear of disaster or sickness, although
I have been diverted so often and so long from
lucrative engagements. Our boys are pleasantly
obtaining an education which is a better patrimony
than riches. If our comforts do not decrease, and
our children have no reason to complain of neglect,
we shall have passed through life happier, and I
hope die better, than we should if my earliest
schemes of wealth had been accomplished."

One trial in which he took part at this time should certainly be mentioned, as Seward's conduct in it exhibited some of the best qualities of his character, — the courage and tenacity with which he pursued, in spite of threats and obloquy, a course which his conviction of right and his sense of humanity dictated. A demented negro named Freeman, just out of the state prison at Auburn, killed, without the slightest provocation and with revolting brutality, a whole family of the neighborhood. He was arrested. The people, roused to a pitch of frenzy, were with difficulty restrained from lynching him. Seward was away at the time. He had recently been counsel in another case where the then novel and unpopular defense of insanity had been set up and maintained by him with some success; and it was feared he might be induced to act for Freeman. Every effort was made to prevent this. To quiet the popular apprehensions on this point, one of the county judges publicly declared that no Governor Seward would interfere to defend Freeman; and Seward's own law partners were persuaded to confirm this assurance, while threats of personal violence, should he appear for the defense, were freely made. Seward, on his return, was present in court when the poor lunatic was brought in to be arraigned; he had no counsel; and thereupon, finding no other lawyer willing to defend him, Seward, though he had full knowledge of the popular feeling and of all that had been said and done as to his appearance in this case, the threats as well as the promises, volunteered to act for him. It is not necessary to repeat the story of the trial. It was a most painful mockery of justice, equally discreditable to the judge, the prosecuting counsel and the jury. Seward was uniformly treated by them all during its progress as a person who was prostituting his great talents in a wicked attempt to save by unlawful means the worst of criminals. But he was apparently unmoved by all this. He bore with seeming composure the taunts and abuse of the prosecuting attorney, the ill manners and injustice of the court, and the gibes and insults of the people. The arduous and painful professional duty he had undertaken was most faithfully discharged. His closing argument was exhaustive and convincing. The insanity of Freeman was proved beyond a doubt. But conviction was a foregone conclusion. The public excitement had made a fair trial and verdict a matter of difficulty. The presiding judge did not hesitate to show that he shared the feelings of the people, and his obvious leaning against the prisoner and his defense made any unbiased consideration of the case by a jury altogether impossible. A higher court, less subject to local pressure and the temporary popular frenzy, set aside the verdict on Seward's application, and ordered a new trial; but before that could take place the poor fellow's mania had so developed that it was impossible to try him again. He lived only a short time, and the examination which followed his death disclosed an organic disease of the brain, from which he had long been suffering.

For his conduct in this case, Seward was at the time to some extent proscribed. "I rise from these fruitless labors," he wrote, "exhausted in mind and in body, covered with public reproach, stunned with protests." Freeman's death, however, and the clear proof of his insanity, caused a revulsion of popular feeling; and in the end, and perhaps especially with those who had been loudest in their denunciations of him, his defense of Freeman brought him far more gain, than loss, of reputation.

Though he was not again a candidate for office until his election to the United States Senate in 1849, declining in the interval every suggestion of a nomination, yet he was never so absorbed by his professional labors as to cease to take an interest in politics. Either from his own choice, or because he was out of favor with his party, he gave little time to public affairs in the year 1843. But in the presidential campaign of 1844 he did his utmost to insure the success of the Whigs. He began on the 22d of February with a speech at Auburn in favor of Clay, who was then recognized as the Whig candidate, though it was not till May that the convention ratified, by a formal vote, the nomination already made by the people. In this election there was but one real issue, the annexation of Texas. Though this had been vaguely threatened for some time, no scheme for effecting it had taken any definite shape until that which Tyler had sprung upon the country, only a few weeks before the nominating conventions of the different parties were to be held.

Adventurers from the Southern States had wrested Texas from Mexico, not to make it an independent republic, but to secure its annexation to the United States and an extension of the area of slavery. There were many intrigues and secret negotiations for this purpose during the earlier years of Tyler's administration, and even before that time; but no decisive step was taken until Calhoun became secretary of state in March, 1844, when he at once negotiated a treaty of annexation, which the Senate rejected by a considerable majority. While it was under consideration, both the great parties held their conventions. The platform of the Whigs was silent as to Texas and slavery, though Clay had declared himself opposed to annexation. The Democrats abandoned Van Buren, who had been their most prominent candidate, because he was known to be against annexation; they nominated James K. Polk of Tennessee, and declared "the re-annexation of Texas a great American measure recommended to the cordial support of the Democracy of the Union." The Liberty party had met the year before and nominated James G. Birney, with a platform of twenty-one resolutions all aimed at the slave system of the South.

During the summer, as the canvass went on, it became evident that the election was to depend on the vote of New York. Whichever of the great parties could carry that State would elect its candidate. The Whigs might reasonably hope to do this, if they could hold the radical anti-slavery members of their party, and induce them to support the regular nominations instead of throwing away their votes on Birney. Seward's advanced anti-slavery opinions, and his unhesitating adherence to the Whig party and its candidates, made him a most efficient worker with men of this description, who were opposed to the admission of Texas, who meant to resist it by their votes, and wished to do so in the most effectual manner; and he spent three months in campaign labors in the strongholds of anti-slavery opinion in northern and western New York. His speeches and letters were of necessity much alike in substance, however they might differ in form. The following passages give an outline of his principal arguments for the support of the Whig candidates: —

"The annexation of Texas is identical with the perpetuation of slavery. Our opponents are for it. The Whig party are against it. If there is a friend of human freedom willing to follow my lead in this sacred cause, I appeal to him to give his suffrage to the Whig candidates, not for the sake of Henry Clay, nor even for the sake of the Whig party, but for our country, for liberty's sake, and for the sake of humanity."

"What will Texas cost? It will cost a war with Mexico, an unjust war — a war to extend the slave trade. You will not go to war for human slavery, will you? You say Henry Clay is a slave-holder. So he is. I regret it as deeply as you do; I wish it were otherwise. But our conflict is not with one slaveholder, or with many, but with slavery. You are opposed to the admission of Texas. Will you resist it by voting for James G. Birney? Your votes would be just as effectual if cast upon the waters of the placid lake."

"Henry Clay is opposed to the coming in of Texas. He is the candidate of the Whig party. They are opposed to the coming in of Texas. The security, the duration, the extension of slavery, all depend on the annexation of Texas. How, then, can any friend of emancipation vote for the Texas candidate, or withhold his vote from the Whig candidate?"

"The integrity of the Union depends on the result. To increase the slaveholding power is to subvert the Constitution, to give [this power] a fearful preponderance, which probably will be speedily followed by demands to which the Demo-cratic free-labor States cannot yield, and which will be made the ground for secession, nullification, and disunion."

Before the convention met in May, Mr. Clay had written a letter in which he deprecated either urging or opposing annexation on sectional grounds, declared an acquisition of territory for the purpose of strengthening one portion of the country against the other to be a scheme pregnant with evil, and insisted that annexation and a war with Mexico were identical, and that such a measure at that time would be dangerous to the integrity of the Union. It was upon this letter that he was nominated and that the Northern Whigs were asked to accept his position on the Texas question as satisfactory. But in August, yielding to the pressure of Southern Whigs in States which he could not possibly carry, Clay wrote a second letter, saying: "So far from having any personal objection to the annexation of Texas, I should be glad to see it, without dishonor, without war, with the common consent of the Union, and upon just and fair terms." The news of this last letter reached Seward while he was canvassing New York on Clay's behalf; its effect was immediately apparent: "I met *that* letter at Geneva," he writes, "and thence here, and until now, everybody droops, despairs. It jeopards, perhaps loses the State. Is there any other way but to go through to the end more devotedly than ever?"

He followed the course he here suggests, finishing his campaign labors with no apparent lack of zeal or courage, but with an inward conviction of the coming defeat. His exertions, however, brought him one satisfaction, the restoration to some extent of the former harmonious relations between the conservative Whigs of the city of New York and himself. The causes of this were twofold. The

mass of the Whigs had moved forward to where
Seward stood, and even the laggards had advanced
much nearer his position; while the more intelligent of his opponents in his own party were becoming aware of the fact, that whatever were his
hopes or beliefs as to the perfect republic, he endeavored to consider and deal with actual public
affairs as a practical statesman rather than as a
Utopian doctrinaire, and would not knowingly sacrifice a possible present gain to a remote and uncertain ideal.

At the close of the campaign he resumed his
professional labors, and remained until the next
presidential election a simple looker-on in politics,
even declining a nomination to the constitutional
convention of his own State.

Detained by professional business at Washington during several weeks in each of the next three
winters, he heard there much talk as to the political questions of the day, — the matter of the
Oregon boundary, which was in dispute between
this country and Great Britain, the Mexican
war and the Wilmot Proviso. But he listened,
perhaps, to more speculations as to the possible
and probable candidates for the next election,
and by March, 1847, he felt that General Taylor's nomination and election scarcely admitted
of a doubt. "I am not prepared to speculate,"
he writes, "upon the consequences of events so
great and unlooked for as these. What will be
their effect upon the ' Great Question of Ques-

tions,' which underlies all present political movements?"

When the nomination was actually made, he accepted it as a "result inevitable, if not the best left within our power to attain," and took comfort in thinking that, "if the Barnburners continued the conflict, they would be able to save the State for the Whigs."

Before the convention took place, Seward's name had been suggested for the vice-presidency; but it was immediately stated that he was not a candidate. Fillmore, who received the nomination, was not the choice of Taylor's supporters, but was a concession to his opponents; and Seward at once predicted that, if Fillmore were elected, that portion of the Whig party of the State, to which he himself belonged, "would be in the position of a faction apparently opposed to the New York leader in the general council of the Whigs of the Union," — a prophecy partially realized during Taylor's life, and thoroughly fulfilled after his death.

Before the Whig convention met, General Cass had been nominated by the Democrats; and when the new Free Soil party had selected as its candidates Van Buren and Adams, the political campaign began.

In 1848 the Whigs repeated the experiment made eight years before. They nominated a military hero, admittedly without political experience, and having at the best but a scanty equipment of political knowledge or opinions. Their convention had no committee on resolutions, and made no declaration of principles. The Democrats proclaimed the war with Mexico "just and necessary;" and the Free Soilers declared that there should be "no more slave States and no more slave territory;" but "Free Soil, Free Speech, Free Labor and Free Men."

It was soon evident that for a second time the election was to depend upon the fortunes of this new third party in the pivotal State of New York. Would it catch enough anti-slavery Whig votes to give the election there to the Democrats; or could Van Buren, by the magic of his name, his personal popularity and his political skill, seduce from their allegiance so many Democrats as to compass the defeat of his old political rival and enemy, Cass? Again, the conduct, the position, the presence and the labors of Seward, a pronounced anti-slavery man, but an equally emphatic Whig, were all-important to his party.

Seward yielded to the numerous demands made upon him, and for six weeks or more spoke constantly in New York, New England, Pennsylvania, New Jersey, Delaware and Ohio. In Boston he and Abraham Lincoln were heard together, and at the close of the evening Lincoln said to him: "I have been thinking about what you said in your speech. I reckon you're right. We have got to deal with this slavery question, and got to give much more attention to it hereafter than we have been doing."[1] Seward's last speeches were made to the anti-slavery men of the Western Reserve in Ohio, endeavoring to persuade them to cast their votes for Taylor rather than to throw them away on Van Buren and thereby assure the election of Cass, and the opening to slavery of the Territories just wrung from Mexico. His friends thought his speech at Cleveland the boldest and best he had made, while his opponents characterized it as the most perverse and dogmatic. He revised this speech for publication, thinking "it would commend itself to consideration." A short summary of it will show his views of the issues between the parties, and of the duty of all opponents of the extension of slavery.

He saw two antagonistical elements of society in America, — freedom and slavery. These elements divided and classified the American people into two parties. One of these, the party of slavery, regarded "disunion as among the means of defense, and not always the last to be employed." The other maintained that the preservation of the union of the States, one and inseparable, now and forever, was the highest duty of the American people to themselves, to posterity and to mankind. "The party of slavery," he said, "declares that institution necessary, beneficent, approved of God, and therefore inviolable. The party of freedom seeks complete and universal emancipation. These two great elements exist and are developed in the

[1] Seward, *Life*, ii. p. 60.

two great national parties of the land." Seward
did not contend that an evil spirit had always possessed one of these parties without exception or
mitigation, and that a beneficent one had on all
occasions fully directed the actions of the other;
but he insisted that a beneficent one had worked
chiefly in the Whig party, and its antagonist had
worked in the other party; and that the Whig party
had been as true and faithful to human freedom as
the inert conscience of the American people would
permit it to be; that inert as that conscience was,
much could be done, everything could be done, for
freedom.

"Slavery," he said, "can be limited to its present bounds, it can be ameliorated, it can and
must be abolished, and you and I can and must
do it. The task is as simple and easy as its consummation will be beneficent and its rewards glo-
rious. It requires only to follow this simple rule
of action, namely, to do everywhere and on every
occasion what we can, and not to neglect or refuse
to do what we can at any time, because at that
precise time and on that particular occasion we
cannot do more. Circumstances determine possibilities. When we have done our best to shape
them and make them propitious, we may rest satisfied that superior wisdom has determined their
form as they exist, and will be satisfied with us if
we then do all the good that circumstances leave
in our power. But we must begin deeper and
lower than in the composition and combinations of

factions and parties. Wherein do the strength
and security of slavery lie? You answer that they
lie in the Constitution of the United States, and
the constitutions and laws of all slaveholding States.
Not at all. They lie in the erroneous sentiment
of the American people. Constitutions and laws
can no more rise above the virtue of the people
than the limpid stream can climb above its native
spring. Inculcate, then, the love of freedom and
the equal rights of man under the paternal roof;
see to it that they are taught in the schools and
in the churches; extend a cordial welcome to the
fugitive who lays his weary limbs at your door,
and defend him as you would your paternal gods;
correct your own error, that slavery has any constitutional guaranty which may not be released
and ought not to be relinquished. Say to slavery,
when it shows its bond and demands the pound of
flesh, that if it draws one drop of blood its life
shall pay the forfeit. Inculcate that free States
can maintain the rights of hospitality and humanity; that executive authority can forbear to favor
slavery; that Congress can debate, that Congress
can at least mediate with the slaveholding States;
that at least future generations might be bought
and given up to freedom. . . . Do all this, and
inculcate all this in the spirit of moderation and
benevolence, and not of retaliation and fanaticism,
and you will soon bring the parties of the country
into an effective aggression on slavery. Whenever the public mind shall will the abolition of

slavery, the way will open for it. I know that
you will tell me that all this is too slow. Well,
then, go faster if you can, and I will go with you;
but . . . remember that no human work is done
without preparation, that God works out his sub-
limest purposes among men with preparation."

If the closing passages of this speech, which
have just been quoted, did not indicate a new departure in what Seward considered the political
aims of the Whig party, they certainly stated these
aims with clearness and emphasis, and are in
marked contrast with the absolute silence of its
platform on the subject of slavery. The mass of
the anti-slavery Whigs at the North, though opposed to the extension of slavery, were not eman-
cipationists, and had by no means reached Seward's position as declared in this speech. The
large majority of them who were not politicians
voted for Taylor, slaveholder though he was, on
the grounds upon which Seward advised it, — that
the Whig party was, after all, the party of freedom, and the personal question a subordinate one,
and that it would be almost impossible to regain
for freedom what would be lost by a Democratic
victory.

Seward had no special gifts of voice or presence.
He was below the average height, with nothing
commanding in his appearance, and his voice was
harsh and shrill; but there was a courage, an earnestness about his campaign speeches of this year,
which made them most effective at the time, and

a tone of conviction, which still vibrates as one reads them after the lapse of nearly half a century.

He returned home the night before the election. The next morning it seemed probable that the Whigs had carried New York; in a week's time Taylor's election was ascertained beyond a doubt.

The campaign over, Seward turned again to the law, and was busily engaged with his cases. But though he wrote on the 16th of November: "Now that I have got into the law again pretty deep, I care nothing for these [political] intrigues," — yet it cannot be doubted that he took a lively interest in the canvass for the United States Senate, which his friends were making on his behalf, and which his opponents in his own party were fighting by the publication of anonymous pamphlets and forged letters, and the manufacture of fictitious interviews. As often happens in such cases, these inventions returned only to plague the inventors, and on the 6th of February, 1849, Seward was chosen senator from New York. He was not at this time forty-eight years old. He had never been in Congress or held any office under the United States, yet he had been four years in the New York Senate, and for an equal time the governor of that State. He was familiar with the machinery of legislation and the workings of a legislative body, and with the conduct of public affairs. He had been from his youth an ardent politician, and his ability had been quickly recognized and used by his political associates. He was but twenty-three when he attacked the Albany Regency, the all powerful clique which then ruled New York, and only twenty-seven when he was unanimously chosen president of a state convention called to promote the reëlection of John Quincy Adams. The defeat of Mr. Adams was a deathblow to the party which supported him, — the National Republicans, — and Seward joined the anti-Masonic party as the most vigorous opponent of Jackson and his followers, and by the anti-Masons he was nominated and elected to the state Senate in 1830. If at the beginning of his four years' service in that body he suffered some embarrassment from the consciousness of his youth and inexperience, this feeling soon disappeared; he rose rapidly in the opinion of his fellow senators and of the public, and before the end of his term was the recognized spokesman of the small minority opposed to the Democracy. His speeches there upon national questions are especially noteworthy for their boldness and intellectual vigor; while in matters of domestic legislation he was the strenuous supporter of all measures which a liberal and enlightened policy suggested for the improvement and growth of the State or the advancement and welfare of the people. At the end of his four years' service he was so far a leader in the new party into which the opponents of Jackson were endeavoring to unite, and which assumed the name "Whig," as to receive its nomination for governor. The party was too new to succeed, and though he led his ticket in all the counties, Seward failed to be elected.

He now found himself, however, for the first time a member of a national party representing upon the pressing national issues what had long been his own cherished convictions. With the principles of the Whig party he was thoroughly imbued. He believed in a liberal construction of the Constitution, in the protection and development of American industries and the policy and duty of the government in the promotion of internal improvements, and held generally the liberal views of those Whigs who were most radical and progressive, and which were in some respects much in advance of the time.

During the four years which intervened before his election as governor in 1838, though he took no active part in politics, yet he spoke from time to time to the people of western New York, insisting upon the necessity of public education for the successful maintenance of republican government, and on the importance of internal improvements for the development of the State; and in the financial crisis of 1837 he gave wise and timely warning of the evil of the government's "pledging its credit by issues of ' Continental money ' to pay its officers and carry on a war." During these four years there was a constantly increasing interest in the slavery question, and a marked development of sectional bitterness between the North and the South. At the North, abolition societies were becoming more prominent and aggressive, and in Congress John Quincy Adams was fighting the battle of the right of petition; while in the South, the postmasters, with the encouragement and approval of the administration, were arbitrarily destroying the abolition newspapers found in the mails, and the President himself was recommending and the Southerners insisting upon the passage of a law punishing the circulation of such publications through the mails in the Southern States. Seward saw the dangers of encouraging these demands, and prophesied that if the South persisted in such monstrous claims and conduct the issue would be fearfully changed for them.

Sectional differences, however, played no part of importance in either the presidential campaign of 1836 or that of 1840, both of which turned upon the economic issues which divided the Whigs and Democrats; but minor incidents and such events as the correspondence between Seward and the Southern governors kept alive and tended to increase the hostile feeling between the two sections, which the proposed annexation of Texas threatened at any time to kindle into an active flame.

The campaign of 1840 was practically the last presidential election which did not turn on the slavery question. From Tyler's accession to power, and his veto of every bill passed by Congress to carry out the financial policy which he had been

elected to support, the questions which, to the mass
of the Whigs of the North, overshadowed and
eclipsed all others in importance and interest were
those of the admission of Texas and the consequent
extension of slavery, and the compliance with, or
refusal of, the growing demands of the slaveholders.
Upon these great questions, in whatever form they
presented themselves, Seward had from the outset
held fixed opinions, while other people were hesitating, and he had never shrunk from expressing
and acting up to them, regardless of any obloquy
he might incur.

In the discussions with the governors of the
Southern States as to persons charged with aiding
slaves to escape, in his arguments before the courts
in defending such cases, and in his political
speeches, Seward was the recognized exponent of
the most advanced views as to the slavery question
of the most advanced Northern Whigs who still
adhered to their party.

It would not be true to say of any one man that
he created the public opinion on the subject of
slavery which at last found its political expression
in the Republican party; but it is true of Seward
that his speeches and arguments at this period in-
culcated the doctrines and instilled into the voters
of the free States the principles on which that
party was built; and that these speeches were the
textbook from which large and continually increasing masses of Northern voters were receiving their
political education. Of the "Conscience Whigs"

in New York he was the representative man, and
it was to his pronounced anti-slavery opinions and
his bold advocacy of them, quite as much as to his
adherence to the other doctrines of his party, that
Seward owed his strong hold upon the people of
New York which caused his election to the Senate
in the winter of 1849.

CHAPTER IV

In the four and a half years between Polk's election and Taylor's inauguration, the policy of the slave States had become distinctly developed, and the political dogmas of their leading statesmen clearly formulated. In 1845 they refused to admit Iowa, which had a sufficient population, unless Florida, deficient in numbers, should be brought in as a State under the same bill. In 1848 Wisconsin came in as a counterpoise to Texas and the great acquisitions of the Mexican war, which were then expected to inure to the benefit of the South and slavery.

In the closing days of Tyler's administration, a joint resolution for the annexation of Texas had been passed by the expiring Congress, and received the President's signature. Before the middle of January, 1846, Polk ordered Taylor to advance into Mexico, and our war of invasion began. In the following winter, while the war was still in progress (February 19, 1847), Calhoun offered in the Senate, and supported by an elaborate speech, resolutions declaring in substance that slavery was national, freedom sectional; that the Constitution authorized and protected slavery in all the national domain, and that neither Congress nor any territorial legislature could legally prevent a citizen of a slave State from migrating with his slaves to any Territory and there holding them in servitude.

During the Mexican war the territory which was ceded to us by treaty at its close had been occupied by our troops and governed by the officers in command of them, who treated the laws of Mexico as still in force, so far as the civil rights and obligations of the people were concerned. With the peace, the military authority properly ceased; and President Polk earnestly recommended Congress to provide some government as a substitute. For California this was an imperative need, for directly the discovery of gold was known, hordes of adventurers of every description had rushed in, and it was absolutely necessary that there should be some authority to repress and punish with a strong hand the disorderly and vicious, and protect the honest and industrious immigrants.

Congress was so divided on the question of free soil or slave labor in these new possessions that all legislation was impossible. The House would pass no bill for their organization without a proviso prohibiting slavery, while the Senate would assent to no bill containing any such proviso; and Congress adjourned six months after the peace, leaving them without a legal government or any provision for forming one. Under these circumstances, the military governors continued, though reluctantly, to exercise the same authority as before, relying for their justification quite as much upon the necessity of the case and the tacit acquiescence of the people, as upon the orders of the President. The acquiescence of the people was an unwilling one; they were much disappointed that no permanent government had been provided for them; but they followed the President's advice, and submitted to the existing condition of things in the expectation that, as he assured them, Congress would give them a proper government before the 4th of March, 1849. As, however, from the inaction of Congress during the winter, these hopes gradually faded away, while the necessity for a strong and permanent government became continually more manifest, the people of California grew more and more restless, and in various localities, San Francisco, Sacramento and elsewhere, the inhabitants made abortive attempts to establish local legislatures and governments. General Riley succeeded in inducing the leaders of these tentative governments to forbear and delay, though he had only persuasion and argument to rely on, the attractions of the mines making it impossible to hold in the ranks on land either soldiers, sailors or marines.

Riley was conscious, however, that he had exhausted his influence; and when he learned that Congress had dissolved, and California was left without legislature or government, he at once (June 3, 1849) issued a proclamation, calling

upon the people to choose delegates to a convention
to adopt a frame of government, state or territorial,
as they might think best.

The insurmountable obstacle to any territorial
legislation in the second session of the thirtieth
Congress, which expired March 4, 1849, had been,
as before, the matter of slavery; the Senate again
rejecting any bill restricting slavery in the Territories, and the House insisting on its absolute
prohibition there. The presidential election of
the previous summer had been fought by the
Whigs with no platform; Northern voters had been
urged to support Taylor as the candidate of the
party most firm and persistent in its opposition to
slavery; while on the other hand it had been contended at the South that absolute confidence could
be placed in him as a Southern planter and the
owner of three hundred slaves. The Democratic
party had enunciated its doctrines on the subject
of slavery in the platform of its convention; and
this platform had been supplemented by a letter
from General Cass, insisting on the right of the
people of a Territory to settle the question of slavery
for themselves. This letter, however, was suscep-
tible of a double construction, — at the North it
was declared to mean that the people of a Territory
could at any time determine for themselves the
question of freedom or slavery there; while at
the South it was relied on as containing the true
Southern doctrine that the people of a Territory
were powerless to take any action in regard to

slavery while in their territorial condition, and could only do so when framing a state government.

Among the solutions of the California question proposed during the winter of 1848–49, the one which had found most favor in the eyes of the South, though it failed to be adopted, was that of authorizing the inhabitants to form a state constitution and apply for admission to the Union. The Southerners thought that, if a convention for this purpose should be called under an act of Congress, with sufficient notice to them, they could flood California with their own people prepared to vote for a pro-slavery constitution, before the more distant Northerners could reach there.   In the mean time, however, they hesitated to carry their slaves thither, partly because they feared that the Mexican laws abolishing slavery were still in force, and that their slaves would therefore be free in California; partly because they were afraid of the passage of a bill prohibiting slavery there; partly also, because, until the discovery of gold, it was very doubtful how far slave labor could be made profitable in California; and for another reason, perhaps of greater weight than all these, that the labor and expense of moving slaves rendered it practically impossible for any Southern planter to compete in the ordinary processes of emigration with the enterprise of the pioneers of the North and West.

When General Taylor arrived in Washington, just before his inauguration, he was greatly disap-

pointed to find that Congress was likely to expire
without any provision for the government of California, and he used his best exertions, Seward acting as his representative and adviser, to secure the
passage of a bill which should give the Territories
some form of legal government. Having failed in
this attempt, he then, with the approval of all the
members of his cabinet, the majority of whom
were Southerners, and with the assent of Seward,
dispatched to California Thomas Butler King of
Georgia, a former member of Congress from that
State, "to encourage the people there to form a
state constitution and ask for admission to the
Union, assuring them of his support should they
do so;" and he took a similar course as to New
Mexico. There is no reason to suppose that he
had any special purpose, to introduce or to prohibit slavery in either Territory. His plan was
that which had already been suggested, to look to
the Territories themselves for the settlement of the
territorial difficulties, letting the people organize
their own governments, since Congress would not
do so for them.[1]

As it turned out, neither General Taylor nor
his messenger had any hand in calling the California convention. General Riley, the military governor, published his proclamation before he had
any communication with either of them. The
proclamation stated that the course he was taking
was advised by the President and by the secreta-

[1] Letter of John Tyler, March 5, 1849.

ries of state and of war; but it is clear from a comparison of dates that the President and public officers to whom he referred were Polk and his secretaries. King never saw Riley till the middle of June, and when the convention met was dangerously ill and unable to be present; the only advice he is known to have given was to recommend that the boundaries of the State be made as large as possible. This was doubtless in accordance with Taylor's view of sweeping into two new States all the territory acquired from Mexico; and this was the course advocated in the convention by the Southern delegates, who may have hoped either to prevent the admission of California with such extensive boundaries, or at a later date to procure her division into two States, one of which would be slave though the other were free. At all events the boundary question was really the only matter in dispute in the convention. There was a due proportion of men from the South among the delegates, but the clause prohibiting slavery was unanimously adopted.

When Congress assembled in December, 1849, it was known that California, with a constitution prohibiting slavery, would at once apply for admission as a State. The Mexican war had been a Southern war, brought about by Southern policy, largely fought by Southern officers and men, with the determination that its final result should be " to adjust the whole balance of power in the Confederacy so as to give the South the control over the operations of the government in all time to come," and with the expectation that the territory acquired by the war would create a new demand for slave labor and a great advance in the price of slaves. The admission of California as a free State would not merely rob the Southerners of what they considered the just political and pecuniary fruits of this war, but also, unless accompanied by that of a slave State at the same time, would destroy that equilibrium of sectional power in the Senate which had been successfully maintained ever since slavery had become a political question.

Party ties were to a certain extent dropped when Congress assembled. The Southern Whigs and Democrats stood together on every question which appeared to them to have any sectional bearing. They were supported by some Northern Democrats, and were also aided by the small knot of Free Soilers in the House, whose violence of language, half justified by the personal attacks on themselves, hindered the cause they professed to have at heart, and helped that party which they said they were seeking to destroy. For a whole month the House of Representatives attempted to elect a speaker,[1] and during this time the talk of the Secessionists was defiant and treasonable.

[1] The Free Soilers were not averse to any speaker who would pledge himself to give the Wilmot Proviso members control of the Committee on Territories, and nearly succeeded in electing a Democrat who had promised in writing to do this. Seward urged the Whigs of the House to stand firmly by Mr. Winthrop, the regular Whig candidate.

When at last the House was organized and the
President's message read, the vital struggle began.
There were several burning questions connected
with the war: the admission of California; the
true limits of Texas, — those which the United
States were bound to recognize; the proper government of New Mexico and Utah.   The President thought California should be admitted, because she had the population and all the other
conditions requisite to form a State.   He hoped
that New Mexico might also come in as a State
with a proper frame of government, and that the
Texas. boundary question might be settled as a
judicial matter before the Supreme Court.   Upon
the last question he doubtless had some feeling and
a very decided opinion, as he knew from his own
personal experience during the war, that, whatever
might have been claimed on paper, Texas had never
actually governed a single inch of the land in dispute.[1]   The only importance of the matter arose
from the fact that if the lands in dispute were a
part of Texas they were already slave territory; if
they belonged to Mexico and became ours by the

---

[1] Texas had advanced claims to a large portion of New Mexico,
cutting off many thonsand square miles where there was no slavery,
and insisting that it was included within her own limits where
there was slavery.   Polk, at the very end of his administration,
issued orders to the officer in command in New Mexico to fall
back before any inroad of the Texans, and surrender possession of
the disputed territory.   These orders Taylor at once revoked, and
directed him to maintain the boundary line as the United States
found it, and as ceded to them by the treaty.

treaty, slavery had been abolished there before we acquired them. It was not, therefore, merely a Texas question, but a slavery question, and as such a sectional one.

There were other matters, the discussion of which served to excite still more the hostile feeling already existing between North and South. Among these were, the question of the abolition of slavery in the District of Columbia, and of the prohibition of the slave trade between the States (neither of which had any such support as to make it of political importance); of the inefficiency of the law for the surrender of fugitive slaves, and of the reluctance of the North to comply with the constitutional requirements on this point; and of the prevention of the use of the District of Columbia as the common slave mart and exchange for the entire South. Though this last was hardly a sectional issue, as it received the support of senators and representatives from all parts of the country, yet it was so closely connected with the slavery agitation that debate upon it was liable to become passionate and personal.

Upon the question of slavery in the Territories, the Southern view was, that the Constitution is a compact of union for limited purposes between several sovereign States, the citizens of each of which have in all the Territories a common property and equal rights with the citizens of every other State, any citizen having the right to carry there all property of every species recognized as such by the laws

of his own State, and therefore slaves, if slaves were
property in the State from which they were taken.
Some Southerners went even farther than this, and
insisted that under the provisions of the Constitution for the return of fugitive slaves to their masters, and for slave representation in Congress,
slaves were a kind of property entitled to special
and peculiar favor, singled out by the Constitution
from the mass of other property, invested with
higher dignity and guarded with greater security,
too precious to be intrusted solely to state law,
and especially under the protecting ægis of the
Constitution; or, as it was forcibly put by one of
the ablest exponents of the Southern doctrine:
" This is a pro-slavery government; slavery is
stamped upon its heart, the Constitution.   No
matter where you place the power to legislate on
the Territory, the power to legislate on questions of
slavery is a legitimate instrument of it.   Slaves
are property — our property.   If it is said slavery
is a peculiar institution against the common law
of mankind, then I reply, our government is a peculiar government, our Constitution is a peculiar
Constitution, for they are both impregnated with
this peculiarity."   In short, it was insisted that,
without any legal enactments, slavery existed by
force of the Constitution in all the Territories of
the United States, and that neither foreign laws
before conquest, nor domestic legislation afterwards, could prohibit or abolish it.

The original opposition of the North to the ex-

tension of slavery to the new Territories was not
founded upon political considerations. The Northerners had submitted, without reluctance, to the
supremacy of the South for two thirds or more of
the whole period of the history of the government,
and were practically indifferent about the matter.
The men of the North were engaged in all sorts
of industrial and commercial enterprises, their interest in politics was limited, and their opposition
to slavery and its extension was in most cases an
objection upon moral grounds. The Southerners,
on the contrary, had few occupations except politics and the ordinary pursuits of a country life,
and they had controlled the government almost
from its foundation, either directly through one
of their own number, or indirectly through some
Northerner designated by them for President.
They saw the possibility, and feared the probability, of this political supremacy slipping from
them, and believed the admission of California as
a free State to be the first fatal step in a path
which would ultimately leave them in a position
of inferiority and subjection to the North in the
government and administration. To them the contest was not merely for a theoretic principle, but
for a positive, actual, valuable right.

General Taylor having been nominated with no
platform or declaration of principles, any policy
which he advocated as to the settlement of the
slavery question might fairly be called the President's policy, and no Whig need feel that, if he

failed to support it, he was breaking loose from his party. There was, indeed, no Whig party, in that sense in which party means a combination of persons agreeing upon certain political principles, and united to carry out a certain political policy. The questions which had united the Whigs were either dead or dormant, and on the only living political issue they had, as a national party, no principles and no policy. Those members of Congress, therefore, who had been always classed as Whigs and were elected as Whigs, felt at liberty to vote as they pleased upon all the questions relating to the Territories.

Taylor was also unfortunate in the fact that he had not the support of the two great leaders of the Whig party, Clay and Webster. Clay thought himself ill-treated by Taylor in regard to the nomination, and never forgave him. He had declined to advocate or support him during the campaign. He was not present at the inauguration. When he took his seat in the Senate in the middle of December, he announced his purpose of taking "the lead of no subject and no party;" yet a few weeks later he made a speech which drew from one of his opponents the observation, that he well knew "the senator from Kentucky formally declined exercising on behalf of the administration a parliamentary leadership, but had no suspicion, until he listened to his speech, that he meditated a regular course of hostilities against those in power."

Webster, the other great leader of the Whig party, had sulked in his tent by the sea the whole summer long; and when he was at last induced to leave his solitude to speak at a political meeting, he only said that Taylor's nomination was one not fit to be made; but that, as he was the Whig candidate, he should support him. He was in Washington when Taylor arrived there, and called upon him at once; but his real feeling towards the incoming President is to be seen in an extract from a letter, in which he says : " Although I would not yield myself to any undue feelings of self-respect, yet it is certain that I am senior in years to General Taylor, that I have been thirty years in public life, . . . have had . . . friends, who have thought that for the administration of civil and political affairs my own qualifications entitle me to be considered a candidate for the office to which General Taylor has been chosen. I feel [therefore] that I shall best consult my own dignity by declining to fill a subordinate position in the executive government." [1]

Before Congress met in December, Taylor's course as to California had alienated the leading Southern Whigs, upon whom he might have thought he could depend ; and either from inclination or necessity he consulted Seward, the only

[1] *Webster's Life*, ii. p. 357. Webster was born in January, 1782, Taylor in September, 1784. A year later Webster accepted a subordinate position, and became secretary of state to Fillmore, who was born in January, 1800, and so was sixteen years younger than Taylor.

Whig senator from the most important State in the Union, and his active supporter in the election campaign. Indeed, confidential relations between them had begun even before the inauguration, and a few weeks later attention had been called to these relations by the publication of a letter from Seward, written to exonerate Taylor from the charge of having used his influence with the Congress which had just expired, in favor of legislation which would have fastened slavery on all our newly acquired Territories. The letter was well intentioned; it had been read and approved by the Cabinet before it was given to the press; nevertheless, its publication was unfortunate. To have public proclamation made that he was taking for one of his chief counselors a radical anti-slavery man like Seward, and one so inexperienced in national politics, injured the President, not only with Clay and the Southern Whigs, but also with Webster and his friends. There was so little apparent necessity for printing the letter, that Seward was taunted with having done this that he might make a display of his confidential relations with General Taylor, and he became in consequence a ready mark for the attacks of all the senators, of whatever party, who were either tacitly or avowedly hostile to the administration.

From the moment of the assembling of Congress the air of the Capitol was heavy with the coming storm. There seemed to be no question the discussion of which was harmless. A resolution to

extend the courtesies of the Senate to Father Ma-
thew, the Irish apostle of temperance, brought on
a discussion as to slavery. A debate upon our
diplomatic relations with Austria soon drifted into
the same channel.

In talking about the subjects to be embraced in
the census, abolition and the abolitionists were
among the topics treated of, and the discussion
was made the occasion for bitter personalities.
Threats of disunion were frequent. These were
partly in earnest, and were partly intended to excite the fears of the people of the North, that they
might yield more readily to the demands of the
slaveholders and assent to the legislation they desired. In many of these debates Seward took
part, and was, when the occasion required, vigorous and outspoken in declaring his hostility to slavery and his hopes of ultimate emancipation. He
made no personal attacks on any one, and replied
once for all to those made on him : " I am here for
public measures, not for private ends, and no im-
putations shall ever put me on a defense of myself
against aspersions or complaints of this kind."

Taylor, though inexperienced in political affairs
or civil administration, was a man of good sense,
single-minded, honest, direct, averse to anything
in the nature of political intrigue or bargain, of
sterling integrity, of undoubted loyalty and unhesitating courage, able and determined to discharge his duty as he understood it, and impatient
at the Southern bluster and threats of disunion,

which he considered treasonable, and in the face
of which what was called compromise seemed to
him a cowardly surrender to disloyalty. He saw
no connection between a bill admitting California
as a free State and acts organizing the other
Territories, or establishing the true boundaries of
Texas; and a combination to secure the passage of
any one bill by arrangement with the friends of
the others seemed to him a base business. He
might have assented to all the measures contemplated by Clay's compromise resolutions, each on
its own merits, but never as a bargain between
contending sections.[1] On the 21st of January,
1850, he sent to Congress a message recommending
the admission of California with the constitution it
had formed prohibiting slavery, confining his message to this subject alone.

Clay, Calhoun and Webster were this year together in the Senate for the last time. Clay
was the man of compromise. He had been the
father of the Missouri Compromise in 1821, had
quieted the threatened nullification outbreak of
South Carolina a dozen years later by another
compromise, and now came forward for the last
time, offering a series of resolutions to be after-

[1] " I would rather have California wait than bring in all the
' Territories on her back.' " Taylor to Webster, Curtis's *Webster*,
ii. 473. Southern Whigs in Congress said the Southern officers
would refuse to obey, if ordered to maintain the line of New
Mexico against Texas. " Then," said Taylor, " I will command
the army in person, and hang any man taken in treason." Schou-
ler, v. p. 185.

wards embodied in appropriate legislation. They were intended to cover all the matters in dispute, and to be a full and final adjustment of all questions relating to slavery. California was to be admitted as a free State; the other territory conquered from Mexico was to have a proper territorial government, with no provision either introducing or excluding slavery; the western boundary of Texas was to be established, and that State paid from the public treasury for the relinquishment of its claims to any part of New Mexico. The resolves further declared that, so long as slavery existed in Maryland and Delaware, it was inexpedient to abolish it in the District of Columbia without the assent of those States; but that it was expedient to prohibit there the trade in slaves brought from without the District; that Congress had no power to interfere with the slave trade between the different slave States, and that more effectual provision ought to be made for the restitution of fugitive slaves.

Clay had been for some time deliberating on the matter of these resolutions. On the 2d of January he wrote to his son James: "I have been thinking much of proposing some comprehensive scheme of settling amicably the whole question in all its bearings, but have not yet positively determined to do so." Before offering his resolves, he went, on a stormy evening, to Webster's house and secured his approval. He introduced them in the Senate at the end of the month, and a little later the great debate began. For two days, to a chamber crowded with an eager and excited audience, Clay spoke eloquently and persuasively in support of his resolves, appealing to the North for concession, and to the South for peace. A month later Calhoun, tall, gaunt, and haggard, with the shadow of coming death on his face, sat in the Senate, while a friend read for him his carefully prepared argument. He opposed Clay's resolutions, and insisted that the South required further legislation for the protection of her peculiar institution, and for the security and maintenance of that equilibrium between the slave and free States, which he asserted was a fundamental condition originally insisted on by the South, in joining the Union. On the 7th of March Webster followed. His speech was not a discussion of the subjects considered in Clay's resolutions; it was an appeal "for the preservation of the Union" and the restoration to the country of quiet and harmony. Penetrated with a deep sense of what the Union had accomplished during the seventy years of its existence, and of the future it promised, if it remained unbroken, he compared slavery to a spot on the face of the sun, and the persons who would break up the government on account of it to those who would strike the light from the heavens, if there were any imperfection in it, and prefer the chance of utter darkness. He endeavored to make the proposed compromises acceptable to the free States, and for this purpose minimized the concessions

required of them, and either wholly omitted or
touched but lightly on their complaints; on the
other hand, he dwelt at length on the wrongs done
the South by the general hostility to slavery, by
the violent language of the abolitionists, and by the
evasion of the constitutional provision for the surrender of fugitive slaves. He would, therefore, he
said, vote for a more stringent law on the last subject; while he should vote against the insertion of a
proviso prohibiting slavery in any bills organizing
governments for the territory acquired from Mexico, because slavery was excluded from those regions by a law of nature, and he would not " reënact
the will of God," or wound to no purpose the pride
of the South. Upon the other subjects of the
resolves he was silent.

This speech was a great disappointment to many
Northern Whigs, including some of Webster's
warmest supporters. It cannot be denied that it
has a very different ring from that in which he
claimed the Wilmot Proviso as his own thunder, or
from his political utterances of the September previous, when he said: "There has for a long time
been no North; I think the North star is at last
discovered. I think there will be a North, but up
to the recent session of Congress there has been no
North, no section of the country in which there has
been found a strong, conscientious, united opposition to slavery; no such North has existed."
Yet, though there was much bitterness of feeling
and criticism, and imputation of base motives at

the time, it is only just to Mr. Webster to admit that the speech may have been inspired by his profound love for the Union and his conviction that it was in great peril ; that his honest apprehensions of its imminent destruction affected the whole tone as well as the conclusions of the argument by which he attempted to undo at once with the Northern voters his own work of many years. The success he met with at the time was a striking tribute to his personal power. In the cities the merchants, manufacturers and business people generally, many scholars and thoughtful persons acting with them, held large and enthusiastic Union meetings, and resolved their approval of Webster's speech and Clay's compromises. But the country folks, the rural districts, held off, and Webster never regained his hold on them. The Whig party at the North split into two factions, the "Conscience" and the "Cotton" Whigs ; and there were in the next Congress an increased number of senators and representatives distinctly opposed to the doctrine of the 7th of March speech and to the measures of compromise, who made the nucleus for the formation of the Republican party.

CHAPTER V

SEWARD, during the winter, was the object of
many attacks and a great deal of personal abuse
from Southern senators, who seemed to go out of
their way to insult him. To these he replied, as
has been said, that he had come to the Senate for
public, not for private ends ; that he should pass
by in silence, as he had before done, all such personal attacks ; that he admitted the purity and
patriotism of the motives of all other senators,
and expected the same justice to be done to himself. He was not on any committee during this
session. He asked to be excused from the committee on patents, to which he had been assigned,
upon the ground that his previous employment as
counsel in patent suits might be embarrassing to
him ; and no other place could be found for him
except by a re-arrangement of all the committees,
which he thought not worth while.

When Clay and Webster spoke, the silver tongue
and personal charm of the one, the majestic eloquence and noble presence of the other, and the national reputation of both, filled the Senate chamber

with their admirers, women as well as men; and
their speeches met with a sympathetic response
from the people of Washington, Southerners and
slaveholders as they were.   Seward had no such
presence, no such eloquence, no such reputation,
and when a few days later he rose to speak, the
Senate was substantially empty.   The President's
message transmitting the constitution of California
was the special order of the day, and it was to the
question of the admission of that State that Seward particularly addressed himself.   It is difficult
to give within moderate limits an analysis of this
great speech.   An intelligent listener said of it, at
the time, that it "was marked by more breadth of
view, more vigor of thought, and a more profound
and masterly treatment of the subject, than was
displayed by either Clay or Webster."

On the other hand, Clay wrote to his son a few
days after its delivery: "Mr. Seward's late abolition speech . . . has eradicated the respect of
almost all men for him."   These different statements represent the extreme divergence of public
opinion at the North and South.   The speech
marked an epoch in discussions on slavery in the
Senate of the United States.   It was the first
time that any senator, regularly elected by one of
the great parties of the country, had made in the
Senate not merely a statement of his own position,
but what was felt to be an authentic declaration
of the attitude as to slavery of a formidable and
growing minority, if not a majority, of the people

of the North. It was the first time that the senators had been called on to recognize the fact, which many of them were striving to ignore, that " a moral question, transcending the too narrow creeds of parties, had arisen, that the public conscience was expanding with it, and the green withes of party associations giving way and falling off."

Seward began by brushing aside the formal and trifling objections brought forward by the opponents of the immediate admission of California, all of which were to be waived if the admission of this free State should be accompanied by sundry irrelevant concessions to slavery, — a new fugitive slave law, a guaranty of the perpetuity of slavery in the District of Columbia, acquiescence in its existence in the Territories of Utah and New Mexico. Passing from these objections, he proceeded to state the reasons which to his mind rendered the immediate admission of California imperative. The substance of these was that California was in fact already a State, and could never be a Territory, colony or military dependence ; that remote as she was on the Pacific coast, with the population that had suddenly filled her borders, she needed a constitution, sovereignty, independence and protection, — either a share of ours, which she had asked for, or her own, which she could assume without our consent, if we rejected her appeal ; and that if we wished to retain her, and Oregon with her, we could not afford to trifle or delay. He then considered the position of those persons who insisted that to the admission of California should be joined fresh compromises on questions connected with slavery. It was to what he had to say on this point that the especial interest and importance of his speech attached. The admission of California was almost conceded. The real struggle was on what should be yielded in return. Declaring himself, for various reasons, opposed to all legislative compromises not absolutely necessary, he took up in turn each of the particular measures proposed, commenting briefly on the incongruity of the subjects tacked together in the resolves. He next examined Calhoun's statement, that nothing would satisfy the South except such legislation as would secure a permanent equilibrium between the free and slave States; this he pronounced absolutely impossible, as it must involve a veto by the minority of the majority, which meant nothing less than a return to the rope of sand of the old Confederacy, and a subjection of the people of the growing States of the North and West to the more stationary population of the slave States.

Speaking of the proposed Fugitive Slave Law, he took the ground not merely that a more stringent law would be useless, as it was opposed to the moral convictions of the people of the North, denied all the recognized safeguards of personal liberty, and converted into a crime that hospitality to the outcast and refugee which all mankind save the slaveholder considered an act of common

humanity ; but he also insisted that, to have the
constitutional provision as to the return of fugitive
slaves honestly carried out, the rigors of the law
must be alleviated, not increased. Referring to
the proposal that, as part of the compromises,
Congress should deprive itself of the power of
emancipation in the District of Columbia, he declared that he would at any time vote for the abolition of slavery there, with a proper compensation
to the slave-owners, and was willing to appropriate
any sum necessary for this purpose.

It was, however, what he said in treating of the
public domain, and of the power and duty of Congress in regard to it, that so greatly stirred the
people of both sections at the time, and has since
been often quoted and misinterpreted by both
friends and enemies.

"The national domain is ours. . . . It was acquired by the valor and with the wealth of the
whole nation. We hold, nevertheless, no arbitrary
power over it. . . . The Constitution regulates our
stewardship ; the Constitution devotes the domain
to union, to justice, to defense, to welfare and to
liberty. But *there is a higher law than the Constitution*, which regulates our authority over the
domain, and devotes it to the same noble purposes.
The territory is a part of the common heritage of
mankind, bestowed upon them by the Creator. We
are his stewards, and must so discharge our trust
as to secure in the highest attainable degree their
happiness. . . . Whether, therefore, I regard the

welfare of the future inhabitants of these new Territories, or the security and welfare of the whole people of the United States, I cannot consent to introduce slavery into any part of this continent, which is now exempt from what seems to me so great an evil, . . . or to compromise the questions relating to slavery, as a condition of the admission of California."

To the argument that the prohibition of slavery was unnecessary, he answered : —

" There is no climate uncongenial to slavery. . . . Labor is in quick demand in all new countries. Slave labor is cheaper than free labor, and it would go first into new regions, and wherever it goes it brings labor into dishonor. . . . Was the ordinance of 1787 necessary or not? Necessary, we all agree; and yet that ordinance extended the inhibition of slavery from the thirty-seventh to the fortieth parallel of latitude. . . . We are told that we may rely on the laws of God, which prohibit slave labor in this new territory, and that it is absurd to reenact the laws of God. The Constitution of the United States and the constitutions of all the States are full of such reënactments. Wherever I find a law of God or a law of nature disregarded, or in danger of being disregarded, there I shall vote to reaffirm it with all the sanction of civil authority."

In all this there is nothing startling, revolutionary or treasonable, nothing even that is novel or original. The same thought had been expressed more than once by English philosophers and writers upon jurisprudence. Two hundred and fifty years before, Bishop Hooker had written those noble and familiar words : " Of law, there can be no less acknowledged than that her seat is in the bosom of God." Already in this very speech Seward had quoted from another political philosopher, " There is but one law for all, namely, that law which governs all law, — the law of our Creator." In any point of view the passage was harmless, for far from antagonizing or contrasting the Constitution and the laws of God, Seward was insisting that they were both in harmony and working to the same noble ends.

Nor was he responsible for introducing into the debate both the " higher law " and the Constitution as conclusive authorities as to slavery and the rights of the slaveholders. Southern senators had already appealed to them. On the day on which Clay introduced his resolutions, Mason, of Virginia, and Davis, of Mississippi, had both insisted that the Constitution carried slavery into all the Territories, and protected it there. A fortnight later, Davis declared slavery to be " a blessing, established by God's decree, and sanctioned by the Bible, from Genesis to Revelation." A few days before Seward spoke, Davis had again rested the Southern case upon the same authorities, saying : " It is the Bible and the Constitution on which we rely, and we are not to be answered by the dicta of earthly wisdom or more earthly arrogance, when we have those high authorities to teach and to construe the decrees of God." It was natural, therefore, it was fit, and it was necessary, that some senator holding the opposite opinions should also appeal to the " higher law " which the Southerners had already invoked, and should say that he did not so read the Bible and the Constitution, though he also found them both in accord, — the one a gospel of freedom, not a decree of bondage, and the other a charter of liberty, not a law of servitude.

The rest of Seward's speech was devoted to considering the argument that the Union was in danger, and could only be saved by compromise. He was but little moved by the threats and passionate talk of dissolving the Union unless satisfactory concessions were made to slavery. He attached, or professed to attach, but little importance to them ; but the Southern leaders and many of their followers were in deadly earnest and meant all that they said. The Southern heart, however, had not yet been thoroughly fired, the slave States had made no preparations for secession, there had been no single act or even fancied aggression of which they could complain ; and they knew that, while Taylor lived, there could be no peaceable separation, that he considered secession to be treason and would not hesitate to treat it accordingly. Ten years' delay, and the complaisance of a President as feeble and vacillating as Taylor was prompt and resolute, were needed to complete their preparations and put them in readiness for action. That Seward saw any part of this is more than doubtful. He thought the Union practically indissoluble, because the centripetal and conservative forces seemed to him much stronger than the centrifugal. It seemed to him that the South, on reflection, would realize that, if there were to be a dissolution, the probable line of cleavage would run north and south, following the great river. He could not believe that the people of the South, when it came to the point, would be willing to say to the civilized world that they had seceded from the Union in order to establish a government of which African slavery should be the corner-stone, and its maintenance and perpetuity the final cause. Animated as he personally was by the conviction that slavery, which he had abhorred since the youthful days of his teaching in Georgia, must give way before the light of modern civilization, he felt confident that the Southerners, looking at the question calmly, would at last prefer that the Union should stand, and slavery " disappear gradually, voluntarily and with compensation," rather than that the Union should be dissolved, and, as he foresaw, " civil war and violent, complete and immediate emancipation follow." The day, he trusted, was far off, when the fountains of popular content should be broken up; but should it ever come, he felt certain that it would show " how calmly, how firmly, how nobly a great people can act in preserving their Constitution."

At this time, Clay, Calhoun, Webster and Seward practically represented all the shades of public opinion in the different sections of the country on the subject of slavery, except the views of the radical abolitionists. Clay, recognizing the existing antagonism between the North and South arising from the various questions connected with slavery, thought that, if some arrangement could be made by which the pending issues could be compromised, no further differences would arise, and this disturbing and dangerous element would be removed from our politics. Calhoun considered any such compromise as a mere palliative. In his opinion the Union was only a compact between two classes of equal, sovereign States, one class having slaves and the other not; and there must be an exact equilibrium of political power between these two classes, or the compact could not be permanent. Webster believed that the gain to mankind by the maintenance and perpetuation of the Union would far outweigh any loss or injury from concessions to, or compromises with, slavery and the slave States. Seward thought that the slave States and slaveholders were entitled to the exact rights and privileges which the Constitution gave them, but to nothing more; that slavery was a moral and political wrong, and that under no compulsion and by no persuasion would he ever consent to give it one hair's breadth of advantage not distinctly secured to it by the compromises of the Constitution.

After a debate, protracted more than two months, Clay's resolutions, with the amendments and the substitutes proposed by other senators, were referred to a committee of thirteen, of which he was chairman. A month later this committee reported three bills. The first of these made two amendments to the Fugitive Slave Bill then pending before the Senate; the second put an end to the use of the District of Columbia as a public slave mart for the States. The third was a bill of thirty-nine sections, — the first four of which provided for the admission of California, the next seventeen gave Utah a territorial government, and prohibited the territorial legislature from passing any law as to African slavery. Seventeen more sections provided a similar government for New Mexico. The last section contained a proposition to Texas as to the settlement of her boundaries. This third bill soon became known as the "Omnibus bill."

Those Southerners who had always opposed Clay's resolutions at once attacked this "Omnibus bill," and all through the hot and sultry summer the debate went on, personal, acrimonious, eager, passionate. The Southern senators were unwearied in their efforts to gain here or there something more than the bill gave them. They endeavored to limit the southern boundary of California to the line of the Missouri Compromise, and to provide for a slave State out of the territory thus cut off, to obtain a distinct recognition of what they claimed to be their constitutional right to carry slaves into New Mexico and hold them there, though the laws of that country abolishing slavery had never been repealed, and also to secure an admission of the power of the territorial legislatures to pass laws for the protection of slavery, but not for its prohibition. Clay, in spite of his years and feebleness, was indefatigable in defense of the committee, and in his endeavors to pass the bill; but all was in vain. By successive amendments it was gradually reduced to a simple act to provide a territorial government for Utah; and so mutilated, it passed the Senate on the last day of July.

Before this happened, Taylor, after a short illness, had died. So long as he lived, Clay had against him, not so much Taylor's active opposition as the knowledge of every senator that this plan was not the President's or approved by him, and that he had said to a senator who was opposed to the compromise measures: "Stand firm, don't yield." But when Fillmore succeeded Taylor, he called to his cabinet Webster and Corwin, the leading compromisers from the free States, and exerted all the influence of his administration to secure the passage of the Omnibus bill. Contrary, however, to the expectation of its advocates, it turned out that the tacking together of so many incongruous matters was a source of weakness, that it served to combine the opponents rather than to unite the friends of the separate measures, and so brought about the defeat of the entire bill.

All the measures recommended by the committee were, however, carried later, each in a separate act. It is the fashion to talk of these as compromise measures, but it is in a certain sense a misnomer; they did not as a whole receive the support of a majority of the committee of thirteen, less than one third of its members voting for all the bills. The separate acts were carried by different combinations of senators, only eighteen senators voting for all the bills as passed; of these, twelve were Northern Democrats, one a Northern Whig from Pennsylvania; four were Southern Whigs, and one, Houston, of Texas, a Southern Democrat. The analysis shows that it was not to be expected that measures, which taken as a whole found so little general support, could be a final settlement of all questions as to slavery.

Had Taylor lived, the compromise measures would probably have failed to pass in any form. The threats of disunion had steeled him against concessions to the demands of the South. " I am pained to learn," said he, " that we have disunion men to deal with.   Disunion is treason."   It seems the very irony of fate that this Southern President, for whom so many Northern Whigs hesitated or refused to vote, because he was a slaveholder and the representative of slaveholding interests, should have been abandoned by the great leaders of the party upon such a question, and should have stood without their support, an immovable bulwark against the slaveholders, in spite of South-

ern pressure and Northern weakness. Webster
thought Taylor's death delivered the country at
that time from the horrors of civil war; and later
writers have said that "the slaveholding States
would have been more able to hold their own in
1850 than they proved to be in 1861." But secession, had it been then attempted, would have
lost the ten years of organization and preparation
secured by delay, and would have encountered the
iron will and firm resolve of a Southern soldier,
who would have acted while others talked, and
whose well known character would have made the
stoutest secessionist hesitate before he took the
fatal step which separates declamation from action. The South did not secede in 1850 because
the masses were not ready to do so, and because
the leaders knew well what they might expect
from the President. Had any State committed
a single overt act of rebellion, there would have
been at once a resort to force. The offenders
would have been quickly reduced to obedience,
but slavery would have been untouched, and the
whole battle would have remained to be fought
out at a later day.

The death of Taylor made a great difference in
Seward's political weight in the Senate; he had
been recognized as the advocate, if not the official
representative of the President's policy, and this
position lent additional importance to his words.
But he had no such relations with Fillmore. On
the contrary, though in their early political days

both Fillmore and Seward had been anti-Masons, and both were original members of the Whig party, yet each of them had his own friends and followers, who looked to him when in office or power for crumbs from the political feast; and there was early established between them or their partisans a rivalry in the prosecution of claims for spoils. When questions as to slavery first became prominent, their opinions seemed substantially the same; but later, while Seward grew more outspoken against slavery, Fillmore became more conservative and cautious. When Fillmore was nominated for vice-president, he was understood to represent the anti-Seward wing of the Whig party; and the probability of difficulties from the counter-claims to office of their respective supporters was so fully recognized, that an attempt was made to effect an amicable arrangement between them as to the division of places; but it did not succeed. Some of Fillmore's friends were first served; but the fact that the governor and state authorities of New York belonged to the Seward wing of the party, which was far more numerous than Fillmore's, and that to this wing Taylor was principally indebted for the vote of the State, made it essential that this wing should be chiefly recognized in the distribution of offices.

The change in the attitude of the administration towards the compromise measures, which occurred on Fillmore's accession to office, did not affect Seward's position regarding them, or that of the

Whigs who were his followers. The Whig papers in the State of New York which had hitherto opposed them continued to do so, and President Fillmore became proscriptive. He removed the Albany postmaster, a friend of the editor of the Albany " Evening Journal," a paper outspoken in its hostility to the compromises ; and the whole influence of his administration was exerted, in vain, to prevent the Whig state convention of New York, in the autumn of 1850, from passing any resolution approving Seward's course. The president of the convention was one of the conservative Whigs, or, as they were afterwards called, Silver Greys ; he appointed a committee on resolutions, so selected as to make it sure that they would let Seward severely alone. But when they made their report, a resolve indorsing Seward's course was moved as an amendment and carried by a handsome majority. The administration members of the convention thereupon withdrew to another hall and indorsed the President and the compromises. In the Senate, within three weeks after Taylor's death, a Southern senator threatened to move Seward's expulsion ; and as he himself wrote : " By the advent of Mr. Fillmore " he " was buried below low-water mark."

The compromise measures, passed as separate bills before the adjournment of Congress in September, 1850, and which were practically all the work of the session, conceded to the North the admission of California as a free State, and the abolition of

the slave trade in the District of Columbia; to the
South, territorial governments for New Mexico
and Utah, with no exclusion of slavery, the adjustment of the boundary line between New Mexico
and Texas, so as to give Texas a large area which
she had never occupied or governed while an independent republic, the payment to her of ten
million dollars for relinquishing a purely paper
and nominal claim to still more of New Mexico,
and the enactment of a new and more stringent
law for the recovery of fugitive slaves. These
measures were proclaimed to be a final settlement
of the whole slavery question, which had thus become a dead issue.

Perhaps the compromises would have allayed
the excitement, and have been accepted at the
North with practical unanimity, but for the Fugitive Slave Law. But this law was odious to the
communities in which it was to be enforced. It
contained no statute of limitations; it permitted
the recapture of runaways, who had been for years
residents in, and had become citizens of, the different free States. The proceedings were assumed
to be analogous to those by which a person charged
with a crime in a State from which he has fled is
surrendered to take his trial there; and the statute
was so drawn that colored persons alleged to be
fugitive slaves could be arrested upon *ex parte*
affidavits and hurried into slavery upon the production of mere formal proofs, with no opportunity
to try the question of their freedom in the States

where they were living and where all the testimony tending to establish this was naturally to be found. While, as if to make the statute still more offensive to the North, it was provided, that the commissioners who were to administer the law should receive a fee, when the alleged fugitive was returned, twice as large as that to which they would be entitled if the captive were discharged. Had the law been less arbitrary and brutal, had it provided some safeguards for freedom, some remedies for mistakes of identity, had it made any concessions to Northern sentiment and to the civilization of the nineteenth century, the people of the free States might have permanently acquiesced in it as a legitimate mode of fulfilling an obligation which the Constitution imposed on them, repugnant to their conscience and feelings as that obligation was. But the actual statute was a mere firebrand flung among the opponents of slavery at the North, and every case that arose added fuel to the spreading flames of the popular excitement against it.

CHAPTER VI

FILLMORE'S ADMINISTRATION

AFTER the passage of the compromise measures, there was a lull in the great contest between freedom and slavery, as often after a battle both combatants seek repose, and time to recruit their strength before renewing the conflict; and this truce lasted, with no signs of any new struggle, until the close of Fillmore's administration in 1853.

The congressional session of 1850–51 was politically unimportant. It was yet too soon for either the North or the South to declare that the compromise measures were not a finality; although in the free States many meetings, with resolutions indorsing the Fugitive Slave Law and declaring an unfaltering determination to execute it, and a deluge of pamphlets and sermons by its supporters, lay and clerical, were found necessary to offset the meetings, speeches and sermons of its opponents, and to endeavor to overcome the hostility of the North to its enforcement. In November, 1850, Mr. Webster wrote to the President from Boston: "There is now no probability of any resistance if a fugitive should be arrested." Yet only three months afterwards a negro, arrested as a fugitive slave, was rescued from the court house there at high noon and successfully carried to Canada; and in spite of the utmost exertions on the part of the government, no one was ever convicted of taking part in his escape. Quite as significant of the public opinion of the North, though in a different way, was the election to the Senate from New York, Fillmore's own State, of Hamilton Fish, an opponent of the compromises, as Seward's colleague; while Ohio sent Benjamin Wade, a most outspoken Free Soiler; and in Massachusetts, though only by a bargain for offices between Democrats and Free Soilers, Charles Sumner, an exponent of the extreme anti-slavery opinion, though not a political abolitionist, succeeded Webster in the Senate.

Though " political ends, and not real evils resulting from the escape of slaves, constituted the prevailing motives for the enactment of the Fugitive Slave Law," yet, in fact, during the first year after its passage, more persons were seized as fugitive slaves than in the preceding sixty years. This statement, however, does not imply so much as it seems to. From many of the New England States no slave had ever been taken back, and, except from Massachusetts, not one from any of them for at least a quarter of a century. There was, even so early as February, 1851, some foundation for the complaint that bad faith threw all kinds of difficulties in the way of the recovery of fugitives, often increasing the cost to the full value of the slave. Charges of this kind became doubtless more and more true as time went on and the constantly growing hostility to the law continually invented new and fresh obstacles to its speedy and peaceful execution. There were other rescues, and an occasional murder either of pursuers or pursued, or the killing by a mother of her children that they might not be sent back to slavery. These, with some kidnappings, and the not infrequent return to slavery, under the summary processes of the law, of free colored persons, kept alive the public feeling, and tended slowly to consolidate into a new party the plain people of the Northern States, who did not live by commerce or manufactures, and had no direct dealings or intercourse with the South.

Even in Congress there was a certain recognition of the fact that the finality of the compromises might be questioned. Before the end of January, 1851, forty-four senators and representatives of different political parties, with Clay himself at their head, thought it advisable to publish a manifesto, declaring that they would support no man for office who did not condemn any disturbance of the compromises or agitation of the slavery question. Yet congressional action on this subject was not always consistent with what this declaration implied. Only a few days later a bill to construe the Fugitive Slave Law so as to increase its rigor was introduced into the Senate, and at

once referred to a committee, while petitions for
its repeal were refused such reference, and immediately laid on the table. Yet even as to these
the rule was not uniform, such a petition presented
by Seward being summarily disposed of, while
similar petitions presented by senators from Maine
and Pennsylvania were appropriately referred.

In a short speech on this matter, Seward, allud-
ing to the charge of being an agitator, said : " I
am one of the members of this body who have
been content with the debates which were had
when this subject came legitimately before us in
the form of bills requiring debate. I have never
spoken on the subject since those bills became
laws. I have been content to leave those measures
to the scrutiny of the people, and the test of time
and truth. I have added no codicils and have
none to add, to vary, enforce or explain what I
had occasion to say during the debates."

This declaration was true, and his conduct in
this matter eminently characteristic. He was no
agitator for agitation's sake. He recognized the
fact that the country was for the moment worn out
with discussion, that it was hopeless to attempt to
rouse the people by declamation, and that only
concrete facts of wrong and outrage, which he felt
sure would not fail to occur, could do this.

There were other subjects besides slavery discussed in the session of 1850–51, — a French Spoli-
ation Bill, which Seward supported in an elaborate
speech, the improvement of rivers and harbors, the

disposition of the public lands, and changes in our
postal system. In his views on this last subject,
Seward was distinctly a reformer, and in advance
of the times. He could not secure cheap postage;
but it was to his exertions at this session that we
owe our street letter-boxes and the first attempt at
delivery by letter-carriers in the cities and towns.

The summer of 1851 saw the opening of the
Erie Railway to the Lakes; the President and
many of his cabinet and Seward with them made
an excursion over the whole length of the road,
and there were banquets and speeches and fire-
works and all the other festivities common to such
occasions. To the "Silver Greys," the Whigs who
had indorsed the administration and the compromises, the chief of the "Woolly Heads" must have
seemed an undesirable addition to the presidential
party on this prolonged excursion; and Seward
himself felt that there might be some embarrassment from his presence. But the construction of
this railway had been one of his early and constantly cherished projects, and he would have been
reluctant to miss "the wedding of the Lakes to
the salt sea with the ring of well wrought iron."
This was his holiday for the year; he spent the
rest of his summer in the trial of an important and
fatiguing criminal case.

Both sessions of the thirty-second Congress
(December, 1851, to March 4, 1853) were in
striking contrast to those of the previous one. Instead of stormy discussion, hard feelings, bitter

words, and unbecoming personalities, there were
courtesy, fair debate, and general kindliness and
good feeling.   In the opening days of the first
session, resolutions were introduced in the Senate
affirming the finality of the compromise measures;
but the discussion of these, except in a single
instance, was carried on between the Southern
senators, and the resolutions themselves were never
pressed to a vote.   In Mississippi, where the issue
had been distinctly raised between secession or the
Union with compromises, Foote, the compromise
Union candidate, was elected governor over Jefferson Davis, the nominee of the pronounced Secessionists.   A South Carolina convention, called to
promote the cause of disunion, collapsed; and, so
far as the South was concerned, it was evident
that no further concessions to the slaveholding
interests were to be asked for at present.   At the
North the number of cases under the Fugitive
Slave Law seemed to diminish.   There was consequently less general excitement about it, though
there were occasional bursts of indignation, when
the popular passions in some locality broke out in
a flame; but the flame never spread into a con-
flagration, and the elections in 1852 showed that,
on the whole, public opinion was inclined to abide
by the compromise measures and not to disturb
them.

The event of the winter (1851–52) which principally excited Congress and the country was the
visit of Kossuth and his companions, who had

been leaders in the Hungarian insurrection of
1848. The efforts of the Hungarians to establish
a republic had seemed on the point of success,
when the forces which Russia sent the Austrian
emperor at his request, joined to his own army,
enabled him to crush the rebellion. The Czar,
who had refused to aid Austria so long as the
Hungarians were merely seeking reforms, justified
his interference when they had undertaken to form
a republic, upon the ground that "the internal
security of his empire was menaced by what was
passing and preparing in Hungary." Upon their
final defeat, Kossuth and other Hungarians escaped
to Turkey. The Sultan, supported by England,
refused to surrender them; and the Congress of
the United States, acting on the belief that these
refugees wished to leave Europe forever, and to
seek new homes here, gave them passage to this
country in a national vessel. Kossuth, however,
leaving the ship at Gibraltar, went directly to
England, where he was received with an enthusiasm
which grew day by day. During his visit there
he put before the people in public addresses of
marvelous eloquence, tinged with Oriental thought
and fancy, and clothed in the language of Shake-
speare, the only English he knew, vivid pictures of
the wrongs and oppression of his country. He
made it evident that it was his purpose to induce
both Great Britain and the United States to acknowledge that it was their duty to protest against
the action of any state which should assist another

to put down an insurrection; and although he did
not expressly say so, he evidently expected them
to be prepared, if necessary, to support their protests by force.   As an earnest of their assent to
this principle, he wished Great Britain and the
United States each to put on record its official and
public condemnation of the recent intervention of
Russia in the affairs of Hungary, and his hope
was, under cover of this declaration, to start a
fresh insurrection there with a better prospect of
success.

After a short stay in England, he sailed for
New York, where he was to arrive early in December.   On the very day that Congress assembled in
that month, a resolution was introduced in the
Senate, at the instance, it was said, of the secretary
of state, providing for the welcome and reception
of the Hungarian patriots.   It was expected to
pass at once and unanimously, but it was opposed,
and was therefore not pressed.   A substitute, offered by Seward, simply giving Kossuth "a cordial
welcome to the capital and the country," was
adopted by both houses after some debate.   The
small minority against it consisted, with a single
exception, of Southerners, whose opposition to the
resolve, as one of them declared, "had been guided
solely by sensitiveness on the subject of slavery."
Some Southerners, whose sympathies had been
excited for the defeated leaders of an unsuccessful
rising in a remote land, and who had been quite
ready to invite them here as "exiles broken in

heart and fortune," desirous only "to spend their
remaining days in obscure industry," were quick
to take alarm when they found Kossuth preaching
a crusade in favor of freedom and the rights of
men, and when they witnessed the effect of his
fervid appeals upon all classes of persons at the
North. For it was not merely the more impres-
sionable and uncritical masses who were carried
away by his eloquence; but grave professors, scholars, and men of letters, the intelligent, refined,
and fastidious people of the land were equally
moved by him; and the slaveholders not unreasonably apprehended that the quickened sense of
the wrongs of a people suffering under the yoke
of a despotism, might intensify and deepen the
growing conviction at the North of the greater
wrongs and sufferings of a people borne down
by the still heavier yoke of slavery. The fact
that the most earnest anti-slavery leaders were
among the most ardent of Kossuth's admirers
naturally tended to increase these apprehensions.
Kossuth made a tour of the South; but though
he preserved a discreet silence on the subject of
slavery, his speeches failed to awaken there any
interest for Hungary.

Some of the men in public life undoubtedly
used the Hungarian question for political purposes; but Seward took it up in dead earnest. He
offered in the Senate a resolution which denounced
the conduct of Russia in invading Hungary without just right, in subverting there the constitution

established by the people, and reducing the country
to the condition of a province ruled by a foreign
power ; and which further declared that the United
States, in defense of their own interests and of the
common interests of mankind, protested against
this conduct of Russia, as a wanton and tyrannical
infraction of the law of nations, and would not in
future be indifferent to any similar acts of national
injustice, oppression, or usurpation, wherever they
might occur.   In a very earnest and elaborate
speech he urged the passage of this resolve.   He
admitted that it would have been better had we
made our protest before the final defeat and surrender of the Hungarians ; but thought this of the
less consequence as the surrender was quite recent,
and there was some prospect of a new rising in
Hungary, which made the protest important and
seasonable.[1]   We had an interest in making this
protest, he said, as one of the family of nations,
and so deeply concerned in their general welfare
that it was not merely our right but our duty to
do this.

Nor did he see any real objection to it.   A protest was "not a declaration, nor a menace, nor
even a pledge of war in any contingency."   It

[1] The final defeat and surrender of the Hungarians was August 10-13, 1849.   This speech was delivered March 9, 1852.   As
neither this country nor England gave Hungary official encouragement there was never any later outbreak.   The ninety thousand
dollars ($90,000) raised in this country by subscription, for the
Hungarian cause, was all spent for the benefit of those who came
over here.

was only "a remonstrance addressed to the conscience of Russia, and an appeal to the reason and
justice of mankind. By the law of nations," he
argued, "no remonstrance justifies a war." If
war should come, the protest would be not a
cause, but a "pretext," and "in a defensive war
levied against us on such a pretext we should be
unconquerable." If Hungary should never rise,
there would be no *casus belli*, and if she should do
so, we should have the right to choose our own
time for recognizing her. He found in our civil
reply to Louis XVI.'s announcement of the formation of the French constitution of 1791, an infer-
ential protest against the foreign intervention then
organized beyond the Rhine, although the reply
was absolutely silent on this point; and he discovered further protests of the same kind in the
friendly official messages sent to the Committee of
Safety of the first French republic.

Washington's policy of avoiding entangling alliances with European countries Seward admitted
to have been wise and necessary in its day; but
he argued that this policy was not intended or
adapted for all time; that Monroe's course as
to the Holy Alliance and the South American
republics was a departure from it; and that his
later expression of sympathy with Greece towards
the close of her long struggle for independence was
inconsistent with it. He spoke with pride of the
instant, though unauthorized, recognition by our
own minister of the French republic of 1848, as

showing the trend of our political relations and influence with the countries of Europe; and he insisted that the resolve he offered was no greater intervention (if it were intervention at all), than what we had done "in every contest for freedom and humanity throughout the world since we became a nation."

Seward had, in fact, found no precedent for any such protest, in any act of our foreign policy as to the domestic difficulties of any European state. The diplomatic history of the country afforded no such precedent. The speech was one in which his sympathies got the better of his reason. It advocated a meddlesome foreign policy, inconsistent with the position, the interests, and the prosperity of the United States. Had his resolution been adopted, it would have been a new departure, at variance with the established practice and traditions of this country, and ten years later might have been relied on by the countries of Europe to justify a more active interference with our course in crushing the Southern rebellion. The sober sense of Congress saved us from the possible consequences of Seward's rash and quixotic proposal.

In forming the standing committees of the Senate, in the Congress which met in December, 1851, Seward was made a member of that on commerce. This brought him into more familiar relations with other senators, and gave him plenty of congenial work. He was always a believer in the development of the country, upon the lines of the policy of the Whig party, and his place on this committee made more effective his endeavors to foster by legislation our domestic and foreign commerce. He advocated government aid to two lines of Atlantic steamers, to the ship canal round the Sault Saint Marie, and to railroads in various parts of the country, declared himself " out and out " in favor of a railway across the continent, while for the benefit of our whalers and trade in the Pacific he strenuously urged a government survey of that ocean.

In the second session of this Congress there were no political debates. When the presidential conventions met, both parties inserted in their platforms an indorsement of the finality of the compromises. That of the Democrats was explicit, and adopted unanimously; that of the Whigs, though more qualified, was opposed by one fourth of the delegates.

In the Democratic convention the struggle for the nomination was long : the party leaders, Cass, Marcy, and Buchanan, were all at last abandoned, and Franklin Pierce of New Hampshire, who had seen some public service both in the House and Senate and been a general in the Mexican war, secured the nomination.

Among the Whigs, Scott was the candidate of the opponents of the compromises of 1850; Fillmore and Webster, of those who supported these compromises. On the first ballot in the convention Webster received only twenty-nine votes, while

Fillmore had a hundred and thirty-one, — enough with Webster's twenty-nine to have given him the nomination. The conservative Northern and the Southern Whigs had together a majority of the convention, and the indorsement of the finality of the compromise measures, including the Fugitive Slave Law, was not unexpected. Indeed the outcome of the convention was but another compromise, a last attempt of the Whigs to preserve their character as a national party. The anti-slavery Whigs of the North secured the nomination, the South the platform. Seward was disheartened. "The North, the free States," he wrote, "are divided as usual, the South united. Intimidation, usual in that quarter, has been met, as usual, by concession, and so the platform adopted is one that deprives Scott of the vantage of position he enjoyed. . . . I anticipate defeat and desertion." He was so discouraged as to feel weary of his position and that he should be glad to get out of it. This feeling continued throughout the summer. "When will there be a North?" he asks; and says again: "I still remain strongly inclined to give up this place and public life. If the state Whig convention adopt the platform, I think I shall be justified in resigning at once."

The result of the election confirmed his forecast. Pierce received two hundred and fifty-four electoral votes from twenty-seven States, while General Scott had only the votes of Vermont, Massachusetts, Kentucky, and Tennessee, forty-two in all.

Pierce's plurality over Scott on the popular vote was more than two hundred thousand, and his majority over all candidates nearly sixty thousand. So far as the election had any political significance, it showed that the Southerners believed the Democrats more subservient than the Whigs to the slaveholding interests; while it also indicated that the majority of the Northern voters were weary of antislavery agitation, and had accepted the compromise measures as a solution of all difficulties, and as the finality which the platforms of both parties asserted them to be.

CHAPTER VII

THE REPEAL OF THE MISSOURI COMPROMISE

PRESIDENT PIERCE's first message, delivered on the 5th of December, 1853, called attention to the " sense of repose and security in the public mind," and gave assurance that this repose should suffer no shock if he had power to avert it. There can be no doubt that, at the time he said this, the President had not the slightest foreboding of the rude shock which this repose was at once, with his own assent and support, to receive at the hands of his own party.

The Louisiana purchase, the territory acquired from France by the Treaty of 1803, extending west from the Mississippi to the Rocky Mountains, first brought into our politics the disturbing factor of the extension of slavery; all our previous holdings being free under the Ordinance of 1787. After a sharp contest the question of freedom or slavery in this territory was settled by a compromise, by which Missouri was admitted as a slave State; and in all the rest of the territory slavery was to be allowed south of 36° 30', while north of this latitude it was forever prohibited.

By this bargain between the sections, the South

secured all the rich and fertile lands from the mouth of the Mississippi to the northern border of Missouri, and left to the North the uninhabited regions beyond, which were abandoned to the hunter and trapper, or gradually given over to Indian reservations. In 1836, Missouri obtained leave of Congress to extend her boundaries westward to the Missouri River, and thus more than three thousand square miles, which the Compromise had made free, became slave territory. Aside from this, however, the Missouri Compromise had remained practically unquestioned from its passage in March, 1820, until the year 1853, and had been regarded as hardly less sacred and binding than the Constitution itself. But the South had now reaped the full benefit of all it had secured by the bargain ; and the inhabitants of the southwestern counties of Missouri, with their twenty-five thousand slaves, were looking with covetous eyes upon the fair lands of Kansas, lying just beyond their own borders.

Several attempts had been made to secure from Congress an act for the organization of a territorial government, in conformity with the provisions of the Missouri Compromise ; but they had all been defeated by Southern votes, ostensibly upon the ground that this Territory could not be opened to settlement without interference with Indian reservations secured by solemn treaties. Within ten days after the delivery of the President's message, with its promise of repose, a similar bill was introduced into the Senate and referred to the Committee on Territories, of which Stephen A. Douglas of Illinois was chairman.   Three weeks later the committee returned it with amendments, accompanied by an elaborate report, in which it was said that it was a disputed point whether the Compromise prohibiting slavery in this Territory was a valid enactment; eminent statesmen holding that Congress had no authority to legislate as to slavery in the Territories, that the Constitution secured to every citizen an inalienable right to move into any Territory with any property, including slaves, and to have the same protected by law, and that any legislation interfering with or restricting this right was null and void.   The committee added that they did not recommend any legislation either affirming or repealing the Missouri Compromise, or declaring the meaning of the Constitution upon this disputed question; but then went on to say that the compromise measures of 1850 rested upon the proposition that all questions pertaining to slavery in the Territories, or in the States to be formed therefrom, should be left to the decision of the people residing therein.

The purpose and effect of this report did not escape the notice of the vigilant anti-slavery press of the North.[1]   Nor was the hint at its close wholly lost on the South.   On the 16th of January, a Southern senator gave notice of an amendment

---

[1] New York *Evening Post*, January 7, 1854 ; *Tribune*, January 11; *Independent*, January 7.

repealing so much of the Missouri Compromise as
prohibited slavery in this Territory, and providing
that slaves might be taken there as if that act had
never been passed.   A week later, after a Sunday's
conference with the President, in which Pierce at
last yielded to the arguments and persuasion of
Jefferson Davis and Douglas, Douglas again reported the bill· from his committee, and now there
was no uncertainty as to its meaning.   It created
two Territories, Kansas the southern one, and north
of this Nebraska.   It provided that slavery in these
Territories should be left to the decision of the
people there, and declared the Missouri Compromise inconsistent with the principle of the acts of
1850 and therefore inoperative and void.   The bill
in this shape passed the Senate by a vote of thirty-
seven yeas to fourteen nays, — all the Southerners,
of whatever party, except Bell of Tennessee and
Houston of Texas, voting for it, and only four
Northern Democrats against it.[1]

When Douglas reported his bill he readily
granted its opponents a week's delay before it
should be brought up for discussion.   In this
interval there was published the address of the
" Independent Democrats," in which the whole
history of the growth and development of the bill
was exposed, the report attacked, and a strenuous
effort made to rouse the people of the North to
a sense of the wrong attempted to be done them,

[1] Seven Whigs including Bell, five Democrats including Houston, with Chase and Sumner, Independents, made up the minority.

and of the threatened danger to freedom.   This
address was signed by Chase and Sumner of the
Senate and three members of the House.   Seward
did not sign it, and it is obvious that he could not
have done so.   He was not an Independent Democrat ; he was a Whig, and there was no reason for
his signing it which did not apply equally to the
other anti-slavery Whigs in the Senate, — Fessenden, Foote, Fish, Smith, and Wade, none of whom
put their names to it.

When the day for the debate arrived, Douglas,
assuming that the delay had been asked to gain
time to stir up sectional agitation at the North,
made a savage attack on Chase and Sumner, the
senators responsible for this manifesto, and on
them, for the time, came the brunt of the battle
against the bill.   Before its final passage Seward
made two speeches upon it.   It was a case, however, where discussion was useless.   Douglas had
brought the bill to its final shape, providing for
the organization of two Territories with no restriction as to slavery, because (if we are to take his
own explanation) he thought some organization of
these Territories a pressing necessity, and was satisfied that the South would assent to no other plan.

The Southerners were perfectly well aware of
what they were doing.   They knew that they were
breaking a bargain of which they had reaped the
advantage, and they were at bottom quite indifferent to the charges of bad faith and to all the
reproaches heaped upon them.   They expected to

gain an immediate substantial advantage for slavery, and did not mind the exposure of the flimsy and shifting pretexts which they offered in justification of their conduct. They had the united Southern vote, which was pro-slavery and " knew no Whiggery and no Democracy where slavery was concerned ; " and they could rely on a sufficient number of Northern Democrats to carry any measure on which they had determined. To the Senate, therefore, argument was vain, and invectives and personalities were useful only to relieve the mind of the speaker. Whatever was said was a mere protest, unavailing where it was spoken. " We were only a few here," said Seward, "engaged in the cause of freedom in the beginning of this contest. All that we could hope to do was to organize and prepare the issue for the House of Representatives, and awaken the country."

Seward's first speech was a simple but exhaustive statement of the whole question in all its bearings, entirely free from personalities, and with little rhetorical adornment. Its tone was one of great calmness, and its calmness made it all the more effective. It has been described as a lawyer's argument. If it were so, the jury to whom it was addressed was the people of the United States, and its effect upon them was all that Seward himself could have desired.

" His words were listened to not only by his followers in New York, but they had a marked influence on all the anti-slavery Whigs in the country.

The speech was translated into German, and exten-
sively circulated among the Germans of western
Texas. It probably affected the minds of more
men than any speech delivered on that side of this
question in Congress." [1] Having stated the history
of the acquisition of the territory and of the passage of the Compromise bill, which had secured it
to freedom, the " universal acceptance of this measure by both parties for more than thirty years, as
a conclusive arrangement, its confirmation over
and over again by many acts of successive Con-
gresses, and the fact that the slaveholding States
had received the full benefit of what the Compromise secured them, while the non-slaveholding
States had practically enjoyed nothing under it,"
Seward went on to consider the nature of the question and the momentous consequences depending
upon its decision. " It was no abstraction that
had brought the Compromise into being. Slavery
and freedom were then active antagonists, seeking for ascendency in the Union ; and the contest
between them had since that day been merely protracted — not decided. By holding fast to the
Compromise, the occupation of the land by freemen, with free labor, would be secured forever ; by
abrogating it, this vast region was to be abandoned
to the chances of slavery, which no one could fore-
tell." He announced his conviction that if ever
the slaveholding States should " multiply themselves and extend their sphere, so that they could,

[1] Rhodes's *Hist. U. S.* i. pp. 453, 454.

without association with the non-slaveholding States, constitute of themselves a commercial republic, from that day their rule would be such as would be hard for the non-slaveholding States to bear; and their pride and ambition would consent to no union in which they should not so rule."

Notwithstanding the compromise measures of 1850, Seward's observation and his natural optimism had made him hopeful that anti-slavery opinion was gaining ground, and the country making slow progress, with occasional drawbacks, towards the gradual and peaceful emancipation which he ardently desired. The introduction of Douglas's original bill at this session of Congress, and the support which it at once received from Northern Democrats, were a rude shock to this hope; and Seward's letters at this time are full of gloomy forebodings. He wrote home: —

"Douglas has introduced a bill for organizing the Nebraska territory, going as far as the Democrats dare towards abolishing that provision of the Missouri Compromise which devoted all the new regions north of 36° 30' to freedom.

"I am heart-sick of being here. I look around me in the Senate, and find all demoralized. Maine, New Hampshire, Connecticut, Rhode Island, Vermont! ! ! All, all in the hand of the slaveholders; and even New York ready to howl at my heels, if I were only to name the name of freedom, which once they loved so much." [1]

[1] January 4, 1854.

To an invitation to a meeting in New York to protest against the bill, he replied: " Nebraska is not all that is to be saved or lost; we who thought, only so lately as 1849, of securing some portion at least of the Gulf of Mexico and all the Pacific coast to the institutions of freedom, shall be, before 1857, brought to a doubtful struggle to prevent the extension of slavery to the shores of the Great Lakes and Puget Sound." [1]   And as the vote was about to be taken in the Senate, before sending the bill to the House, he wrote again : " Heaven be thanked that since this cup of humiliation cannot be passed, the struggle of draining it is nearly over. . . . This triumph of slavery, the greatest and the worst, is the consummation of thirty-four years of compromise." [2]

In Mr. Welles's " Lincoln and Seward," which was written rather from a controversial than a historical point of view, he prints a letter from Mr. Montgomery Blair, in which Mr. Blair says: " I shall never forget how shocked I was at Seward's telling me that he was the man who put Archie Dixon, the Whig senator from Kentucky in 1854, up to moving the repeal of the Missouri Compromise as an amendment to Douglas's first Kansas bill; and had himself forced the repeal by that movement, and had thus brought to life the Republican party.   Dixon was to out-Herod Herod at the South, and he would out-Herod Herod at the North.   He did not contemplate what followed.

[1] January 28, 1854.   [2] March 3, 1854.

He did not believe in the reality of the passions he
excited, because he felt none himself.   He thought
it all a harmless game for power." This statement
of Mr. Blair's, though apparently relied on by
some careful writers, seems to show so great forgetfulness or ignorance of historical facts, or such a
reckless disregard of them, as greatly to impair, if
not wholly to destroy its claim to serious consideration; but as a malignant posthumous attack on
Seward, it justifies, if it does not require, even at
the risk of repetition, some notice here.

The principal historical facts, which dispose of
Mr. Blair's charge that Seward forced the repeal
of the Missouri Compromise by putting up Dixon
of Kentucky to move it, are as follows: early in
December, 1853, Dodge of Wisconsin introduced
into the Senate a bill for organizing into one Territory, to be called Nebraska, the whole country
stretching west from Missouri to Oregon and Utah.
All this region had been declared free by the
Missouri Compromise, and Dodge's bill assumed
this to be constitutional and still in force, unaf-
fected by any subsequent legislation.   His bill
was referred to the Committee on Territories, of
which Stephen A. Douglas of Illinois was chairman, and that committee, on the 4th of January,
1854, reported the bill in a new draft, or, to speak
accurately, substituted for Dodge's bill one of
their own.   They also submitted an elaborate
report, in which they said that "it was disputed
whether the law prohibiting slavery in Nebraska

was valid ; that there was involved in it the question whether Congress had the constitutional power
to regulate the domestic institutions of the Territories, — the same issue which produced the struggle of 1850, — that they thought it wise not to
depart from the course pursued at that time, and
would not recommend either affirming or repealing
the Missouri Compromise, or the passage of any
act declaratory of the meaning of the Constitution
on this point." Nevertheless their bill, when it
first appeared in print as an act of twenty sections,
on the 7th of January, 1854, contained provisions
borrowed from the laws organizing Utah and New
Mexico, by which, whenever this or any part of
this new Territory should be admitted as a State,
its admission should take place without regard to
the fact that its constitution permitted or prohibited slavery. This provision was a violation of
the spirit, if not also of the letter, of the Missouri
Compromise, and an application to this Territory
of the doctrine of squatter sovereignty as established by the compromise measures of 1850.

Three days later (January 10, 1854), there was
printed an additional section (the twenty-first),
said to have been omitted by a mistake of the
copyist in the original draft of the bill. This section contained several paragraphs. It declared
that it was the intent of the act, so far as slavery
was concerned, to carry into effect the principles
established by the compromise measures of 1850 ;
and specified as the first of these principles that

"all questions pertaining to slavery in the Territories, and in the new States to be formed therefrom, are to be left to the decision of the people
residing therein, through their appropriate representatives." If there had previously been any
doubt as to the purpose and effect of Douglas's
bill, this new section made its scope and object
perfectly clear; and Douglas was quite right when
he said at a later date that "the bill, in the shape
in which it was at first reported, as effectually
repealed the Missouri restriction as it did when
the repeal was put in express terms." The country
understood the bill in this way, and leading newspapers at once exposed its character.

Seward so understood it, and before the 10th of
January (the day when the additional section first
appeared) had written of it as "this infamous
Nebraska bill, an administration move;" and
called attention to its clause protecting Indians in
their rights of property, which he declared to be
"an equivoque to cover the slaves the Indians own,
and so sanction slavery by implication." He had
also written as to meetings and legislative resolutions to remonstrate against it, and expressed a
hope that Clayton might be induced "to lead an
opposition to *the repeal of the Missouri Compromise.*" [1]

On the 16th of January, eight days after the
date of this letter, Archibald Dixon of Kentucky,
who had been elected to the Senate as a Whig,

[1] Letters, January 8, 1854.

but who openly declared that upon the question of slavery he knew no Whiggery and no Democracy, that he was a pro-slavery man, was from a slaveholding constituency, and was there to maintain their rights, gave notice of an amendment which he proposed to offer, expressly repealing so much of the Missouri Compromise as prohibited slavery in this new Territory. Sumner on the next day proposed an amendment of an exactly opposite character. The bill was recommitted; the following week Douglas reported it substantially as it was finally passed; and we find Seward writing to his wife: "The great news of the day I suppose you have anticipated. The 'Hards,' finding fault with Douglas's equivocations in his first bill, insisted on the repeal of the Missouri Compromise. Douglas conferred last Sunday with the cabinet; and the matter resulted in a unanimous agreement to concede the demand, and to put the bill right through, before the country could be aroused, and so silence agitation of freedom by leaving no more for slavery to demand. I shall not speculate yet on the consequences."

The course of events in the Senate and the accounts contained in these letters correspond with one another. Douglas meant to repeal the prohibition of slavery contained in the Missouri Compromise, but hoped to do it indirectly, in such a way as to satisfy the South without rousing the attention or exciting the opposition of the North. He made two attempts for this purpose, — the second (by the restoration of the suppressed twenty-first section) more explicit than the first. But the friends of freedom had seen his object from the beginning; they believed, as he did, that he had accomplished it in his original bill, and at once began to endeavor to rouse public opinion at the North. The Southern slaveholders and the Northern pro-slavery Democrats (the Hards) would not, however, be satisfied with anything less than a direct repeal in clear language. They persuaded the President to assent to this course, and Douglas reported his final bill. Dixon's motion was an incident of no special importance. Before it was made the committee had determined that their bill should open the Territory to slavery, and believed that it had done so in the way to attract least attention. The South insisted on more explicit language on this point, and the committee yielded to their persistence. The final shape of the bill, proposing the organization of two Territories instead of one, may have been expected to facilitate its passage, as it left room for the argument that there was to be a division between the North and the South, as often before, and that though Kansas, which was next Missouri, would be a slave State, yet Nebraska was not likely to be so. Nebraska it was then quite safe to talk about, as its only denizens were Indians on their reservations, and our hunters and the game they were pursuing; and there was no immediate prospect of any more stable population.

What Seward actually said to Mr. Blair, which enabled him to make the statement he has printed, can never be known, since Mr. Blair, however shocked he was, never mentioned the matter during Seward's lifetime, when Seward might have explained or denied it, but reserved it for an attack on him after his death.   To any one who has studied Seward's life, the suggestion that in his opposition to the extension of slavery he was playing a part in " a harmless game for power," is simply absurd.   Slavery was abhorrent to him from his early experience in Georgia.   Later in life he abandoned a journey in Virginia because the daily contact with slavery was so repulsive to him.   He believed it a moral wrong and a political mistake, and his whole course in politics rested upon this conviction.   The substance and the tone of the letters we have quoted, his whole correspondence at the time, and his speech on the Kansas-Nebraska bill are absolutely inconsistent with his having " put up Dixon " to moving the repeal of the Missouri Compromise.   There were no confidential relations between Seward and Mr. Blair which would have naturally led Seward to make him the sole depositary of this secret; Blair himself had no such tender regard for Seward's reputation as would have caused him to hesitate for an instant to speak of this, if, at the time, he really understood what he at last brought himself to state in this letter.   There were in Congress, when the Kansas-Nebraska bill was under discus-

sion, many of its opponents who did not like, or
always agree with, Seward, and who did not shrink
from criticising him, or saying sharp and unpleasant things about him. If there were any back-
ground of facts to warrant Mr. Blair's charges, we
may be quite sure that some rumor of them would
have been then circulating in Washington, and
that we should not have waited till twenty years
after the events happened, when all the actors were
dead, before hearing this story for the first time.
Nor, if there were any foundation for Mr. Blair's
charge against him, if he had any share in Dixon's
motion, could Seward himself, when the facts were
fresh, and when the evidence to convict him of
falsehood, if what he was stating were untrue, was
right at hand, have written as he did in the letters
we have quoted, or have publicly said in a speech
on this very bill : " The shifting sands of compromise are passing from under my feet, and they are
now, *without agency of my own*, taking hold again
on the rock of the Constitution."

In the House of Representatives there was more
opposition to the bill; there seemed a possibility
of its defeat, and more than a possibility of some
amendments unacceptable to the slaveholders. But
it was at last forced through, without material
changes, by the parliamentary skill and the unhesitating audacity of Alexander H. Stephens of
Georgia, who succeeded most ingeniously in cutting off all possible amendments and stopping all
debate.

A change, which the Southerners were prepared
to accept, made it necessary to return the bill to
the Senate, that it might be put on its final passage there.   It was on the night before this final
vote was taken that Seward made his second
speech ; and the despondency betrayed in his correspondence is even more manifest here.

"The sun has set," he began, "for the last time
on the guaranteed and certain liberties of all the
unsettled and unorganized portions of the United
States.   To-morrow's sun will rise in dim eclipse
over them.   How long that obstruction shall last
is known only to the Power that directs and con-
trols all human events.   For myself, I know only
this, that no human power will prevent its coming
on, and that its passing off will be hastened and
secured by others than those now here, and perhaps only by those belonging to future generations.
. . . By the passage of this bill, freedom will endure a severe, though, I hope, not an irretrievable
loss. . . . . The slave States are in earnest in
seeking for and securing an object, and an important one.   I do not know how long the advantage
gained will last, nor how great and comprehensive
it will be. . . . There is suspended on the issue of
this contest the political equilibrium between the
free and the slave States.   It is no idle question,
whether slavery shall go on increasing its influence
over the central power here, or whether freedom
shall gain the ascendency. . . . I believe that, if
ever the greater ascendency of the slave power

shall come, the voice of freedom will cease to be heard in these halls, whatever may be the evils and dangers which slavery shall produce. . . . When freedom of speech on a subject of such vital interest shall have ceased to exist in Congress, then I shall expect to see slavery not only luxuriating in all new Territories, but stealthily creeping into the free States themselves. Believing this, . . . I am sure that this will be no longer a land of freedom and constitutional liberty, when slavery shall have thus become paramount." It was, therefore, rather with the courage of despair than with the confidence of hope that he said: "Come on, then, gentlemen of the slave States. Since there is no escaping your challenge, I accept it in behalf of the cause of freedom. We will engage in competition for the virgin soil of Kansas, and God give the victory to the side which is stronger in numbers as it is in right."

The only gleam of satisfaction that he could see came from his conviction that the so-called final arrangements with the South, made only to be broken, were forever at an end.

CHAPTER VIII

THE vote on the Nebraska bill again demonstrated that all questions touching the interests of slavery lay outside of the creeds of parties and the ties of party associations. The disintegration of the Whig party seemed inevitable. Every Northern Whig, in either House or Senate, voted against the bill; while of the Southern Whigs, twenty-one voted for it and only eight against it. Among the Democrats the sectional lines were not so sharply drawn; fifty-eight Northern Democrats voted for the bill, and forty-eight against it; while from the South but three voted against it, fifty-eight for it.

From the Northern Democracy, as an anti-slavery party, there was nothing to be hoped, and the people as well as the politicians were discussing whether it was more advisable to make a fight against slavery under the Whig name and organization at the North, or to form a new party. Already, before the passage of the bill, there had been meetings in Wisconsin to consider a fusion of the Whigs, Free Soilers, and anti-slavery Democrats into a new party, for which the name "Republican" had been suggested. The day after the passage of the bill some thirty members of Congress agreed together upon the necessity for a new party, and adopted the same name; and in the summer there were in several States, under varying forms, fusions between the anti-Nebraska members of the different parties, and elections to local offices of candidates who represented the various organizations which had united to form a common opposition to the constant demands of slavery. In Michigan the new organization was complete. It held a regular convention, called itself the "Republican party," nominated its candidates, and elected them.

Something had been said, even before the passage of the bill, as to calling a convention of all the free States; and Seward in reply to this suggestion had given his opinion that "we were not yet ready for a great national convention;" that the States were the places for activity. "Let us make our power respected, as we can, through our elections in the States, and then bring the States into general council."

The difficulties in the way of any fusion of the old parties were much greater in the East than in the West; for at the East the animosities were much stronger between the various political elements from which the opponents to the Nebraska bill were drawn.

There were several distinct bodies. The Northern Whigs, who on this question were a unit, were divided into at least two groups, — those who had

opposed the compromises of 1850, the Seward
Whigs we may call them, — and those who had
favored those compromises, the Webster Whigs.
The former were the more numerous, and had been
recruited by the addition of most of the young
Whigs ; the strength of the latter was in the cities
and with the older, richer, and more influential
classes. Of the former Seward was the leader ;
but by the latter he was looked upon with distrust
and dislike. If the houses of some of the conservatives in New York were again opening to him,
the Webster Whigs of Boston ignored his existence even at a later period ; when he came to
Massachusetts in December of the following year
(1855) to deliver an oration at Plymouth, no one
of them called upon him, though his arrival had
been announced in the newspapers, and he passed
a day in Boston, alone in a hotel parlor, reading
Lewes's "Life of Goethe." For the Whigs of
this class he had gone too fast and too far. To
the Free Soilers who had been Democrats, and to
those Democrats who had opposed the Nebraska
bill, he was objectionable, as having been always,
upon all the economic questions which had divided
the two great parties, a pronounced Whig. For
the successful formation of a new national party,
it was essential that Seward should lend to the
movement his active assistance, if he must not indeed lead in it ; yet the politicians were too much
afraid of the opposition to him from various
quarters to put him at its head, and, as he thought,

would have liked him to do the work and decline
the honors. He wrote to his wife : " I have letters
of all sorts ; . . . the amount of which is that, in-
somuch as I am too much of an anti-slavery man
to be proscribed by anti-slavery men, and yet too
much of a Whig to be allowed to lead, that I am
in the way of great movements to make a Democratic anti-slavery party . . . which would revo-
lutionize the government at once.

" Then again, I am so important to the Whig
party that it cannot move without me ; but that
party (the Webster part of it) is so jaundiced
toward me, that I am expected to decline being
a candidate right off, and go in for some other
Whig candidate, and so carry the election for
the Whig party.

" The Free Soilers are engaged in schemes for
nominating Colonel Benton and dissolving the
Whig party ; . . . and there are not less than half
a dozen parties coming to negotiate with me as if
I were a vendor of votes."

All that he saw and learned increased his doubts
whether the various opponents of the Nebraska
bill were yet prepared so to subordinate their
differences as to work together harmoniously and
earnestly for a common end, and confirmed his
opinion that the time was not ripe for a national
experiment, but for separate efforts in the States,
where success would be more probable and more
encouraging, and where failure would be less disastrous and demoralizing. This course seemed

all the more judicious, as there was no national contest this year, and separate congressional districts could arrange, each in its own way, for the election of anti-Nebraska congressmen, more effectually than if they were in any degree under the control of a new party organization.

It presently appeared also that there was a new element to be taken into account in any political calculation : — the mysterious apparition of a new party, the " Dark Lantern," the " Know-Nothing " or " Native American " party, which was both a political organization and a secret order, whose ostensible purpose was to check the power and restrict the numbers of foreign-born citizens by a rigorous enforcement and the ultimate modification of the existing naturalization laws, to purify the ballot, and to resist all attempts to exclude the Bible from the public schools; in other words, it seemed to be a union of American Protestants against Irish Roman Catholics. It originated in New York in 1853, and its avowed objects appealed to many people in that and other large cities of the East, where the influx of illiterate foreigners was the greatest, and abuse of the naturalization laws most frequent. Conservative men all over the country who had been Whigs, and who realized that their party as a national organization was dead, joined the order in the hope that questions as to slavery might be put aside by these new issues, which had nothing sectional about them. It was the only refuge for a

Southern Whig; and Northern Whigs, who could
not bring themselves to strike hands with Seward
and the advance guard of their old party, found
here an escape from so doing. It became distinctly a Union-saving party in November, 1854,
when it introduced into its ritual a third, or Union,
degree, and conferred it on the initiates with an
imposing ceremonial. Before this time, however,
there were not wanting zealous anti-slavery men
who had seen that the Know-Nothing organization
might be used as an instrument in breaking up
the old parties and aiding the formation of a new
one, and who joined it for this purpose. They
were sufficiently numerous in many States to influence the nominations, and to take care that the
candidates for Congress should be in harmony
with their views.

The Know-Nothings were badly defeated in
Virginia in the spring of 1855, and their national
council, in June of that year, was hopelessly divided by sectional strife; yet in the elections of
1854 they had been formidable opponents, all the
more so because nothing was known of them, of
their methods, their power, or their numbers. In
Philadelphia, where they were supposed to be very
numerous, Douglas denounced them bitterly in a
campaign speech, hoping in this way to deter Democrats from joining the organization, and to secure
for his party the full Irish vote.

Seward, whose hostility to any political proscription on account of birth, race, or religion was

of long date and had often been stated by him in
public addresses and letters, took no part in the
campaign. His silence has been criticised. But
whether considered with reference to his own personal interest in his reëlection to the Senate or to
the success of the party, it seems to have been judicious. It may be doubted whether, when the
largest national issue to which he could address
himself was practically that of his own reëlection,
he would have thought it becoming the dignity of
his position to enter the lists as a campaign speaker
on his own behalf. It was well understood, too,
that many Whigs, who looked on him with jaundiced eyes, had joined the new, mysterious company with its secret affiliations. The Whig party
of New York had declined all alliances whatsoever, adhered to its old organization, and placed
itself squarely on anti-Nebraska ground; nothing
that Seward could have said would have detached
a single "Silver Grey" neophyte from his allegiance to the new order, though it might have lost
him the vote of some Know-Nothing, who had a
more vivid interest in the struggle against a manifest and growing evil at home than in a crusade
to secure the freedom of a region so remote as
Kansas. In the State of New York the Whigs
carried their ticket by a plurality of only three
hundred in a vote of nearly half a million. A
change of one hundred and fifty-five votes would
have elected the Democratic candidates.

Early in February of the following year, Seward

was reëlected senator; and this reëlection, considering his antecedents, was as severe a blow as could have been dealt the Know-Nothings at that time. The earnest members of that party had set their hearts on his defeat; but the result showed that, when an issue was raised between anti-slavery and Americanism, there were members of that party, at least in the legislature of Seward's own State, who were opponents of slavery before they were Know-Nothings.

This campaign and election, which seemed to Seward a victory for himself as well as his party, was to bear for him most bitter fruit. Horace Greeley, who was generally considered at that time an unselfish patriot, but had at bottom an unsatisfied desire for a nomination, as a recognition from his party, had set his heart on being the Whig candidate for governor; and had, as both he and his friends thought, every reason to expect this. In spite of Greeley's ability, his advocacy of various hobbies and crotchets of his own had led so many sensible people to doubt his judgment, that it was feared that his name on the ticket, when success was at the best so uncertain, would insure its defeat, and he did not receive the nomination; while, to make matters worse, a rival editor — Henry J. Raymond, of the New York "Times" — was nominated and elected as lieutenant-governor. For all this Greeley chose to consider Seward responsible, and he wrote him a letter, which Seward took for a momentary ebullition of temper, but

which was in truth a declaration of undying hostility.   Greeley bided his time; and in 1860 went
from New York to Chicago as a " delegate from
Oregon " to the Republican Convention, that he
might do all in his power to get even with Seward
and defeat his nomination for the presidency.

The defeat of the Know-Nothings in Virginia,
and their domestic disorders in Philadelphia, were
unmistakable signs of waning strength.   The auspicious moment for the formation of a new party
in those States which had clung to their old organizations appeared to have arrived.   In Ohio, Pennsylvania, Massachusetts, and New York, Republican
conventions were called and candidates nominated.
To this movement in New York Seward gave his
hearty adhesion and a strong impulse.   In a speech
at Albany he summed up the case for the Northern
opponents of the extension of slavery, by a most
graphic sketch of the changes of attitude of the
slaveholders, from their assent to the dedication to
freedom of all our public lands by the ordinance of
1787, to their steady encroachments and constantly
increasing demands as to our newly acquired territory from the time of the Louisiana purchase to
the repeal of the Missouri Compromise; and he
showed the necessity of a new party organization
to resist the future exactions of this privileged and
persistent class.

The result of the autumn elections, however, indicated that the Northern seceders from the Know-
Nothing party had underestimated its strength,

and justified the boast of the New York leader of
its pro-slavery faction : that, though they had ex-
pelled thirty thousand members for supporting
Seward's reëlection, they could still muster votes
enough to carry the State. The outcome of these
elections, as a whole, was somewhat disheartening
for the Republicans ; the Democracy recovered
New Jersey, Pennsylvania, Indiana, and Illinois ;
and the pro-slavery American party, with the
"Silver Grey" Whigs, who voted for its candidates, carried New York, California, and Massachusetts. If any conclusion is to be drawn from the
result in New York, it would seem to be that,
had Seward surrendered his own judgment to the
opinions of those who advocated the formation of a
new national party the year before, and had he
abandoned the Whig organization at that time,
the Know-Nothings or the Democracy would have
carried the State, he would have returned to private life, and the country would have lost his great
services during the trying six years to come.

The Republican party having been organized in
the various Northern States, the next step was to
give it a national character and prepare for the
presidential campaign of the following year. A
preliminary matter, to which much consideration
was given by some of the leading men, was the
question of the recognition of the Know-Nothings,
either in the call for the convention, the platform,
or the candidates, and an alliance, if not a fusion,
of the two parties.

Just at the close of the year, at a conference to which Seward was invited, but which he declined to attend, it was proposed to have a convention, half Republican and half Know-Nothing, and he was told that all the free States except New York either had acquiesced in it or would do so. Seward declined to assume any responsibility as to the action of his State; but for himself protested against any such combination, saying that if it were carried out, he should disavow all connection or sympathy with it. The prospect of some such understanding he thought increasing as time went on, and regretted that the tone of anti-slavery sentiment was becoming daily more and more modified under the pressure of Know-Nothing influence, feeling as if he himself were half demoralized by it. The question had a personal bearing with him from the outset. He would have liked the presidential nomination, if the new party were to put itself squarely on a ground of principle and not of expediency; but he could not accept it if there should be any taint of Know-Nothingism, either about the convention or the platform. At the conference which has been spoken of, it was stated that Fremont and Chase were both candidates; and it was also said on Weed's authority that Seward was not so. This Seward confirmed, so far as it related to a nomination by the joint convention then proposed; but he by no means abandoned either the hope or the desire for the nomination, though he put himself as to that in

Weed's hands, trusting to his political sagacity to decide what was best. The trend of opinion in favor of Fremont was so strong that early in April Seward wrote that it had ripened into the general impression that it would be expedient to nominate the California candidate; but his apprehensions of some arrangement with the Know-Nothings were by no means relieved. " I am content and quiet on the personal question," he wrote to Weed, " and when the array of the battle shall be set and fixed, I shall decide upon my own line of duty, so as to save my independence without the exhibition of personal susceptibilities."

A preliminary convention, on the 22d of February, had announced the organization of the Republicans as a national party; its nominating convention was to be held at Philadelphia on the 17th of June. As this time drew near Seward's uneasiness increased; he thought the indications decisive of a compromise which would be embarrassing to him, and " even more injurious to the great cause in whose name it was to be made." He had not, however, nor had the people generally, abandoned all expectation of his being the nominee of the convention; and though he learned — and with apparent surprise, tracing no connection between Greeley's conduct and his letter — that Greeley had struck hands with his enemies, and sacrificed him for the good of the cause, and that Weed had concurred in this; yet it was not till the day the convention met that he absolutely declined the

Thurlow Weed

nomination, upon the ground that the convention was not prepared to adopt all his principles, and that he would not modify them to secure the presidency.   Chase's name was also withdrawn, and the only candidates practically before the convention were Fremont and McLean.   The latter was the choice of Pennsylvania, the only man, it was said, who could carry that State, where the Republican party contained a large admixture of Know-Nothings, to whom Seward was impossible and Fremont unacceptable.   But on the first ballot Fremont received a decisive majority, and his nomination was at once made unanimous.   The platform, contrary to Seward's expectation, contained nothing to which he could not cordially assent. The result of the convention was, as he himself expressed it, "a complete Seward platform with new representative men upon it."

It is certainly very doubtful whether, if Seward himself had personally urged his claims for the nomination at this time, and his friends had done all in their power to procure it for him, he could have carried the convention.   He was not then so strong in the country as he was four years later ; in the Republican party, especially in Pennsylvania and Indiana, there were many seceders from the Know-Nothings to whom he was particularly objectionable ; the opposition of the delegates from these States in the convention four years later had a powerful, if not a conclusive, effect against him at that time, and their influence would have been greater in 1856 than it was in 1860. Moreover, his anti-slavery views were more advanced than those of a large number of Republicans, who were opposed to the extension of slavery, but by no means believers in emancipation in the District of Columbia, or in taking any steps towards ultimate emancipation in the slave States, even with their consent and with compensation. He was really, in 1856, the candidate of the original anti-slavery men, the pioneers of the army of freedom.

Two years earlier Seward had objected to a national convention, on the ground "that it would bring together only the old veterans." Now the ranks of the anti-Nebraska party were filled with new recruits, young men; they were the bone and sinew of the party in the country, and the delegates at Philadelphia represented them. Fremont was their choice. All that was known of him, his pluck, energy, persistent endurance, and skill as an explorer, justified their attributing to him the qualities which the times and the triumph of the Republicans would require. His career appealed to them; his adventures roused their interest and excited their admiration; there was a romance about his marriage which touched their sympathies, and there had been an element of martyrdom in his treatment by the government which enlisted in his behalf the lovers of justice. He was personally handsome and attractive; a Southerner by birth, and a son-in-law of Benton, who, as an opponent — though on grounds peculiar to himself — of the

repeal of the Missouri Compromise, had more or
less close relations with the Republican leaders.
Everything told in his favor. To those delegates
who were.looking only to the promotion of the
principles of their party, as well as to those who
were eager for success, and to the mass of the
people, Fremont appeared an ideal candidate. He
was invested by them with the qualities of a hero;
and of all the names presented to the convention,
or suggested elsewhere, his was doubtless the most
potent to conjure with.

The nomination of Buchanan was the strongest
that the Democrats could have made, and was dis-
couraging to the Republicans. "The temper of
the politicians" (i. e., the Republican), wrote Seward, "is subdued by Buchanan's nomination, and
indicates retreat, confusion, rout in the election."
Early in August he found that "there was no
Republican organization or life in eastern Pennsylvania or New Jersey," and that "the well-informed
despaired of both these States, and so of the election
itself." There was a pressure on him to take the
field; nevertheless he did not make any campaign
speech till October. Congress was late in adjourn-
ing. The two houses disagreed as to the army
appropriations, — the Representatives passed the
bill with a proviso, prohibiting the employment of
troops to enforce the laws of the fraudulent legislature of Kansas; the Senate refused to concur; and
so the session ended. The President immediately
called an extra session, and, after laboring ten

days with the recalcitrant Democrats, succeeded in forcing through the House, by the narrow majority of three, the bill without the proviso. Seward took a month's needed rest, then spoke at Detroit, and devoted the time till the election to the work of the campaign at various and widely separated places in his own State. Of these speeches only two have been preserved in any permanent form.

In that at Detroit he drew a vivid picture, hardly exaggerated, of the slaveholders' entire possession of the government in all its branches, — the executive, from the President and the heads of the various departments to the humblest tide-waiter in the Customs, the most unimportant consul in our foreign service, and the merest scrivener in the army of clerks; the legislative, through their control of the Senate, with the aid of their Northern Democratic allies; and the judicial, by having a majority of the justices of the Supreme Court from the slaveholding States. He also showed how fidelity to the slaveholders' policy was the test required of all Northern Democrats who wished to share even the crumbs that fell from the government's table.

His speech at Auburn repeated his opinion that the conflict was not merely for "toleration, but for absolute political sway in the Republic, between the system of free labor with equal and universal suffrage, free speech, free thought, and free action, and the system of slave labor with unequal franchises, secured by arbitrary, oppressive, and tyrannical laws;" and emphasized again his conviction that "the State, the nation, and the earth were to be, in the fullness of time, the abode of freemen, and its hills and valleys to be fields of free labor, free thought, and free suffrage."

New York responded handsomely to Seward's arguments and appeals; though Fremont carried the State only by a plurality, he had eighty thousand votes more than Buchanan, and his majority over Fillmore was greater than Fillmore's entire vote. Of the sixteen free States, eleven voted for Fremont. He received only twelve hundred votes in the slave States, and these came from Delaware, Maryland, Virginia, and Kentucky. Buchanan was elected by the solid South, with the aid of five free States (New Jersey, Pennsylvania, Indiana, Illinois, and California). In the free States Buchanan had a hundred and twenty thousand less votes than Fremont, and by the popular vote of the country was in a minority of nearly three hundred thousand. There were votes for Fillmore in all the States where the people chose the electors;[1] but they were so distributed that, though he was the choice of nearly nine hundred thousand voters, he received only the eight electoral votes of the State of Maryland.

The elections of the year had an ominous aspect. In the House of Representatives the speaker was chosen for the first time by a purely sectional

[1] In South Carolina they were chosen by the Legislature.

majority, no Southern man voting for the successful candidate, and no Northerner for his opponent.
The issue in the presidential campaign had been
solely sectional, — the surrender of the Territories
to slavery or its exclusion from them. Buchanan,
though a Pennsylvanian, was the nominee of the
South, and the representative of the slaveholders'
policy. The new party had carried nearly three
fourths of the free States, had given to Douglas,
as a colleague, an anti-Nebraska senator, and substituted for General Cass a radical Republican
from Michigan. If the South had won the victory,
it was one that boded ill for their future control of
the country.

CHAPTER IX

AFTER the passage of the Kansas-Nebraska bill, the political struggle during the remainder of Pierce's term and for a large part of Buchanan's was as to slavery or freedom in Kansas. On the one side were arrayed the administration with its patronage and appointments, the solid South, with its members of Congress, its Democratic supporters in the North and the border ruffians from Missouri; on the other were the free-state settlers in Kansas, who were largely in the majority there, and the Republican party in Congress and in the country. The battle was fought in the Territory between the settlers and immigrants from the North, and the invaders from Missouri and the South; in Washington, by the President and his advisers at the White House, by senators and representatives at the Capitol. But as the members of the lower house are more numerous and more frequently elected, the change in the public opinion of the North caused by the passage of the bill was more quickly shown there, the opposition to the administration was stronger in the House, and the part played by the representatives during the struggle was in some respects more prominent and important than that of the Senate, with which Seward was directly concerned. The story of the struggle cannot, however, be omitted here, nor can any one part of it be told without the other.

The repeal of the Missouri Compromise had thoroughly roused all the Northern people except the Hunker Democrats. Angry at the South's breach of faith in accepting the benefits of a bargain and then repudiating its obligations, the North determined to save for freedom, if possible, the territory secured by the Compromise. The South recognized the struggle as a vital one. " If Kansas is abolitionized," wrote Atchison, " Missouri ceases to be a slave State, New Mexico becomes a free State, California remains a free State. But if we secure Kansas as a slave State, Missouri is secure, New Mexico, and southern California, if not all of it, becomes a slave State ; in a word, the prosperity or ruin of the whole South depends on the Kansas struggle."

One or more emigrant aid societies had been organized at the North before the passage of the bill, and others followed afterwards. Among the earliest was the New England Emigrant Aid Society, a Massachusetts company, which assisted five hundred free-state men to emigrate and settle in Kansas within a year, and about three thousand during the entire struggle. The administration was prompt in opening the Territory to settlement, and had purchased, while the bill was still pend-

ing, several reservations lying nearest Missouri,
from the Indian tribes to whom they had been
secured by treaty.   These purchases were known
to the people of Missouri before the rest of the
country had learned of them ; and, within a few
days after the bill became a law, hundreds of Missourians entered the Territory in small bodies at
various points, staked out, each man for himself,
his quarter section or more, and marked it.   The
different companies then held meetings, at which
they resolved that slavery already existed in the
Territory, and urged slaveholders to bring in their
property at once ; while they also voted to afford
no protection to abolitionist settlers.   To offset the
emigrant aid societies of the North, associations
called "Blue Lodges," "Sons of the South," and
other similar names, were organized in western
Missouri, to take possession of Kansas in behalf of
slavery, and to assist in removing any emigrant
who might go there under the auspices of the
Northern societies.

The first territorial governor appointed by President Pierce was Andrew H. Reeder of Pennsylvania, whose loyalty as an administration Democrat
was unquestioned.   An election for a delegate to
Congress was had by his orders at the end of
November, 1854, and of the twenty-eight hundred
ballots then cast, more than seventeen hundred
were the illegal votes of invading Missourians.   In
one polling precinct six hundred and four votes
were thrown, of which only twenty were legal.

There was no concealment about the matter; what was done was done openly, and was encouraged and approved. "When you reside within one day's journey of the Territory," said Senator Atchison in a public speech before this election, "and when your peace, your quiet, and your property depend upon your action, you can, without any exertion, send five hundred of your young men who will vote in favor of your institutions. Should each county in Missouri only do its duty, the question will be decided quietly and peaceably at the ballot box."

After ascertaining by a census the number of legal voters in the Territory, Governor Reeder appointed a day for the election of a territorial legislature. The evening before, about a thousand Missourians, armed with rifles, pistols, and bowie-knives, and supported by two pieces of artillery, arrived at Lawrence, a free-state town. They distributed their men among the different election precincts, overawed the judges of election, and, reinforced by other men of Missouri, chose their candidates in all but two of the districts. The census had shown twenty-nine hundred voters; but more than six thousand ballots were cast, only eight hundred of which were legal. In some of the districts, where protests were seasonably made, the governor declined to issue certificates of election, and ordered a new poll; but the legislature refused to admit the free-state men chosen on this second ballot, and gave the seats to the persons to whom the governor had refused certificates. The legislature thus chosen adopted by a single act all the Missouri statutes (to save time), and then proceeded to pass, notwithstanding the governor's veto, a criminal code, by which nearly all offenses connected with slavery, including that of aiding a fugitive to escape, were made punishable with death.

Reeder's course as to the election and his vetoes made it clear that he was not a sufficiently pliant tool; the President, yielding to the pressure from the South, removed him, and appointed in his place Wilson Shannon of Ohio, who signalized his arrival in the Territory by declaring in a public speech that he was "for slavery in Kansas." Isolated acts of violence had taken place from time to time, before and during Reeder's administration; a free-state settler had been occasionally murdered; the pro-slavery newspapers had given warning that they "would continue to lynch and hang, tar, feather, and drown every white-livered abolitionist who dared pollute the soil;" and Lawrence had been threatened by a party of more than two hundred Missourians. Under Shannon's misgovernment such outrages became the rule; Lawrence was plundered; its printing-offices and hotels were burned by a troop of about eight hundred men, partly from the South and partly from Missouri, armed with weapons from the United States arsenal, and commanded by General Atchison, United States senator from Missouri; whilst later the town of Osawatomie was sacked and burned by a similar force headed by Whitfield, the territorial delegate to Congress.

Meantime, the free-state settlers, seeking relief by a thoroughly American process, had called a convention, which framed a constitution prohibiting slavery. This was ratified by the actual settlers, a governor and legislature were chosen, and a memorial was forwarded to Congress praying for the admission of Kansas as a free State under this constitution. The President's annual message, sent in on the last day of the year (1855) dismissed the subject of Kansas with a word; but less than a month later, when he had determined to give a thorough-going support to the Southerners, although nothing new had happened in the interval, he sent a special message in which he characterized the proceedings of the free-state settlers as revolutionary and treasonable,[1] and announced his purpose of upholding the fraudulent legislature and enforcing its laws by federal authority; and, in accordance with the policy thus declared, the legislature at Topeka was dispersed by United States regulars in the following July.

[1] It was nothing revolutionary or even unprecedented for the people of a Territory, without any previous authority from Congress, to form a state constitution and ask for admission to the Union. Michigan did this and was admitted; California had done it and been admitted; and the reasons for the action of the people of Kansas, though of a different nature, were quite as strong as those which existed in either California or Michigan.

A guerrilla war was carried on during the summer of the year 1856 between bands of free-state and pro-slavery men.   In August the administration, unable longer to endure the scandals of Shannon's misgovernment, and fearing lest these should lose them the presidential election, removed him, and appointed John W. Geary of Pennsylvania in his place.   Geary endeavored to restore order and to do exact justice, leaning neither to one side nor the other; but, finding that this impartiality was not what the administration required, he resigned in the following March.

Whatever may have been President Pierce's ideas when he assented to Douglas's bill and accepted the doctrine of popular sovereignty, in his actual treatment of Kansas he had been not the honest exponent of that policy, but the active and unhesitating agent of those Southerners who were determined, by fair means or foul, to make that Territory a slave State.   He finds his severest condemnation in the course of the governors appointed by him.   The two who were men of character, and who were not willing to use their power to defeat the wishes of the actual settlers and to drive the free state men from the Territory, were forced out of office, and became most active opponents of his policy, unsparing in their exposure and denunciation of the frauds and violence which he was seeking to hide ; while the third, who had been at first the ready tool of the border ruffians of Missouri, and acceptable to the whole South, was at last unable to satisfy their demands, was distrusted by them, despised by the other party, and removed in disgrace by the administration that had appointed him.

In the Congress which met in December, 1855, the House had a majority hostile to the administration, but composed of heterogeneous elements. There were Democrats and pro-slavery Whigs, both pro-slavery and anti-slavery Americans, and Republicans. No one party had the control, and it was not until the 3d of February, 1856, that its organization was perfected by the choice of a speaker. Meantime, both houses had taken action on the Kansas question, the Senate by resolutions of inquiry, calling on the President for information as to the troubles there; and the House by the passage of a resolve demanding the restoration of the Missouri Compromise. In the Senate, the President's special message concerning Kansas, and his answer to the resolutions of inquiry, were referred to the Committee on Territories, of which Douglas was chairman. The committee presented two reports; that of the majority, prepared by Douglas, was very severe upon the settlers from the free States and upon the Emigrant Aid Society, who were made responsible for all that was wrong in Kansas; while the fraudulent legislature, he insisted, was a proper law-making body, whose acts were legal statutes binding upon the people. The minority report was signed only by Senator Collamer of Vermont, who justified the Topeka convention and the proceedings under it as a peaceful and constitutional effort for the redress of grievances.   The Emigrant Aid Society was vindicated from Douglas's attack, as soon as the reading of the reports was finished, by Sumner's spirited protest that it had not offended, either in letter or spirit, the Constitution and laws of the land.   It had sent men to Kansas, "and it had a right to do so.   Its agents loved freedom and hated slavery, and they had a right to do so."   "This, and no more, was its offense."

In the House Governor Reeder, who had been elected by the legal voters of Kansas as territorial delegate, presented a petition claiming the seat held by Whitfield, the delegate fraudulently chosen by the Missourians; and this petition, after some debate, was referred to a committee empowered to investigate generally the Kansas troubles.   The exhaustive report of this committee, with the accompanying evidence, is a storehouse of information as to the history of the times.   On the same day that this committee was appointed in the House, Douglas addressed the Senate in support of his report and of the bill in which its conclusions were embodied, which authorized the people of Kansas to form a state constitution, when they should have sufficient population to entitle them to one representative in Congress.   For this bill Seward proposed, as a substitute, the immediate admission of Kansas under the Topeka constitution.   Of his speech in support of this substitute, one hundred and sixty-two thousand copies were sent out on the day it was published.

Such defense as could be made for the invaders of Kansas, for the rule they had established there, and for the government's support of it, had already been set forth in the President's message and in Douglas's report; and a large part of Seward's speech was devoted to a scathing criticism of the President's message, and an unsparing exposure of his misrepresentations and concealment of facts, of his unjust aspersions on the North, and of the flimsy pretexts and hardly specious arguments by which he attempted to justify his course. It might almost be called, in this aspect, an arraignment, trial, and conviction of the President, upon the charge of prostituting his official power to sustain in Kansas a government which he knew, from his own representatives, had been forced upon the Territory by the frauds and violence of the people of Missouri. Seward proved to a demonstration, by the declarations of the leaders of the border ruffians, by the statements of independent observers, as well as by those of the free settlers of Kansas, and by the public avowals of the territorial governor, whom the President himself had appointed, that "Kansas had been invaded, conquered, subjugated by an armed force from beyond her borders, trampling under foot the principles of the Kansas bill and the rights of suffrage;" and that the President of the United States was aiding and abetting this wrong, upholding with all the

resources of the administration and all the powers
of the federal authority the perpetrators of this
outrage upon republican government, and main-
taining by force of arms the tyranny they had
established. Seward then turned to the question
of how these wrongs were to be redressed. His
contention was unanswerable, that the only sure
remedy was the immediate admission of Kansas
as a State, under the constitution presented by the
actual settlers. The objections urged to this course
were practically only formal, and might be waived
by Congress in this case, as they had been in
others. Touching the very heart of the controversy, he said : " Congress can refuse admission to
Kansas only on the ground that it will not relinquish the hope of carrying African slavery into
that Territory;" . . . and asked : " Have we come
to that stage of demoralization and degeneracy so
soon ? "

The speech was the masterly argument of a
statesman. If he sometimes showed a fondness
for philosophical generalization and theorizing,
there was nothing of that here ; it was an eminently practical speech. Any remedy, other than
that which he urged, was at the best doubtful.
Any plan authorizing the calling of a new convention, and the formation of a new constitution,
because of defects or uncertainties about the one
adopted at Topeka, must be carried out by the
authorities actually in power in Kansas, the crea-
tures and tools of the border ruffians who elected

them, and under the supervision of an administration whose partisan character and absolute
disregard of justice and of the pledges of the organic law of the Territory had already been
abundantly manifested. But the truth was, as
Seward suggested, that neither the administration
nor the South was prepared to relinquish one inch
of the advantage which slavery had already gained
in the Territory, whether acquired by force or
fraud; both were still confidently expecting to
make it a slave State; and the majority of the
Senate were supporters of the South and of the
administration.

The debate on Kansas continued till the close
of the session in August; it resulted in no legislation; but the speeches of the opposition, circulated
by hundreds of thousands all over the North, had
an immense effect in forming and stimulating
public opinion, and produced a reaction even in
Congress. This was increased by the assault upon
Sumner in the senate chamber itself, by the burning of Lawrence, and by the publication of the
report of the committee of the House, charged to
investigate the Kansas troubles.

For two whole days Sumner addressed the Senate in denunciation of the crime against Kansas.
His speech was not merely an unsparing philippic
against slavery, but most bitter in its personalities.
He spoke of Atchison, stalking like Catiline into
the Senate, reeking with conspiracy, and then like
Catiline skulking away to join and provoke the

conspirators, "murderous robbers from Missouri, hirelings, picked from the drunken spew and vomit of an uneasy civilization;" of Butler of South Carolina, "with incoherent phrases, discharging the loose expectoration of his speech;" and of Douglas, as "switching out from his tongue the perpetual stench of offensive personality." It was a speech in this aspect to make the judicious grieve, and feel a keen regret that Sumner should have descended to such a level. It would hardly have gained converts to the Republican party save for the assault by which it was followed.

Two days later, while he was writing at his desk in the senate chamber, just after the adjournment, he was attacked in a most brutal and cowardly manner by Preston S. Brooks, a member of the House from South Carolina, who inflicted on him injuries from which he never wholly recovered. The Senate, when Seward moved for a committee to investigate this assault, so far forgot the common parliamentary courtesies, the requirements of decency, and the gravity of the occasion, as to choose a committee composed wholly of Sumner's personal and political enemies, who performed the service expected of them, and reported that there was nothing for the Senate to do. The subservient judiciary of Washington disgraced itself by inflicting on Brooks a paltry fine, and even in the House of Representatives there were not to be found the necessary two thirds to secure his expulsion. Any difference of opinion there may have been at the North as to the wisdom or good taste of Sumner's speech disappeared at once, forgotten in the universal outburst of sympathy for him and indignation at the assault; the recollection of which, even to-day, heightens Sumner's fame, by investing him with somewhat of the glory of martyrdom.

"The blows that fell on the head of the senator from Massachusetts," said Seward, "have done more for the cause of human freedom in Kansas and in the Territories of the United States, than all the eloquence which has resounded in these halls, from the days when Rufus King asserted that cause in this chamber until the present hour." It was not regarded merely as an attack upon an individual, it was an assault on the freedom of debate, a violation of the privileges and dignity of the Senate, an insult to the State that Sumner represented, and through that to all the other States of the Union.

The same day that Sumner was speaking in the Senate, the free settlers' town of Lawrence in Kansas was attacked and burned. A little later came the report of the House committee, accompanied by evidence which proved, beyond question, that the territorial elections were carried by fraud, the Legislature unlawfully constituted, and its acts without a color of legality. Under these circumstances it was felt by some Southern senators that there must be further concessions to the public opinion of the North, some fresh attempt at a settlement of the Kansas question. Various amendments to Douglas's original bill were proposed, and other measures introduced; these were all referred to the Committee on Territories, who reported a bill which was, in substance, one that had been offered a few days before by Senator Toombs of Georgia. Upon its face it was a fair proposition. There was to be a new census in Kansas, only actual male inhabitants of full age were to be registered as voters, and they were to elect delegates to a constitutional convention. Commissioners were to supervise the census and the registration; and frauds and irregularities at the election were to be prevented. Had the measure been proposed in January instead of July, its details might have been modified, where they were open to criticism, and the bill have become a law; but it was brought in too late. The presidential election was approaching, and Seward thought, and doubtless others with him, that the change from denunciation to compromise proceeded only from the alarm of the Democrats.

The Republicans objected to the bill as a snare and a delusion. It did not directly annul the enactments of the usurping legislature. On the contrary it recognized that body as a regularly chosen law-making assemblage, and left it uncertain whether any of its so-called laws were abrogated, remitting the determination of this question to the territorial judges, whose partisan character had been already abundantly demonstrated. The

proposed bill continued the existing régime in
Kansas, until a new census should be had, delegates elected, a convention held, a constitution
formed, and Kansas admitted as a State, thus
perpetuating the tyranny established by fraud
and violence, and only maintained in power by
the arms of the United States. It provided that a
census should be taken and an election held under
the direction of commissioners, to be appointed by
a president who had already shown by the appointments he had made, by the officers he had retained,
and by those he had removed, how unevenly he
held the scales of justice in the Territory, how little
freedom of action he was allowed by his masters,
and how he lacked courage to assert himself against
the hot-headed Southerners who prescribed his
policy and his conduct. All this and more, which
made it " a sham, evasive Kansas bill," Seward
showed in his speech on an amendment, offered
by Wilson, proposing the immediate repeal of all
the spurious laws of the so-called Legislature, —
an amendment which the Southern and Democratic
majority of the Senate at once rejected.

The proofs of the wrongs done in Kansas were
quite different now from what they had been when
Seward spoke in March. There was no more need
of argument or inference, and no room for denial
or doubt. The evidence taken by the House committee established conclusively not only the public
wrong committed by the invaders from Missouri
and ratified and sustained by the President of the

United States and his territorial officers, but also the private violence and crime by which settlers from the free States had been robbed of their property, their houses burned, their cattle destroyed, and they themselves either murdered or compelled to flee for their lives; and it was not to be expected that the Republicans would accept as satisfactory a bill which converted the illegal oppressors of the Territory into its rightful governors, and substituted for the election guaranteed by its organic law a ballot to be taken after the settlers from the free States had been driven from Kansas, and under conditions which would permit the people from Missouri to come into the Territory, according to their avowed plan, " in time to acquire the right to become legal voters for the purpose of determining the domestic institutions of the new State."

The bill passed the Senate, but not the House. The House bill, admitting Kansas as a State, under the Topeka constitution, was rejected in the Senate, and Congress adjourned without giving any relief to the people.

CHAPTER X

THE DRED SCOTT CASE — THE FINAL STRUGGLE FOR KANSAS

THE closing session of the Congress which expired with Pierce's administration was, like most of the short sessions ending with a presidential term, absolutely colorless and unimportant; and Buchanan was inaugurated with the hopes of many Northern Whigs and Democrats, who had voted for him with hesitation, that he would have a just and tranquil administration, a reign of law and order in Kansas, and no further slavery agitation. But two days had not elapsed before the country was shaken to its centre by the extraordinary intervention of the Supreme Court in the slavery discussion. The statement in Buchanan's inaugural, that "the point of time when the people of a Territory can decide the question of slavery for themselves" would be "speedily and finally settled by that court," had not at all prepared the public for what was to follow. It was known that a case was pending before the Supreme Court, in which one Dred Scott, a person of African descent, and once a slave, was claiming his freedom, on the ground of a residence with his master in Minnesota,

a Territory made free by the Missouri Compromise, and of a shorter stay in Illinois, where
slavery had been prohibited by the ordinance of
1787. To maintain his action it was necessary
that the plaintiff should be a citizen of the United
States; if he were not so, the federal courts would
have no jurisdiction of the case. The first objection raised by the master was to Scott's citizenship, upon the ground that this was a white man's
government, and that no person of African blood
could be a citizen. This objection was not sustained by the court in which the suit was originally
brought, and the trial went on; but the court
finally decided that Dred Scott was not entitled to
his freedom. The case was then taken up to the
Supreme Court and had been twice argued there.
A few days after the inauguration that court announced its decision. The majority of the judges
held that Dred Scott was not a citizen, because
he was of African blood, and that the courts of
the United States had, therefore, no jurisdiction
of his suit. This was the end of the matter, so
far as Dred Scott was concerned. From this judgment there was no appeal. Two judges, however,
dissented from the judgment. In their opinion
Dred Scott, though of African descent, was a
citizen of the United States, and the court had
jurisdiction of his suit. Having reached this conclusion, it became necessary for them to examine
all the facts of the case, to consider the constitutionality of the Missouri Compromise and of the

ordinance of 1787, and the effect of the plaintiff's living in Minnesota and Illinois; this they did in a most exhaustive manner, and, affirming the constitutionality of both these enactments, decided in favor of the plaintiff's claim to his freedom.

The Southern and pro-slavery members of the court were unwilling to let the statements and reasoning of these dissenting opinions go out to the country without some reply on their part, and induced the chief justice to violate the recognized and established judicial proprieties, by adding to his opinion a statement of his political views upon the relations between the Constitution and slavery, as if this were a part of the judgment of the court. It was a flagrant abuse of a judicial position, and drew from one of the dissenting justices, in no way a sympathizer with the Republican party or the anti-slavery agitators, this emphatic rebuke: "I dissent from the assumption of authority by the majority of the court to examine the constitutionality of the act called the Missouri Compromise. Having decided that this is a case to which the judicial power of the United States does not extend, they have gone on to examine the merits, and so have reached the question of the power of Congress to pass this act. On so grave a subject as this, I feel obliged to say that, in my opinion, such an extension of judicial power transcends the limits of the authority of the court."

The political declaration of the chief justice was

in substance a repetition of Calhoun's doctrine,
that the Territories were the common domain of
the several States, in which each had equal rights;
that therefore the people of every State could
legally carry into any Territory, and lawfully hold
there, any property recognized as lawful in any
State; and that all legislation, congressional or
territorial, limiting or interfering with the full
and perfect enjoyment of this right, was unconstitutional and void.   If this statement had been
necessary to the judgment of the court in the case,
it would have been a hard blow to the Republican
party, whose avowed object was the exclusion of
slavery from the Territories; but it was so obviously a pure piece of politics that, stigmatized as
it had been by Mr. Justice Curtis, it only impressed the people of the North as a fresh and
most convincing proof of the demoralizing influence of the slave power, roused them to more
strenuous efforts to make Kansas free, and enven-
omed still more the bitterness already existing
between the two sections of the country.

Judge Curtis had shown the Republicans that
the chief justice's politics were no part of the judgment of the court; that they were only the political views of a judge upon questions not at the time
judicially before him, and of no binding force
whatever.   Lincoln and Seward made another suggestion.   The judgment settled the case of Dred
Scott; but it might be reversed in some other suit,
as other judgments had been, and one mission of

the Republican party should be to hasten this result.

It was evident from the President's inaugural that he had been privately informed of what the court was to do, and it was believed and asserted by Republican leaders that the decision had been withheld until after the election, lest it should injure or destroy the chances of Democratic success; and that nothing would have been heard of the monstrous doctrines of the chief justice had Fremont been chosen president. Lincoln, in a public speech in Illinois, attacked the court for its attempt to render nugatory the right of choosing between freedom and slavery, which the Kansas-Nebraska act assumed the people of the Territory to possess. Seward charged the court with forgetting, "in this ill-omened act, its own dignity, which had always before been maintained with just judicial jealousy," and both the court and the President with failing to remember "that judicial usurpation was more odious and intolerable than any other among the manifold practices of tyranny."

The resignation of Governor Geary, President Pierce's last appointee in Kansas, took effect at the close of the presidential term, leaving Buchanan free to make his own appointment. After much persuasion, he induced Robert J. Walker, of Mississippi, to accept the post. Walker was a Pennsylvanian by birth, who had removed to Mississippi soon after he began practicing the law. He had been in Congress, was Polk's secretary

of the treasury, had exercised a large influence
with several Democratic administrations and with
the Democratic party, had advocated the annexation of Texas and counseled a vigorous prosecution
of the Mexican war, and was a man of much more
prominence, of larger experience in public affairs,
and of greater ability than is usually to be found
in the office of governor of a Territory.   In his
inaugural address, Buchanan had given the assurance that any constitution, framed by a convention
in Kansas, should be submitted to the people; and
before Walker left for the West, he understood
that the President agreed with him that the territorial act required this to be done.   The fraudulent legislature had called a convention, and appointed a time for the choice of delegates.   Walker
arrived in the Territory before the day fixed for the
election, and endeavored to induce the free state
men to vote.   They were afraid to trust him, and
suffered the election to go by default; a little more
than one fifth of the registered voters chose the
delegates.[1]   The convention met at Lecompton,
but immediately adjourned until after the regular
election of a new territorial legislature.   Meantime, the governor, having satisfied himself that
Kansas was lost to slavery, though he still hoped

---

[1] Had there been no frauds and had the free-state men voted,
as the governor urged them to do, they would have elected their
own candidates as delegates, notwithstanding that about seventeen counties, settled principally from the North, had been practically disfranchised by omitting them from the census.

she might be honestly saved to the Democracy, if
the two wings of the Democratic party, the free-
state and pro-slavery Democrats, would unite, bent
his energies to accomplishing this, and to inducing
the free-state men to vote at the regular territorial
election.   With some difficulty they were persuaded to do so.   The election was, on the whole,
a fair one.   In one precinct, where there were
about a hundred voters, the returns showed sixteen
hundred votes for the pro-slavery candidate; in
another more than twelve hundred similar votes
represented about twenty settlers entitled to the
ballot.   Walker courageously threw out these returns, and the result gave the free-state party the
control of both branches of the territorial legislature.

The Lecompton convention met, pursuant to its
adjournment, and framed a constitution, which, by
its terms, could not be amended till 1864, and its
provisions as to ownership in slaves not even then.
The article entitled "Slavery" declared: "The
right of property is before and higher than any
constitutional sanction, and the right of the owner
of a slave to such slave and its increase is the
same, and as inviolable, as the right of the owner
of any property whatever."

Since the great majority of the people of Kansas
considered the members of this convention as ma-
lignants, and its whole proceedings as an insult, it
was evident that to submit its constitution to a popular vote would be merely to insure its rejection.

To avoid this, the convention determined that the vote should be only upon the question whether the constitution should be adopted with slavery or without it.   If the majority should be for the constitution with slavery, the article quoted was to remain; if for the constitution without slavery, then that article was to be stricken out; slavery was no longer "to exist in the State, except that the property in slaves already in the Territory should not be interfered with."   This was not such a submission of the constitution to a vote of the people as Walker had promised.   No pressure from Washington could induce him to accept it as a fulfillment of the requirements of the law and of the assurances he had made with the President's sanction and approval.   He left the Territory, and, on arriving at Washington, finding himself at issue with the President on this vital point, resigned, rather than be a party to what he did not hesitate to pronounce a vile fraud.

At the election ordered by the convention, the total vote was less than seven thousand.   For the constitution without slavery there were five hundred and sixty-nine votes; for the constitution with slavery, sixty-one hundred and forty-three, of which three thousand and twelve were fraudulent.[1]

When Walker left the Territory, the secretary, Frederic P. Stanton, of Tennessee, also a Southerner and a perfectly fair and upright man, became

---

[1] Wilder, *Annals of Kansas*, p. 156.

acting governor. At the instance of the people of Kansas he summoned the newly elected legislature to meet in December. One of its first acts provided for a direct vote on the Lecompton Constitution, and at the election held for this purpose it was almost unanimously rejected, receiving only one hundred and sixty-two votes, out of ten thousand four hundred. On learning of Stanton's action, Buchanan at once removed him.

In defense of his course as to Kansas the President insisted that, as the vital question, whether they would have the constitution with or without slavery, had been submitted to the people, it was the same thing as if they had been allowed to vote directly on its adoption or rejection. He persisted in this statement in spite of his knowledge that the election ordered by the convention was not open to all qualified voters, but that every citizen, before he could deposit his ballot, was obliged to take an oath to support the Lecompton Constitution.[1] He also knew that it had been proved that the settlers there were opposed to this constitution, by its rejection by an almost unanimous vote at an untrammeled election.

When Congress met in December, it was quite understood that any Democrat who did not favor the admission of Kansas with the Lecompton Constitution would come under the ban of the administration; and Washington was full of speculations as to what Douglas would do. The numbers and

[1] Lecompton Const. Schedule, Sect. 7.

position of the Republicans in both branches of
Congress had been constantly improving. "It did
look well," wrote Seward, "to see the array of
twenty solid men" on the floor of the Senate.
There was no longer any attempt at the ostracism
of which they had heretofore been the victims.
"All personal antipathies and prejudices against
the party and its members seemed to have disappeared." The Southern and Democratic opposition in social circles had given way, and society of
all classes was profuse in its courtesies. As an
illustration of the changed conditions, we find
Seward, before the session is over, acting as peace-
maker between Jefferson Davis and Senator Chandler of Michigan; and, in connection with Crittenden and Jefferson Davis, settling a difficulty, in
which Wilson of Massachusetts and Gwin of California were the opposing parties. The thorny,
solitary path which the Republicans had heretofore pursued was now abandoned to Douglas.
The Southern Democrats transferred to him their
former hatred of the Black Republicans, and their
courtesies to the old anti-slavery men served to
emphasize their treatment of the deserter.

Arriving in Washington before the meeting of
Congress, Douglas called on the President to discuss the Kansas question. Buchanan said that he
should recommend the admission of Kansas under
the Lecompton Constitution; Douglas answered
that he should denounce it in the Senate; and on
the 9th of January he did so. "What can equal

the caprices of politics!" wrote Seward. "The triumph of slavery [in 1850] would have been incomplete, indeed it could not have occurred, had it not been for the accession to it of Stephen A. Douglas. . . . By that defection he became soon, and has, until just now, continued (under the favor or fear of successive administrations) legislative dictator here, intolerant, yet irresistible. . . . That was his position yesterday morning. . . . Yesterday he broke loose from all that strong host he had led so long, and although he did not at the first bound reach my position, as an ally, yet leaped so far towards it as to gain a position of neutrality altogether unsafe and indefensible."

Seward welcomed all accessions from the Democrats to the anti-Lecompton forces. "Since Walker, Douglas, and Stanton," he wrote, "have been converted, at least in part, we are sure to hear the gospel preached (though with adulteration) to the Gentiles." And, while many of the Republican leaders were distrustful of Douglas, he took the opposite view, saying: "God forbid that I should consent to see freedom wounded, because my own lead, or even my own agency in serving it, should be rejected. I will cheerfully coöperate with these new defenders of this sacred cause in Kansas, and I will award them all due praise for their large share of merit in its deliverance."

The administration had staked its all upon sustaining the Lecompton Constitution. Buchanan's message, transmitting it to Congress, showed his entire surrender to the extreme Southern opinion. "Kansas," he said, "is at this moment as much a slave State as Georgia or South Carolina." Before his message was sent in, Denver, who had succeeded Walker as governor of Kansas, had endeavored to dissuade him from sending to Congress the Lecompton Constitution, advising him strongly against his proposed policy. Buchanan answered that he had already shown his message and that the advice came too late.

It was hardly to be expected that the debate on this question should add anything to what had already been said. The Southerners fell back on the doctrines of Chief Justice Taney, insisted that all the anti-slavery agitation had been aimed at the constitutional rights of the South, and that both the Missouri Compromise and the Wilmot Proviso were unconstitutional.

In a speech, made early in March, Seward gave a highly colored sketch of a coalition between the executive and judicial departments of the government, to undermine the legislature and the liberties of the people, and of whispered conferences between the chief justice and the incoming President before the delivery of the inaugural, which heralded, not the decision of the Dred Scott case, but the extra-judicial exposition of the Constitution, which the chief justice was about to promulgate. This drew from Judge Taney the declaration that, if Seward were elected president, he should decline to administer to him the oath of

office, and from both Taney and Buchanan indig-
nant denials of any such conferences. But these
denials did not meet the substance of the charges
then made, not by Seward alone, but by many Republican leaders. These charges were, that the
political passages were added by the chief justice
after the result of the presidential election was
known, and that their substance was communicated
to Buchanan just before the 4th of March, to enable him to make the announcement which he did
in his inaugural address. Known facts justified
the accusation, even though they did not conclusively prove it. It was understood that a majority
of the judges, having reached the conclusion that
Dred Scott, being of African descent, was not a
citizen, and had therefore no standing in the courts
of the United States, an opinion stating this conclusion and the reasons for it, and nothing more,
had been prepared, to be read as the judgment of
the court; that the chief justice afterwards, and
not long before the delivery of the judgment,
added to his opinion the statement of his political
conclusions, which — if they had been in any sense
a decision of the court — would have fastened slavery irrevocably upon every foot of the territory of
the United States. Buchanan's inaugural address
substantially foreshadowed these conclusions as the
result of the case, and it was known that the passage in which he did this was added after his arrival in Washington. It was insisted that it was
quite incredible that he should have written this

at that time unless he had received authentic information of what the chief justice was to say.

His long and unblemished judicial career and his patriotic motives have been urged as an excuse or apology for the chief justice's course in this case, and it is perhaps only fair to him to suppose that he may have thought his political statement would be quietly accepted by the North as an authoritative and binding construction of the Constitution, and would put an end to all anti-slavery agitation there; while, as it conceded to the South all that they could gain by separation, the motives for secession would no longer exist, and the Union would continue undisturbed.

Other persons disapproved of Seward's speech for reasons of an opposite character. The aim of the Republicans was to secure Kansas to freedom; and in the struggle of the moment — the question of its admission under the Lecompton Constitution — they had the support of several Democrats, among whom was Douglas, the author of the repeal of the Missouri Compromise, and for that reason, as well as for his qualities as a debater, a most powerful auxiliary. Seward had already publicly welcomed the accession of these new allies, and announced his cordial coöperation with them; and in this speech, after declaring his opinion that "it would be wise to restore the Missouri prohibition of slavery in Kansas and Nebraska," he went on to say: "But I shall not insist now on so radical a measure as the restoration of the Missouri

prohibition. I know how difficult it is for power
to relinquish even a pernicious and suicidal policy
all at once. We may obtain the same result, in
this particular case of Kansas, without going back
so far. Go back only to the ground assumed in
1854, the ground of popular sovereignty. Happily for the authors of that measure, the zealous
and energetic resistance of abuses practiced under
it has so far been effective, that popular sovereignty in Kansas may now be made a fact, and
liberty there may be rescued from danger through
its free exercise." It is difficult to see in this
passage anything more than a recognition of the
facts as they actually existed; but it gave offense
to some persons, who thought it implied a readiness to condone the repeal of the Missouri Compromise, and to welcome the coöperation of Douglas, who, they considered, should have been received with reluctance, hesitation, and distrust.

His speech on the Lecompton Constitution and
convention is not one of Seward's best. It drags
here and there; but the wrongs of Kansas, as material for a speech, had already been worn thread-
bare. There are certain passages, however, to
which the South might well have given heed: —

"The nation has reached the point where intervention by the government for slavery and slave
States will no longer be tolerated. Free labor has
at last apprehended its rights, its interests, its
power, and its destiny, and is organizing itself to
assume the government of the republic. It will

henceforth meet you boldly and resolutely here; it
will meet you everywhere, in the Territories or out
of them, wherever you may go to extend slavery.
. . . The interests of the white races demand the
ultimate emancipation of all men.   Whether that
consummation shall be allowed to take effect with
needful and wise precautions against sudden change
and disaster, or be hurried on by violence, is all
that remains for you to decide. . . . It is for
yourselves, not for us, to decide how long the contest shall be protracted before freedom shall enjoy
her already assured triumph.   I would have it
ended now. . . . But this can be done only in
one way, — by the direct admission of the three
new States [Kansas, Minnesota, and Oregon] as
free States, . . . and by the abandonment of all
further attempts to extend slavery under the federal Constitution.''

The Kansas question, however, was not to be
decided by argument, or by any sense of justice.
The best men of the South did not venture to
defend the Lecompton Constitution, or the proceedings by which it came before Congress, or the
course of the administration.   The necessity of
making Kansas a slave State was the governing
motive with those who supported the bill.   A few
Southerners, notably Bell and Crittenden, opposed
it.   But the administration controlled the Senate,
and its patronage and proscription were freely employed to enable it to carry the House.   The outcome of the whole matter for this session (1857–58)

was the passage of a bill, — a new compromise, —
by which the Lecompton Constitution was to be
again submitted to the people of Kansas for adoption or rejection.   If it should be adopted, the
Territory would receive large grants of public lands,
and be admitted at once as a State.   If it should
be rejected, Kansas was to remain a Territory for
an indefinite period.   The people spurned the
bribe; the constitution was a second time rejected
by an overwhelming majority.   Yet it was only
when some Southern senators had already vacated
their seats that the struggle was ended in January,
1861, by the admission of Kansas as a free State.

There was another matter before the Senate this
winter, in which Seward's course was most severely
condemned by some of his own party.   The Mormons of Utah were in a state of open, if not of
avowed rebellion.   Troops were needed to compel
their obedience and to maintain the authority of
the government.   The administration wished to
raise two additional regiments for this purpose.
The Republicans, distrusting the President and
remembering the use to which the army had been
put in Kansas, were opposed to giving him any
such power.   Seward thought the troops necessary
for the purpose for which they were asked, and
that the President should have the authority he
desired.   "It is," he said, "with a view to save
life, to save the public peace, to bring the Territory
of Utah into submission to the authorities of the
land without bloodshed, that I favor the increase

of force which is to be sent there." A letter from Senator Fessenden shows us how the Republicans of the Senate looked at the matter. "Some of our people," he wrote, "are frightened by the idea of refusing supplies in time of war. Seward, I understand, is to make a speech for the bill. He is perfectly bedeviled. He will vote alone, so far as the Republicans are concerned; but he thinks himself wiser than all of us." Hale spoke of him as the Judas Iscariot of the little company of Republicans in the Senate. Nevertheless he persisted in his opinion, and spoke and voted in favor of the bill, carrying out in his conduct the policy which he had insisted was correct at the beginning of the Mexican war a dozen years before, when he was still a private citizen. The bill, however, after being amended, was at last defeated by a vote which had no party significance or character, Toombs voting with Seward, and Mason and Slidell with Fessenden and Hale. Coercion of the Mormons became for the time unnecessary, as a truce was patched up between them and the government.

Subsequent events, however, showed that Seward was right in his views of the necessity of reducing to strict obedience the Latter Day Saints; and had this been done earlier there would have been fewer or no unpunished outrages upon Christians, no Danite bands, no cowardly midnight murders in Utah. Seward himself must have felt amply rewarded for his speech and action in the

matter, when three years later he learned from
more than one war Democrat that this speech
had taught him to disregard unpatriotic party
counsels, and to stand by the government and the
Union.

The historical interest of the political campaign
of the summer and autumn of 1858 is practically
confined to the debates between Lincoln and Douglas; but Seward in his speech at Rochester struck
the keynote of the contest when he spoke of "*The
Irrepressible Conflict between Freedom and Slavery.*" The idea was not a new one, though the
expression was. If we read his speeches we shall
find him often before struggling with a similar
thought, but never till now finding the apt words
which would best convey his meaning, and coining
a phrase which became at once a part of our popular speech.

The substance of the Rochester address was an
indictment of the Democratic party as sectional
and local, with its principal seat in the slave
States and its constituency almost exclusively
there, but having in the free States a number of
supporters sufficient to modify its sectional appearance without altering its sectional character,
committed therefore to the policy of slavery, and
which had carried that policy to its then alarming
culmination. The accusation was followed by a
statement of the historical facts justifying it, and
the speech had great weight in the autumn elections. In the year before, the Republican party

had suffered a grievous setback; but the course of
the President in endeavoring, by all the means at
his command, to crowd through Congress and force
upon Kansas a constitution odious to its inhabitants, and so tainted with fraud that even his own
officers there, Southerners and slaveholders as they
were, refused to sustain him, had done for the
opponents of the administration what they could
not have done for themselves.   The Congress
chosen in the autumn of 1858 elected, though only
after a prolonged struggle, a Republican speaker.
To the Senate no Northern Democrat was returned
except Douglas, and the Republicans there now
numbered twenty-four.

Nothing was done in the short session ending
on the 4th of March, 1859.   The endeavors of the
South to obtain a vote to put thirty millions of
money into the hands of the President, in order
to pave the way for a favorable negotiation as to
the purchase of Cuba, signally failed; and a homestead bill, granting moderate quantities of public
lands to actual settlers, and warmly pressed by the
Republicans, shared the same fate.   The antagonism between the North and South was never more
conspicuous than in the discussion of these measures.   The House, it was known, would not pass
the Cuba bill, if sent down to them, but they had
already passed the homestead bill, which was before the Senate, and Seward urged laying aside
Cuba to take up the homestead bill, saying: "The
Senate may as well meet face to face the issue.

. . . The homestead bill is a question of homes
for the landless freemen of the United States.
The Cuba bill is the question of slaves for the
slaveholders of the United States." Toombs re-
torted that, much as he despised senators who
were demagogues, he despised still more those who
were driven by demagogues, and who met a great
question of national policy by the cry of land for
the landless; on which Wade cried out: "Shall
we give niggers to the niggerless or land to the
landless? When you come to niggers for the
niggerless all other questions sink into perfect in-
significance."

The summer and autumn of 1859 Seward passed
in Europe. When he returned, the John Brown
raid in Virginia had ended in the execution of its
leader; Congress had assembled, and the two
months' contest for the election of speaker was
well under way. The several parties were already
beginning to take their positions for the coming
presidential campaign. The Senate was practically under the control of the extreme pro-slavery
leaders, who were determined to drive Douglas out
of the Democratic party as a punishment for his
opposition to the admission of Kansas under the
Lecompton Constitution. For this purpose, Jefferson Davis offered a series of resolutions embodying the political doctrines enunciated by Judge
Taney in the Dred Scott case, and the most extreme deductions to be made from them. These
resolves were meant to be a complete statement of

the true creed of the Democratic party on the subject of slavery, as revised by the chief justice.
The fundamental article was this: —

"*Resolved*, That neither Congress nor a territorial legislature, whether by direct legislation, or
legislation of an indirect and unfriendly character,
possesses power to annul or impair the constitutional right of any citizen of the United States to
take his slave property into the common territories,
and there hold and enjoy the same while the territorial condition remains."

Special interest attaches to this resolution, from
the fact that in the Democratic national convention
of 1848 a resolve, offered by Mr. Yancey of Alabama, declaring: "That the doctrine of non-inter-
ference with the right of property of any portion
of the people of this confederacy, be it in the States
or Territories thereof, by any other than the parties
interested in them, is the true republican doctrine
recognized by this body," was rejected by a vote
of two hundred and sixteen to thirty-six; while
against this resolution of Jefferson Davis, introduced in the Senate eleven years later, there was
only one Democratic vote, that of Mr. Pugh of
Ohio.[1] The attitude of the Democracy as regards
slavery was clearly not stationary. If the Republicans were advancing in the path of modern civilization, the Democrats were even more rapidly
retrograding towards a government which should
rest on slavery as its base. The Republicans stood

---

[1] Douglas was absent throughout, from illness.

aloof, and left Davis's resolutions to be discussed by the Democrats.   They were adopted by a strict party vote.

Seward's most important speech during the session was on the bill for the admission of Kansas under a new constitution, framed by a convention held at Wyandot and composed of delegates from the actual settlers of the Territory.   In this speech he discussed the general state of the country; and in a sketch of the difference between the slave and free States, defined the former as States where the slave was regarded and protected, not as a man, but as the capital of another man, a special kind of capital entitled to be politically represented by its owners, and which, with the increase in slaves, had become a great political force; while in the free States the laborer, invigorated and developed by the rights of citizenship, was himself the dominating political power.   He therefore classified the slave States as capital States, and the free States as labor States.   Running a historical parallel between these two classes, he showed by the debates on the Missouri Compromise, — the first great struggle between them, — how easy it was to combine the capital States in defense even of their external interests, and how difficult to unite the labor States in any common policy; that the labor States were naturally loyal to the Union, while the capital States were quick to alarm that loyalty by threats of disunion, and either could not or would not distinguish between legitimate,

constitutional opposition to the creation of new
capital States out of the common territory, and unconstitutional · attacks upon slavery in the States
where it already existed. The history of the two
parties proved, he contended, that the Democratic
party was generally found sustaining the policy of
the capital States; while the Whigs, being usually
an opposition party, had practiced some forbearance towards the interests of labor, until, in an
evil hour, the Whig representatives of the capital
States concurred in the passage of the Kansas-
Nebraska act, and the Whig party instantly went
down, never to rise again.

To the charge that the Republican party was a
sectional one, and that its success would therefore
justify secession, he answered: "Is the Democratic
party less sectional? Is it easier for us to bear
your sectional sway than for you to bear ours? Is
it unreasonable that for once we should alternate?
But is the Republican party sectional? Not unless the Democratic party is. The Republican
party prevails in the House of Representatives
sometimes, the Democratic party in the Senate
always. Which of the two is most proscriptive?
Come, if you will, into the free States anywhere,
address the people, submit to them fully all your
complaints of Northern disloyalty, oppression,
prejudice, speaking just as freely and loudly as
you do here; you will have hospitable welcomes
and ballot-boxes for all the votes you can win. . . .
Extend to us the same privileges and I will engage

that you will have very soon in the South as many
Republicans as we have Democrats in the North.
. . . Our policy of labor in the Territories was not
sectional during the first forty years of the republic; it will be national again during the third forty
years, and forever afterwards." He minimized
the dangers of disunion, not because he underrated
the earnestness of the leaders of secession, but because he believed that, refine as one might about
the nature of the Constitution, calling it a compact
between States, a breach of any article of which
by one State would absolve all the others from
their allegiance, yet it would be found, on any
attempt to subvert it, to be a government of the
whole people, in which every member was conscious of his interest and power, and which was
indestructible from the millions of fibres by which
it was interwoven with the affections, the ambi-
tions, and the hopes of all citizens of all classes.

CHAPTER XI

THE Democratic national convention of 1856 had determined to hold that of 1860 at Charleston, South Carolina; it accordingly met there towards the end of April. The irreconcilable difference between the supporters of the administration and the followers of Douglas made any agreement as to a platform impossible; and, on the failure of the resolutions proposed by the South, forty-five of the one hundred and twenty Southern delegates withdrew. The convention adjourned to Baltimore and there nominated Douglas for the presidency; Herschel V. Johnston, of Georgia, being afterwards added as the nominee for vice-president. The seceding delegates held a separate convention, and chose as their candidates John C. Breckenridge of Kentucky, and Joseph Lane of Oregon. The Constitutional Union party, the survivors of the Native American organization, put John Bell, of Tennessee, at the head of their ticket, and gave the second place to Edward Everett, of Massachusetts.

The Republican convention assembled at Chicago on the 16th of May. The organization,

preparation, and adoption of the platform occupied
the first two days, and it was the general expectation both of his friends and opponents that Seward
would be nominated on the following morning.
It was known that there was opposition to him,
yet it was thought that the different elements composing it would not be able to unite on any candidate.   But on the third ballot Abraham Lincoln,
of Illinois, was nominated, a change of four votes
of the Ohio delegation from Chase to Lincoln giving him the requisite majority.   There is no question that to the Republican party, as a whole, this
nomination was at the time a bitter disappointment.   Lincoln was a man comparatively unknown.   He had served in one Congress without
distinction, and would gladly when his term was
over have accepted a subordinate office.   Four
years earlier he had received a respectable vote on
an informal ballot as a candidate for vice-president
on the ticket with Fremont; but this was hardly
remembered at the time of his nomination in 1860.
His campaign with Douglas had brought him into
more prominence, had shown him to be a clear
thinker, and very ready and formidable in debate;
but the interest in that discussion was comparatively limited; and he was best known at the East
by his address at the Cooper Institute in New
York, on the 27th of February, 1860.   He was a
very popular local politician, but was hardly recognized elsewhere as a rising man with anything
that could be called a national reputation.   The

opposition to Seward, adopting the policy pursued in previous conventions by the opponents of the great men of the respective parties, united on Lincoln as a more or less colorless candidate.

So far as the success of the Republican party in 1860 was not the inevitable outcome of the constantly increasing demands and pressure of the South, and the consequent resistance of the North, it was the work of William H. Seward more than of any other single individual. He had labored to this end for many years; his speeches had been printed in different languages, and circulated by millions, and had produced the deepest and widest effect on public opinion. At the South he was fully recognized as the leader of his party, the price set on his head there being fifty thousand dollars, while only twenty-five hundred was offered for that of any other prominent Republican.

A Southern newspaper did no more than justice to his position, when its editor wrote: "Mr. Seward is a great political leader. Unlike others who are willing to follow in the wake of popular sentiment, Seward leads. He stands head and shoulders above them all. He marshals his forces and directs the way. The Abolition host follow. However we may differ from William H. Seward, we concede to him honesty of purpose, and the highest order of talent. He takes no halfway grounds, he does nothing by halves. . . . He is at once the greatest and most dangerous man in the government. . . . For eighteen years he has

stood forth in the Senate of the United States, the
great champion of freedom, and the stern opposer
of slavery." If one turns from the estimate of
opponents to the judgment of his political friends,
the words of Governor Andrew of Massachusetts,
in indorsing the nomination of Lincoln, do not
exaggerate the appreciation of Seward at that time
in the Republican party: —

"The affection of our hearts and the judgment
of our intellects bound our political fortunes to
William H. Seward, — to him, who is the highest
and most shining light of this political generation,
— to him who, by the unanimous selection of the
foes of our cause, and our own, has for years been
the determined standard-bearer of liberty." A
Democratic newspaper announced the result of the
convention in an article entitled "Actæon devoured
by his own Dogs;" and this heading had quite
enough truth in it to give it point, and to need no
explanation for even the dullest and most obtuse.

Seward's failure to obtain the nomination at
Chicago was due to a variety of causes. The influence to be attributed to the defection of Horace
Greeley was probably exaggerated at the time;
and the episode is mostly interesting for the light
it throws upon the characters of the two men.
Greeley was commonly thought to be an unselfish
patriot, but he had at bottom a hunger for office,
and, as his conduct to Seward shows, a strong
appetite for revenge. As has been already stated,
he was very much disappointed at not receiving

the nomination for governor of New York in 1854, and still more chagrined that his old associate and subsequent rival, Henry J. Raymond, was nominated for lieutenant-governor by the very convention in which he himself had been defeated.   There is nothing to show that Seward personally had anything to do with this result, though Weed, believing it essential to success, had undoubtedly done what he could to bring it about; there were, however, so many objections to nominating Greeley, that it may be doubted whether Seward's active intervention in his behalf would have been of any avail.   The election was extremely close.   A change of less than two hundred votes would have altered the result; and the party was evidently wise, in so close a contest, in declining to handicap themselves with a candidate of such pronounced opinions, the eager advocate of so many visionary schemes as Greeley was considered to be.   Greeley himself subsequently admitted that he could not have been chosen.   Just after the election, when he was still extremely sore, he wrote Seward a letter, complaining of the treatment he had received, notifying him that he could no longer rely on his support, and that the so-called partnership of Seward, Weed, and Greeley was at an end. So far was Seward, however, from penetrating Greeley's real meaning, that he shortly afterwards wrote to Weed: "I have a long letter from Greeley, full of sharp, pinching thorns.   I judge, as we might indeed well know, from his, at the bottom,

nobleness of disposition, that he has no idea of
saying or doing anything wrong or unkind; but it
is sad to see him so unhappy. Will there be a
vacancy in the board of regents of the Univer-
sity of New York this winter? Could one be
made at the close of the session, could he have it?
Raymond's nomination and election is hard for
him to bear. . . .. I think this a good letter to
burn. I wish I could do Greeley so great a favor
as to burn his."

Seward did not suffer this letter to interfere
with the personal relations between himself and
Greeley; and though Greeley opposed Seward's
nomination in 1856, yet, if his opposition was
based on personal grounds, he carefully concealed
them. Ten days after the convention of that year
he called on Seward in Washington, and wished
to be congratulated on having done the very best
thing in the very best way. In the spring of 1859
he succeeded in satisfying a politician so astute as
Weed that he was all right politically and "seeking to be useful" in California, whither he was
going; and he dined with Seward on the eve of
his departure.

He was not a delegate from New York to the
Republican convention of 1860; but he procured
an appointment as substitute from Oregon, and
going to Chicago in this capacity, devoted his time
and energy to defeating Seward. He nominally
advocated the candidacy of Edward Bates of Missouri, but was ready to support anybody to beat

Seward; and it has been said that, when Seward was actually defeated, he openly gave thanks that he was even with him at last.

Seward had shown Greeley's letter of 1854 to no one; but after the convention there began to be rumors of its existence, and Greeley himself finally printed it in the "Tribune." Its publication drew from Weed an article in which he said: "Having remained for six years in blissful ignorance of its contents, we should have much preferred to have ever remained so. It jars harshly upon cherished memories. It destroys ideals of disinterestedness and generosity which relieved political life from so much that is selfish, sordid, and rapacious." The impartial reader, who wishes to think well of Greeley, will probably agree with Weed.

Greeley's unaided exertions would hardly have resulted in Seward's defeat. There were other more powerful elements at work for that end. The body of the Republican party was composed of old Whigs; but even among these there were not wanting some conservatives who had joined the party late and half reluctantly, and who still thought Seward almost dangerously radical. To those who had supported Fillmore in 1856, his nomination would not have been acceptable; and the Democratic Free Soilers of '48, who had voted for Van Buren, and were now in full Republican communion, were at heart strongly opposed to Seward. They might put their opposition nominally on various grounds; but the fundamental reason

was that he had always been a Whig, till that party
perished, and never a Democrat. Those members
of the convention who had been members of the
Know-Nothing party remembered Seward's steady
and uniform opposition to and denunciation of
that party and its proscriptive doctrines. Many
Republicans in Pennsylvania and Indiana were
still Know-Nothings, slightly covered with a thin
varnish of Republicanism; and the respective candidates for governor in these two States professed
to think it impossible to succeed at their state elections in October, if Seward were the national candidate, and were therefore earnest to defeat his
nomination; Cameron of Pennsylvania, who was
thought to favor Seward, did not appear at the
convention and took no steps in his behalf, and
Ohio had a favorite son, Chase, whom she preferred to him. Some Republicans of more or less
prominence nominally placed their opposition to
Seward on the ground of their distrust of a New
York politician; they objected to his connection
with Weed; they admitted him to be personally
honest, but thought him not sufficiently averse to
jobs for his friends. These objections came mainly
from persons who, had they fully expressed their
minds, would have given other reasons why they
wished he should not be nominated. If they had
any effect upon the action of the convention, it
was so trifling that it need not be taken into account. The nomination was determined by other
and quite different influences.

Lincoln was most ambitious for the nomination, and had been working eagerly for it for months. He was personally a much more adroit politician than Seward, who practically, during his whole public life, relied on Thurlow Weed to manage for him. Lincoln's forces were well organized; he had an earnest committee, determined to succeed, and not over-scrupulous as to the means; and as the convention was at Chicago, they were on their own ground and supported by all the local influences. The question was how to consolidate upon Lincoln all the elements of the opposition to Seward. This difficulty was solved on the night preceding the nomination, by the chairman of Lincoln's committee promising to Caleb Smith, of Indiana, a place in Lincoln's cabinet in return for the vote of that delegation, and giving a similar pledge in favor of Simon Cameron to the delegation from Pennsylvania, on the assurance of its support; the votes of these two delegations, with a change of votes by a few wavering members from Ohio, secured Lincoln's nomination. Lincoln had telegraphed his committee to make no bargains for him; nevertheless he did not afterwards repudiate their promises, and Caleb Smith and Cameron were both in his first cabinet.

When the news arrived at Auburn, and no one else there had the heart to prepare for the "Daily Republican" newspaper a paragraph approving the nomination, Seward himself wrote: "No truer or firmer defenders of the Republican faith could

have been found . . . than the distinguished . . .
citizens on whom the honors of the nomination
have fallen." None the less keenly, however, did
he feel himself to be "a leader deposed by his own
party in the hour of organization for decisive battle." Yet instead of merely acquiescing in the
result of the convention, and remaining quietly at
home, as he might fairly enough have done, he
put forth all his energies to insure the success of
his party, and devoted five weeks to a political
campaign in New York and the Northwest, especially in those States which had been his ardent
supporters in the convention.

CHAPTER XII

THE narrative of the events of the winter suc-
ceeding the election of Lincoln forms one of the
most mortifying and melancholy chapters in our
national history. The withdrawal of the Southern
Democratic leaders from their party convention,
and their nomination of a separate candidate in
the summer of 1860, was a mere prelude to the
secession of the States they represented. It rendered the election of Lincoln certain, and thus
furnished the pretext they wanted for carrying out
their long cherished scheme of breaking up the
Union and forming a new Southern confederacy,
of which slavery should be the corner-stone and
cotton the king. They were not alarmed at the
prospect of any injury to their property in slaves,
or of any diminution of their material prosperity
in consequence of the Republican victory. The
Democratic control in Congress not only made
them absolutely secure from attack, but left the
incoming Republican president powerless to appoint a single public officer, from the members of
his cabinet down, who would not be satisfactory to
the South, — or to carry any measure, or pursue

any policy, which did not have its approval.
Moreover, there were practically no open issues,
by the decision of which the interests of the South
could be materially affected. The Dred Scott
case, it was claimed, had settled the right to hold
slaves in all the Territories of the United States;
it could not be modified until the political com-
plexion of the Supreme Court should be changed,
and this would be, of necessity, a process requiring
many years and a succession of presidents of the
same political opinions. The excitement, both
North and South, about the Fugitive Slave Law
had practically died out; and the secession movement had no strength in the border States, the only
ones having a material interest in the observance
of this law, or suffering from its evasion.

The real grievance was one which could not well
be formulated or put forward as a ground for
breaking up the Union. For half a century the
cotton States and Virginia had governed the country; they had controlled its policy, made its wars,
annexed new territory, nominated presidents, and
filled the government bureaus and departments.
They foreboded from this election the end of their
political domination, and determined to go off by
themselves, having faith that the world's need of
their great staple would bring them, should the
United States use force to prevent their carrying
out their plans, the recognition of their independence by the leading countries of Europe, if not
more material support. "Our leaders and public

men, who have taken hold of this question," wrote
Alexander H. Stephens, "do not desire to continue
the Union on any terms.   They do not wish any
redress of wrongs; they are disunionists *per se*,
and avail themselves of present circumstances to
press their objects."[1]

South Carolina was in the van of the movement.
Preliminary conferences had been held in Charleston as early as September, 1860, and at a private
meeting of the leading men on the 25th of October
it was unanimously resolved that South Carolina
should secede in the event of Lincoln being chosen
president.   To the legislature which assembled on
the 5th of November, the day before the presidential election, the governor in his message declared
that, should the Republican party carry that election, the only course for South Carolina would be
to secede from the federal Union; that political
indications justified the conclusion that other States
would immediately follow her, and that the long
desired coöperation for which they had been waiting would soon be realized.   From this time South
Carolina marched forward in her revolutionary
course with steady steps, and, as the governor had
foreseen, the other cotton States were not slow to
follow.   Before the end of November the preliminary steps had been taken in eight Southern States;
within two months afterwards, six of them —
South Carolina, Georgia, Florida, Alabama, Mississippi, and Louisiana — had passed ordinances

[1] November 30, 1860.   . .

of secession; by the middle of February Texas had united with them to form a Southern Confederacy, which had chosen a complete set of officers to administer its government. They had also seized for their own use all the forts, arsenals, and other public property and moneys of the United States in the South, unfortunately left without guard or protection, except Fort Sumter, off Charleston, which Major Anderson was holding with a handful of men, and Fort Pickens, at Pensacola, into which a gallant subaltern, Lieutenant Slemmer, had thrown himself with his company.

The moment selected for the outbreak of the secession conspiracy was most auspicious. The administration at Washington had no sympathy whatever with the Republican party or the dominant sentiment of the North. Four of Buchanan's cabinet were from the South, and three of these were either open or ill-disguised secessionists, — while every one of the Northern members was a pro-slavery Democrat, untainted by any of the heresies which had split the party in 1848, and either indifferent to, or else a supporter of, the violence and fraud by which the South had undertaken to gain Kansas for slavery, as well as of the administration's policy toward that Territory. All the departments swarmed with Southern rebels. Washington society was a hot-bed of treason and secession, wholly Southern in its sympathies; and extremists from the South were the closest companions and friends of the President. His term was nearly over, and the secession leaders relied on his political and personal proclivities and intimacies, and on his general reluctance to take responsibility, increased, as they knew it would be, by the fact that he was merely holding over until the inauguration of his successor, as sufficient to prevent any aggressive action on his part.

The President's annual message, sent to Congress on the 3d of December, did not disappoint these anticipations. It took the Northern States and people severely to task for the existing condition of things, for which, it said, they were wholly to blame. Secession was unlawful; of that there could be no question; but the coercion of a State was equally unlawful, and in the political dilemma, which he had thus reached, the President left the subject to Congress and the country. It was generally known that these views had not merely the support of the cabinet, but were the conclusions of the attorney-general, submitted to the President in a labored opinion. Thus encouraged, the Southern leaders had little hesitation in following their inclinations, and crossing, one by one, the narrow Rubicon which divides idle declamation, vaporing threats, and empty braggadocio from actual rebellion and treason. Within a month matters had gone so far that South Carolina, having removed the buoys and extinguished the lights in her harbors, and occupied by hostile troops all the forts except Sumter, was sending commissioners to Washington to treat with the government as a

foreign power. She insisted, as a preliminary to
all negotiations, upon the immediate evacuation of
Sumter, on the ground that the presence of the
United States troops there was a standing menace
to her sovereignty. Under these circumstances
the attorney-general revised his opinion; and approaching the questions presented him from a different point of view, reached the conclusion that
it was the President's clear constitutional right
and duty to defend the public property, to resist
by force any attempt to drive the troops of the
United States from any of its fortifications, and
to use both the army and navy, if necessary, for
the purpose of aiding the proper officers in the
execution of the laws. Had he been convinced of
this a month earlier, and satisfied the President's
mind then, it is possible that the rebellion might
have been nipped in the bud; though it is extremely doubtful if the small force disposable for
this purpose would have been sufficient to effect
much, unless the message and the proceedings of
the government had evinced such a resolute purpose that the Southern leaders would have hesitated
about precipitating a conflict. By the end of the
year they had gone too far, and kindled their own
and their people's passions to such an extent that
retreat was no longer possible.

The attorney-general succeeded, however, after a
severe struggle, in bringing the President to his own
standpoint. The cabinet was purged of the secessionists (Cobb of Georgia, Thomas of Maryland,

who succeeded him, Floyd of Virginia, and Thompson of Mississippi), and their places were filled by Dix, Stanton, and Holt; the White House ceased to be the rendezvous of Benjamin, Mason, Slidell, and Jefferson Davis, the conspirators of the Senate; and the efforts of the administration were loyally and vigorously bent towards keeping the government intact for delivery to its regularly elected successors.

Meantime, the bold and defiant attitude of the cotton States and their hasty and rapid strides towards secession had caused much alarm and a good deal of vacillation of opinion and feeling at the North, even among the supporters of Lincoln. Leading Republican newspapers were suggesting that our erring brethren should be allowed to go in peace. There were meetings in the large cities recommending concessions to save the Union, — the concessions suggested amounting in some cases to an abandonment of everything for which the Republican party had contended; and in the press and elsewhere there were from time to time hints that, should there be any attempt at coercion, the men from the North might find from their homes a fire in their rear.

When Congress assembled, the aspect of affairs inspired the loyal members of both Houses with profound gloom and anxiety. They knew that Washington was the centre of innumerable plots and intrigues, all having for their object the destruction of the Union. They felt themselves

absolutely powerless, and the administration, which
was then controlled by its Southern leaders, they
considered worse than powerless, believing it to be
the mere tool of the enemies of the country.   In
this great crisis no man distinguished himself as
a leader.   Many men of experience in public affairs, of character, resolution, and intelligence,
seemed hopelessly bewildered; they made speeches,
proposed and voted for measures, and took positions, which are only to be explained by their desire to postpone any violent outbreak until after
the 4th of March, lest on that day Washington
should be in the hands of the rebels, and Lincoln
trying to find some safe retreat where he might
take the oath of office as president of the United
States.   This fear was by no means a groundless
panic, but a well justified apprehension.   From
early in January, 1861, the senators from seven
Southern States were sitting in a room at the
Capitol, as a revolutionary council, directing every
movement toward secession, and preparing the
programme to be carried out in the formation of
the Confederacy.   There were several months when
the capture of Washington by surprise would have
been perfectly feasible; but so long as Buchanan,
the President whom the South had elected, and
who had faithfully done its bidding, was in office,
it was not easy to find a pretext for seizing the
capital.   To do so would have been, not the assertion of independence, but an act of offensive warfare, for which the seceding States were not yet

prepared; and so they delayed; the chances for
the success of a sudden attack were constantly
diminishing, yet it was never certain until some
time after Lincoln's inauguration that such an
attack would not be made, and Washington be
captured.

It needs but little reflection to convince one that
the plan of letting our erring brethren depart in
peace was impracticable and visionary; that it
would have merely postponed till after the recognition of their secession and independence the settlement of difficulties, which would then surely have
given rise to war.   An independent North would
never have consented to return a fugitive slave to
the seceded South; yet the Southern Confederacy
must have insisted at all hazards on some provision
for this purpose, in any treaty of separation, or
they would have lost rather than gained by secession.   The policy of conciliation, however, acquired new strength from its advocacy in various
New York papers, and especially from an editorial
by Thurlow Weed, which was supposed to have
been inspired by Seward, and to represent his
views.   Seward had in fact no knowledge of the
article before its publication, and Weed was alone
responsible for it.   But the personal and political
relations between Seward and Weed naturally
gave rise to suspicions of his connection with it,
and these were confirmed by the positive statement at the office of the New York "Tribune"
that Seward not only wrote the article, but was

meditating a great compromise after the fashion of
Clay and Webster. This whole statement, whether
malicious or not, was absolutely false, and it annoyed Seward extremely. He had nothing in view,
no plan but to wait, drifting like the rest. "I am
thus far silent," he writes to his wife,[1] "not because I am thinking of proposing compromises,
but because I wish to avoid, myself, and restrain
other Republicans from intermeddling just now,
when concession, or solicitation, or solicitude would
encourage, and demonstrations of firmness of purpose would exasperate;" and again, a day or
two later, he says: "Another day in the Senate.
Vaporing by Southern senators; setting forth the
grievances of their section, and requiring Northern
senators to answer, excuse, and offer terms which
they are told in the same breath will not be accepted."[2]

He was desirous, if possible, to find some solution of the "difficult task of trying to reconcile
the factious men bent on disunion, reckless of civil
war, to the ascendency of an administration based
on the principles of justice and humanity." But
he had no faith that any constitutional amendment
that might be proposed would be of any avail.
He had written earlier: "No amendment that can
be proposed, and would be satisfactory, can get
two thirds of both houses, although just such
amendments might pass three fourths of the States
in convention."

[1] December 8, 1860.   [2] December 11, 1860.

Besides his conviction that the Fabian policy was the best, Seward had another reason for silence. He must have shared the general expectation that he would be offered a seat in Lincoln's cabinet, and was therefore unwilling to make or assent to any proposals which might not meet the approval of the incoming president, or be in accord with the policy of his administration. Ten days after the meeting of Congress a letter from Mr. Lincoln invited him to become secretary of state; and he left Washington that he might consult his wife and Weed before coming to a decision.

He was by no means certain what he had better do, and wished for some more definite knowledge as to who were likely to be his associates in the cabinet, and as to Mr. Lincoln's general policy. Weed had already been asked to come to Springfield for a conference with the President-elect, and at Seward's suggestion he decided to go at once. While he was there Mr. Lincoln talked to him with entire frankness, and Weed in return stated his own opinions with absolute freedom. Weed came away, satisfied that Chase was to be secretary of the treasury, and Bates attorney-general, that Indiana was to have a place in the cabinet, and that Pennsylvania would probably be represented there by Cameron, that Gideon Welles was to be secretary of the navy, and that the only remaining post was likely to be offered to Montgomery Blair. Against these last two nominations

Weed protested strongly. Many men might be named, he said with perfect truth, any one of whom would be more satisfactory to New England, and better qualified to be secretary of the navy, than Mr. Welles. He was satisfied, however, that what he said did not affect Mr. Lincoln's previous decision, though he did not learn till much later that this appointment was made at the vice-president's special request. To Blair he objected, because he represented nobody and had no following; because his appointment would be obnoxious to the Union men of Maryland, who were old Whigs, while he had been always a Democrat, and till 1858 an office-holder under Buchanan; and also because, though he was now called a citizen of Maryland, he actually lived in the District of Columbia. To appoint both Welles and Blair would, Weed urged, give an undue prominence in the administration to the Democratic element among the Republicans, as it would leave the Whigs, who were a majority in the party, in a minority in the cabinet. It was evident to him, however, "that the selection of Montgomery Blair was a fixed fact," unless some Union man from one of the more southern States, who was of undoubted loyalty and acceptable to Lincoln, could be prevailed on to take the place. At Weed's instance, Mr. Lincoln made the attempt to induce a gentleman of this description to come into the cabinet, but the hopelessness of keeping these States in the Union made all efforts in this direction fruitless.

On his journey home Weed saw Seward, told him all he had learned as to the plans for the cabinet, and also the concessions which Lincoln was willing to make for peace and harmony. Seward returned at once to Washington, and after thinking over the matter for two or three days, in the light of the information he had received from Weed, whose conclusions as to the composition of the cabinet were subsequently shown to be absolutely correct, he wrote to Mr. Lincoln that, after due reflection and with much self-distrust, he had concluded that, should he be nominated and confirmed as secretary of state, it would be his duty to accept the appointment.

During Seward's absence at Auburn, Crittenden had offered in the Senate a series of resolutions proposing various constitutional amendments. The Missouri Compromise was to be restored, and extended to the Pacific; the Fugitive Slave Law was to be amended, so that the government should pay for a rescued slave; there were to be constitutional provisions, prohibiting Congress from abolishing slavery in any place under its exclusive jurisdiction in a slaveholding State, — or in the District of Columbia (so long as slavery existed in Maryland or Virginia); and from interfering with the transportation of slaves by land or water from any one slave State or Territory to any other slave State or Territory.

The resolutions were referred to a select committee of thirteen, of whom Seward was one, who

were "to consider the grievances between the slaveholding and non-slaveholding States, and to suggest if possible a remedy." At the close of the
first day's session of this committee, he wrote to his
wife: "We came to no compromise, and we shall
not." Toombs makes Seward responsible for this
result. "I supported Crittenden's compromise,"
he says, "heartily and sincerely, although the sul-
len obstinacy of Seward made it almost impossible
to do anything. . . . At length I saw that the
compromise must fail. With a persistent obstinacy that I have never yet seen surpassed, Seward
and his backers refused every overture. I then
telegraphed to Atlanta: ' All is at an end. North
determined; Seward will not budge an inch. Am
in favor of secession.' "

On his first meeting with the committee Seward
offered, with the unanimous consent of the other
Republican members, three propositions embodying the concessions which they understood Mr.
Lincoln would sanction. These were: *First*, A
constitutional amendment providing that the Constitution should never be altered so as to authorize
Congress to abolish or interfere with slavery in the
States. *Second:* A modification of the Fugitive
Slave Act so as to secure to any alleged fugitive
from service a trial by jury in the State where he
was arrested. *Third:* A recommendation to all
the States to revise their legislation concerning
persons recently resident in other States, and to
repeal all such laws as were in contravention of

the Constitution of the United States or of any law of Congress in pursuance thereof.[1] And later, with the concurrence of the other Republicans, he offered a fourth resolution: That Congress should pass a law to punish all persons engaged in the armed invasion of one State from another or in complicity with such invasions.

Nothing, however, came of Crittenden's resolutions, or of Seward's propositions. Neither the Senate committee of thirteen, nor a more numerous committee appointed by the House for a similar purpose, nor a Peace Convention assembled in Washington later in the winter at the invitation of Virginia, were able to make any suggestions which would be acceptable to the North, and would also induce the South to abandon its scheme of secession. The only effect of all the conferences and discussions was to postpone any further overt acts by the South and to enable Buchanan to see his successor inaugurated as the nominal President of the whole United States. The Republicans expected nothing more, and were only fearful lest this should not be safely accomplished. The seceding South meant to break up the Union, and could only have been diverted from its purpose by the acquiescence of the North in the substance of the demands set forth in the resolutions offered by Jefferson Davis in the Senate's select committee,

[1] This was aimed at the personal liberty bills of the North, the laws of South Carolina as to colored seamen and the similar statutes of other States.

which proposed: "That it should be declared by an amendment of the Constitution, that property in slaves, recognized as such by the local law of any of the States of the Union, shall stand on the same footing in all constitutional and federal relations as any other species of property so recognized; and like other property shall not be subject to be divested or impaired by the local law of any other State, either in escape thereto, or by the transit or sojourn of the owner therein. And in no case whatever shall such property be subject to be divested or impaired by any legislative act of the United States or any of the Territories thereof."

"The people of the South, all of the Southern States," wrote Seward, "are in the lead of reckless politicians. They are bent on coercing the free States into a recognition of slavery, and failing that, into a civil war and disunion." To this recognition, whether by amendments to the Constitution or otherwise, no Republican could assent.

The debates of the winter, the wide-spread publicity given to the pretensions of the South, the peremptoriness and arrogance with which its claims were insisted on, and the rejection of every scheme of compromise or adjustment proposed by any Northern senator or representative, brought home to the people of the free States a realizing sense of the impossibility of preventing the South from attempting to break up the Union, unless they were prepared to concede that this was a government in every part of which negroes might be lawfully held in bondage, and which had for the object of its existence the maintenance and perpetuation of African slavery.

In this winter of talk Seward made a speech, on the 12th of January, in which he endeavored to set before the country a picture — drawn in colors as glowing as possible — of the advantages of the Union; to describe what it had done for us, how under it we had grown from feeble colonists to a great nation, happy and prosperous at home, respected and feared abroad; and to contrast with this the result which would follow the dissolution of the government into several confederacies, each of which would be unimportant and disregarded; each would have its own policy, and would endeavor to stipulate with other countries for arrangements advantageous to itself, though injurious to its neighbors. Their mutual jealousies would encourage civil wars, which must ultimately result in the loss of their liberties and the destruction of their independent republican governments. Neither North nor South would suffer the other section to possess our entire national domain, nor would any peaceable division of this be possible. The resources of the slave States might be called on to put down risings of the slaves, or possibly to meet invasions more extensive and formidable than John Brown's attack upon Harper's Ferry. Dissolution would arrest the growth of the country, paralyze its industries and commerce, and substitute, for the brilliant constellation of our United States, the feeble light of small groups, or the uncertain glimmer of solitary stars.

While not even for peace and the maintenance of the Union would he make concessions that involved "any compromise of principle or any advantage of freedom," yet he would "meet prejudice with conciliation, exaction with concession which surrenders no principle, and violence with the right hand of peace." He suggested in the Senate the propositions he had already offered in the committee of thirteen, and urged the immediate admission of Kansas, as settling all that was vital or even important as to the question of slavery in the Territories.

In a second speech a few weeks later he further explained his position upon this question. The Territories of the United States, he said, contained more than a million square miles, over which a slave code had been in force for twelve years; but though during this time the courts, the legislature, and the administration had maintained and guaranteed slavery there, yet only twenty-four African slaves were to be found in that whole region, one slave for every forty-four thousand square miles. He had, therefore, no further fears as to this great public domain. Slavery there had ceased to be a practical question.

Afterwards, during this same session, when Colorado, Dakota, and Nevada were carved out of this

vast country, the acts organizing them as territories, which were reported by a senator from
Missouri, a strong supporter of the Breckenridge
Democracy, and which contained no prohibition
of slavery, received the votes of such stalwart anti-
slavery men as Sumner, Wade, and Chandler of
the Senate, and Thaddeus Stevens, Owen Lovejoy,
and the radical Republicans in the House; no one
of whom thought it worth while to explain or justify the omission of the proviso prohibiting slavery,
which they had so long and hotly contended was
of vital importance.

It was said on the one hand that Seward in
these speeches had "surrendered his principles and
those of his party to avert civil war and the dissolution of the Union;" on the other hand he was
denounced because he would "give up nothing at
all, not even his prejudices or caprices, to save
peace and the Union, the most inestimable of all
blessings;" whilst there were others who thanked
him for his attempt to save the Union, "without
damage to the sacred cause of freedom, and the
safeguard of its laws."

He himself considered the "concessions" in his
speech "not compromises but explanations." And
as they were substantially only assurances that he
was prepared to abide by the Constitution as it
was and would not seek to amend or alter it except
by a convention duly called for that purpose, his
own conclusion may be fairly accepted as correct.

To the charge that he had made a Union speech

and not an anti-slavery one, Seward replied: "Twelve years ago freedom was in danger, and the Union was not. I spoke then so singly for freedom, that short-sighted men inferred that I was disloyal to the Union. . . . To-day, practically, freedom is not in danger; and Union is. With the loss of Union all would be lost. Now, therefore, I speak singly for Union, striving if possible to save it peaceably; if not possible, then to cast the responsibility upon the party of slavery. For this singleness of speech I am now suspected of infidelity to freedom. In this case, as in the other, I refer myself not to the men of my time, but to the judgment of history."

Perhaps the clearest insight into Seward's hopes and expectations at this time is to be gained from a letter of Lord Lyons, the British minister at Washington, to Lord John Russell, then secretary of state for foreign affairs. "Mr. Seward's real view of the state of the country," he writes, "appears to be, that if bloodshed can be avoided until the new government is installed, the seceding States will in no long time return to the confederation. He seems to think that in a few months the evils and hardships produced by secession will become intolerably grievous to the Southern States; that they will become completely reassured as to the intentions of the administration, and the conservative element which is now kept under the surface by the violent pressure of the secessionists will emerge with irresistible force. From all these

causes he confidently expects that, when elections
for the state legislatures are held in November
next, the Union party will have a clear majority,
and will bring the seceding States back into the
confederation. He then hopes to place himself at
the head of a strong Union party having extensive
ramifications both North and South, and to make
' Union or Disunion,' not ' Freedom or Slavery,'
the watchword of political parties."

Seward himself had expressed something of the
same thought in the closing passages of his speech
at the dinner of the New England Society in New
York on the 22d of December, just after he had
learned from Weed Mr. Lincoln's views, the concessions he was willing to make, and his tone
toward the South. He said: "The necessities
which created this Union are stronger to-day than
they were when the Union was cemented; these
necessities are as enduring as the passions of men
are short lived and effervescent. The cause of
secession was as strong on the night of November 6, when a president and vice-president were
elected who were unacceptable to the slave States,
as it has been at any time. *Fifty days have
passed; and I believe that every day the sun has
set since that time, it has set upon mollified passions and prejudices; and if you will only await
the time, sixty more suns will shed a light and
illuminate a more cheerful atmosphere.*"

Taken in its connection, the meaning of the passage in italics is obvious. Sixty days more will

see the inauguration of a new president, whose
administration will dispel doubts, clear the air,
purge the government of secessionists and conspirators, and cheer the heart of every loyal lover of
the Union.   But, wrested from their context, these
words were tortured into a prophecy that the war
of secession would be at an end in sixty days, and
were constantly quoted to show how false a pro-
phet, how blind to the signs of the times, and how
untrustworthy a guide Seward was.   Even if this
had been their real meaning, he would not have
been alone at that time in his opinion that the
war, if it came, would be a short one.   An ob-
server equally intelligent, with equal, if not superior, opportunities of seeing and knowing the
actual condition of the South and Southern opinion, General Grant himself, has left on record a
statement that during the winter of 1860–61, and
indeed until after the battle of Shiloh, he believed
that the war would be over in ninety days.[1]

It was not Seward's natural optimism which led
him and many others with him to the belief that
the advent of Lincoln's administration would bring
a brighter outlook for the Union.   Secession was
as yet confined to the cotton and Gulf States.   It
was believed that, unless joined by others, these
States alone had not the power to break up the
Union.   In the other slave States there were
marked indications of a strong Union feeling; in
several, a distinct Union majority.   At the North

[1] Grant's *Autobiography*, i. p. 222.

the hope was very generally entertained that Lincoln's inaugural and the whole tone of his administration would allay the passions and calm the fears of the people of those slave States that had not passed secession ordinances, and that they would remain loyal.   But those who had this hope did not reckon upon the strength of the family affections and the wide ramifications of family ties among the dominant class in the slaveholding States.   They overlooked the natural effect of the slaveholders' loyalty to one another, of their strong sectional sympathies, and of their fidelity to their supposed common interest in slavery.   They forgot the Southerners' dislike to the North, the feeling they had that they were looked down upon as slaveholders, were treated as inferior in civilization and humanity, and the belief, common in the slave States, that Northern intermeddling with their domestic institutions was the cause of all their difficulties.   Nor did those people who were still hopeful of the Union in any way anticipate the expedients to which the secessionist leaders would resort to drag any doubting State into disunion, or to stifle the voice of the majority when they feared it was against them.

CHAPTER XIII

DURING the winter Mr. Lincoln had endeavored without success to select some Southern man as a member of his cabinet. When he reached Washington on the 23d of February, there was still one place which was supposed to be open; and, in the scramble and intriguing for this, there was a moment when it seemed as if Seward would withdraw. The President's decision to nominate Montgomery Blair for this post was no surprise to Seward. The statements of Weed on returning from Springfield in December had quite prepared him for this as well as for all the other cabinet appointments. He had no personal objections to Mr. Blair, and no reluctance to serve with him as a colleague. The selection, however, gave great offense not only to the leading Whigs, the most numerous body of Lincoln's supporters, since it left them a minority of the cabinet ministers; but also to many Republicans of Democratic antecedents, who, while recognizing the ability of the Blairs, both disliked and distrusted them. It was also especially objectionable, for the reasons already given, to the Union men of Maryland, by

whom Mr. Blair was not recognized as a Mary-
lander, and of whom, as they were substantially
of old Whig stock and descent, Mr. Blair, as a
Democrat and a stranger, was in no sense a representative. Under these circumstances, Blair's
friends were naturally uneasy, lest the President
should for some reason change his mind before the
nomination was actually made; and, when rumors
of such a change were flying about Washington
three or four days before the inauguration, one of
these gentlemen, a personal friend of the President, asked him if they were true. Mr. Lincoln
answered, "No, — if that slate is broken again, it
will be at the top." This was where Seward's
name stood.

There can be but little doubt that this speech of
the President was at once reported to Seward, and
that it had much to do with the abrupt manner in
which on the 2d of March he wrote to Mr. Lincoln, thanking him for his kindness and confidence, but declining the office of secretary of state.
The other considerations inducing him to this
course, and of which he speaks in his letter of
March 8, presently to be quoted, may have been
in his mind for some time; but they had not moved
him to any definite action. Something of a different nature must have suddenly come to his knowledge, which caused him within forty-eight hours
before the inauguration to write to Mr. Lincoln,
withdrawing his previous acceptance of the first
place in the cabinet. His short note bears quite

as strong marks of wounded feelings as of changed
convictions.   The coldness of its tone is in marked
contrast with that of his other letters to the President.

WASHINGTON, March 2, 1861.

MY DEAR SIR: — Circumstances which have occurred since I expressed to you in December last
my willingness to accept the office of secretary of
state seem to me to render it my duty to ask leave
to withdraw that consent.

Tendering to you my best wishes for the success
of your administration, with my sincere and grateful acknowledgments of all your acts of kindness
and confidence towards me, I remain very respect-
fully and sincerely,

Your obedient servant,

WILLIAM H. SEWARD.

The Hon. ABRAHAM LINCOLN, President-elect.

Lincoln got this note on Saturday, and on Monday, inauguration day, handed his answer to his
secretary, saying that he "could not afford to let
Seward take the first trick."   This mode of speech,
with which the country afterwards became familiar, seemed at the time more undignified and offensive than pithy and expressive; and many persons found it, in the President of the United
States, as unpleasant as it was novel.   As Seward
did not persist in his refusal, one may be quite sure ·
that the discreet secretary did not repeat to him
the remark with which the President accompanied

the delivery of the note. Seward was not considering the administration as a game in which he was trying to take the first or any other trick; nor did he wish his name on a slate which the President had any inclination to break; he was not so hungry for place that he would submit to any indignities, if he might thereby enjoy either the honors or emoluments of office; he was under no obligations to Lincoln to accept any appointment. The obligation, if there were any, was the other way: Lincoln had taken from Seward the first trick at Chicago, and Seward had done his best to enable him to win the game in the country. He went into the cabinet from no motive less noble than the desire to perform for his country the best public service he could. He might not unreasonably have hesitated about becoming a member of an administration composed of such discordant and heterogeneous materials as Mr. Lincoln had got together, — a cabinet which the caustic tongue of a veteran Republican described as "an assortment of rivals whom he had appointed out of courtesy [Seward, Chase, and Cameron], one stump speaker from Indiana [Caleb Smith], and two representatives of the Blair family [Mr. Bates, for whom General Frank Blair was said to be responsible, and Montgomery Blair]."

After the inauguration Lincoln had a long talk with Seward, who at last agreed to take office, and on the following day was nominated and confirmed as secretary of state.

In writing home at this time (March 8, 1861), Seward says: "The President is determined that he will have a compound cabinet; and that it shall be peaceful, and even permanent. I was at one time on the point of refusing — nay, I did refuse — to hazard myself in the experiment. But a distracted country appeared before me, and I withdrew from that position."

The cabinet, as finally constituted, consisted of Chase, Welles, Cameron, and Blair, Democrats; Seward, Bates, and Smith, Whigs. Some of these have already been spoken of, and of others there is no occasion to speak. The attorney-general, Edward Bates of Missouri, was known as a gentleman of spotless reputation, as an old conservative Whig of distinct anti-slavery opinions in a State where the holding of such views was as courageous as it was rare, as a man who avoided rather than sought office, and as a respectable rather than an eminent lawyer. Mr. Welles was a Democrat from Connecticut. If he had any position or prominence in his party, it was practically confined to his own State; he was not known throughout New England, of which section he was the representative in the cabinet. He had been a newspaper editor, and held a facile pen, had been in one of the departments at Washington, and postmaster at Hartford; but he brought to the cabinet neither increased strength within, nor additional support from without. The vigorous and successful administration of the navy during the war was substantially due to the energy and executive ability of Captain G. V. Fox, the assistant secretary in that department.

Lincoln, in entering upon the duties of his office, was confronted by problems as appalling and perplexing as any government was ever called upon to face. The seven States which had undertaken to secede and break up the Union had formed their new Confederacy. In the month before Lincoln's inauguration they had elected a president, and adopted a constitution, whose fundamental difference from that of the United States was in its provision for the most "ample and avowed protection to property in slaves." Their government was complete on paper; the machinery of their state governments was the same as before the secession ordinances were passed, was in the hands of the same officers, and running on without change. They had banished the sovereignty of the United States from all places within their jurisdiction, except Forts Sumter and Pickens; the safety of which, insufficiently garrisoned and provisioned as they were, must be at once provided for by the administration, unless they were to be abandoned.

On the morning after the inauguration, before any member of the cabinet had assumed the duties of office, the War Department communicated to the President information just received from Major Anderson at Sumter, stating that he had only a month's provisions, that newly erected hostile

batteries commanded his position, that the channels and harbor had been obstructed, that patrol
boats and other Confederate vessels guarded the
approaches to his post and watched his every
movement; and that it would take twenty thousand
men to relieve and hold the fort. General Scott
and the other army officers confirmed this opinion.
The relief of Fort Pickens was a much simpler
affair, if it were only done promptly. But an expedition for Sumter on the scale which these officers thought requisite to insure success was simply
impossible. The President had at his disposal no
forces adequate for such an undertaking. A vague
direction to General Scott by word of mouth, that
he was "to exercise all possible vigilance for the
maintenance of all military posts, and to call upon
the departments for the means necessary for this
purpose," and a request to him to reconsider carefully the matter of the relief of Sumter, were all
that could be done for the moment. Four days
later the whole matter was laid before the cabinet,
and on several days following there were consulta-
tions with officers of the navy as well as of the
army. The latter adhered to their opinion as to
the force required to succor and hold Sumter; the
former thought that a small expedition of light-
draft steamers might successfully carry supplies.
The President hesitated. He took from General
Scott an order for the evacuation of the fort, but
did not sign it; and on the 15th of March he
called upon the members of his cabinet to give

him in writing their opinions, whether, if it were possible to provision Sumter, it would be wise to attempt to do so. The form of the question shows that it was the political, not the military, problem which was submitted to their consideration.

Only two members of the cabinet, Chase and Blair, favored the attempt to provision the fort, assuming it to be possible to do so. The other five, Seward, Bates, Cameron, Welles, and Smith, were opposed to it. Seward in his answer assumed that "the government was to maintain, preserve, and defend the Union, peacefully, if it could, forcibly, if it must, to every extremity." It was by our standing on the defensive, he thought, that the border States had so far been kept loyal, and a perseverance in this policy was in his opinion the only means of assuring their continuing so. He expressed his fear that with a daily press, daily mails, and incessant telegraph, the design to supply the fort would become known in Charleston as soon as preparations should begin, and the garrison fall by assault before the expedition could reach the harbor.

To obtain more certain and definite information both as to the condition of Sumter and the existence of any Union feeling in South Carolina, the President dispatched to Charleston Captain Fox, the author of the relief plan proposed by the navy, and two other gentlemen. Returning before the end of the month they reported that there was but one avowed Union man in Charleston; and while

Captain Fox was more confident than ever of the success of his plan, he had been unable to convince either his companion, who visited the fort, or Major Anderson, that it was in any way a feasible one.

Just after their return Lincoln received from General Scott a memorandum, advising the abandonment of Fort Pickens, as a measure of conciliation which would soothe the eight remaining slave States, and render perpetual their cordial adherence to the Union. A cabinet meeting was called, and with this memorandum and all the other information before them, the members of the cabinet gave the President their written opinions as to both forts. Of the seven members of the cabinet who, a fortnight before, had answered his question as to Sumter, Blair had been then the only advocate of that plan for its relief of which his brother-in-law, Captain Fox, was the author; though Chase had doubtfully answered that the fort should be relieved if possible. But now, when the situation of both forts was considered (only six members of the cabinet being present), Chase and Welles joined with Blair; Bates thought Sumter should be "either provisioned or evacuated," and they all, except Blair, were of opinion that Pickens should be reinforced. Having heard the views of his constitutional advisers, the President determined to attempt the relief of Sumter; and, as he was uneasy at the want of news from Fort Pickens, for the reinforcement of which he had already taken specific measures, he resolved to send an expedition there also. The preparations for the Sumter expedition, which were made through the Navy Department and followed its usual routine, were more or less guessed at by the public and disclosed in the newspapers. Notice of this expedition was officially communicated to the governor of South Carolina in accordance with an assurance the President had previously authorized to be given, that he would give such information, if it should be decided to provision the fort. But before this notice reached Charleston, two telegrams had already made the plan known and its precise details had been ascertained by the treacherous rifling of Major Anderson's mail bags. The bombardment began before the first vessel of the relief expedition had reached the rendezvous off Charleston harbor; a violent storm prevented the arrival of the tugs which were essential to success, and the expedition was a failure.

Seward has been criticised for detaching and sending to Fort Pickens the Powhatan, which the secretary of the navy had ordered on the Sumter expedition. But Seward's responsibility in the matter, if any at all, is very slight. Captain Fox asked for the Pocahontas for Sumter, and the President ordered her to be given him. Mr. Welles substituted the Powhatan. The President, knowing nothing of this change, gave to the officer in charge of the Pickens expedition a direct order for the Powhatan, and he carried her off. The loss of this vessel did not in fact have anything to do with the failure of the Sumter expedition, the causes of which have been already stated.[1]

The Fort Pickens expedition succeeded, and gave us during the war the control of that fort, of Key West, and of the Dry Tortugas. This expedition was fitted out under the direct orders of the President without the knowledge of the Navy Department, and the secret was kept so perfectly that the first actual knowledge of it was derived from the report of the commander on his return. This mode of proceeding was, of course, all wrong and irregular, but secrecy was vital to success, and it may well be doubted whether in the then existing condition of affairs secrecy would have been possible had the Navy Department directed or even been cognizant of the preparations.

The Sumter expedition failed of its ostensible object, but it brought about the Southern attack on that fort. The first gun fired there effectually cleared the air, put an end to discussions and differences of opinion, and placed Lincoln at the head of a united people, resolved, at whatever cost, to maintain the integrity of their country. There were no more doubts or hesitations. The border States chose their sides. The struggle had begun.

---

[1] The President's orders to Fox were, "If on your arrival at Charleston you shall ascertain that Fort Sumter shall have been attacked by an opposing force you will return here forthwith." The Baltic, with Fox on board, the first vessel to reach the rendezvous off Charleston, arrived there just in time to hear the opening guns of the bombardment. *N. & H.*, iv. pp. 35, 54.

CHAPTER XIV

JUSTICE CAMPBELL AND THE REBEL COMMIS-
SIONERS

AT the time of Lincoln's inauguration there were in Washington commissioners accredited by the "Confederate States of America" to the government of the United States as a foreign power, and instructed to open negotiations "with a view to the recognition of the independence of the Confederacy and the concluding of treaties of amity and good will between the two nations." So far as its avowed objects were concerned their mission was wholly fruitless. They never saw the President or any member of his cabinet. They lingered in Washington for their own purposes, until on the 8th of April they took from the State Department a copy of a memorandum which Seward, unwilling to give them even such recognition as is implied by the writing of a letter, had filed there on the 15th of March, and which they knew had been waiting for them since that time. In this memorandum he distinctly but civilly declined to receive them, and gave some reasons for so doing. As they assumed to be foreign ambassadors, they should have addressed themselves in the first in-

stance to the secretary of state; but, feeling doubts
as to their reception, they induced a senator from
a border State that had not yet seceded, to ask if
the secretary would see them informally; when
Seward declined to do this, they sent a formal application, with the final result that has just been
stated. This is the whole story of these commissioners, so far as the nominal and declared object
of their appointment is concerned; but Southern
historians have accused the government of having
adopted "a policy of perfidy" toward them; and
Justice John A. Campbell, of Alabama, — who
still retained his place on the Supreme Court,
although he was in fact the intermediary of the
Southern commissioners and Confederate authorities, — has devoted much labor to an attempt to
prove that Mr. Seward in his intercourse with him
was guilty of duplicity and equivocation.

Judge Campbell's intervention began in this
way. When Seward had written the memorandum which has been spoken of, declining to receive the commissioners, he directed a copy of it
to be prepared and given them; but before this
had been done two justices of the Supreme Court,
Nelson of New York, an old acquaintance and almost neighbor of Seward, and Campbell of Alabama called upon him together. Campbell, it is
said, had his resignation already prepared and was
to have sent it in on that very day (March 15,
1861).[1] Instead of doing this, however, he had

[1] Stanton to Buchanan, March 10, 1861.

determined to withhold it for a time, that, as he
wrote Jefferson Davis, he might avail himself of
his position to give him access to the administration, which he could not otherwise have.[1]   He
probably thought the breaking up of the Union a
mistake, and was therefore not a disunionist; but
he was a states-rights Southern Democrat, who believed that his State had a claim on him paramount
to any obligation which he owed to the United
States government, whose sworn officer he was.
Alabama had seceded, and he meant to follow her.
He also believed, however, that if the United
States were to abandon Sumter and Pickens and
let the Confederacy go its way unmolested, war
might be avoided, and a more satisfactory conclusion of the questions between the two "governments" be speedily reached.   Seward knew nothing of this.   He only knew that Campbell was
a justice of the Supreme Court of the United
States; and if he had harbored any suspicions as to
his loyalty, or had felt the need of any assurance
of this beyond the guaranty of his official position,
any such doubts would have been dispelled, and
every requisite assurance given, by his coming as
the companion of Judge Nelson, whose support of
the government was absolutely unquestioned.

Seward, Nelson, and Campbell each wished to
preserve the existing condition of things, and to
postpone as long as possible any outbreak, in the
hope that a resort to force might be at last avoided.

[1] April 3, 1861.

Their reasons for wishing so and the objects they had in view were, however, quite different. Seward's position and hopes were well known. He thought that, if any clash of arms could be postponed until the border States should realize the scrupulous care with which Lincoln would respect and maintain the just rights of the South, they would remain loyal, and that secession, confined to the seaboard and Gulf States, would fail from its own weakness. Nelson dreaded a war, had grave doubts as to the legality of some coercive measures which it was rumored that the government might adopt, and feared that, should there be a resort to arms, our constitutional government might perish in the struggle. As to Campbell's position, perhaps enough has been already said. He considered the Confederacy an established fact; but he knew that peace was very important for the new government, and he was willing to work for it in the interests and as the intermediary of Jefferson Davis and his cabinet.[1] Whether Campbell had seen the commissioners before calling on Seward seems uncertain. His visit with Judge Nelson was made for the purpose of inducing Seward to reconsider the matter, and to write to the commissioners, stating the desire of the government for a friendly adjustment, and saying that "every effort would be made and every forbearance exercised before resorting to extreme measures." This Seward declined to do, and told the judges

[1] Davis's Message, May 6, 1861.

that the cabinet would never assent to it. On Seward's part the conversation was frank and friendly; but, considering that Judge Campbell was a Southerner from a seceded State, it was unwise and indiscreet. That there was any difference between Campbell's relations and feeling towards the government and those of Judge Nelson, seems not to have occurred to Seward at the time; certainly no suspicion ever crossed his mind that Campbell was in fact a secessionist going out with his State, but lingering in Washington and keeping his place, that he might better serve the interests of the rebel authorities.

It had already been announced half officially in the newspapers that Sumter was to be evacuated;[1] and Campbell asked Seward point-blank if this was so. Campbell says that Seward replied that Sumter would be evacuated within five days. Leaving Seward, Campbell went at once to the rebel commissioners and reported to them the result of his conversation. He urged them to give a reasonable delay before demanding an answer to their request for an interview, telling them that, if they pressed for it at once, they would receive a civil but firm refusal. As to Fort Sumter, he said he felt perfectly confident it would be evacuated within five days. The commissioners were not quite open with Campbell; he found them apparently impatient of delay; they seemed to yield

[1] *New York Herald*, March 10. *National Republican*, March 12, 1861.

to his wishes reluctantly, and only after they had satisfied themselves that all his information had come from Seward; they required him to put his statement as to Sumter in writing and to sign it. Their reluctance, however, was more apparent than real. Their secret instructions were to "play with Seward and gain time," until the South was ready. They meant to make a peremptory demand for their reception or rejection on the very first day that Jefferson Davis and his cabinet were ready to meet the consequences; but not till then, if they could avoid it. Campbell's intervention gave them just the excuse they desired. It enabled them to stay in Washington and pick up such crumbs of information and gossip as could be found in the corridors of the hotels or in other places accessible to them, and to secure time for the Confederacy to make the necessary arrangements for its defense. Their course was approved, and they were instructed to make no formal demand for an answer so long as the United States continued its hesitating, uncertain, and vacillating policy.

After seeing the commissioners, Campbell the same evening (March 15) wrote to Jefferson Davis: "Before this reaches you Sumter will have been evacuated, or orders will have been issued for the purpose." This he says that Seward authorized him to do; he also says that he sent to Seward the same evening the substance of the memorandum which he had given to the commissioners. The memorandum and his statement as to that are to be found in his letter to Seward of April 13, 1861. Campbell's statement that Seward authorized what he wrote to Davis was never made public until after Seward's death.

The conversation, memorandum, and letter to Davis are all to be referred to the same day (March 15), the very day of the decisive vote in the cabinet (five to two) against holding Sumter; when Lincoln had already in his possession the order for its evacuation, which only needed his signature. Seward, therefore, had not the slightest doubt that the matter was settled. He communicated to his visitors the confidence he himself felt. It was an unguarded statement on his part, yet not fairly subject to any severe criticism. What Judge Campbell stated, on the faith of what he heard from Seward, he might almost equally well have said upon the faith of what is admitted to have been the almost official utterance of the government organ; his attempt to torture Seward's statement into a promise and to charge him with duplicity in not carrying it out wrests the words from their natural meaning and from the sense in which the judge understood them at the time. He knew perfectly well that it was not in Mr. Seward's power to carry out any policy or to control the situation in any way; that all that he could do, and what he was doing, was to state the conclusion, which he understood to have been reached at the time, but which at any moment before it was acted upon might be reversed, against his own

judgment and contrary to his expectation, as in
this case actually happened. Moreover, Judge
Campbell seems to forget, — when he speaks of
this statement as a promise, and charges Seward
with bad faith in not fulfilling it, — that a promise
necessarily implies two parties who are on opposite
sides, and that in charging the secretary with bad
faith he assumes not merely that he himself was,
as afterwards appeared, a rebel emissary, but that
he was then known as such to Mr. Seward; whereas
just the reverse is true. It had never occurred to
the secretary that he might find under the robes
of a United States judge an emissary of Jefferson
Davis. The two judges who were present at this
interview on the 15th of March seemed to have
come on the same errand and were presumed to be
in the same position. Mr. Seward's conversation
was with both alike; whatever he said was said to
both; whatever assurances or promises he made
were given to one just as much as to the other; if
he was guilty of any bad faith, he was equally so
to both judges. Judge Nelson approved Judge
Campbell's memorandum which has been quoted,
but we have yet to learn that he ever gave to
Campbell's charges against Seward any countenance or indorsement.

When five days had gone by, Campbell, whose
true relations, if there were still any shadow of
doubt about them, are thus made absolutely clear,
requested the rebel commissioners to telegraph
Beauregard at Charleston and ascertain what had

been done as to vacating Sumter. Beauregard answered that there had been no change; thereupon Judge Campbell, taking Judge Nelson with him, went twice to see Mr. Seward (March 21 and 22) and on the same days wrote for the commissioners two memoranda giving the results of these interviews. In the first he says that his confidence in the evacuation of Sumter is unabated; in the last, that of March 22, he repeats this statement, and adds, "*I shall have knowledge of any change in the existing status.*"[1] At this point Judge Nelson withdrew from further connection with the matter; he had probably begun to suspect Campbell's real relation to the Confederate authorities, and was afraid of being drawn into a false position by continuing to follow him further. Here it becomes important as well as interesting to note the difference in Judge Campbell's language when he speaks of a promise actually made him, and that which he used in stating his own conclusions from what had been said in conversation. He does not say now that he is convinced he shall have knowledge of any change; he asserts positively, "I shall have knowledge of any change in the existing status." This new mode of expression was not accidental; it corresponded to the new situation. He

---

[1] In his letter of April 13 to Mr. Seward Judge Campbell attempts to paraphrase this sentence so as to restrict it, and make it mean that as regards Fort Pickens he was to "have notice of any design to alter the existing status there." This is not so in the original memorandum, and this construction is not warranted by the context there.

now for the first time had a promise, which Seward had been authorized by the President to make, and the difference in his phraseology only repeated the difference in Seward's. The President had been informed by Seward of his conversation with Nelson and Campbell on the 15th of March. He had weighed the matter deliberately, and Seward's statement to Campbell on the 22d, that he should "have knowledge of any change in the existing status," embodied, as Mr. Lincoln's biographers tell us, the conclusion which the President himself had reached and which he had authorized Mr. Seward to communicate to Judge Campbell.

The President was at this time deeply considering his duty with reference to the whole situation and especially as to Sumter. He had said in his inaugural address: "The power confided to me will be used to hold, occupy, and possess the property and places belonging to the government." It might be true that it would require a force greater than he could command to hold Sumter against a hostile attack, and that to send any reinforcements thither might provoke an attack; the garrison already there was quite sufficient for a time of peace, but its provisions were nearly exhausted. Should he undertake to throw in fresh supplies by sea, following a plan which naval officers assured him was practicable; or should he, notwithstanding his public declarations, withdraw the troops, and evacuate the fort without making a single effort to supply the needed provisions?

To determine this matter to his own satisfaction, the President felt that he must have further and more accurate information, and to obtain this he sent to Charleston three gentlemen on whose judgment he thought he could rely. One of them, Marshal Lamon, besides visiting the fort and seeing Major Anderson, had an interview with Governor Pickens, in which he made such inquiries as to the best mode of removing the garrison, and whether they would be permitted to depart in peace, that the governor fancied the evacuation definitely determined on, and was constantly expecting to see signs of preparation for it. Becoming impatient after a few days, he wrote to Beauregard, whom the Confederate authorities had sent to command at Charleston: "If Lamon was authorized to arrange matters, Anderson ought now to say so." Failing to learn anything through Beauregard's inquiries, the governor, on the 30th of March, telegraphed to the Confederate commissioners at Washington. They sent at once for their intermediary, who carried the dispatch to Seward on Saturday afternoon and left it, saying that he would return on Monday. When they met on that day, Campbell, after some unimportant talk, asked Seward what he might say to Governor Pickens on the subject of Sumter. Seward wrote: "The President may desire to supply Fort Sumter, but will not undertake to do so without first giving notice to Governor Pickens," and handed this to Campbell. According to a more detailed narrative of this interview given by Campbell (from whom, it should be observed, our only accounts of all these interviews come), Seward, in reply to a further question, stated that he did not believe the attempt to throw in supplies would be made, and that there was no design to reinforce the fort. To which Campbell answered that he had that assurance previously, and added that it was already difficult to restrain South Carolina, and that he "would not recommend an answer that did not express the purpose of the government." Thereupon Seward went out, saying he must see the President; and returning presently, modified the memorandum so that it read, "I am satisfied the government will not undertake to supply Fort Sumter without giving notice to Governor Pickens."[1] With this, as the definitive reply to his inquiry as to what he "might say to Governor Pickens," Campbell departed; and the interviews between him and Seward were brought to an end. If there is any substantial difference between the two papers written by Seward at this time, it is, that the probability of an attempt to provision the fort is more strongly suggested by the second, which Campbell carried off, than by the first. A person comparing the two, and considering the change of phraseology, might naturally find the explanation of it in a more than half-formed, though not fully ripe purpose in the President, by

[1] Campbell to Seward, April 13, 1861. Reb. Rec. I. Doc. p. 426.

whom the alteration had evidently been made, to endeavor to supply the garrison of Sumter.

The day before Campbell went to Seward with the telegram from Governor Pickens the cabinet had held its second meeting as to Sumter. At this meeting Chase, Welles, and Blair had given their opinions in favor of relieving the fort, by force if necessary, and Bates had stated his conclusion that the time had come either to evacuate or to relieve it, while Seward and Smith thought that it should be abandoned. The President had given no definite orders for an expedition to Sumter, though he had issued some preparatory directions, which were probably known only to the secretaries of war and of the navy, who were each necessarily cognizant of them. It is clear from his letter of April 1 to the President, which is presently to be spoken of, that Seward either did not know them, or had no belief that they would lead to any consequences. If there was any rumor of these preparations in Washington, it was not sufficient to excite serious uneasiness in the Confederate commissioners before the 6th of April, the day on which the President gave to Captain Fox his final orders for the Sumter expedition, and sent to Charleston a confidential messenger with the promised notice to Governor Pickens of his intention to provision the fort.

By the morning of Sunday, April 7, however, the commissioners had become so disturbed that they again invoked Campbell's assistance; he at

once wrote to Seward and received from him this
brief reply: "Faith as to Sumter fully kept; wait
and see." This of course meant that notice had
been given to the governor, as agreed, of the attempt to provision the fort, and that Campbell, if
he would only wait, would see this. It is evident
that Campbell at the time so understood it, for on
the same day, after receiving this line from Seward, he wrote the commissioners: "I believe that
my assurances to you, that the government will
not undertake to supply Sumter without notice
to Governor Pickens, will be fully sustained by
the event." A further extract from the draft of
a letter written by him on the same day will show
that, while he knew and shared the common opinion in Washington as to the uncertainties and
vacillations of the administration, he also anticipated what was to be its ultimate decision as to
Sumter. He says: "Such government by blind-
man's-buff, stumbling along too far, will end by
the general overturn. Fort Sumter, I fear, is a
case past arrangement."

The same Sunday evening at nine o'clock the
commissioners' secretary called at Seward's house
to ask that the answer to their request for an interview, which they knew had been waiting their
pleasure at the State Department for more than
three weeks, might be delivered to them at two
o'clock the next day. This was done. On the
9th of April, they sent to Mr. Seward a reply,
which had previously been submitted to Judge

Campbell and modified at his request, and on the
11th they left Washington. They had gained the
delay which they were instructed to obtain. If
their hopes of a peaceful solution of their difficulties by the administration's abandonment of Sumter and Pickens seem to have been at times somewhat too sanguine, and their communications to
the Confederate authorities too rose-colored, yet
their telegram of March 22 — "And, what is of
infinite importance to us, notice will be given of
any change in the existing status" — shows that
they themselves were not over-confident of the fulfillment of their own prophecies of evacuation and
of peace. Jefferson Davis and his cabinet never
put any faith in these. On the 1st of March the
Confederate secretary of war wrote to Beauregard
at Charleston: "Give but little credit to the rumors of an amicable adjustment. Do not slacken
for a moment your energies;" and this represents
the attitude and action of the authorities at Montgomery from that time forward.

The news of the bombardment of Sumter reached
Washington on the 12th of April; the next day
Campbell addressed to Seward a letter complaining that the equivocating conduct of the administration was the proximate cause of this great calamity. To this letter Seward properly made no
reply. A week later Campbell inclosed a copy of
it in another communication, in which he said that
he insisted upon an explanation, adding that in
case of refusal he should not hold himself debarred

from placing these letters before such persons as were entitled to an explanation from him. This letter also remained unanswered. Shortly afterwards Campbell gave his own version of the matter to Stanton, who, after hearing Campbell's whole story, wrote to Buchanan that he did not believe any deceit or double dealing could be justly imputed to Seward, that he had no doubt that Seward believed that Sumter would be evacuated, as he stated it would be; but that the war party overruled him. With Judge Campbell's later statements, founded upon his recollections after the lapse of ten years, there is no need to concern ourselves; so far as they conform to the contemporary records they are unimportant, so far as they modify them they are less trustworthy. Nor is this the place to discuss what must be regarded as Judge Campbell's equivocal and unfortunate position in the whole affair. As an historical episode, the incidents have but little importance, though they are not devoid of interest as the story of a single Southern intrigue; as the basis of a serious accusation against Seward they seem to justify this somewhat full statement of them.

Seward's natural optimism and his earnest desire to avoid the "civil war, and the violent emancipation" which he had long before prophesied as its inevitable consequence, may have made him over-confident that some peaceful settlement would be reached; he may have expressed this confidence too strongly to Judge Campbell, with whom, as subsequent events showed, he talked more freely than was judicious, misled, as other people were, as to Judge Campbell's loyalty, by his retaining his seat in the Supreme Court of the United States notwithstanding the secession of Alabama, and by his selection of Judge Nelson of New York, a familiar acquaintance and almost neighbor of Seward, as the companion of his visits. The only independent contemporary opinion as to Seward's conduct in these transactions is that of Mr. Stanton, who was then far more disposed to criticise the administration than to commend it, and to find fault with Seward than to excuse or justify him; and who reached his conclusions solely from Judge Campbell's own story, told him while the whole matter and every detail of it was fresh and vivid in the judge's mind. Under these circumstances, it is no more than justice to Seward that these conclusions should be accepted as final, and that he should be relieved from any imputation of deceit or double dealing in the whole affair.

CHAPTER XV

BEFORE the close of Seward's first month as secretary of state there was another incident which there is reason to believe has been misinterpreted, and has consequently subjected Seward to criticisms both harsh and unjust.

On the 1st of April he submitted to Mr. Lincoln a paper entitled "Some Thoughts for the President's Consideration," in which he stated that at the end of a month's administration we were "without a policy, either domestic or foreign." But, though he admitted this condition to have been unavoidable, the presence of the Senate and the pressure of the office-seekers having prevented attention to graver matters, any further delay to adopt and prosecute our policies for both domestic and foreign affairs would, he said, not only bring scandal upon the administration, but danger upon the country.

As to domestic policy, he suggested that "we must change the question before the public from one upon slavery, or about slavery, for a question upon union or disunion." The occupation or evac-

uation of Fort Sumter being regarded as a slavery
or party question, although it was not so in fact,
he "would terminate it, as a safe means of chan-
ging the issue;" and he deemed it "fortunate that
the last administration created the necessity."
He would reinforce and defend all the forts in the
gulf, have the navy recalled from foreign stations
to be prepared for a blockade, and put Key West
under martial law.

As to foreign nations, — he "would demand explanations from Spain and France categorically,
at once;" and would convene Congress and declare war against them, if the explanations were
unsatisfactory; he would also "seek explanations
from Great Britain and Russia, and send agents
into Canada, Mexico, and Central America to
rouse a vigorous continental spirit of independence
on this continent against European intervention."
"But," he added, "whatever policy we adopt,
there must be an energetic prosecution of it. It
must be somebody's business to pursue and direct
it incessantly. Either the President must do it
himself, and be all the while active in it, or de-
volve it on some member of his cabinet. It is not
in my especial province, but I neither seek to evade
nor assume responsibility."

This paper was first printed, eighteen years after
Seward's death and a quarter of a century after
that of Lincoln, by Nicolay and Hay.[1] Its existence had been forgotten by those who had ever

[1] *Abraham Lincoln, a History*, iii. pp. 445–447.

known of it, and it had apparently never been seen
or spoken of from the day when Mr. Lincoln received and answered it, nearly thirty years before,
until it fell into the hands of his biographers.
Every one, therefore, knowing the close relation
existing between them and Mr. Lincoln naturally
accepted without question their account of the matter and their comments upon it.   This was done
in the first edition of this book; the paper was
treated as a thunderbolt out of a clear sky, — the
secretary appearing to recommend to the President that, in the midst of a civil convulsion which
threatened the destruction of the republic, he
should initiate a foreign policy which would apparently involve us at once in a war with at least
three first-class European powers, and to suggest
further that it would not be amiss, if the President
had any hesitation about carrying out this scheme,
that he should step aside and leave the secretary
to manage the whole business.   But since the publication of that edition, it has been stated to me
on unquestionable authority [1] that, when Seward
wrote this paper, he knew not merely of the revolution in San Domingo, in which the Spanish flag
had been hoisted, but also, — not from newspaper
reports, but from members of the diplomatic body
with whom he had personal and friendly relations
— that France and Spain were actively discussing schemes for invading Mexico and establishing
a European protectorate there, also that Great

[1] Letter of F. W. Seward.

Britain and Russia had been sounded on this subject; that he thought the surest way to keep the peace with France and Spain, and to break up their plans before they were fairly committed to them, was to put on a bold front and insist on knowing at once their intentions, while we at the same time endeavored to rouse in the other American republics and in Canada an active spirit of opposition to any interference by the Continental powers of Europe with the absolute independence of any country in America; that he believed that the manifestation in Canada of a strong public sentiment of this kind might have an almost decisive weight in determining the course of England, and would at all events greatly diminish the probability of her acquiescing in any such schemes; that, if the republics of Central America could be made to see that a successful attack upon any one of them by a European power would be the precursor of the downfall of all, they would be induced to unite for the repulse of the first invader, and that the apprehension of this union would tend to deter the European powers from attempting such conquests.[1]

From England and Russia it will be observed that Seward proposed in his memorandum not to demand but to seek explanations; and this difference of phraseology shows that he hoped that these explanations would be of a friendly and reassuring character. Happily for us the Mexican scheme

[1] Letter of F. W. Seward.

was abandoned for the time, and there was therefore no necessity for any further consideration of Seward's suggestions in this respect. It is certain, however, that these were intended to work for peace and not for war, and to meet an emergency apparently threatening at the time, but which fortunately passed by; that the President understood the circumstances, and knew to what condition of affairs they were intended to apply and the results they were expected to secure.

The paper was written by Seward himself, was copied that it might be legible, and was then laid before the President and left with him; it was a confidential memorandum written for Mr. Lincoln's personal use, intended to aid, not to antagonize him, and did not differ in character and purpose from other similar memoranda from all the members of the cabinet written to serve as reminders of views expressed in conversations or in cabinet meetings.

Seward's suggestion of his readiness to assume further responsibilities, if called upon to do so, was simply a declaration of his readiness to be helpful in any way that he could, and was without any selfish or ambitious purpose on his part. It was intended to assist, not to embarrass, the President, and its importance and its sincerity were fully proved a few weeks later, when the administration began to realize that our self-preservation required some arbitrary proceedings by the government, — the arrest without legal authority of individuals suspected of plotting its destruction, and a search for and seizure of the telegrams and correspondence of such persons. There was no warrant of law for such acts, and any officer who should assume the responsibility for them ran the risk of being compelled to pay heavy damages, as well as that of incurring public reprobation and odium. Therefore, while the necessity of such proceedings was fully recognized, every one shrank from tasks so troublesome and involving such unpleasant possibilities; until Seward, finding that no one else in the cabinet was willing to undertake them, consented to do so. His conduct was recognized by the loyal citizens and by the government as eminently patriotic, a self-sacrifice on his part in aid of other overworked departments, and was cordially accepted as such by these departments.

Those persons whose relations with Seward were most intimate, who enjoyed his entire confidence, who were in Washington at the time, and in daily and hourly communication with him, state as a matter of absolute certainty within their own knowledge, that this is the true meaning, and all the meaning, that there is in the last two sentences of his paper; that Mr. Lincoln understood perfectly well that this was what was meant; and that the idea of asking the President to allow him or any one else to usurp the presidential functions and authority, and to rule in his stead, never entered Seward's mind.[1]

[1] Letter of F. W. Seward.

An apparent difficulty in accepting this explanation arises from the fact that, though all his suggestions as to a policy in which he was to take an active part were made with reference to our foreign affairs, which were precisely those of which he had charge, yet, in speaking of what he recommends and offers to do, he says, "It is not my especial province." It is natural, therefore, to ask what this statement means, unless his purposes of management extended to other departments than his own. The answer is obvious; the diplomatic correspondence was his province, but the sending of unaccredited agents to excite public opinion in Canada and the American republics — a plan like that which he afterwards effectively pursued, with Mr. Lincoln's approval, in England and France — was not his province, and required the previous authority of the President before he could move in it. There is really nothing, therefore, upon the face of the paper inconsistent with what the only persons now living who have a right to speak as to Seward's intent and meaning, knew at the time to be its purpose. So understood, it is in harmony with Seward's own declarations in a letter of somewhat later date to some political supporters,[1] and in accordance with all that we know of Seward's character, disposition, and conduct; while on the other hand, if this incident is to receive the construction which Seward's critics first put upon it long years after his death, it stands

_____
[1] *Life*, ii. pp. 50, 51.

quite apart from the rest of his life and in flagrant contradiction to it, is inconsistent with his own declarations, and is denied by the authoritative statements of those who are qualified to speak on his behalf.

"The affair never reached the knowledge of any other member of the cabinet, or even the most intimate of the President's friends."[1] All that Mr. Lincoln ever said about it is to be found in his note to Mr. Seward written on the same day.

Lincoln was a person exceptionally politic and shrewd, and, taking these qualities into account, it may be contended that his letter is not absolutely inconsistent with his understanding Seward's memorandum in the sense afterwards attributed to it by the critics; but at the same time it must be admitted that there is nothing in this letter incompatible with his acceptance of the memorandum as meaning exactly what Seward intended it to mean. If either Mr. Lincoln believed the intent and meaning of the memorandum to be what his biographers assume that it was; or if Seward had either so intended it, or had any suspicion that Mr. Lincoln so understood it, it seems quite impossible that there should not have been some temporary embarrassment between the President and secretary, if not on Mr. Lincoln's, at least on Seward's side, — some interruption, however slight and momentary, in the harmony of their relations. But there was nothing of the sort; during these

_____
[1] *N. & H.*, iii. pp. 448, 449.

very days Seward was engaged with the President
in most confidential work entirely unconnected with
his department; and all that is known goes to
show that their relations were never for a single
instant changed or even clouded, that Mr. Lincoln's confidence in Seward's loyalty and upright-
ness of purpose was never shaken in the slightest
degree, that their mutual regard for one another
grew steadily, and that their personal relations
became continually more close, affectionate, and
trustful until they were severed by death.

To sum up all that is now known about this
matter: On the one hand the precise and emphatic
statements of those who speak with both knowledge
and authority effectually dispose of the charge that
Seward in his memorandum intended any disloyalty whatsoever to his chief; while on the other
hand Mr. Lincoln's uniform conduct towards his
secretary both at the time and afterwards gives no
indication that he ever misunderstood Seward's
intentions, or questioned the good faith and recti-
tude of purpose of "Some Thoughts for the President's Consideration."

Something has already been said of the condition of our public service at the beginning of Lincoln's administration. But it is quite impossible
for any one not at that time in active life to realize
the extent of the disintegration and demoralization
which then prevailed in every department. The
civil service contained many men who thought the

betrayal of their trusts no shame. The South found its most distinguished officers in deserters from our army and navy. Before the close of Buchanan's administration one of our generals had not only treacherously surrendered to the secessionists the public property of the United States confided to his charge, but had attempted to carry with him into the rebel service the troops under his command. Another officer, whose loyalty was not put to the test till later, received and transmitted the orders for the disposition of the troops when there were apprehensions of a night attack on Washington, and the same evening fled and joined the hostile forces. In the diplomatic and consular services there were men who, while holding the commission of the United States, negotiated purchases of arms for the rebels, and others who assisted their cause by more indirect and less conspicuous means. Four, certainly, of Buchanan's foreign ministers returned home only to accept commissions in the Southern army, and one of these had not even the common excuse of going with his State, for his State never seceded. In his instructions to Mr. Adams, written a day or two before the attack on Sumter, Seward gives a vivid and forcible picture of the situation: —

"The party which was dominant in the federal government during the period of the last administration embraced practically and held in universal communion all disunionists and sympathizers. It held the executive administration. The secretaries

of the treasury, war, and the interior were disunionists. The same party held a large majority
in the Senate, and nearly equally divided the
House of Representatives. Disaffection lurked,
if it did not openly avow itself, in every department and in every bureau, in every regiment and
in every ship of war, in the post office and in the
custom house, and in every legation and consulate
from London to Calcutta. Of four thousand four
hundred and seventy officers in the public service,
civil and military, two thousand one hundred and
fifty-four were representatives of States where the
revolutionary movement was openly advocated and
urged, even if not actually organized." . . . The
new administration "found the disunionists perse-
veringly engaged in raising armies and laying
sieges around national fortifications situate within
the territory of the disaffected States. The federal marine seemed to have been scattered everywhere except where its presence was necessary,
and such of the military forces as were not in the
remote States and Territories were held back from
activity by vague and mysterious armistices, which
had been informally contracted by the late president or under his authority, with a view to postpone conflict . . . at least until the waning term
of his administration should reach its appointed
end. Commissioners . . . sent by the new confederacy were already at the capital, demanding
recognition of its sovereignty and a partition of
the national property and domain. The treasury,

depleted by robbery and peculation, was exhausted, and the public credit was prostrate.

"The period of four months, which intervened between the election which designated the head of the new administration and its advent, . . . assumed the character of an interregnum, in which not only were the powers of the government paralyzed, but even its resources seemed to disappear and be forgotten."

From the time when his secretary of state transmitted to our ministers abroad Buchanan's message of December, 1860, which contained the statement that in his opinion secession was a revolutionary, not a constitutional right, but that the federal government had no power to interfere with, restrain, or coerce any State attempting to carry out this revolution, no general instructions as to their duties in the grave crisis through which we were passing were issued to our foreign ministers, until the 28th of February, 1861, less than a week before Lincoln's inauguration. During this whole period the pernicious doctrines of this message, which gave to secession all the countenance and encouragement its friends could expect, were permitted to make their way unchecked throughout the various countries of Europe, encouraging their rulers in the belief that the ill contrived governmental machine, the United States, which its own president declared to be held together only by the mutual consent of its several parts, was fast falling to pieces, if indeed it were not already broken up.

At length, after this long silence, but not until
the very close of his official term, the Democratic
secretary of state wrote to our representatives
abroad a circular, in which, after reiterating
Buchanan's declaration that there was no constitutional right of secession, and stating again the
sectional character of the election and the consequent apprehensions of the defeated party, he instructed our ministers that the President expected
them to use such means as might in their judgment
be necessary and proper to prevent the success of
any attempts to secure from the European powers
the recognition of the new confederation, declaring that such an acknowledgment by any European government would tend to disturb the friendly
relations existing between that country and our
own.

One of Seward's first acts on entering upon the
duties of his office was to endeavor to reinforce
the formal and perfunctory directions of this dispatch, and to counteract its statement of the issues
and results of the election, — a statement which
seemed half to apologize for the conduct of the
seceding States.   For this purpose he wrote a circular dispatch more bold and vigorous in tone, in
which he inclosed Lincoln's inaugural address.
In this circular he expressed his entire confidence
in the maintenance of the Union, and strove to
impress foreign powers with the conviction that its
perpetuity was more for their advantage than its
division into several distinct nationalities would

be; while he also called upon our ministers to exercise the greatest possible diligence to prevent the designs of those who would invoke foreign intervention to embarrass or overthrow the republic.

To purge our diplomatic and consular service of all persons whose loyalty was uncertain was, however, his most urgent duty; in many cases it was not enough that our representatives abroad should "speak only the language of truth and loyalty, and of confidence in our institutions and destiny," but it was of the utmost consequence that they should be persons selected with especial regard to their ability and fitness for the posts assigned them. It could hardly be expected that Lincoln, who not unnaturally considered our difficulties as a domestic quarrel with which foreign nations had no concern, should be so keenly alive to the importance of these nominations as was Seward; but the President gradually brought himself to attach more weight to fitness than to pressure in his selection from the candidates proposed, and was willing to accept the responsibility for several of them being "huddled up and coming from a small section of the country." There may have been differences of opinion between the President and secretary as to who would best fill some of the vacant places; but the appointments were as a rule exceptionally good, and the most important one, which we know from the President's own statement to have been made at Seward's pressing instance and on his responsibility, that of Mr. Adams to England, proved the wisest possible.

With the actual outbreak of the rebellion, the mode of dealing with our Southern ports became a matter of the first importance, requiring an immediate decision. To leave them open to commerce, as they were, was out of the question. It would enable the seceding States, by the export and sale of their cotton, to raise money to sustain the insurrection, and would allow the unrestricted importation of all sorts of arms, equipments, and munitions of war, as well as of such articles of daily use as those States did not themselves manufacture. Two ways of closing these ports were suggested. One was their discontinuance as ports of entry, so that any vessel landing her cargo there would violate the laws of the United States. This course had the advantage of ease and simplicity. It required only a notice from the Executive that Charleston, Savannah, Mobile, New Orleans, and the other Southern cities where there had been United States custom houses, were no longer ports of entry. It had this disadvantage, that if any vessel paid no heed to the notice, and ran in with her cargo, she had simply violated a revenue law, and could only be punished by proceedings in a federal court of the State and district where the offense was committed; and these courts were all in the hands of the insurgents. There were also well grounded apprehensions that other nations would consider the closing of the ports by procla-

mation an evasive attempt to establish a paper
blockade, would certainly remonstrate against it,
and would probably disregard it; and that it would
therefore be wholly ineffectual.[1] The other method
was an actual blockade. The advantages of this
were, that, as it closed the ports by physical force,
it must necessarily break up foreign commerce,
and that any vessel violating it could be captured
and condemned as prize in any admiralty court
of the United States, or in that of any foreign
country, with the assent of its government. The
objections urged against it were, that a blockade
was strictly an act of war, and that to proclaim it
would either convert the insurgents into enemies
and the domestic insurrection into a war; or that
the blockade would be declared unlawful by the
courts, and vessels violating it could not therefore
be condemned; that no nation had ever attempted
to establish so extensive a blockade, and that we
had no naval force at all adequate for the purpose.

Seward was earnest in advocating a blockade,
and it has been said by one of his associates in the
cabinet that he was principally responsible for the
adoption of this alternative. The wisdom of this
course was amply justified by the result. The
legal objection was not sustained, the supreme

[1] These apprehensions were subsequently shown to be well
founded. When Congress in the summer of 1861 passed a law
authorizing the President to close the Southern ports by proclamation, it was at once made a subject of remonstrance by both
England and France, though nothing whatsoever had been done
under it.

court deciding that a blockade of their coast was a legitimate mode of dealing with insurgents. The practical difficulties proved to have been exaggerated; the coast was extensive, but the important harbors were few. The validity of the blockade was never seriously questioned; and as it became continually more effective, it more and more crippled, and in the end practically destroyed, all foreign commerce at the South, cutting off both their resources and supplies for carrying on the military operations of the rebellion. Of the two million four hundred thousand bales of cotton, the crop of 1861, the largest part of which should have found its way across the Atlantic by the summer of 1862, only about fifty thousand bales ever reached Europe;[1] of these England received the lion's share. In December of that year (1862) one of the Confederate cabinet ministers spoke of "the almost total cessation of foreign commerce for the last two years" as producing a "complete exhaustion of the supply of all articles of foreign growth and manufacture;" and this statement was confirmed by Lord Russell's almost simultaneous declaration, that "the United States were enabled by the blockade to intercept and capture a great part of the warlike supplies which were destined to the Confederate States from Great Britain."

[1] Bernard's *Neutrality of Great Britain*, pp. 286–87.

CHAPTER XVI

BEFORE the breaking out of the rebellion the question of the probable attitude of the great European powers, in case of the government's resort to force to maintain the Union, had occasioned no uneasiness at the North. If there was any public opinion there on the matter, it was hardly more than a vague notion that we should be left to settle our own quarrel in our own way, the North, as representing the cause of freedom and of legitimate government, having the sympathy of civilized Europe, while the South would labor under the odium of having stirred up a rebellion solely for the purpose of perpetuating and extending African slavery. The tone of the foreign newspapers warranted this belief. In leading articles, which showed their writers to be familiar with our Constitution and the relations between the federal and state governments, any attempt to destroy the Union, whether by individuals or by States, was declared to be treason.

The South was at the same time warned that a proposal to intervene in their behalf in a struggle against the Union would be scouted nowhere with more scorn and indignation than in those districts of England which would most benefit by free trade with the United States; that the dissolution of the Union, so far from being hailed as a profitable transaction, would be lamented; and that any policy would miscarry, which assumed that England could be coaxed or bribed into a connivance at the extension of slavery. The English government was in the hands of the Liberals, — the party of reform, the authors and advocates of an extended suffrage, and of the emancipation of the slaves in the British West Indies. No important questions were open between this country and Great Britain, and the North assumed that, as it would in any event remain the United States of America, the friendly relations then existing would not be interrupted. The French emperor had been, it was thought, especially cordial in his expressions of good will to the United States at his New Year's diplomatic reception (January 1, 1861), and the French press had expressed its hopes for the safety of the great American republic and the gradual diminution of slavery. There was a prevailing notion that the French would feel a decided sentiment of regret at the disintegration of that Union, which France had so largely aided to establish, and that the seceding States would meet at her hands nothing but discouragement.

At the South, on the contrary, the confidence of the leaders in their speedy recognition as an independent nation inspired them with a conviction of success, and encouraged them to hasten the work of secession.   They argued that Cotton was King, and that the loss of their great staple would cause such distress and disaffection in the manufacturing districts of both England and France that the two governments would be forced to insist that any war which interfered with its production and free exportation should cease.   They also relied on the cupidity of the European commercial world, to which they proposed to offer the bribe of free trade, while they would exclude the North from their markets as a punishment, if their peaceable secession should be opposed.

The course of events in the winter and early spring of 1861 had a marked effect on European opinion.   First came Buchanan's declaration that there was nowhere any power to prevent the withdrawal of any State from the Union.   This was followed, during the remainder of his administration, by an inaction which was broken only by an abortive attempt to reinforce Sumter, when the steamer carrying the troops was fired on by South Carolina militia.   The federal government tamely submitted to the insult and made no further attempt to strengthen the garrison; in Congress nothing was done to prepare for the emergency of a forcible resistance to the federal authority, Northern statesmen and newspapers were earnestly advocating concessions and peace, and the people seemed to accept the situation with tranquillity.

During the month after Lincoln's inauguration there were no signs of any more vigorous policy; the government was apparently still hesitating and drifting. On the other hand, the secessionists had been making steady and regular advances. The Southern States had formed a new confederacy, organized its government and elected its officers, had ousted the United States from all jurisdiction over its territory, and by the seizure of forts, arsenals, custom houses, and mints, had turned against the federal government its own strongholds, arms, and resources. The Confederate soldiers were being drilled, instructed, and commanded by officers who had abandoned the government that had trained and educated them; and the work of organizing and administering the civil affairs of the Confederacy was in the hands of experienced public men, who had hardly ceased to hold office under the United States.

The South was an oligarchy; the people were accustomed to follow their leaders, and were not so sluggish and reluctant to move as were the masses of the free States. The South was roused and in earnest, the North still apathetic and inert. When Sumter was attacked, it was generally believed in Europe that the Union was at an end, that the South had practically secured its independence, and that the North would soon admit this. With most of the European governments the result was a matter of comparative indifference; but with England and France this was not so; the prospect

that this great republic might break in pieces was
soon followed by a wish that it would do so.   The
vast majority of the great governing classes in
England thought that the division of the United
States would be a fresh proof of the inability of
a republican government to weather a storm, and
would therefore give additional strength and sta-
bility to their own institutions.   Some of them,
who had condemned African slavery as a foul blot
upon this country, excused their support of the
slaveholders' rebellion by insisting that the South
was fighting for independence, the North for supremacy.   The mill owners and manufacturers of
both countries were anxious lest a war between
the sections should bring on a cotton famine and
the distress which would accompany it; and the
apprehension of this probably had the greatest
effect in determining the attitude of France at the
outset of the struggle.   Perhaps the feeling prevalent among the average Englishmen, that the
Americans were a boastful and conceited people,
and that it would do them no harm to have their
pride taken down,— though it may not have shaped
the government's policy, — had more effect than
any other cause upon the tone and attitude of most
of the English press, which changed from that of
friendliness towards the North to bitter hostility
and contemptuous sneers.

Seward possessed a certain knowledge of Europe; he had traveled there and met some of her
leading statesmen; he had served several years

on the Senate's Committee on Foreign Affairs, and knew the diplomatic relations between this country and the great European powers; he was from the State of New York, had long been interested in the development of the commercial connections of its metropolis with foreign countries, and knew the extent and closeness of these connections with both England and France, and especially with the former. What complications might arise abroad, growing out of our difficulties at home, he could not foresee; but it was evident to him that the seceding States would make all possible efforts to obtain recognition as a nation, and were entirely confident of their speedy success. He thoroughly realized the necessity of our being represented abroad by our ablest and fittest men, especially in England, where he expected the Confederacy would make its first and most strenuous appeal, and would not cease to renew its efforts so long as a possibility of hope remained.

Early in the spring Jefferson Davis had sent abroad commissioners to negotiate for the recognition of the Confederacy; but their presence in England seemed to furnish no cause for anxiety, as we were still confident of the good will of both its government and people, and had moreover the assurance of Lord John Russell, the secretary of state for foreign affairs, that "the coming of Mr. Adams would doubtless be regarded as the appropriate occasion for finally discussing and determining the question" of the attitude to be taken by

Great Britain towards the rebellion.   The Confederate agents baited their hooks judiciously, and had the audacity to tell Lord John that it was not any apprehensions as to slavery, but the protective tariff on which the North insisted, that had made it necessary for the Southern States to secede, since free trade was essential to their prosperity. It was not believed at the time in this country that this assertion could impose upon any one, or have any effect, unless its flagrant disregard of truth should excite a smile.   No importance was attached to it, for neither our government nor our people were at all prepared to believe that Great Britain's policy towards us was to be that of a nation of shopkeepers, who would justify their course by saying that, though they objected to slavery, they wanted cotton, and disliked the Morrill tariff.

Seward's first serious anxiety as to our foreign relations was caused by learning, through Russia, that the French emperor had proposed to England that they should act in concert in their course towards this country, and that England had assented; that Russia had been invited to join this league, and had declined; but that it was confidently expected that the smaller European powers, and those having less interest in the matter, would follow the lead of France and England.   This intelligence showed him that our quarrel was not considered only our own affair; that we were not to be permitted to settle it in our own way; but were possibly to be threatened with a combined pressure from the European powers, which we could not resist, and which might ultimately force us to acquiesce in the breaking up of the Union. Upon learning this arrangement, Seward immediately took the only means in his power of averting the difficulty, by notifying our ministers that this government would not recognize any such understanding between France and England, and would decline to receive any communications as joint proposals from these two, or any two or more countries. He adhered to this resolve; and when, later in the year 1861, the British and French ministers called upon him together for the purpose of communicating their dispatches at a joint interview, he insisted on receiving them in separate interviews at different times, and on treating each dispatch as if it were a distinct matter, wholly unconnected with the other.

The knowledge of the agreement between these two great powers had not at all prepared Seward for the first decided step taken by them together; or it is perhaps more exact to say that the statement of Lord John Russell already quoted had given him absolute confidence that nothing would be done until Mr. Adams had arrived and had the opportunity of laying before the ministry the views of the new administration, with which he was fully in accord. The recognition of the rebels as belligerents, made after Mr. Adams was known to have sailed for England, and the publication, on the very day of his landing, of the queen's proclamation enjoining her subjects to observe a strict neutrality in the civil war then existing between the Northern and Southern States, seemed to Seward, in the moment selected for this action, when a few days' delay could have done no possible harm, a breach of good faith, an act of national discourtesy and of personal disrespect to our minister. In substance, too, he thought the proceeding of the British government unprecedented and unjustifiable, and under the influence of these feelings he wrote a fiery dispatch, which might have produced a rupture between the two countries, had the paper been treated, according to the usages of diplomatic correspondence, as a message from one government to the other, and read in full to the British secretary of state. But when it was submitted to the President, Mr. Lincoln, besides suggesting various modifications softening its tone, advised its being sent to Mr. Adams for his own guidance, not as a dispatch to be read, and that this should be distinctly stated in the letter itself. The wisdom of this was apparent; it was done, and Seward's original draft with these changes made by the President, and a few other unimportant verbal alterations, conveyed to Mr. Adams, in language which did not admit of a doubt, the views of our government as to the course of the English ministry.

Without undertaking to discuss elaborately how far the United States had just cause for a serious

complaint against Great Britain on account of her
recognition, on the 6th of May, 1861, of the Confederacy as a belligerent, it may fairly be said
that the action of that government was unprecedented and precipitate, and could only be regarded
by us as ungracious, if not intentionally offensive.
As has already been stated, early in April Lord
John Russell had suggested to Mr. Dallas, who
was then our minister in London, that the coming
of his successor, Mr. Adams, would be the suitable
time for discussing any question between the two
countries connected with the rebellion; and again,
on the 1st of May, referring to the rumors of a
proposed blockade, he agreed that the time for
discussion would be on the arrival of Mr. Adams,
who was to sail on that day. Under these circumstances the publication, on the very day of Mr.
Adams's landing, of the queen's proclamation
notifying her subjects of their duties and obligations as neutrals in the civil war then raging in
this country, whether it arose from an accidental
forgetfulness, or an intentional disregard by Lord
John of his conversations with Mr. Dallas and his
assurances then given, was alike ungracious and
offensive both to Mr. Adams and to the country
he represented. It shut the door in his face, and
precluded the discussions which Lord John had
suggested; it was obviously intended to do this.

That Great Britain's recognition of the Confederates as belligerents was unprecedented is not to
be denied. One of the principal grounds on which

it was attempted to justify this recognition was, that an insurrection of so many provinces, with organized governments, and a central confederate administration and army in existence at the outset, had been hitherto unknown. Mr. Adams, replying to this contention, reminded Lord Russell that there had been within a century a revolt of thirteen provinces corresponding in every particular, except that of the numbers involved, to Lord Russell's description; but that, notwithstanding all these points of identity, Great Britain had not been met at the outset in 1774 with the announcement by any foreign power of a necessity for the immediate recognition as belligerents of her insurgent American colonies; and he added that there was not the smallest ground for believing that Great Britain would have tolerated for one moment any such proceeding, if it had been attempted. The only historical precedent, to which Lord Russell ever referred as a vindication of his course, was that of the recognition of the Greeks as belligerents in 1825, after they had maintained during four years the struggle for independence; yet, when, after this lapse of time, such recognition was granted them, the Turkish government complained of it, — but Great Britain answered that a people who, in a contest of arms, had already covered the sea with their cruisers, must either be acknowledged as belligerents or treated as pirates, and that this latter character England disclaimed for Greece. It is obvious that this so-called precedent bears no analogy to the case of the Southerners in May, 1861. The cruisers of Greece had scoured the Mediterranean and forced the English government to take a decided stand for the protection of Great Britain's commerce and merchantmen. The Confederates in May, 1861, had done no harm at sea, were then utterly incapable of doing any such harm, and, if left to themselves, without the aid of British intervention and British ships, would have remained, until the insurrection was crushed, as powerless at sea as when Great Britain first created them maritime belligerents.

It is equally clear that the action of the British government was precipitate. Though France and England had determined to act in concert, France made no proclamation, no public declaration of any kind, till a month later. It is hardly credible that Lord John Russell, when he was agreeing with Mr. Dallas on Wednesday that the arrival of Mr. Adams a fortnight later would be the appropriate time to discuss the questions of policy as to the Southern Confederates, should have been at the same moment seriously considering the propriety of at once recognizing them as belligerents. Yet he did so recognize them publicly and officially, on the following Monday, in a speech in Parliament, and in dispatches to the British minister at Paris, as well as to Lord Lyons, in both of which he speaks of the *late* Union. The only reason he assigned in his speech or in either of his letters for this recognition was, that the Southern

insurgents had established a government which
was carrying on in regular form the administration
of civil affairs.   But this is an explanation which
does not explain the British ministry's haste.
The organization of the Confederacy took place
before the end of February.   It was no new fact;
it had been known in England for weeks.   It was
not, however, even in May absolutely true that
the Southern Confederacy was performing all the
functions of the federal government; for one of
the most important of them, the carrying of the
mails, was done by the United States throughout
the entire South until the 1st of June.   Between
Wednesday, the 1st, and Monday, the 6th of May,
nothing had happened, no new intelligence had
been received; which could either justify or account for the ministry's sudden change of front.
Yet on that day the Southerners, who up to that
time had been insurgents, became belligerents,
and the fact of their recognition as such was
announced in Parliament.   The queen's proclamation, a week later, was merely a domestic publication, cautioning British citizens to govern themselves accordingly.   The ministry had, on the 1st
of May, all the knowledge as to the proposed
blockade of the Southern ports by the United
States, and the issuing of letters of marque by
Jefferson Davis, which they possessed on the 6th.[1]

---

[1] See Lord John Russell's letter of May 1st to the Commissioners of the Admiralty.   *Correspondence concerning Claims
against Great Britain*, i. p. 33.

They had not at either date any official or authentic information as to these matters, and they did not at the time refer to either of them as a reason for their conduct.   They knew that the proclamation as to each was merely a declaration of an intention to do something at a future day, official notice of which might justify a formal remonstrance, but would afford no excuse for any such hasty action; and it is a significant fact that the blockade was first officially mentioned as a reason for this sudden announcement of the existence of a civil war in America in the letters of Lord Russell to Mr. Adams at and after the close of the rebellion in 1865.

In its haste to recognize the Southerners as belligerents the English ministry almost anticipated the Confederate Congress, whose act declaring the existence of a war between the United States and the Confederacy was first published on the same day on which Lord John Russell announced in the House of Commons that Great Britain considered the Southern insurgents a belligerent power.

In the four days between Lord John's interview, with Mr. Dallas, which left our minister with the understanding that nothing was to be done until Mr. Adams arrived, and the government's declaration in Parliament, there was only one significant incident, — the unofficial meeting of Mr. Yancey and the other Southern commissioners with Lord John, at which they assured him that it was the heavy duties which the North had

forced the South to pay, and not the attacks upon
slavery, that had driven their States to secession;
that the new Confederacy had abolished the slave
trade, was opposed to a high tariff, and wished
only to sell its cotton to Europe and make its purchases there.   This interview took place on Saturday; on Monday the letters to Lord Cowley and
Lord Lyons were written, and it was announced
in Parliament that the government had come to
the conclusion that the Southern Confederacy must
be treated as a belligerent.

The real motives for this hasty action can only
be conjectured. So far as the debates in Parliament at this time throw any light on the matter,
they indicate that, foreseeing that Englishmen
would be likely to avail themselves of Jefferson
Davis's offer of letters of marque, the British
government determined to settle by anticipation
the question of the character of such adventurers,
and after consulting the law officers of the crown
decided to recognize at once the Confederates as
belligerents, in order to prevent any privateers-
men who were British subjects being treated as
pirates. This consideration, together with the
prevailing idea — probably strengthened to a conviction by the efforts of the rebel commissioners
at their interview with Lord John Russell — that
the schism was complete, the Southern seceders
already a perfect confederacy, and cotton sure to
come more quickly, if there should be some act on
the part of England which could be interpreted

as the expression of a wish for, and a belief in,
the speedy success of the South, may perhaps be
fairly assumed as the leading motives for the sudden and decisive action which followed so closely
the representations of the Southern agents.

Seward's strong feeling as to the matter was
not uncalled for or unnatural. He realized what
British recognition meant, what courage and confidence it would give the seceders, how great an
increase to their strength and resources; while he
also knew that it would add incalculably to our
difficulties and indefinitely prolong the struggle.
His repeated remonstrances and unceasing endeavors to have this hasty step recalled were therefore
no more than his duty, and, if ineffectual, were in
no way unreasonable.

Mr. Motley, who was on the spot and in a position to form an opinion about it, thought that,
had this recognition been delayed only "a few
weeks or even days," it would never have been
made. Possibly he was right; but at all events
we may moderate our natural resentment at this
early unfriendliness of England by considering
that our actual blockade a few weeks later would
have justified, in point of law, though it would not
have required, her declaration that the secessionists were belligerents. In judging of her conduct
at this time we should also bear in mind the natural inclination of the citizens and government of
a free country to sympathize with any people in
rebellion, to assume that they have good reason

for their insurrection, and are really striving to
secure some right which is wrongfully withheld
from them.   Our own political history furnishes
more than one instance of such sympathy on our
part.   And it is only fair to Great Britain to
make some allowance for the influence which this
feeling had in bringing about the hasty and impul-
sive step of her government on the 6th of May.
Its action can be called fortunate for us only in
one aspect.   It prolonged the struggle, and so
brought about emancipation.   Had the rebellion
been crushed quickly, slavery, the cause of all our
trouble, would have remained, and sooner or later
the battle would have had to be fought over again.

CHAPTER XVII

NEGOTIATIONS AS TO THE TREATY OF PARIS — SUSPENSION OF THE HABEAS CORPUS

By the articles of the Treaty of Paris, which was made at the close of the Crimean war in 1856, the leading powers in Europe agreed — in order to mitigate the severities of maritime warfare and assimilate its usages more nearly to those of war on land — that privateering should be abolished, and that both enemy's property, not contraband of war, on board a neutral vessel, and neutral property, not contraband of war, on an enemy's vessel, should be exempt from capture and condemnation as prize. They invited other countries to subscribe to these articles, with the hope of making them in this way rules which should govern naval warfare for the whole civilized world, stipulating, however, that every nation's assent must be given to them as a whole, or not at all. The United States, whose position was usually that of a neutral, wished to extend the exemptions from condemnation to all private property not contraband of war, and, postponing its assent to the treaty as it stood, opened negotiations for this purpose, which, though apparently

fruitless, had not been abandoned at the close of
Mr. Buchanan's administration.   On the 24th of
April, 1861, Seward instructed our ministers to
England and France, as well as to other countries
which had assented to these articles, to ascertain
whether the governments to which they were sev-
erally accredited were disposed to negotiate for
the accession of the United States to this treaty,
adding that the assent of these governments was
to be expected, as we should accept the articles
precisely in the form in which they had been proposed to us.   These instructions were given before
the British recognition of belligerency, and when
there was no anticipation of any such action.
France had not yet proposed to England the adoption of a common line of conduct towards this
country in its difficulties; and though a week before (April 17, 1861) Jefferson Davis had published his offer of letters of marque to any one
wishing to engage in privateering on behalf of the
Confederate States, no such letters had been issued
or applied for.

Our negotiations seemed to open prosperously.
They were delayed on various grounds; but by the
middle of July Mr. Adams was officially informed
that the English ministry would advise the queen
to conclude the necessary convention, so soon as
they should be informed that a similar convention
had been agreed on with the French emperor, so
that both might be signed on the same day.   But
ten days later, when Mr. Adams notified them that

our minister to France had returned to Paris to
propose there the same arrangements, Lord Russell wrote him: "On the part of Great Britain
the agreement will be prospective, and will not
invalidate anything already done." The meaning
of this somewhat enigmatical sentence was made
clear a few weeks later, by the announcement that
Great Britain proposed to add to the convention
already agreed on a declaration, "that by execut-
ing that convention Her Majesty did not intend
to undertake any engagement which should have
any bearing, direct or indirect, on the internal
difficulties prevailing in the United States." Seward approved Mr. Adams's course in declining to
sign the paper with this addition, which there
seemed reason to believe an afterthought; and this
ended the negotiations, the French government
desiring to attach a similar condition to its assent.

Seward's objects in proposing our assent to this
treaty were, probably, to declare our purpose of
conducting our contest with the South under the
humane rules agreed on by the leading nations of
the world, and also to preclude the recognition
of privateers under Jefferson Davis's letters of
marque as vessels having any legal status. Before
the declaration of May 6th this result might have
followed the unqualified acceptance of our assent
to this treaty; but after recognizing the Confederacy as a belligerent both Great Britain and France
were in honor bound to take no step which might
impose on them obligations inconsistent with this

position. Seward was equally right in declining
to accept the arrangement proposed. It would
not have been the Treaty of Paris to which we
should thus have become parties, but a different
and special convention with England and France,
implying an acquiescence in the assumption of
these governments that we were no longer the sovereign of the States in insurrection, and had no
power to treat for them, an admission which would
have been irreconcilable with our position, that
the integrity of the republic was unbroken and
the government of the United States supreme, so
far as foreign nations were concerned, as well for
war as for peace, over all the States, all sections,
and all citizens, the loyal not more than the disloyal, the patriots and insurgents alike.[1] Seward
was of opinion, however, that the real objection of
the English government to giving an unqualified
assent to our adherence to the Treaty of Paris was,
that by the middle of August it was well understood that any vessels cruising as Confederate
privateers would be English ships, and that Great
Britain, while opposed to this mode of warfare in
the abstract and on principle, was perfectly willing
to become the patron of privateering when aimed
at our devastation.

Though they knew that Jefferson Davis, after
his call for privateers, would not assent to the provisions of this treaty as a whole, — the only way
in which there was any provision in the treaty

[1] Seward to Adams, July 25, 1861.

itself for its acceptance, — the British ministry
thought it sufficiently important to secure his adherence to the other articles (those relating to
neutral and enemy property and to blockade) to
open negotiations with him, for the purpose of
obtaining this. They selected as their agent in
this matter an Englishman, — their own consul at
Charleston, accredited to the United States, whose
exequatur was unrevoked. Voluntarily to open
direct negotiations with the insurgents was a proceeding sufficiently contemptuous of the United
States, and encouragingly near to complete recognition; and so Mr. Bunch, the consul, an active
sympathizer with secession, considered it. He
successfully performed the mission intrusted to
him, and obtained the adhesion of the Confederacy
to these articles; but was indiscreet enough to
claim much more. The bearer of his letters to
his government, having crossed the Union lines
without permission, was arrested, his papers were
taken from him, and among them was found a
letter saying, "Mr. B. on oath of secrecy communicated to me also that the *first step* to recognition
was taken. . . . This is the first step to direct
treating with our government, so prepare for active
business by 1st January." The whole matter having in this way come to Seward's knowledge, he
remonstrated, protesting against Great Britain's
employing one of their public officers accredited
to and recognized by the United States, and still,
in the legal view of both governments, exercising

his functions there, to conduct a negotiation with insurgents in arms against this government, whether the insurgents were to be considered as simple rebels, as we viewed them, or to be treated as belligerents, as Great Britain had acknowledged them. The English government expressed neither regret nor apology. They maintained the supercilious tone which characterized much of their correspondence during the war, until Gettysburg and Vicksburg demonstrated that the suppression of the rebellion was merely a question of time. The whole proceeding shows how illogical and inconsistent was the attitude of England and France during our domestic difficulties. The rebels were parties to a war; they were amenable to, and to be governed by, the laws of war; they were sufficiently a nation to be asked to become parties to a treaty, yet not so far a nation as to permit negotiations for this purpose to be conducted in any regular manner.

Not long after the attack on Sumter, the President, acting upon the opinion of the attorney-general that he had the power to do so, suspended the writ of *habeas corpus* without any special legislation authorizing it. Chief Justice Taney held this suspension illegal; thereupon, when a British citizen residing here, arrested and held without regular process, was unable to obtain relief by applying for this writ, Lord Russell undertook to open a diplomatic discussion as to the constitutionality

of the President's action. Seward courteously but
peremptorily declined to enter upon any such discussion, or to permit the constitutionality of any
act of the administration to be called in question
by any foreign power, and the attempt was not
renewed. Nevertheless every foreigner arrested
by arbitrary process naturally appealed to his minister, in the hope that diplomatic influence might
procure his discharge. Most of these foreigners
were Englishmen; their cases occupied a great
deal of time, and were a constant source of worry
and anxiety to Seward during the greater part of
the war. At first, and until Mr. Stanton became
secretary of war, all these arrests, as well of our
own citizens as of foreigners, were under the direction of the State Department, and during this
period Seward was earning with the disloyal and
their friends the name of a tyrant with his hands
full of despotic orders of arrest and imprisonment,
— a reputation which clung to him long after he
had ceased to have any charge of these matters.

The accusation of officious intermeddling, which
has been to some extent taken up as a popular cry
against him, has its origin in these and other acts
of his during the first year of the rebellion, when
the War Department was much disorganized by
the desertion of Southern officers and clerks, and
was also excessively overworked. There were many
things which needed to be done — some of them
disagreeable, — which did not properly belong to
the secretary of state, but which no one else seemed

able to find time or inclination to do.   At the
President's request and to the entire satisfaction
of all loyal citizens, Seward undertook the responsibility and burden of some of these matters.   In
doing so, he was no more guilty of officious intermeddling than were the "great war governors,"
whose zealous loyalty induced them to overstep
the strict line of official duty and endeavor to relieve the War Department of some of the burdens
of the equipment and transportation of troops,
which properly belonged to the general government.   There is no reason to believe that Seward
had any motives for what he did other than patriotic ones; he had in a high degree the fervor and
lofty spirit which then animated and dignified the
country.   The time had arrived of which he had
spoken, when we were to see "how nobly, how
firmly, a great people could act in preserving their
Constitution."

CHAPTER XVIII

THE TRENT

THE summer of 1861 wore away without further serious diplomatic trouble. The defeat at Bull Run, and the later repulse at Ball's Bluff, confirmed the general European opinion of the ultimate success of the seceding States. It had severely taxed Seward's optimism and ability, to minimize in his dispatches to our ministers the character and effect of these failures. Our successes in the West were too remote to offset them with the public; and the importance of the capture of the forts and garrisons at Hatteras Inlet, Port Royal, and Hilton Head, and of the occupation of these points by the Union forces, was too little understood to check the tide of European opinion, which was running strongly against us. There was a time in the autumn when Seward, fairly disheartened, wrote home: "I have had two weeks of intense anxiety and severe labor. The pressure . . . which disunionists have procured to operate on the cabinets of London and Paris has made it doubtful whether we can escape the yet deeper and darker abyss of foreign war. . . . I have worried through and finished my dispatches. They must go for good or evil. I have done my best."

The moment which Seward thought so gloomy seemed to Jefferson Davis auspicious for a vigorous and determined effort to obtain from England and France the full recognition of the Southern Confederacy as an independent nation; and early in the autumn he sent James M. Mason, of Virginia, to England, and John Slidell, of Louisiana, to France, as commissioners to open negotiations for this purpose. Slidell was a Northerner by birth, who had made his fortune in Louisiana, and who, while still United States senator from that State, had been, during Buchanan's administration, a most zealous and efficient worker in the cause of secession, using his official position to break up the government of which he was a member. Mason, if less conspicuous, had been no less earnest, and had done all in his power to prevent a free, honest, and independent vote in Virginia on the question of the secession of that State. If the United States were a government and not a mere voluntary association, both were traitors, and both were especially odious and infamous in the eyes of the loyal people of the country. On a dark night in October these envoys with their families and secretaries ran the blockade at Charleston in the little steamer Theodora, and arrived safely at Havana, where, after receiving much attention from the authorities, they embarked on the British mail steamer Trent for St. Thomas, proposing to sail thence for England. The United States frigate San Jacinto, commanded by Captain

Charles Wilkes, boarded the Trent between Havana and St. Thomas; but instead of putting on board a prize crew and sending the steamer to a port of the United States, that the question of her liability to condemnation, as a neutral carrying contraband of war, might be settled in a prize court, Captain Wilkes, out of consideration for the convenience of the other passengers and for the regular business of the steamer, contented himself with taking on board his own ship the commissioners and their secretaries, leaving the Trent to continue her voyage with her other passengers and her mails.

When the news of this reached England the excitement was intense, public opinion was unanimous, and the public passion at fever heat. The British flag had been insulted; the prisoners must be given up and a suitable apology made. Troops were at once ordered to Canada and ships of war were made ready for sea; in the arsenals and dockyards the business of preparation was pushed forward day and night and even on Sunday; and the first transport left the Mersey with the regimental band playing "I wish I was in Dixie." The British ministry had some time before received information from a source which they professed to think worthy of belief, that the government of the United States was expecting Mason and Slidell to embark on the Trent, and had given express orders for their capture. On the receipt of this information the law officers of the crown had been consulted, and had advised the ministry that a United States man-of-war overhauling the Trent, capturing her and carrying her into port, would be exercising a recognized belligerent right; but that if she merely took the Confederate commissioners and their dispatches and let the steamer go, she would be clearly wrong; or, as has been said, "if the British flag were more grossly insulted there would be less or no cause of complaint." After exact information of what had been done was received in England, the queen's legal advisers, being again consulted, reiterated their opinion; so that upon the actual facts the British case appeared quite perfect. The English ministers had been told by Miss Slidell that the officer who boarded the Trent stated that the commander of the San Jacinto had no instructions, but was acting solely on his own responsibility. They, however, permitted the receipt of this information and even an authentic confirmation of the officer's statement to be denied by the party press, though they communicated it to the queen when the dispatch, as originally drafted, was shown her. The queen was distressed at the peremptory tone of this paper; at her request Prince Albert prepared a memorandum embodying her views, and the dispatch was modified to conform to them. A pathetic interest attaches to this incident from the fact that Prince Albert was at the time suffering from the illness which shortly afterwards proved fatal, and that this memorandum was the last thing he ever wrote.

The officer who boarded the Trent had stated the simple truth, — Wilkes was acting solely on his own judgment and responsibility. The first knowledge that either our government or people had of the matter was by a telegram from Fortress Monroe, where the San Jacinto touched for coal (November 15, 16, 1861), and proceeding thence directly to New York was met in the harbor there by orders to carry the prisoners to Boston, and deliver them to the commandant at Fort Warren. By universal consent Wilkes became at once a hero; the newspapers and the people praised him as if he had won a great naval victory; he was feasted in Boston, and honored in New York. The secretary of the navy on receiving his report wrote him: "Especially do I congratulate you on the great public service you have rendered in the capture of the rebel commissioners. . . . Your conduct in seizing these public enemies was marked by intelligence, ability, decision, and firmness, and has the emphatic approval of this department." The annual report of the Navy Department repeated and indorsed this approval, and when Congress met, the House of Representatives voted Captain Wilkes a gold medal for his good conduct in promptly arresting the rebel ambassadors.

Except the letter from the secretary of the navy, and the passage in his report which may be fairly taken as representing his own opinion at the time, there is little if any contemporary evidence as to what the President or any member of his cabinet

thought about the matter when the news of the capture of the commissioners first reached them. In writing from his recollection ten years later, Mr. Welles, whose object at that time was to depreciate Seward, said "that no man was more elated or jubilant than Seward at the capture of the emissaries, and that for a time he made no attempt to conceal his gratification and approval of the act of Wilkes." Without actually indorsing this assertion of Mr. Welles, or bringing forward a single fact in its support, Mr. Lincoln's biographers say: "Mr. Seward was doubtless elated by the first news that the rebel envoys were captured." So far as can be ascertained, there is nothing to justify either statement.

Dr. Russell, the correspondent of the "London Times," who was in Washington when the news of the capture reached there, says that "at the State Department there was a judicious reticence observed about it." Mr. Sumner, arriving there for the opening of Congress, writes: "I learned from the President and from Mr. Seward that neither had committed himself on the Trent affair, and that it was an absolutely unauthorized act. Mr. Seward told me that he was reserving himself in order to see what view England would take." Even to his family Seward said nothing. The only allusion to the affair that appears in any domestic letter prior to the settlement of the case is contained in a single line, "The Mason and Slidell affair will try the British temper."

His son, then the assistant secretary of state,
and in daily confidential relations with him, and
who was also his biographer, whose narrative of
the whole transaction is founded not upon his
recollection, but upon notes made at the time,[1]
speaks of his abstaining from all conversation on
the subject. Seward did see McClellan on the
17th of November.[2] There seems to be no reason,
however, to suppose that McClellan was volunteer-
ing his advice, as he has been charged with doing;
on the contrary, it has been said on trustworthy
authority that Seward sent for McClellan when he
first learned of the capture, and asked him what
we could do if Great Britain made a peremptory
demand for Mason and Slidell, and the alternative
was either their surrender or war; that he was
told in reply that if we went to war with England
we must at once abandon all hope of keeping the
South in the Union; and that he thereupon said
that, "if the matter took that turn, they must be
at once given up."[3] It is further to be observed
that the subject was not alluded to in the President's message, and, Mr. Sumner tells us, was not
touched upon in the cabinet or in conversation.

The first thing which Seward is known to have
said or written about this affair is his confidential
letter to Mr. Adams, on November 27, in which
he cautiously refrains from expressing any opinion,

[1] Letter of F. W. Seward, February, 1896.
[2] *McClellan's Own Story*, pp. 175, 176.
[3] R. H. Dana, Jr., to the writer, January, 1862.

and says: "I forbear from speaking of the capture of Messrs. Mason and Slidell. The act was done by Commodore Wilkes, without instructions, and even without the knowledge of the government. Lord Lyons has judiciously refrained from all communication with me on the subject, and I thought it equally wise to reserve ourselves until we hear what the British government may have to say." Seward repeated this in an official dispatch of November 30, which was communicated to the British government, but which, as has already been said, was not suffered to find its way to the public, while its statements were denied by the ministerial press. From the day when the capture was first known Mr. Seward and the British minister did not meet, until on the 19th of December Lord Lyons came to the State Department, and acquainted Mr. Seward in general terms with the tenor of Lord Russell's dispatch.

The reserve of Seward and Lord Lyons, and their avoidance of each other during this month of waiting, show how strongly both felt the gravity of the situation, and their apprehension of most serious consequences. If Seward hoped that the British demand might leave some loophole for negotiation, he had evidently foreseen the possibility that the English might take a tone which left us only the alternatives of the surrender of our prisoners or of war, and had decided upon his course if this should be the case.

It was insisted in Lord Russell's dispatch that

the forcible taking of the commissioners from a
neutral ship pursuing a lawful and innocent voyage was an affront to the British flag, and a violation of international law; and a confident hope
was expressed that, when the matter was brought
under the consideration of our government, it
would voluntarily offer the only redress that could
satisfy the British nation, — the restoration of the
captured persons to British protection, and an
apology for the aggression committed. The demand for an apology was not pressed, and no apology was ever made. That for the return of the
prisoners, if not uncourteous in tone, was absolute
and peremptory. Two sets of private instructions
to Lord Lyons accompanied the dispatch. Both
these, however, were at the time unknown to our
government and to Seward. The first of them
gave to the demand the character of a threat. It
directed Lord Lyons, if it should not be complied
with in seven days, to close the legation, remove
the archives, notify the admiral of the British
Atlantic fleet and the governors of the North
American and West Indian colonies, and return
home; but the second private note, written later,
and apparently intended to soften the public dispatch as well as the earlier instructions, gave him
a discretion which would tend to avoid a war, and
expressed the wish that he would not formally deliver the dispatch at once, but prepare the way,
and ask Mr. Seward before its delivery to settle
with the President and cabinet the course they

would propose. Acting upon these suggestions,
Lord Lyons on December 19 called at the State
Department, as has been said, and stated to Mr.
Seward the substance of the British demands, and
on the Monday following (December 23) read to
him his dispatch, and left with him a copy. In this
interval the secretary had not been idle. The manner in which he employed the time leaves no room
for doubt that he had already carefully considered
the situation and studied the law of the case, and
had determined not only what he should answer if
the British demand were for an absolute surrender
of the men, but also the grounds on which he would
rest his compliance. Shutting himself in his room,
and barring his door against all interruption, he
began at once the draft of his reply.

The cabinet met on Christmas day (Wednesday),
and Seward read them his proposed answer. He
writes: "It (the case) was considered on my presentation of it on the 25th and 26th of December.
The government, when it took the subject up, had
no idea of the grounds upon which it would explain its action, nor did it believe it would concede
the case. Yet it was heartily unanimous in the
actual result after two days' examination, and in
favor of the release."[1] Two other members of
the cabinet have given us accounts of these meetings which are entirely in accord with this statement. Mr. Bates, the attorney-general, in his

[1] Letter to Weed, January 2, 1862. *Memoirs of Thurlow Weed*,
ii. p. 409.

diary says: "Seward read his proposed dispatch; it was examined and criticised by us with apparently perfect candor and frankness. All of us were impressed with the magnitude of the subject. . . . I urged the necessity of the case, — that to go to war with England is to abandon all hope of suppressing the rebellion. . . . The maritime superiority of Britain would sweep us from all the Southern waters. Our trade would be utterly ruined and our treasury bankrupt. There was great reluctance on the part of some of the members of the cabinet — *and even the President himself* — to acknowledge these obvious truths; but all yielded to, and unanimously concurred in, Mr. Seward's letter, . . . after some verbal and formal amendments." [1] Mr. Chase wrote in his journal: "I give my adhesion, therefore, to the conclusion at which the secretary of state has arrived. It is gall and wormwood to me. But I am consoled by the reflection that . . . the surrender under existing circumstances is . . . simply giving the most signal proof that the American nation will not, under any circumstances, . . . commit even a technical wrong against neutrals." [2]

Mr. Lincoln's biographers and other writers have assumed or claimed that the settlement of the Trent case was substantially his work, that his judgment favored the surrender of the prisoners, and that he intimated to Seward the need

[1] *N. & H.* v. p. 35.
[2] Warden's *Life of Chase*, p. 394.

of finding good diplomatic reasons for so doing. Whatever Mr. Lincoln said, thought, or did about this matter can neither greatly add to nor detract from his fame, which rests upon other and wholly distinct grounds; but justice to Seward demands that he should receive in this matter the credit to which he is fairly entitled. It is only so far as they are consistent with what we know from contemporary evidence that Mr. Lincoln actually said or did at the time, that credit should be given to the personal recollections of the popular writer, who tells us that on the day when the news of the capture of the commissioners reached Washington he went to the White House in company with a treasury official and saw the President, who said to him: "We must stick to American principles concerning the rights of neutrals. We fought Great Britain for insisting by theory and practice on the right to do precisely what Captain Wilkes has done. If Great Britain shall now protest against the act, and demand their release, we must give them up, apologize for the act as a violation of their doctrines, and thus forever bind her over to keep the peace in relation to neutrals, and so acknowledge she has been wrong for sixty years." [1]

This story was first published more than seven years after the transaction took place, and nearly three years after Lincoln's death. It has never been confirmed; though it has been quoted again and again by writers of history and biography,

[1] Lossing's *Pictorial History of the Civil War*, ii. pp. 156, 157.

who sometimes give credit to Mr. Lossing and
sometimes do not. Whatever one may think as
to the substance of the alleged conversation, it is
evident that the language as reported is Mr. Lossing's own, and not that of Mr. Lincoln; and it
will be quite as apparent, when'we come to examine what we do really know about Mr. Lincoln's
conduct in this matter, that, if he said anything
which justified Mr. Lossing's statement, it was a
mere passing thought, not the expression of any
fixed conviction. The anecdote related by Mr.
Welles was so often told at the time that it may
fairly be considered as supported by contempora-
neous proof. "The President," says Mr. Welles,
"was from the first impressed with the gravity of
the situation, and thought the capture embarrassing. His chief anxiety was as to the disposition
of the prisoners, who, to use his own expression,
would be elephants on our hands that we could
not easily dispose of. Public indignation was so
overwhelming against the chief conspirators that
he feared it would be difficult to prevent severe
and exemplary punishment, which he always deprecated." This opinion is quite different from
what Mr. Lossing reports to have been the President's views expressed to him on the same day,
even if the two accounts are not absolutely inconsistent with one another.

Of the President's subsequent reticence we have
already spoken. Sumner, after his arrival in
Washington, writes that he has "seen him almost

daily and most intimately ever since the Trent question has been under discussion,[1] and that he has pressed upon him arbitration." But, though he speaks of the President as being "essentially honest and pacific in disposition, with a natural slowness," he does not give us in his published letters the slightest hint that he had heard him express any opinion as to the affair of the Trent.

After Lincoln's death there was found among his papers the draft of a letter proposing arbitration as a solution of the difficulty. This was probably written under the influence of the interviews in which Sumner urged this course. It was never submitted to the cabinet, but it is an authentic piece of evidence in his own handwriting, that he was seriously considering this aspect of the matter.

The intimation that there were confidential interviews between the President and Seward as to this case, of which no record has been kept, and the further suggestion, that the President intimated to Seward, while he himself was considering the desirableness of arbitration, that, as only a few days of the grace allowed by the British government for our ultimate decision of the matter remained, he should find good diplomatic grounds for the surrender of our prisoners, are both gratuitous. There is no foundation for either of them. The latter falls to the ground, as neither the President nor the secretary had any knowledge at the time that Lord Lyons was instructed absolutely to

[1] *Life*, iv. p. 60.

require his answer within a limited period, much
less that that period had nearly expired. The
former is inconsistent not only with Seward's own
statement in his letter to Weed already quoted,
but also with the President's reluctance, as shown
by Mr. Bates, to acquiesce in the conclusion of
Seward's dispatch and the surrender of the prisoners; and it is further practically contradicted
by Seward's biographer, who tells us — from his
memorandum made at the time — that when the
cabinet separated on Christmas day after discussing Seward's dispatch, the President said to him:
"Your answer states the reasons why they ought
to be given up; now I 've a mind to try my hand
at stating the reasons why they ought not to be
given up;" but told him the next day that he could
not make an argument that satisfied his own mind,
and that this proved to him that Seward's ground
was the right one.

The contemporary evidence all points one way:
it shows that Lincoln took no lead in the decision of the matter, but acquiesced, as the members
of the cabinet did, in the reasoning and conclusions of Seward's dispatch, convinced, though
against his will, that the result which Seward had
reached could not be avoided.

Seward's dispatch, whatever be its merits or
defects, is distinctly a technical document. It
has been called an attorney's plea. The question
was one of law, and he properly treated it as such.
His paper bears evidence of a most careful and

exhaustive study of the adjudicated cases, and of the discussions in the text-books and elsewhere having any bearing on the question at issue; the internal evidence as well as the historical facts show that, both in its general scope and in its details, it was the work of one mind, and that Seward's alone. The cabinet, as we know, adopted it after discussion, making only some verbal and formal amendments, and on the same day it was delivered to Lord Lyons.

Before considering the argument of the dispatch, a few words on international law and the political situation of the country at that time may not be amiss. The sources of public international law are to be found in those practices universally admitted and recognized as legitimate by the usage of civilized nations, in historical precedents, and in the decisions of the prize courts. In every war there are two or more belligerents. Other countries, not engaged in the war, are known as neutrals. Neutral nations naturally desire, if they are commercial people, to have their merchantmen free from liability to capture and condemnation, and their trade with any belligerent as secure and untrammeled as possible. They constantly endeavor to procure such mitigations of the established rules of international law, and such liberal interpretations of these rules, as will enable them to extend in every way the uniformly profitable commerce of neutrals in war time. On the other hand, belligerents, if maritime powers, contend

for a strict construction and rigorous enforcement
of these rules, in order that neutral trading with
the enemy may be reduced within the narrowest
limits.

From the time of the formation of our government we had uniformly contended for the largest
extension of the rights of neutrals, for in all the
European wars we had been a neutral nation.
But now the positions were reversed. We were
engaged in a contest for the suppression of a formidable rebellion; and were employing for that
purpose all the recognized methods of modern
warfare, both on land and at sea. Other nations
had declared the insurrection a war, had recognized the insurgents as belligerents, and proclaimed
their own neutrality. Commercial intercourse with
the insurgents was of immense profit to these nations, especially to Great Britain, and was of vital
importance to the States in rebellion. We had
established a blockade to put a stop to this commerce. Whatever claims we might have previously put forth as neutrals, we could not now
afford to make concessions impairing any right
heretofore claimed by belligerents, much less any
undisputed right. If Mason and Slidell were to
be surrendered, care must be taken in stating the
grounds for their release that no admission was
made and no position taken which in any future
contingency could be turned against us.

The successful enforcement of our blockade depended on the energy, vigilance, and prompt and

courageous action of the officers of our navy. It
had been charged that these officers were not sufficiently alert and watchful. If the zeal of Captain
Wilkes should meet with anything like a rebuff
or rebuke, it would certainly tend to discourage
other commanders, and induce them to slacken
their exertions, which it was important to quicken.
The secretary of the navy and one branch of Congress had already thanked Wilkes for what he had
done; it was most undesirable that anything should
be said which could be interpreted as a reflection
upon their action. The whole country had lav-
ished on him unstinted praise; men of eminence
and intelligence, with hardly a dissenting voice,
had maintained the legality of his capture and
conduct; this universal outburst of patriotic feeling and concord of public opinion were not to be
rudely checked or wholly disregarded. The people
did not understand the military exigencies of the
situation, and they were entirely unprepared for
the surrender of our prisoners; the reasons for
giving up the rebel envoys must be so put that they
would, at the same time, both satisfy the judgment
and save the pride of the nation. To do this was
not an easy task; but Seward's dispatch met these
various requirements so far as possible.

Lord Russell had assumed that in what had
been done we claimed to be exercising a right, —
similar to that on which Great Britain had relied
to justify her taking from our vessels persons alleged to be her seamen, — a sort of ocean police

for municipal purposes over vessels of a foreign country, which would authorize any belligerent to take from a neutral vessel rebels, criminals, deserters, or even the citizens of a hostile country.

This Seward at once disclaimed. After reciting the facts as stated by Lord Russell and adding what seemed necessary to the correct understanding of the matter, he went on to say that, instead of being a flagrant act of violence on the part of Captain Wilkes, what he did was undertaken as a simple, legal, and customary belligerent proceeding, the arrest of a neutral vessel engaged in carrying contraband of war for the use and benefit of the insurgents. He then proceeded to enumerate and discuss the questions involved. These were, as he stated them: Were the commissioners and their secretaries with their dispatches contraband of war? — Could Captain Wilkes lawfully stop and search the vessel for those persons and their dispatches? — Did he exercise that right in a legal and proper manner? — Having found the contraband persons on board and in presumed possession of the contraband dispatches, had he a right to capture the persons? If so, did he exercise this right in the manner allowed and recognized by the law of nations?

It was not denied that persons in the military or naval service of the enemy are contraband. The question was, whether ambassadors, their suites and their dispatches, fall within the same category. Mr. Seward maintained the affirma-

.tive, relying principally on the opinion of an eminent expounder of prize law, Sir William Scott, judge of the British Admiralty Court, that: "You may stop the ambassador of your enemy on his passage. Dispatches are not less clearly contraband, and their bearers fall under the same condemnation; . . . when it is of sufficient importance to the enemy that persons shall be sent on the public service at the public expense, it is only reasonable that it should afford equal ground of forfeiture against a vessel that it has been let out for a purpose so intimately connected with hostile operations." It was contended by Mr. Sumner, in his speech on the Trent case delivered in the Senate a few weeks later, that neither Mason nor Slidell, not being persons in the military service, nor their dispatches, were contraband of war. But it may be questioned whether, though neutrals might take this ground, Sir William Scott's doctrine may not be defended, if not as a universal rule, at least as one of limited application. While all dispatches may not be contraband, there are some dispatches which it would be an insult to common sense not to declare contraband. It would have been a great mistake for Seward to have conceded, while we were in the midst of a war, that under no circumstances could the ambassador of a belligerent and his dispatches be contraband, — even though their successful transit in a neutral vessel might give more aid and comfort to an enemy than many thousand stands of arms. The

right of Captain Wilkes to detain and search the
Trent, though she was proceeding from one neutral
port to another, Mr. Seward justified by the maritime law as expounded by British magistrates and
uniformly maintained by the British government.

That the right of search, if it existed, was exercised in a lawful and proper manner was hardly
disputable, nor, if it were once admitted that the
envoys and their dispatches were contraband, was
there any question of the Trent's liability to capture.

There remained only the inquiry whether Captain Wilkes had exercised his right of capture in
conformity with the law. The law requires that
the captor should bring the captured vessel into a
convenient port, and there subject the validity of
her capture and condemnation to the adjudication
and decision of the proper admiralty court. If an
overwhelming necessity prevents his doing this,
the captor is excused, but not otherwise. In this
case, upon the captain's own admission, a consideration of the derangement and disappointment it
would cause innocent passengers had operated, perhaps more powerfully than any other motive, in
inducing him to remove to his own ship the persons claimed to be contraband, and to suffer the
Trent to proceed on her voyage. Though in so
doing he followed exactly the practice of the British officers in carrying off from our merchant vessels sailors whom they claimed to be British subjects, against which we had so often protested in

vain; yet by converting his quarter deck into a
court of law, and constituting himself a judge in
his own case, he violated the established rule that
questions of prize are not to be decided on the
spot by the captor, but are to be determined upon
a full and impartial investigation before a competent and regularly organized judicial tribunal.
The United States had always insisted upon this
course, and had so uniformly protested against
just such proceedings as took place in this case,
that it was impossible for us to admit their suffi-
ciency and regularity; the prisoners must, therefore, be returned.

It was upon this narrow ground that the surrender of Mason and Slidell was determined. The
merits of this mode of dealing with the case were:
that it yielded no point of international law on
which we might at any time desire to rest a claim
as belligerents, but made the decision depend on
a doctrine and practice universally recognized in
modern civilized warfare as the only lawful mode
of treating a prize; that it gave due credit to
Wilkes for all the qualities which we wished our
naval officers to cultivate and exhibit, and only
indirectly criticised and lamented his courtesy and
leniency; that it appeared to follow to their legitimate conclusion the doubts suggested by the secretary of the navy as to the possible consequences of
Wilkes's failure to bring in the Trent; that it
showed, therefore, that the government had from
the outset been conscious of the weak point of the

case, and that its first official utterance in Secretary Welles's letter to Captain Wilkes was not inconsistent with the final conclusion of the secretary of state.

As the dispatch followed precisely the argument, and reached precisely the conclusions of the British crown lawyers, on exactly the grounds on which they relied, though this was not then known to us, it weakened any criticism on the part of the British government. From the whole transaction we gained this advantage, — that the surrendering of these men so promptly and with so little discussion made both the ministry and the people of England ashamed of their violence and haste; and Messrs. Mason and Slidell instead of being England's heroes became her "white elephants," not ours. They were quietly taken early one winter morning from Fort Warren to Provincetown, where they were delivered on board the British frigate Rinaldo. They arrived in England, January 29, 1862. For seven weeks they had been heroes; but the tide was already running against them, and the English did not require the encouragement of the "Times" to "let the fellows alone."

When exactly what Captain Wilkes had done was known in England, the law officers of the crown were again consulted. Somewhat modifying their former opinions, they then advised the ministry, that enemy's dispatches and their bearers were contraband; but that if the dispatches were so successfully concealed as to escape discovery and seizure, the bearer, whether an ambassador or any other person, could no longer be taken.

In his original demand Lord Russell had made no allusion to the supposed diplomatic character of Mason and Slidell. The complaint of the British government was simply that one of our cruisers had forcibly stopped a neutral vessel on an innocent voyage, and taken from her two persons. In his reply to Mr. Seward, written after the surrender of the prisoners, Lord Russell denied that ambassadors were contraband of war subjecting the vessel to seizure. Mr. Seward, as has been stated, had maintained the contrary. The case therefore leaves that question exactly as it was before.

The surrender of our prisoners being placed upon the well settled rule, that a captor cannot take out of a prize either persons or property as contraband without bringing in the vessel for adjudication, unless he is necessarily prevented from so doing, the decision settled in this respect no new principle of international law. But Lord Russell persisted in his original contention, that a belligerent cannot on any pretense take persons out of a neutral vessel, thus not merely admitting but insisting on what we as a nation had claimed for years; this doctrine, therefore, for which we had so long contended in vain, must now be considered an established rule of international law.[1]

[1] Dana's Wheaton, p. 649, note.

CHAPTER XIX

INTERVENTION — CABINET DIFFICULTIES — EMANCIPATION

FROM the time that Seward learned that France had invited both England and Russia to act in concert with her as to our affairs, and that, though Russia had declined, England had agreed to do so, he was very uneasy as to the possible consequences. He feared that this arrangement might lead to offers of mediation, and, if these were not accepted by our government, to a recognition of the independence of the South, if not to more positive intervention on its behalf. He was not aware that M. Mercier, the French minister to this country, had already in March (1861) advised the emperor to recognize the Confederacy, and two months later had recommended the raising of the blockade; nor did he know that in October of that year, when our summer's campaign had ended in disaster, there had been a correspondence between the British secretary of state for foreign affairs and the prime minister, in which Earl Russell had written to Lord Palmerston that while it would not do for England and France to break a blockade for the sake of getting cotton, yet he felt sure that France would join England in saying to both North and South, as had often been said to European belligerents, "Make up your quarrels; we propose fair terms of pacification; if your adversary accepts them, and you do not, you must expect to see us your enemies." To which Palmerston had answered that the best policy for Great Britain was to go on as she had begun, and keep quite clear of the conflict. Seward had at the time no knowledge of these occurrences, but the discussions in Parliament, the general tone of the foreign press, his information as to the activity and persistent efforts of Jefferson Davis's emissaries both in France and England, and the letters of our ministers, made him keenly alive to the constantly increasing danger of some such movement on the part of these countries as had now been proposed.

To correct the representations of the Southern agents and counteract their influence, he determined to send abroad some gentlemen without official position, who, through the press, and by social intercourse with as many different circles and classes of people as possible, as well as with the leaders of public opinion, might produce more favorable impressions of our situation and prospects. Accordingly, in October of this year, before the incident of the Trent, he dispatched for this purpose, with the President's sanction, Archbishop Hughes, the distinguished Roman Catholic prelate of New York, — whose position especially fitted him for such a mission in France, — Bishop McIlvaine of the Protestant Episcopal Church, and with them his own intimate friend, the veteran politician and editor, Thurlow Weed. Their presence in Europe was an advantage to us in the storm that arose on the news of the capture of Mason and Slidell; for though they had no knowledge of this matter that was not possessed by everybody, they were able, and especially Mr. Weed from his intimacy with Seward, to contradict the stories which were widely circulated and eagerly believed, that the secretary had the utmost animosity to Great Britain, and a serious purpose of bringing on a war between the two countries.

The affair of the Trent absorbed for a time the entire attention of the British ministry and public. After our surrender of the rebel commissioners no further demands upon us from England were expected for the moment. But a dispatch from the French minister for foreign affairs, received at the beginning of the new year, showed conclusively the extent of the arrangement between the two countries, and that, although neither the honor nor the interests of France were in any way affected by Captain Wilkes's conduct, yet the emperor had been prepared to make the quarrel his own, and that we should have had both countries to contend with had there been a rupture between us and England.

When the case of the Trent was disposed of, our foreign ministers, while expressing their satis-

faction at the temporary relief which this gave
them, wrote Seward that nothing but very marked
evidence of progress toward success would restrain
for any length of time the hostile tendencies of
England, which this affair had developed.   Fortunately for us, the New Year (1862) opened with a
series of successful movements.   Important points
on the Southern coast were, one after another, taken
and occupied by United States troops, and New
Orleans was captured.   In the West and Southwest a succession of victories restored to the government's control large portions of several of the
States which the Confederacy had claimed as its
own.   It needed only the capture of Vicksburg,
which then seemed close at hand, to open the Mississippi and cut the Confederacy in two.

During the whole war Seward had the habit of
writing from time to time to our foreign ministers
accounts of the military situation, as well of our
losses as of our gains; and these accounts, though
colored by his natural optimism, and strenuously
cheerful when our prospects seemed gloomiest,
give excellent general descriptions of the important
military movements and situations.   He had protested strongly against the recognition of the South
as belligerents, and now, encouraged by our achieve-
ments and prospects, he exerted all his powers of
argument and persuasion to induce the European
governments to withdraw this concession.   But
France declined to retract, upon the ground that
it would be shabby to deprive the South, when it

seemed weak, of the assurance that had been given when it appeared strong; and England also refused, giving as her reason that, although our immediate success then seemed probable, it would be better to wait until the victory had been actually won.

The Northern gains in the early months of 1862 were followed by a series of reverses. The advance on Richmond, for which such enormous preparations had been made, terminated in the withdrawal of the Union troops, after a series of bloody and destructive battles. The Confederates moved forward both in the East and West, not merely with the purpose of repossessing themselves of the places they had heretofore occupied, but of actually invading the North. They were at first successful. At the West the Northern troops retreated in Kentucky and Tennessee, the Confederates advanced, and Ohio was seriously threatened; in the East the Southern forces fought their way through Virginia, and actually invaded Maryland. They were driven back at Antietam, and compelled to retreat. Their forward movement in the West was checked, and there also they were obliged to withdraw. Before this was known in England, when only the news of the Confederate successes had reached there, it was agreed by Lord Palmerston and Lord Russell in the early autumn of 1862, that the proper moment for intervention had arrived, and that, if the United States declined the proposed mediation, the Southern Confederacy should be recognized as an independent nation. A little later, a ministerial circular was prepared, describing the result of the summer's campaign, and setting forth these views; but before the whole cabinet met, towards the end of October, it was evident that the scheme for recognition had failed; the tide was setting against mediation; the Southern victories were seen to be barren of results, and the opinion was gradually gaining ground that the superior resources and population of the United States would enable it eventually to subdue the rebellion.

In November of the same year the French emperor proposed to both England and Russia to join with him in offering to arrange terms of peace. Both countries declined to do so, and he made the proposition alone. It was communicated to Mr. Seward early in February, 1863, at a moment of great discouragement; to the failure of our summer campaign had been added the disaster of Fredericksburg and the political defeat of the administration in the November elections; and under these disheartening circumstances Seward wrote his reply, refusing the offered mediation. His letter is remarkable for its dignity and courage, for its forcible presentation of the situation in which the insurrection found us, and of what had been done to insure success, and for the absolute reliance which it shows on the patriotism of the people and on their determination, at whatever cost, to maintain the Union in its integrity.

"This government," he wrote, "has not the least thought of relinquishing the trust which has been confided to it by the nation under the most solemn of all political sanctions; and if it had any such thought, it would still have abundant reason to know that peace, proposed at the cost of dissolution, would be immediately, unreservedly and indignantly rejected by the American people. It is a great mistake that European statesmen make, if they suppose this people are demoralized. Whatever, in the case of an insurrection, the people of France would do to save their national existence, no matter how the strife might be regarded by, or might affect, foreign nations, just so much, and certainly no less, the people of the United States will do. If those now exercising their power should, through fear or faction, fall below this height of the national virtue, they would be speedily, yet constitutionally, replaced by others of sterner character and patriotism."

No further suggestion of mediation was ever made. But apprehensions of some form of foreign interference, especially from Great Britain, were felt from time to time till nearly the close of the war. It was only on the 24th of March, 1865, ten days before our troops entered Richmond, that Mr. Adams was able to state with confidence that "no further apprehension need be felt by us of any aggressive policy" on the other side of the Atlantic Ocean.

Aside from the grave questions connected with

the war, the diplomatic events of the eighteen months after the surrender of Mason and Slidell, in which Seward found the greatest satisfaction, were a treaty with Great Britain for the "extirpation of the African slave trade at once and forever,"[1] and the opening of diplomatic intercourse with Hayti and Liberia.

In the summer of 1862, when the army before Richmond seemed too reduced for any effective movement, Seward left Washington, carrying with him a letter from the President, intended to supplement his own personal efforts with the loyal governors and leading men at the North, to induce them to urge the administration to issue a fresh call for troops. The President could have made such a call without being asked; but the military situation was critical, our prospects were gloomy, and he feared that if he did so "a general panic and stampede would follow." Seward did his work successfully. Soon after his return to Washington, he was called upon by Mr. Seaton, the editor of the "National Intelligencer," who began the conversation in this way: "Now really, governor, this is a time to say something." Seward began to speak of the need of reinforcements, and the promptness with which they were arriving; but, either induced by what Mr. Seaton said, or guessing the object of his visit, he turned to personal matters, and added that "every rumor of a division of counsels, and of a conflict about

[1] April 8, 1862.

generals, tended to defeat this (the arrival of reinforcements); that he therefore felt at liberty to
state that he had never exercised a power or duty
in the progress of the war with which he was not
specially charged by the President, and in the per-
formance of which he was not always in free communication with him.   That to no one had he ever
expressed distrust of the President, or of any of
his associates in the government; but on the contrary had uniformly supported them.   That he
had not been quick or willing to entertain complaints against any general, but had exerted his
best endeavors to sustain them all.   That he had
never introduced or encouraged in the cabinet any
test question concerning men or measures; had
never seen any intemperance of debate there; nor
had one word of unkindness or distrust ever passed
between the President or any of his official advisers
and himself."

This interview shows not only that the charges
against Seward, which came to a head in December of this same year in the action of a caucus of
senators requesting his removal, were in July the
gossip of Washington, but also that they were
perfectly well known to him at that time, and that
he understood their object; for he went on to say
that he was "content to remain where he was so
long as the war continued and the President required it; but would not prolong his stay one hour
beyond the time when the President should think
it wise to relieve" him.

It was to Seward a summer of intense anxiety. Continued defeats were likely to bring on a recognition of the independence of the Southern Confederacy, which must be either acquiesced in or met by war. To avert the defeats, "what could we do but to push recruiting, and, that failing, to provide for a draft?" "I go to Congress and implore and conjure them," he writes to his wife. "They give me debates upon the errors of the past, and quarrels about who is to blame. These disputes involve policies about dealing with slaves, upon which Congress angers itself and the country; and the governors of the States write, ' You can get no recruits.' I ask Congress to authorize a draft. They fall into altercation about letting slaves fight and work. Every day is a day lost, and every day lost is a hazard to the country." The letter shows that his relations with Congress were at this time not altogether harmonious. A dispatch of the same month to Mr. Adams gives us a further insight into his state of mind: —

"It seems as if the extreme advocates of African slavery and its most vehement opponents were acting in concert together to precipitate a servile war, — the former by making the most desperate attempt to overthrow the federal Union, the latter by demanding an edict of universal emancipation as a lawful and necessary, if not, as they say, the only legitimate way of saving the Union."

As an official dispatch, this communication was unwise, if not unjustifiable, and was not helped

by the word "confidential" at the top. It was
really no dispatch, but a private, personal letter,
expressing strongly a feeling then quite prevalent
in parts of the country, which Seward might fairly
enough have held, and which he had a perfect
right to communicate in private correspondence to
a friend. His own object at this time was to secure, as soon as possible, a victory which should
be to Europe a demonstration of the certainty of
our ultimate success. For this troops were needed,
and every day occupied by Congress in discussing
political problems, instead of taking measures to
fill up our armies, was, to his mind, a day lost to
us. He knew that each day so lost increased the
chances of foreign intervention. He thought that
the questions as to slavery might wait, but that
our successes could not do so; and he was impatient of anything which might endanger or delay
them. Before the meeting of Congress this dispatch had become public. Mr. Lincoln said that
it had not been submitted to him. It made no
reference whatever to either the House or Senate,
and no allusion to Congress. Seward spoke of
"the extreme advocates of slavery" and of "its
most vehement opponents." These terms described
classes, not Congressmen; nevertheless the radical
anti-slavery senators and representatives were in-
dignant at what they chose to consider an affront
offered them by a cabinet minister in an official
document written without the knowledge of the
President.

When the session began in December, every one was depressed about the military situation, and the Republicans very sore at the results of the November elections. The administration had lost everywhere. New York, Seward's own State, had elected as governor a peace Democrat; and had the new Congress met at once, some peace would probably have been patched up, either with or without foreign intervention. The change in the popular vote was to be attributed largely to the failure of our military operations at the East. There was a general feeling that the administration was mainly responsible for this, by its interference with, and mismanagement of, the conduct of the war. Some thought that our misfortunes were owing to the fact that the government had intrusted important commands to officers who had not decided anti-slavery opinions, and were not, therefore, it was charged, thoroughly in earnest in their work. It was evident that the emancipation proclamation, which is presently to be spoken of, had further divided, instead of uniting the people. The nation had given a distinct vote of want of confidence; and the Republican senators wished to regain the popular favor. They assumed that Seward had been the controlling mind in the administration, the premier, in the talk of the day; that he was practically responsible for its domestic as well as its foreign policy, for all its mistakes and misfortunes, civil, political, and military, and had dominated, in a heterogeneous

and discordant cabinet, even the President himself.

It is idle to speculate upon the origin or causes
of this opinion. It is enough that it existed at
the time, and was not confined to Congress. It is
not easy to find any foundation for it. From the
time that supplies were ordered to Sumter to the
close of his life, Lincoln was the head of his own
government, and Seward recognized this fact.
"There is but one vote in the cabinet," he said,
"and that is cast by the President." "The President is the best of us all," he wrote to his wife in
June, 1861. Lincoln listened to Seward's opinions, as he did to those of the other members of
his cabinet, but the decision was always his own;
if anybody interfered with the military operations
and the disposition of the troops, it was the President and secretary of war, not Seward.

It was thought, however, that some change must
be made; and acting on their preconceived notions,
a caucus of Republican senators voted by a small
majority to request the President "to dispense
with the services of the secretary of state." Believing that their object might be equally well attained by a resolve less personal, supported by a
larger majority, the caucus on the following day
adopted, with only one dissenting voice, a substitute, recommending the President to partially re-
model his cabinet, and appointed a committee of
nine, — six radicals and three conservatives, — to
wait on him and present this resolution. That

there might be no doubt as to the object of the resolve, eight of these nine committeemen were known to think "Seward a serious obstacle to the prosecution of the war." Seward, learning of the doings of the caucus, anticipated the action of the committee by sending in his resignation. Chase disapproved the action of the caucus; he was unwilling to be a party to an attack upon Seward, and finding the reason given by the senators for their action broad enough to extend to all the members of the cabinet, he also sent in his resignation. The whole thing disturbed Lincoln; he was displeased with the attempt at congressional dictation, and greatly annoyed at the inability to grasp the situation which the proceeding displayed. Seward and Chase represented the opposite extremes of the Republican party, and it was necessary that he should have in his cabinet the support of both. He was relieved from all embarrassment on that score when he received Chase's resignation, and, one might almost say, ordered them both to go back at once to their posts, because the public good required it. Speaking of the matter a year later, he said: "If I had yielded to that storm and dismissed Seward, the thing would have slumped over one way, and we should have been left to a scanty handful of supporters."

As our armies advanced into the seceding States, the questions of the effect of the war upon the slaves found within our lines, as well as upon slavery itself, became of constantly increasing interest and importance. General Butler's ingenious application of the term "contraband" to the slaves coming within our lines, was of great service in solving the former; but the latter, the vital question of slavery or emancipation, still remained, and upon this there were great differences of opinion. There were many persons, not necessarily radicals, who, looking at the matter only from a moral point of view, considered constitutional scruples wholly idle, that if slavery were not abolished the war would be not merely a crime but a blunder, and that public proclamation of immediate emancipation should be made at once, without regard to consequences, and however ineffectual it might in fact be. Our foreign ministers — while they thought military successes essential, if we would prevent the recognition of the South by the governments of Europe — admitted that a proclamation of emancipation, which should give to the war the aspect of a crusade against slavery, might be of advantage to us; and some of them were urgent that this proclamation should be made at once.

At home those persons who believed in the supremacy of the Constitution, and that the maintenance of the Union was the object of the war and its only justification, were in a state of great doubt both as to the duty and the powers of the federal government. Many of them, as the war went on, had come gradually to the conviction that it must end in the abolition of slavery, and that the

struggle would be futile or worse if in the result
this cause for sectional strife should not disappear
forever; yet they saw no ground for the government's interference with slavery in any State, except as a military necessity for the purpose of more
quickly and successfully putting down the rebellion.
They were very doubtful whether an emancipation
proclamation would have this effect, — whether it
would not more strongly unite and give fresh courage to the South, while it would bring into opposition to the government all those elements at the
North which, united in their support of a war for
the Constitution, were more or less indifferent to
slavery; and whether it would not, by thus divid-
ing the Northern people, make the successful prosecution of the war no longer possible; or in other
words, whether it would not add an enemy in the
rear to those already in the field.

His own doubts upon this point, and his conviction that he had no right to convert the war into
a crusade against slavery, had made the President
hesitate long. As he declared in words often
quoted: "My paramount object in this struggle is
to save the Union, and is not either to save or to
destroy slavery. If I could save the Union without freeing any slave, I would do it; and if I
could save it by freeing all the slaves, I would do
it; and if I could save it by freeing some and
leaving others alone, I would also do that. What
I do about slavery and the colored race, I do because I believe it helps to save the Union; and

what I forbear, I forbear because I do not believe
it would help to save the Union. I shall do less
whenever I shall believe that what I am doing
hurts the cause, and I shall do more whenever I
shall believe doing more will help the cause."

More than a month, however, before he wrote
this letter, he had submitted to his cabinet the
draft of an emancipation proclamation. The discussion which followed showed that there was between the secretaries the same difference of opinion
that existed among the people. The attorney-
general and Stanton favored the immediate issuing
of this proclamation; the secretary of the navy
was silent; Mr. Chase said it was a measure of
great danger, would lead to universal emancipation, and went far beyond anything he had recommended; and Mr. Blair prophesied that it would
cost the administration the next elections. Nothing was said, however, that affected the President's decision, until Seward suggested that the
depression of the public mind, in consequence of
our repeated reverses, was so great that this might
be considered the last resource of an exhausted government, a cry for help, the government stretching
forth its hands to Ethiopia, instead of Ethiopia
stretching forth her hands to the government; and
that the proclamation had better be postponed
until it could be supported by military successes,
instead of coming upon the heel of great disasters.
The wisdom of this struck Mr. Lincoln so forcibly
that he put the paper away, and waited till our

partial victory at Antietam had, to some extent,
redeemed the failures of the summer.   The proclamation was then issued; and when the days of
grace which it gave to the seceding slaveholders
had expired, its assurances were fulfilled.   As our
armies advanced, the government in all its branches
recognized and maintained the freedom which the
proclamation promised, and the interests of humanity became identified with the cause of the
country.

CHAPTER XX

DIPLOMATIC QUESTIONS OF THE WAR

WHEN Lincoln entered upon the duties of his office the troops at his command were too few to permit him even to consider the question of properly reinforcing and holding Fort Sumter. Our navy consisted of forty-two ships fit for immediate service, thirty of which were dispersed in different parts of the world, leaving only twelve for use at home. To suppress the rebellion took us four years. At its close we had an army of a million men, and a navy of nearly six hundred ships, seventy-five of which were ironclads. It was, of course, impossible that a contest of this magnitude, as to which the great European powers had proclaimed their neutrality almost before it began, could be carried on by sea and land for so long a period without giving rise to an infinite number and variety of diplomatic questions and complaints. The published correspondence of the State Department for this period fills thirteen volumes; the mere enumeration of the matters treated of would be extremely tedious. It may be said in general, that Seward claimed for us as belligerents the fullest exercise of all the rights upon which Great

Britain had insisted when at war; but that, without waiving these, he at times made concessions for the purpose of relieving the tension between this country and the leading European powers, and of diminishing if possible the hostile feelings of their citizens. His mode of dealing with the mails found on captured blockade runners is an illustration of this.

These vessels often had mails on board; the question of the disposition to be made of these was important and troublesome, and involved a good deal of feeling. Should we open them and examine their contents? They might contain official dispatches or private letters having important information; but, to ascertain this, it would be necessary to pry into domestic letters of a strictly personal character. Was this permitted by the laws of war? The governments under whose flags these vessels sailed insisted that the mail bags should be forwarded unopened to their destination; our Navy Department contended that they were liable like the cargo to examination for contraband. Seward, after some consideration, agreed that the public mails of any friendly or neutral power should be forwarded unopened. The secretary of the navy thought this a weak yielding to an unreasonable demand. Seward made the concession not as a matter of right, but of expediency, and was unquestionably wise in so doing. In any event the advantages to us would have been slight and rare; the irritation of other governments and of their citizens, whose private correspondence might have been tampered with, would have been constant and extreme, and might have led to most serious consequences.

The permission granted, at the request of their government, to the French, who wished to do so, to leave New Orleans by passing through the blockade is another instance of the same policy. The abuse of a similar privilege by a British consul and the commander of an English man-of-war, which had been authorized for a special purpose to enter a blockaded port, shows the extent to which their sympathy with the South could carry two British public servants. They permitted the Confederate government to ship and send to England by this vessel gold for the payment of its obligations there, that it might in this way escape any risk of capture. When Seward remonstrated, the consul was dismissed from the service; but the mischief had been already done.

The blockade gave rise to many complaints, most of them depending on questions of fact, as to which it was not always easy to ascertain the truth. Though the investigation of these cases occupied a great deal of time, they hardly furnished any cause for serious anxiety; but our attempt in the autumn of 1861 to obstruct some of the channels of Charleston harbor by sinking old hulks loaded with stones — the stone blockade, as it was called — seemed at one moment to threaten difficulties of a graver character. Similar modes of closing the entrance to a harbor, by quasi-permanent obstructions, were not wholly unknown. The British in the war of the Revolution had done something of the sort at Savannah; the Confederates during their four years' struggle placed such obstructions in many harbors. But on learning of our stone blockade Earl Russell's temper seems to have got the better of his courtesy. He instructed Lord Lyons to remonstrate with Mr. Seward against this as a "cruel plan, which could only be adopted as a measure of revenge and of irremediable injury against an enemy;" and to say further that, "even as a scheme of bitterest and sanguinary war, such a measure would not be justifiable; that it would be a plot against the commerce of all maritime nations and against the free intercourse of the Southern States of America with the civilized world."[1] How far Lord Lyons in his interview with Mr. Seward softened the offensive phraseology of this letter cannot be known. Mr. Seward's position in the matter, according to Lord Lyons's report to his government, is exactly what he himself stated it to be in a dispatch of February 17, 1861, to Mr. Adams, in which he said: "I am not prepared to recognize the right of other nations to object to the manner of placing artificial obstructions in the channels of

---

[1] Lord Russell had probably forgotten that a provision of the treaty of Utrecht (1713) inserted in favor of England stipulated for the filling up of the harbor of Dunkirk, and that this was done soon after the execution of the treaty.

rivers leading to ports which have been seized by
insurgents in their attempts to overthrow this government. I am nevertheless desirous that the ex-
aggerations on that subject which have been in-
dulged abroad may be corrected." He adds that
he has applied to the Navy Department for information, and has learned that there are two ship
channels in which no artificial obstructions have
been or are to be placed, and which are guarded
only by the blockading squadron. Nothing further was heard from Great Britain on the subject.
The sunken hulks were gradually washed away by
storms, and the necessity for the discussion disappeared with the obstructions.

The personal questions as to foreigners were
not confined to matters having their origin in our
blockade. There were numerous complaints of
unjust imprisonment or of hard usage as to their
persons or property by resident foreigners of various nationalities. Care and patience were requisite for the examination of these, and tact and
good sense for deciding them; but they were all
disposed of without hard feeling, except those
arising out of General Butler's government at
New Orleans. The foreign population there, of
which a majority was French, had strong secession sympathies, and was not disposed to submit
quietly to Butler's arbitrary proceedings. Complaints from the foreign ministers came thick and
fast; some were of a very serious nature, involving
claims for large amounts of property confiscated,

of money seized, without apparent justification, together with demands for indemnity for personal insults and injuries. They engrossed half Seward's time, and were seriously endangering our friendly relations with the great powers of Europe, until, "to relieve their uneasiness," Banks was sent to succeed Butler. Butler's proceedings were gratifying to the vindictive feelings of the North towards the secessionists, and at the time were much approved. They may have been necessary for the maintenance of public order; if they were not so, it was certainly injudicious to run such risks of a rupture with France, which would probably have involved one with England also. It is not impossible that the action of the State Department on some of these complaints of the foreigners at New Orleans may have been the alleged "interference with our generals," which was urged as one of the reasons for asking Seward's removal.

There is a wide difference between a proclamation of neutrality in the case of a war between two states already recognized as belonging to the family of nations, and a similar proclamation in a case where bands of insurgents, or provinces in revolt, are seeking to wrest their independence from their government. In the former case the proclamation makes no change in the existing status, it is a mere cautionary notice of undisputed facts, which are thus called to the attention of the subjects of the government issuing it, to remind them of their rights and duties. In the latter it alters the previous conditions, and, so far as the citizens of the country issuing it are concerned, actually creates what it only professes to recognize, either calling into being as a full-grown nation (if it acknowledges their independence) a body of people who had previously no political existence whatever, or turning a rebellion into a war, if it only calls them belligerents. It is really not a declaration of neutrality, but a mild form of intervention on behalf of an incipient revolution, and when made jointly by several powerful nations at the same time, is a pretty efficacious one; it is also distinctly an act injurious to the government endeavoring to put down its rebellious citizens. The only way for any foreign nation to maintain a real neutrality in such a struggle is to leave the rebels alone to gain their independence if they can, and their government undisturbed to crush the insurrection if it is able. It was not this absolute neutrality which England and France assumed to maintain towards us during the rebellion. Their proclamations at the outset gave countenance to the South, and the hope of something more.

Our complaints of these proclamations at the time they were issued have already been spoken of. It soon appeared that, so far as England was concerned, the immediate and principal effect of her course was to stimulate all her industries and manufactures, and to encourage her people to do their utmost to supply the needs of our States in rebellion, whose only resources were agricultural, whose main dependence for everything essential to carrying on their struggle was the workshops and factories of Great Britain, and who, without the supplies received in this way, would have been speedily subdued. The perception of these facts quickened and intensified our sense of the wrong done us by England at the outset; it gave rise to a general conviction that the British government was not reluctant to gain advantages for its own citizens at our expense, and was the source of a widespread belief that to secure this result had been the purpose of its original action.

We also complained that England persistently violated in various ways the duties and obligations of the neutrality she had declared. We charged her with doing so by permitting the Confederates to use, first Nassau in the British Bahamas, and later Bermuda, as military bases, and depots for their arms, ammunition, stores, and equipments. Against this use of these ports Seward protested strenuously; but his remonstrances produced no effect. If England had made no proclamation of neutrality, such assistance to unrecognized rebels would not have been tolerated; but under the circumstances it is doubtful if it was a technical breach of neutrality, though if it had clearly been so, it could not have done us more grievous harm.

Our complaints against England's violations of neutrality, however, went far beyond this. We charged her with gross breaches of it in permitting

rebel cruisers, intended to prey upon our commerce, to be built in her ship-yards, equipped
and armed from her workshops, provisioned and
manned by her sailors and subjects. Early in
1862, complaint was made to the British government as to the construction of a vessel for this
purpose. She was finished, registered as an English ship, and cleared as such for Palermo. She
never went there, but appeared at Bermuda, eventually ran the blockade into Mobile, where she was
armed, successfully escaped from there, and cruised
as the Florida. She made many prizes in the
Atlantic, and having burnt one of our ships off
the Irish coast, went in to Brest to land its crew
and make some repairs, and, in spite of our remonstrances, was there allowed to ship a fresh
crew for herself and start again. She ended her
career in October, 1864, at Bahia. She was cut
out from under the guns of a Brazilian battery
and the broadside of a guard-ship, by the United
States steamer Wachusett, and brought into Hamp-
ton Roads, where she fortunately solved a diplomatic difficulty by springing a leak and sinking.
Brazil accepted our apology for the violation of
her sovereignty in the attack on the rebel ship,
and the removal of our consul who had advised it,
with the sending of the commander of the Wachusett before a court-martial, as sufficient amends
for the offense.

·Towards the end of June in the same year
(1862), Mr. Adams informed Lord Russell that

a new and more powerful steamer was nearly ready to leave Liverpool on the same errand as the Florida. She did not in fact sail until the 29th of July, but the British government was not able during this whole month to satisfy itself, until it was too late, that there was any evidence which would justify her detention. This vessel was the Alabama. She slipped out of port and waited off the coast until she had received a crew of forty men sent to her in a tug from Liverpool; off the Azores she was met by two vessels, which had sailed directly from England, bringing all her armament, clothing for her crew, a supply of coal, and her captain and officers. As British ships are British territory, it seems that in this case the vessel was built, equipped, armed, and manned under the British flag and protection; and that the breach of neutrality and the violation of the spirit, if not of the letter, of the municipal law of England were complete in every particular before she hoisted the Confederate colors. It has been admitted by a British jurist, that "had the whole series of transactions which finally placed her on the ocean armed, manned, provisioned, and commissioned for war, been within the knowledge of the British government, and within its power of control, she would never have left the Mersey;" and, if it be conceded that the display of the Confederate flag and the exhibition of a Confederate commission, under the circumstances stated, so changed her character that she could no longer be proceeded against and condemned in any British court, it may fairly be claimed that a due regard to the neutrality they professed, to the dignity of the crown, and to the spirit of their laws would have more than justified the British ministry in refusing to this vessel, English in everything but the name, an asylum in any harbor under their jurisdiction. Instead of this she was received at every British port she chose to visit, and met there a liberal hospitality quite different from the bare toleration which was grudgingly given to our men-of-war. She began her predatory cruising in August, 1862, and finished it twenty-two months later, in June, 1864, when she was sunk off Cherbourg by the United States steamer Kearsarge after an hour's action. During her cruises she captured and destroyed about sixty American vessels, most of which were merchantmen employed in foreign voyages.

Applications to the ministry having proved ineffectual to prevent the sailing of the rebel cruisers, Seward wrote to Mr. Adams: "As one more resource, it is deemed advisable that an effort be made to secure the enforcement of the enlistment laws through the action of the courts" (April 2, 1863). In pursuance of these instructions Mr. Adams furnished the British government with such evidence that proceedings were begun against the owners of the steamer Alexandra. At the trial there was no dispute about the facts. The vessel was built under a contract with the agent of the

Confederate government and was intended for use as a man-of-war. She was not finished at the time the proceedings were begun; and the jury were instructed that, to bring the case within the provisions of the foreign enlistment act, her equipment must have been so far completed in British territory that she was capable of hostile operations; or that, if it were not already so complete, it must be proved that it was intended that it should be completed in British territory. They were also told that, although the vessel had been built and was to be used as a cruiser, if it was intended to put the arms on board at a place beyond British jurisdiction there would be no violation of the foreign enlistment act. Upon these instructions the jury found for the defendants. The subsequent action of the judge who presided at the trial was such as, under the English forms of procedure, precluded any final, authoritative decision as to the construction of the statute. The case left the Confederates at liberty to violate without substantial inconvenience the spirit of international law, and to evade both the letter and spirit of the municipal statutes.

The gravity of the situation was at once appreciated here, and Seward wrote to Mr. Adams that, if the law of this case was to regulate the action of Her Majesty's government, the United States would be without any guarantee against the unlimited employment of capital by British subjects in building and sending forth ships of war from

British ports to make war against the United States, and that this would be, in effect, "a war waged against this country by a portion at least of the British nation, and tolerated, though not declared, by the British government." He suggested to the English ministry, whether Parliament would "not consider it just and expedient to amend the existing statute in such a way as to effect what the two governments actually believed it ought to accomplish;" and he added, that if Her Majesty's government should desire such a proceeding, the President would not hesitate to apply to Congress for an equivalent amendment of the laws of the United States. Mr. Adams made the suggestion, and Earl Russell expressed his willingness to propose amendments, on condition that they should also be adopted in the American act; but when Mr. Adams informed him later of the assent of our government to this proposal, he was told that Her Majesty's government had reconsidered the matter and declined to suggest any amendments. This closed the negotiations; the act remained unchanged till the end of the rebellion.

The English government, however, became more ready to exert themselves to prevent the construction and sailing of Confederate cruisers. Two rams that were building in Liverpool, under the supervision of the officer in charge of the Confederate naval bureau of construction there, were seized and detained, and were finally bought by the crown. The only vessel of importance which subsequently got away was the Shenandoah, whose depredations were continued long after the Southern armies had surrendered and peace had been restored. In October, 1864, when Sherman had already taken Atlanta, Farragut had captured Mobile, and the fall of the Confederacy was evidently a mere question of months, she left London as the Sea King. Off a little island near Madeira she met by appointment another steamer direct from Liverpool, from which she received her arms, ammunition, and stores; she raised the Confederate flag and started on her cruise as the Shenandoah. In January, 1865, she put in at Melbourne, filled up her crew, and proceeded to the Arctic Ocean, where she destroyed the American whaling fleet, continuing her depredations until she learned in August from an English ship that the Confederacy had ceased to exist. Returning to Liverpool, she was taken possession of by the crown, and was subsequently delivered to the government of the United States.

All these vessels, not only those that have been mentioned, but others that have not been named, though called Confederate cruisers, were built to overhaul, plunder, and destroy unarmed merchantmen, but, as the captain of one of them frankly admitted, not to fight, "unless in a very urgent case." Their operations occasioned an enormous amount of diplomatic correspondence and negotiation, which lasted after Seward ceased to be secre-

tary of state.   So long as Mr. Adams remained in
England it was conducted by him, upon general
lines laid down by Seward, but with the largest
discretion given to Mr. Adams.   For a time each
new vessel destroyed was made the subject of a
fresh complaint, until this constant repetition of
similar demands drew from Lord Russell the impatient declaration, "that he wished to say once
for all, that Her Majesty's government disclaimed
any responsibility for these losses, and hoped they
had made their position perfectly clear."   Nevertheless a subsequent ministry expressed Her Majesty's regret for the escape of these vessels from
British ports and for the depredations committed
by them, agreed to submit to arbitration the question of Great Britain's liability for these, and
consented that the arbitrators should accept as the
law which should govern their decision the rules:
that a neutral power is bound to use due diligence to prevent the fitting out, arming, or equip-
ping within its jurisdiction of any vessel which it
has reasonable grounds to believe is intended to
cruise or carry on war against any power with
which it is at peace; that it is bound in the same
way to prevent the departure from its jurisdiction
of any such vessel which has been either wholly or
partly fitted there for such warlike use; that it
cannot permit a belligerent to use its ports or
waters as a base of naval operations against his
enemy, or for the purpose of renewing or increasing
his arms or other military supplies, or of enlisting

men; and lastly, that it must exercise due diligence as to all persons and places within its jurisdiction to prevent the violation of these obligations. By the award of the arbitrators to whom was submitted the question of Great Britain's liability under these rules for the acts of the Confederate cruisers, she was compelled to pay fifteen million five hundred thousand dollars ($15,500,000) for property actually destroyed by them. This sum was intended as a compensation to American shipowners and citizens for the loss of their property; but for the heaviest loss to the country, and one from which it has never recovered, that of its share in the carrying trade of the world, no compensation was made. It was this trade to which Mr. Adams referred when he wrote to Mr. Seward early in the war, that "the English people would be gratified at anything which would inflict an injury on American commerce, of which they are very jealous."

The building and depredations of the Alabama and her sister ships were not, however, the only matters of diplomatic correspondence and complaint as to these cruisers. Their reception in foreign ports, the right of coaling, and other privileges accorded them there, and the courtesies alleged to have been shown to their officers, but refused to ours, were the subject of constant remonstrances from the State Department; and though some of these matters might seem trifling, and the complaints unavailing, Mr. Seward's repeated criti-

cisms served to make the colonial governors of the
various European powers more cautious about over-
stepping the bounds of neutrality, and to lessen
the instances in which they actually did so. On
the other hand, it was charged that our naval officers pursued blockade runners into neutral waters,
lay in wait for Confederate cruisers in foreign
harbors, and often failed to observe the courtesies
expected from ships of war in friendly ports; and
every such complaint required to be investigated,
and explained or answered, or an apology made
whenever there was shown to be just ground of
offense.

There were also other matters as to which we
considered that Great Britain gave us good cause
of complaint.

Towards the close of the war, in October, 1864,
a few men, coming as ordinary travelers from
Canada to St. Albans, Vermont, were met there
by others arriving from Chicago; the two bands,
having joined forces, attempted unsuccessfully to
set the town on fire; they robbed the banks of
their specie and then crossed the frontier into Canada, where several of them were arrested. Seward
endeavored in vain to obtain their extradition as
criminals. British writers have admitted that,
had they been caught in Vermont, they would have
had no claim to be treated as military prisoners;
but the Canadian court refused to surrender them,
on the ground that what they had done was not a
crime, but an act of war. Somewhat similar occur-

rences took place on board steamers on the lakes or on coastwise voyages on the Atlantic. When parties of apparently innocent passengers threw off their disguise and seized and plundered the steamers on which they had embarked, their surrender was refused on similar grounds, the court saying: either this is an act of piracy on the high seas, in which case the men can be tried here; or of war, in which case they cannot be tried anywhere.

It is certainly not for the interests of civilization that acts of this character, done by bands of desperadoes for their private gain and without authority, should be treated as acts of war by a neutral. It is doubtful whether any one connected with any of these expeditions held any regular commission from the Confederate authorities; it is quite certain that no one of the men was at the time a soldier in the Confederate service, and there was no evidence that any of the expeditions were in pursuance of the orders of the Confederate government or of any of its agents. They were the work of marauders. The Canadian government was so ashamed of the conduct of its judiciary that it refunded the gold value of the paper money stolen at St. Albans, which by order of court had been given back to the thieves, from whose possession it had been taken by the police.

Aside from the diplomatic difficulties directly connected with the rebellion, the state of affairs

in Mexico was a source of great anxiety during
Lincoln's administration. We were not only uneasy as to the temporary effect which the troubles there might have upon our foreign relations,
but we were also apprehensive lest they should
have a serious influence upon the future of our
country.

Mexico in 1861 was indebted to citizens of
France, England, and Spain, who complained that
they could not obtain payment of the money due
them. The governments of these three countries,
realizing that our domestic difficulties were their
opportunity, made an alliance in the autumn of
that year, the purpose of which was, not merely
to enforce the payment of these debts, but also to
secure a better protection for foreigners resident in
Mexico. A month after the treaty was executed
we were invited to join in it. Seward declined
the invitation. He suggested that we might guarantee the Mexican debt, and that in this way the
necessity for foreign intervention would be avoided.
This suggestion was not accepted; it was said that
it would leave untouched one of the objects of the
alliance, — security for the future good treatment
of foreigners living in Mexico. The original scheme
of the three powers evidently contemplated a temporary and limited occupation of the territory, if
nothing more. In declining to become a party to
the treaty, Seward stated our strong interest that no
foreign power should acquire territory in Mexico,
or gain any peculiar advantage there, or exercise

any influence to interfere with the free choice by the Mexicans of their own form of government.

It soon became evident that Louis Napoleon had aims quite different from those of the other powers, and early in April, 1862, the Spanish and English commissioners, finding that the French were giving military aid to the monarchical party, withdrew from coöperation with them, and the alliance was dissolved. Mexico at this time was divided between the church party, which was monarchist and conservative, and the liberal party, which was republican. The actual government was republican and liberal, but it was weak and unstable. Napoleon's plan was to use his power and influence in favor of the monarchists, and to obtain, at an election to be held under the auspices and the control of the French troops, a *plébiscite* creating a monarchy and calling a foreign prince to the throne. He knew that it was the settled policy of this country not to permit the establishment by a European power of any monarchy in America, and that, if our condition permitted it, we should interfere, by force if need be, to prevent it. But our hands were tied, and he took advantage of our necessities to attempt to carry out his project. Before the departure of the first expedition for Mexico, rumors that this was the emperor's scheme were rife in Europe; but the French ministers in conversations, apparently frank, with our representatives, and in their diplomatic correspondence, not only at that time but during the whole French occupa-

tion of Mexico, persistently denied that there was
any foundation for these reports, or that the emperor had any purpose of forcing a government
upon that country. Though it was difficult to
reconcile these statements with the reports of the
English and Spanish commissioners, Seward in
his correspondence accepted them as true, and instructed our minister to say that we relied on them
as such; and that while we recognized the right
of France to make war against Mexico, and to determine for herself the cause, we had "a right and
interest to insist that she should not improve the
war to raise up in Mexico an anti-republican or
an anti-American government, or to maintain such
a government there."

An assembly of notables, convened July 10,
1863, by direction of the French general, voted
to establish an imperial government and elected
the Archduke Maximilian of Austria to the throne.
In a dispatch of September 26, 1863, Seward
stated with great distinctness the views of our
government upon this matter. He said that the
United States had neither a right nor a disposition
to intervene by force in the internal affairs of
Mexico, either to maintain a republic or to overthrow an imperial government, if Mexico chose to
establish the one or the other; but that our government knew that the inherent normal opinion of
Mexico favored a republican and domestic government in preference to any monarchy imposed from
abroad, and that if France should determine to

adopt in Mexico a policy adverse to these views, it would probably scatter seeds which might ultimately "ripen into collision between France and the United States and other American republics." It was intimated to Seward that the early acknowledgment of Maximilian's government by this country would tend to shorten, or perhaps to end, the French occupation of Mexico. To this intimation he replied that the French government had been already informed that in the opinion of the United States the permanent establishment of a foreign and monarchical government in Mexico would be found neither easy nor desirable; that this opinion remained unchanged; and that, so long as the United States continued to regard Mexico as the theatre of a war, which had not yet ended in the subversion of the existing republican government with which this country remained in relations of peace and friendship, we were not at liberty to consider the question of recognizing a government which, in the further chances of war, might come into its place.

In all his diplomatic correspondence after the recognition of the Confederates as belligerents by Great Britain, Seward was hampered by a sense of the possibility of a combination between one or more of the great maritime powers with the insurgents, and an apprehension of the probable effect of such a combination upon our contest for the preservation of the Union; and his efforts were directed to preserving peace with all other nations without impairing the dignity of his own country. He had stated with entire frankness, and with unmistakable distinctness, though in courteous language, our position as to the French intervention in Mexico, yet had been careful to avoid using any expressions which could be construed into a threat, or give France an opportunity for breaking with us. The members of the legislative department of the government were not so wise. Resolutions upon this subject were introduced into both the House and Senate in the winter of 1864. In the Senate they were laid on the table on the motion of Sumner, who said that if they meant anything, if they were not mere words, they meant war. The House, however, voted that they were unwilling by silence to "leave the world under the impression that they were indifferent spectators of the deplorable events transpiring in the republic of Mexico, and thought fit to declare that it did not accord with the policy of the United States to acknowledge any monarchy erected in America upon the ruins of any republic, under the auspices of any European power."

This action naturally excited the French government, and brought from it the direct inquiry to our minister, "Do you mean peace or war?" When this question was put to him he had heard nothing from home, and could only answer that the terms of the resolution were opposed to the instructions contained in his dispatches. The French government, however, considered the resolves as a serious matter, and the secessionists in Paris were jubilant until some days later a dispatch was received, in which Seward said, that the question of the recognition of a monarchy in Mexico was a purely executive one, the decision of which constitutionally belonged "not to the House of Representatives, or even to Congress, but to the President of the United States;" that, while the President received a declaration from the House of Representatives with the respect to which it was entitled, he did not contemplate any departure from the policy he had hitherto pursued as to France and Mexico; and that the French government would be seasonably apprised of any change which he might at any future time think proper to adopt.[1] Fortunately this declaration calmed the French government, and the new war, which Congress seemed to court, without considering that in all probability it might have been fatal to our success in the struggle we had already on hand, was averted by the good sense of the President and Seward.

Maximilian never obtained the popular vote calling him to the throne, upon which he had at first insisted as a condition precedent to his acceptance of the crown. He went to Mexico in the summer of 1864. Negotiations were had from time to time between this government and France to in-

---

[1] April 7, 1864. *Dip. Corr.*, 1865, pt. 3, pp. 356–357. See, also, Williams v. Suffolk Ins. Co., 3 Sumner, 372, 13 Peters, *U. S. Sup. Ct. Reports*, p. 415.

duce the emperor to withdraw his troops. After the collapse of the Confederacy, attempts were made to persuade the administration to force France to withdraw her troops at once; but Seward thought it wiser to give her the opportunity to act in the matter, in appearance at least, upon her own judgment, and not under compulsion. He succeeded in doing this. The French troops were gradually withdrawn during the year 1867, without our having assumed any position which could wound the pride of our old Revolutionary ally. When they left, Maximilian declined to desert his Mexican supporters. He was captured by the republican army. Seward interfered in vain to procure his release and liberty to return to Europe; the soldiers insisted on his execution, and the Mexican President did not dare to refuse their demand.

If among Seward's dispatches during the course of the war there are some that deal with generalities, and seem prolix and dull, yet his discussions of the actual questions submitted to him are open to no such criticism. They are vigorous, simple, direct, and to the point, and always manly and dignified. Lord Russell said no more than the truth, when he spoke of the singular and varied ability exhibited in them. They are a credit to American diplomacy, a monument to Seward's unwearied powers of work, and to his intellectual capacity and resources.

Tried by its results, the success of his diplomacy during the four years of Lincoln's administration is entitled to the highest praise. We were engaged in a domestic struggle which was taxing our resources to the utmost, and in which we had not the cordial good-will of a single one of the great nations of the world, unless it were Russia. The opportunities for differences with these countries were numerous, the dangers of the interference or intervention of one or more of them, or of the outbreak of a war between us and any one of them, were almost constant. Seward conducted us safely through all these perils, with no breach of the peace and no sacrifice of the honor or dignity of the country.

CHAPTER XXI

SECRETARY OF STATE UNDER JOHNSON — RETIREMENT FROM PUBLIC LIFE

THE Union troops entered Richmond on the 3d of April, 1865. Two days later Seward was thrown from his carriage; his right shoulder was dislocated, his jaw broken on both sides, and he was otherwise so badly injured that for a time his life was despaired of. Nine days afterwards, late at night, when only his nurse and daughter were with him, an unknown man succeeded in entering the house, burst open the door of his chamber, rushed to his bedside, and with a bowie-knife slashed and stabbed him in the face and throat, till, alarmed by the wakening household, the would-be assassin hastened to escape, fled through the open door, mounted his horse, and rode away. This assault was one act in the conspiracy of which the supreme tragedy was the murder of Lincoln in the theatre.

Seward survived; but for more than a year he was compelled to wear mechanical appliances to retain the broken jaw in its place. Before he could leave his bed he insisted on trying to work, and scrawled on scraps of paper directions for his letters; so soon as he could be moved he was carried daily to his chair in the State Department, where he sat, the shrunk, maimed, and disfigured semblance of his former self. The injuries which he survived brought on him the great sorrows of his life. Mrs. Seward, who had been for some time an invalid, hastened from Auburn to Washington on learning of his accident. On the night of the assault she was roused by the screams of her daughter, and rushing from her room found her husband in the state we have described. The shock was too much for her; she survived it only two months, dying on the 21st of June. The tributes of praise to her knew no exception. Seward's friends and foes alike recognized her charm and her worth, and knew that for him the loss was irreparable. But this was not the only life that was sacrificed to the assault upon him. His only daughter, who, next to her mother, was the person dearest and most important to him, was in his room, saw the attack, his struggles and attempts, in spite of his feebleness, to shield her from any blows, and the scenes of that night killed her. She lived little more than a year; and her death left Seward very desolate.

Though for some days after his injuries Seward's life was in great danger, yet thanks to his vigorous constitution, his unfailing courage, his excellent physical condition, and his equable temperament, his recovery was rapid, and less than four weeks after the attack on him he was able to

receive the President and cabinet at his house.
In this short time there had been a revolution in
our political world. The Southern Confederacy
had ceased to exist, its government had collapsed,
its officials were dispersed, its soldiers had been
paroled and sent home by our victorious generals.
The questions of the true relation of all the seceding States to the Union, and of the proper treatment of these States, had therefore to be dealt with
at once, — whilst their secession had been more
gradual, some of them having been the ringleaders
in rebellion, and others having followed with more
or less reluctance and hesitation. It had been
Mr. Lincoln's idea that no uniform rule should be
established, to be applied indiscriminately to the
rehabilitation of all these States; but that each
one should be treated as seemed wisest with reference to its own people and condition, without
regard to the others, always bearing in mind the
declared object of the contest on our part, — "the
maintenance and preservation of the Union," —
and troubling ourselves as little as possible with
theories as to the effect of their attempted secession upon the relations of these States to the federal government. He also believed that it was
for him, as President, to determine when the rebellion had been so far crushed that military rule
could come to an end, the troops be withdrawn,
the ordinary machinery of civil government put in
motion, and the State left to itself; each house
of Congress having, as to any of the States in

rebellion, the same constitutional right that it has as to all the States, to be "the judge of the elections, returns, and qualifications of its own members." He had already put in practice in Louisiana a scheme which seemed to him satisfactory for that State, and two representatives chosen there in the autumn of 1862 had been admitted as members of Congress in February of the following year. A similar experiment was tried in Arkansas about the same time.

In his annual message in December, 1863, the President made a full statement of what he had done to bring about the resumption of the national authority in the States where it had been suspended, and transmitted with the message a copy of an amnesty proclamation, granting a pardon to those persons concerned in the rebellion, who would take an oath to support the Constitution of the United States, the Union of the States thereunder, and all acts of Congress with reference to slaves passed during the rebellion, "so long and so far as not repealed, modified, or held void by Congress, or by decision of the Supreme Court." Six classes of persons were excepted from the promised pardon. Whenever in any of the States in rebellion a number of voters, not belonging to any of the excepted classes, and equal to ten per cent. of those voting for President in 1860, should have taken the required oath, he was willing to trust them to form a state government, and, if it were such a republican government as the Constitution provides that the United States shall guarantee to every State in the Union, to recognize it as the true government of the State. He was careful to say that he did not intend this to be a Procrustean bed to which exact conformity was indispensable, and that he would by no means exclude consideration and adoption of other plans.

The message and proclamation were not well received by Congress. There was a general feeling of irritation that the President should have assumed upon his own responsibility the initiative and power of decision in a matter which, it was said, was either exclusively a subject for legislation, or one about which Congress should at least have been consulted. In the Senate Sumner offered a resolution declaring that a State pretending to secede from the Union, and "battling against the general government to maintain that position, must be regarded as a rebel State subject to military occupation, and without representation . . . until it has been re-admitted by both houses of Congress." The Senate was not yet ready for so strong a statement, and a resolve that "the rebellion was not so far suppressed in Arkansas as to entitle that State to representation in Congress" was substituted and passed. The definitive action, however, in reply to the President, was a bill, — the first reconstruction act, — passed on the last day of the session, July 4, 1864. This act required the President to appoint a provisional governor for each of the States which had been declared in rebellion, who, when military resistance ceased, should make an enrollment of the white male citizens. If a majority of them should take an oath to support the Constitution, the governor was to order an election of delegates for a constitutional convention. This convention was to declare on behalf of the people of the State their submission to the Constitution of the United States, and also to insert in the constitution to be framed for the State, articles providing that no office-holder under the Confederate government, except civil officers merely ministerial and military officers of inferior grades, should ever vote for, or be, either governor or a member of the state legislature; that no rebel war debt, state or Confederate, should ever be paid, and that slavery was forever prohibited. When a constitution containing these provisions should have been adopted by a majority of the popular vote, the governor was to certify the fact to the president, and the president, after receiving the assent of Congress, was to recognize the state government as established.

This act was not signed by Mr. Lincoln, and a few days after the adjournment of Congress, he made public his reasons for this, which were, that he was not willing to commit himself to one inflexible plan of restoration; or to discourage and repel the loyal citizens of Louisiana and Arkansas, and set aside their free state [1] governments; or

---

[1] Slavery had already been abolished in both these States by constitutional amendments.

to declare Congress constitutionally competent to abolish slavery in the States. He said, however, that if any States chose to adopt the plan proposed in the bill, he would render them all possible executive assistance and would appoint military governors to act according to its provisions. Wade of the Senate, and Henry Winter Davis of the House, replied to the President in a paper personally vituperative; and reflecting on his motives, which the country knew to be above suspicion. Lincoln was reëlected. Congress at its next session (February 4, 1865) passed a joint resolve declaring certain States not entitled to representation in the electoral college. This resolve excluded Arkansas and Louisiana, and was intended as a rebuke to the President. It was sent to him for his signature. He returned it, signed, but with a message stating that he signed it "in deference to the views implied in its passage and presentation," though he thought Congress had complete power to exclude all electoral votes which it deemed illegal, and that the President could not by his veto obstruct or defeat the exercise of this power. He disclaimed all right of interference, and said that by his signature he expressed no opinion on the recital of the preamble, and no judgment upon the subject of the resolve.

This short statement shows the substance of what had been done in the way of reconstruction before Lincoln's death, and makes sufficiently clear the radical difference already existing between the

President and Congress, and the measures adopted by Congress to assert and maintain its right of control in the matter of reconstruction. Lincoln was very desirous to avoid a personal issue, and willing to make any concessions which did not involve a sacrifice of his convictions, or of what he believed to be the prerogatives and duties of his office. In his last public utterance, only a few days before his death, he reaffirmed his faith in the wisdom and justice of his course, and his conviction that any inflexible plan of reconstruction would be a mistake. He had originally called for troops to suppress a resistance to the execution of the laws, too powerful to be overcome by the ordinary judicial processes. There is no question that it is for the president alone to determine when the emergency has arisen which authorizes him to require the aid of the soldiery for this purpose; and in the absence of any express provision of law, it seemed to Lincoln a legitimate conclusion, that it was also for him to decide when the exigency had ceased and the enforcement of the laws could safely be left to the civil authorities; and that it was his duty, therefore, to ascertain, by whatever means seemed to him best adapted for the purpose, the facts necessary for his decision upon this point.

All that Lincoln did as to reconstruction may be explained and justified as being the means he adopted to satisfy himself as to the public opinion and temper of the South, and to determine whether

the troops could be withdrawn, and the execution
of the laws of the United States safely intrusted
to the ordinary civil government. To secure this
it was necessary that the leading men of the South
should accept without reservation all the results of
the failure of their attempted revolution, should
honestly endeavor to make the best of the situation, should be ready to take the hand that Lincoln
was holding out to them, and to coöperate heartily
with him to bring about the harmonious restoration
of the Union. If they would not do this, either
they must be disfranchised and the work intrusted
to less competent hands, or the military rule must
be prolonged until there should be some satisfactory security that the rebel States had not merely
laid down their arms, but that they would not try
to evade the new conditions imposed upon them
by the emancipation of their slaves and the abolition of slavery. Possibly, if Lincoln had lived,
their confidence in his candor, his integrity, his
magnanimity and kindliness, aided by his own rare
tact and knowledge of men, might have caused
his plan to be honestly accepted by the Southern
leaders. If he had succeeded in this, it is more
than probable that he would have had the support
of a majority in the thirty-ninth Congress (March
4, 1865, to March 4, 1867), which, as we shall see,
was at first induced with some difficulty to overrule
Johnson's vetoes; if his plan had not worked satisfactorily, he would have been open-minded enough
to recognize its failure, and wise enough to modify

or even to abandon it, as the case might require.
Whether he would ever have assented to imposing
upon the South the emancipated slaves as voters
is more doubtful. He would not have excluded
any one from the ballot on account of his color;
but he never went farther than to suggest that it
was worthy of consideration whether the franchise
might not be conferred as a special privilege on
some of the more capable and deserving of the
colored citizens. He would have been extremely
reluctant to subject the white population of the
South to what he would have realized they must
feel as so gross a wrong and humiliation, or to
impose on them as voters an ignorant proletariat
of a different race, the mass of whom were totally
unfit for the ballot, whose number in all the seceding States taken together was only one fifth less
than that of the whites, while in three of them it
was actually greater. In the end Congress gave
the colored people the ballot, as essential to their
protection; but the race problem at the South,
even though the outlook should be thought hopeful, is by no means yet settled.

There were persons both in Congress and in the
country who thought that the accession of Johnson
to the presidency would save us from the consequences of what seemed to them Lincoln's ill-ad-
vised leniency and trust. A caucus of politicians
holding these views was held on the very day of
Lincoln's death, to consider the questions of a
new cabinet and of a less conciliatory policy; and

on the next morning the chairman of the reconstruction committee said to the new President: "Johnson, we have faith in you. By the gods, there will be no trouble now in running the government."

Both before and after his inauguration, Johnson had talked of treason as a crime to be punished, and this and similar sayings of his had created an impression that he would make harder terms with the States in rebellion, before permitting them to get back into their "proper practical relations with the Union," than Lincoln would have done. But no such inference is fairly to be drawn from what he had said. He was speaking, not of harshness to communities, but of the punishment of individuals, and hoped for convictions for treason just as he desired the condemnation of Mr. Lincoln's assassins. The legal and practical difficulties in the way of obtaining such convictions he realized later.

The thirty-eighth Congress had expired with the close of Lincoln's first administration; and unless the President should call an extra session, it would be nearly nine months before the new Congress met. Johnson did not call it together sooner; in this he followed the plan of Mr. Lincoln, who had thought it fortunate that there was to be so long an interval between the end of the rebellion and the coming together of Congress. Johnson's constitutional opinions were well known. He believed the Union intact, and that it included

as well the States which had undertaken to secede
as those which had remained loyal. "It is the
doctrine of the Constitution," he had said, "that
no State can go out of this Union, and moreover
Congress cannot eject a State from this Union."
He had resigned his seat in the Senate of the
United States, and gone to Tennessee at Mr. Lincoln's solicitation, as military governor, to facilitate the resumption by that State of her proper
relations to the federal government; he had initi-
ated the measures necessary for this purpose, accepting and acting upon the policy which Lincoln
had employed in Louisiana, — that civil government should be substituted for military rule whenever armed resistance had ceased, and the president, as commander-in-chief, was satisfied that
the people of a State were prepared loyally to accept and abide by the results of the struggle, however bitter they might feel them to be.   It would
have been impossible for Johnson to hold any
other opinion upon the constitutional questions
involved in the rebellion.   Only upon the theory
that Tennessee, in spite of the ordinance of secession, was still an integral part of the Union could
he properly have retained his seat as senator from
that State, or been nominated and elected as vice-
president, or be now discharging the duties of
president of the United States.   This opinion was
not the outcome of his controversy with Congress;
it was his settled conviction before any controversy
arose, and it governed all his official action on the

different reconstruction measures that came before him.

Early in May, 1865, he issued a proclamation announcing that hostilities had ceased. Three weeks later he published a proclamation of amnesty, the terms of which were identical with those granted by Lincoln, except that he added seven more to the classes of persons excluded from the benefits of the former proclamation. No criticisms were made as to any of these additions, unless it be as to the last, which shut out from the right to a pardon "all voluntary participants in the rebellion having more than twenty thousand dollars worth of taxable property." He has been charged with having inserted this for the purpose of striking at a class of men "whom he personally hated;" but the accusation seems unjust. This exception would not strike the aristocratic slaveholders, who had lost everything by the extinction of slavery, and of whom Johnson might personally complain, but the prosperous business men and traders, earnest Southern sympathizers, active and influential in promoting the rebellion, of whom Johnson had just had experience in Tennessee, who were not included in any of the previously excepted classes, but who were in his opinion equally undeserving of pardon.

There was also added to this proclamation a clause that special application for pardon might be made by any one belonging to the excepted classes, and that such clemency would be extended

him as might be "consistent with the facts of the
case and the peace and dignity of the United
States." It has been said that this clause was inserted at Seward's instance, and that he favored
it for various petty reasons, as it is also asserted
that he resisted as long as he could the previous
clause excepting men of property. What foundation there may be for these assertions it is difficult
to ascertain, but the imputation of low motives is
a purely gratuitous aspersion. The final clause
is an extremely proper one, and should not have
been omitted. It was substantially copied by Congress when it had succeeded in obtaining control
of the whole subject of reconstruction;[1] and the
reasons for its insertion were in each case the same.
That the clemency sanctioned by this clause was
abused is unquestionable; but this would not
justify omitting the clause itself. The pardoning
power is often unwisely exercised, but the necessity for its existence is everywhere recognized; and
it cannot be denied that Congress as well as the
President made mistakes as to some of the persons
restored to the rights of citizenship.

On the day that this proclamation was issued,
Johnson appointed a provisional governor for North
Carolina, and before the middle of July had made
similar appointments for the other rebel States for
whose government there were no existing provisions. These officers were directed to take measures to call conventions to be composed of dele-

[1] Fourteenth Amendment to Constitution, Sec. iii.

gates chosen by the loyal voters of the respective
States. These voters were defined to be those
persons, possessing the qualifications required by
the laws of the State before its secession, who were
entitled to the benefits of the amnesty proclamation, and who had taken the prescribed oath.
These requirements followed the precedents established by Lincoln in Louisiana, Arkansas, and
Tennessee, and restricted the suffrage to white
men. The object of each convention was declared
to be to secure to its State that republican form
of government guaranteed by the Constitution of
the United States; the insurrection having de-
prived the States in rebellion of all recognized
civil governments. The convention, or the subsequent legislature in each State, was to prescribe,
it was said by the President, "the qualifications
of electors, and the eligibility of persons to hold
office under the constitution and laws of the State,[1]
*a power the people of the several States composing
the federal Union have rightfully exercised from
the origin of the government until the present
time.*"

This last sentence emphasizes one point in the
differences between Congress and himself. The
bill of the previous July had insisted that the state
constitutions to be adopted must provide that no
Confederate officer of rank or importance, civil or
military, should ever vote for, or be, governor, or

---

[1] Lincoln took a similar view as to the work of the Louisiana
convention. *N. & H.* viii. p. 434.

a member of the legislature; and the President now declared that in his opinion these were matters to be determined not by congressional dictation, but, as they always had been, by the several States, each for itself, and that the Southern States had not by the rebellion lost the right to do this. Both the President and Congress, however, were agreed that something was required, as proof that the rebellion was really over, before the troops could be properly withdrawn and the people of any seceding State be permitted to organize a civil government and resume their old relations to the Union; they were also agreed that some oath should be required of these people. The President during this summer had further insisted with each of these States upon its abolition of slavery, its ratification of the thirteenth constitutional amendment, which forever prohibited slavery, and its absolute repudiation of all rebel war debts, declaring that he could "not recognize the people of any State as having resumed the relations of loyalty to the Union, who admitted the legality of obligations contracted or debts created in their name to promote the war of the rebellion."

In all that he was doing the President assumed to act in the exercise of the war power, and by virtue of his authority as commander-in-chief. For any legislation by Congress authority must be found either in the Constitution itself, — where the only clause which seemed to have any bearing on the matter was that which makes each house the judge of the elections, returns, and qualifications of its own members, — or in the assumption that the seceding States had forfeited all their constitutional rights, were to be treated like any conquered people, and that therefore Congress had absolute authority over them. This assumption is the ground upon which the constitutionality of the reconstruction act of March 2, 1867, is to be defended; yet in this very act Congress showed its want of confidence in the soundness of this theory. It recognized these States as constituent members of the Union for the purpose of voting on the fourteenth constitutional amendment, while with a palpable inconsistency it denied them their right of representation, unless they voted in a particular way. This theory was originally propounded by Thaddeus Stevens in the House and by Sumner in the Senate, in the resolve already quoted. It was never thoroughly accepted even in Congress, was not sustained by the Supreme Court, was never believed in by Lincoln, and was denied by many leading statesmen and jurists.[1]

To get the votes of those who could not accept Stevens' theory, the reconstruction acts were declared to be an exercise of authority under that clause of the Constitution by which the United States is to guarantee to every State in the Union a republican form of government. This declaration afterward found support in the opinion of Chief Justice Chase in Texas v. White (7 Wallace, 700). To maintain this view, however, seems to oblige one to do violence to the natural and obvious meaning of this clause, and to give it an effect certainly never contemplated by the makers of the Constitution.

It has been asserted that Johnson, after he became president, changed his whole opinion of the proper policy to be pursued towards the seceding States, and that this change was owing to Seward's persuasive powers and the immense influence he had thereby acquired over the President.[1] The two statements depend on each other; if there was no such change in the President, then it was certainly not caused by Seward's influence. The real difficulty with Johnson was exactly the opposite one, — the obstinacy with which he adhered to his policy towards the South, after it became evident that it was a mistake and a failure. The persons who charge the President with reversing his entire policy towards the South have confounded two things which Johnson himself kept quite distinct, the proper treatment of individual wrongdoers, the leaders in rebellion, for whom he thought no punishment too severe, and the leniency to be shown to the communities who had followed their guidance, whom he was always disposed to treat with the utmost consideration. His opinions upon constitutional questions were those he had maintained before his election as vice-president. He believed that the Union was indissoluble; that the Constitution secured certain rights to the States as well as to the federal government; that though the exercise of these rights on the one side or the

---

[1] This is the view of Mr. Blaine; but General Grant, whose relations with the President entitle his conclusions to much more weight, "thought the plan the child of Johnson's own brain."

other might be for a time suspended or prevented, the rights themselves could not be forfeited or lost; and his course as president and all his vetoes were not merely consistent with this view, they depended upon it and were its logical outcome. In appointing provisional governors of the several rebel States, and in all that he did towards bringing them back to their true position as an integral part of the Union, he believed himself to be carefully following in Lincoln's footsteps. He undoubtedly hoped and expected in this way to convert repentant rebels into loyal Unionists; yet before Congress met, he had ample evidence, if he had chosen to heed it, that the Southerners were neither loyal nor submissive, but absolutely unregenerate and untrustworthy. Had he been a man of a different nature he would have seen this, and would have modified his treatment of them when he found that it was resulting in the restoration of authority to insurgents, who, while laying down their arms, retained their hostility to the government that had compelled their submission. But he had neither the perception, nor the flexibility, nor the breadth of mind necessary for this. He was a person essentially narrow, obstinate, and conceited, was coarse and vulgar, and possessed of a very bad temper which caused him to lose his head when it got the mastery. Like many common men he was conscious of his defects, very sensitive to ridicule or to any mark of disrespect, and easily affected by attentions or even gross flattery. He had made an unfortunate exhibition of himself on inauguration day, and never forgot that Sumner had urged that, in consequence of this, he should be requested to resign. His first message in December, 1865, shows, however, that he had then no wish or expectation of quarreling with Congress. But in little more than a month after the beginning of the session, a resolution offered by a Republican, expressing confidence in the President and in his coöperation with Congress in restoring to their equal position and rights the States lately in insurrection, was buried by sending it to the committee on reconstruction; and Johnson felt most keenly the indignity thus offered him by his own party.

In his message in December the President had stated correctly the alternative modes of dealing with the Southern States. Either they must be retained under military subjection for a period longer or shorter as circumstances might require, or they must be brought back into practical relations with the Union, as quickly as possible, by methods which necessarily implied a trust in the loyalty of the people. The objections to the former scheme were, that it was opposed to all our ideas as to the right of self-government, and that it assumed that the seceding States were practically out of the Union, and the South a conquered country over which we had full power. The objections to the latter course were, that it seemed to impose no penalty on rebellion, and that its

success depended upon the existence at the South
of a sufficient body of people loyal to the United
States, and prepared to accept the results of the
war.   Lincoln and Johnson both believed in the
existence of such a body, large enough to form
and organize state governments and to serve as
a nucleus round which the mass of the citizens
would crystallize.   Time showed that they were
mistaken in this belief, and that the four years of
war had substantially extinguished for the time
the Union sentiment in the seceding States, as it
had destroyed the peace Democracy at the North.
The congressional plan of reconstruction, which
was finally adopted, assumed that the North had
prevailed in a war of conquest, and had the con-
querors' right to deal with the Southerners as a
subjugated people.   Johnson opposed this plan by
all the means in his power.   The contest between
him and Congress was most bitter; it was carried
on by vetoes on the one side, and by the passage
of bills over these vetoes on the other, by attacks
of the President on Congress in various public
addresses, while in Congress there were attacks
upon him, equally bitter and unjustifiable, which
resulted in an impeachment and a trial, upon
which no man not a partisan can reflect without a
sense of shame.

Before Lincoln's death an act of Congress had
established the freedmen's bureau.   Early in 1866
a bill was passed enlarging the powers of this
bureau, and extending the period of its existence.

This bill the President vetoed on constitutional and other grounds, and his veto was sustained. A second bill was then introduced, drawn not with a view to overcoming the President's objections and obtaining his approval, but with regard to the ability to pass it over his veto, which was done on the same day that the veto message was received (July 16, 1866). "It required, however, potent persuasion reinforced by the severest party discipline to prevent a serious break in both houses against the bill," and to carry it over the veto.

In April, before the passage of this act, a civil rights bill, giving to the colored people in every State equal civil rights with the whites, had also been passed over the President's veto; but to secure the majority required to do this, it had been found necessary to unseat by a strict party vote a Democrat, who would otherwise have retained his place in the Senate, and to insist upon a vote, when one of the Republicans who sided with the President was ill and unable to be in his seat. In December, 1865, Congress had passed the thirteenth amendment to the Constitution. This prohibited slavery everywhere. In June, 1866, they passed the fourteenth amendment, which declared all persons born or naturalized here to be citizens, prohibited any State from abridging their privileges or immunities, and proportionally reduced the representation in Congress and in the electoral college of any State which denied to any of its male citizens the right of suffrage. This amendment also prohibited any person who, having taken an oath to support the Constitution of the United States, had engaged in insurrection, from holding any office under the United States or in any State, unless this disability should have been removed by a two-thirds vote of both houses of Congress. The proposed amendment was no affair of the President's, but he very unwisely sent to Congress a message expressing his disapproval of it.

By a series of offensive speeches, beginning on Washington's Birthday and culminating in those which he delivered at various places during a summer tour in 1866, Johnson had succeeded in utterly disgusting the people, and had wholly lost the confidence of the country. The autumn elections went decidedly against him, and gave to his opponents a free hand. In the following year Congress passed the military reconstruction bill, which laid down the conditions required of any State to obtain the admission of its senators and representatives to Congress, and the counting of its votes in the electoral college. These conditions were: the adoption of a constitution which granted universal suffrage, which abolished slavery forever, which prohibited the payment of any rebel war debt, which secured absolute equality between all classes of citizens; and the ratification by the State of both the thirteenth and fourteenth amendments to the Constitution. To these was added one further condition. No State in insurrection was to be admitted to representation in Congress or in the electoral college until the thirteenth and fourteenth amendments had become part of the Constitution by the ratification of two thirds of the States. Meantime the Southern States were divided into various military districts, several States being united for this purpose, and placed under a single commander. This bill was vetoed by the President, but was passed over the veto.

This was the plan of reconstruction which was finally carried out. Whether it would have worked satisfactorily had the President and Congress been cordially at one in endeavoring to promote its success, is uncertain. Before it was adopted the President's plan had failed. Unrepentant rebels had got control of state governments which he had recognized; there were outrages and riots, and, though slavery had been technically abolished, vagrant and apprentice laws had been passed in several of the Southern States, the purpose and effect of which was to reduce the colored people to a condition analogous to that from which they were supposed to have been freed. The seceding States at last accepted the terms which Congress had prescribed, but only because they found there was no escape from doing so, if they wished to be represented in the House and Senate. In 1868 they all, with the exception of Virginia, Mississippi, and Texas, yielded to the requirements of the law, and the three States last named made their submission in 1870. Although the States had accepted these conditions for the purpose of obtaining their old rights, they felt that they were not bound to observe in good faith the obligations which had been forced upon them, and for several years they resorted to all sorts of expedients to deprive the freedmen of the free and fair exercise of the suffrage to which they were legally entitled. The success of the congressional reconstruction scheme was therefore by no means an unqualified one. It was disapproved of at the time by some of the leaders and by a number of the members of the Republican party, and it had a considerable influence in inducing many of the most conservative of them to join at last the ranks of the Democracy.

Though the President's reconstruction policy was not inspired by Seward, but had its origin in Johnson's own convictions as to the proper construction of the Constitution and the true position of the seceding States, and was in harmony with that which he had with Lincoln's approval pursued in Tennessee, yet it was the logical sequel of the doctrines reiterated by Seward again and again in his dispatches as secretary of state.[1]

It would have been obviously impossible for Seward, after having labored for four years to

[1] In Senator Sherman's *Recollections*, published since this chapter was written, he says: "After this long lapse of time I am convinced that Mr. Johnson's scheme of reconstruction was wise and judicious." [Vol. i. p. 361.] Was it not the hostility between Congress and the President, rather than Johnson's policy, that encouraged the subdued secessionists to try to evade the legislation of four years and escape the consequences of their unsuccessful rebellion?

satisfy the governments of Europe that the Union was intact, that we were engaged in quelling an insurrection and were not embarked in a war of conquest, to deny his own instructions and assent to the new congressional theories and to the legislation which followed them. He thought the course of Congress unwise as well as unconstitutional; he knew the President's honesty of purpose and hoped to restrain his impetuosity of speech or to modify its consequences; he believed in the soundness of his constitutional views and the correctness of his vetoes; he regretted extremely the dissensions which had arisen from the differences of opinion as to the best mode of reconstruction; but did not consider these differences or dissensions as of primary importance. He had no doubt that the States which had ceased their resistance in the field would in some way, after no long delay, come again into the full enjoyment of their privileges as members of the Union; and that time would not merely heal the wounds of the war, but would also efface any bitterness which might follow the harsh measures of Congress; and so believing, he was not a violent partisan of either party. Speaking at the Cooper Institute on Washington's Birthday, he said: "I am not here as an alarmist; I am not here to say that the nation is in peril or danger — in peril if you adopt the opinions of the President; in peril if you reject them; in peril if you adopt the views of the apparent or real majority of Congress, or if you reject them. Nor do I think the

cause of liberty and human freedom, the cause of
progress or civilization, the cause of national ag-
grandizement present or future, material or moral,
is in danger of being long arrested, whether you
adopt one set of political opinions or another.
The Union has been rescued from all its perils.
The noble ship has passed from tempest and bil-
lows within the verge of a safe harbor, without a
broken spar or a leak, starboard or larboard, fore
or aft. There are some small reefs yet to pass as
she approaches her moorings. One pilot says that
she may safely enter directly through them. The
other says that she must back, and, lowering sail,
take time to go around them. That is all the
difference of opinion between the pilots. I should
not practice my habitual charity if I did not admit
that I think them both sincere and honest. But
the vessel will go in safely, one way or the other.
The worst that need happen will be that, by taking
the wrong instead of the right passage, or even
taking the right passage and avoiding the wrong
one, the vessel may roll a little, and some honest,
capable, and even deserving politicians, statesmen,
president, or congressmen may get washed over-
board. I should be sorry for this, but if it cannot
be helped, it can be borne. If I am one of the
unfortunates, let no friend be concerned on that
account."

Seward remained in the cabinet, however, not
so much to take part in the process of reconstruction as because he wished to dispose of the diplo-

matic questions which the war had left unsettled, and thus to finish his work; he knew that he would have freedom of action in dealing with foreign powers, and thought it his duty under the circumstances to remain at his post, and there is no reason to suppose that he ever regretted doing so. The labors of his office he found much less onerous than during the war, and more fruitful and agreeable in their results. He made treaties with the various states of Central and South America for the settlement of all outstanding claims, and a convention with Nicaragua, containing stipulations for a transit between the Atlantic and Pacific oceans, the Nicaragua Canal. As has already been stated, the French were induced by negotiations, and without a resort to war on our part, to withdraw their troops from Mexico, and the republican government was reëstablished there, though its advent to power was stained by the execution of Maximilian, whose life Seward's exertions were unable to save.

The European governments had always denied the right of any native-born subject to cast off his allegiance to his own country and to become a citizen of an adopted one. Our naturalization laws permitted a foreigner to do this, and personal complications were constantly arising on account of this difference. Seward succeeded, at first with Prussia and afterwards with various other countries of Europe, in arranging this matter on a satisfactory basis. He also made a treaty with

the island of Madagascar which opened to us trade
and commerce there, and under which this country
absorbed about two thirds of the entire foreign
business of that island, and retained it until the
recent conquest and annexation of Madagascar by
France.

Any practical discussion of the Alabama claims
was negatived by Lord Russell's emphatic refusal
to admit England's liability on this account; this
matter therefore remained in abeyance until the
change of ministry in 1868. Mr. Adams had
resigned at the close of the previous year, and
Reverdy Johnson had been sent to England in his
place. He negotiated with Lord Clarendon a
treaty for the settlement of these claims, which
was known as the Johnson-Clarendon treaty. It
gave to the United States, in substance, all that
it got by the treaty of Washington; but it was
rejected by the Senate, upon the ground that it
belittled, by its form, the work to be done, ignored
the greater national grievances, and contained
no word of regret for the fact that American commerce had been swept from the sea by the rebel
cruisers, and for the enormous loss thus inflicted
on the country. Though the actual treaty failed to
be ratified, Seward had secured by it the essential
concession, — an admission of the principle of
arbitration for the settlement of our claims against
Great Britain for the losses occasioned by these
cruisers; and, this concession once made, a satisfactory treaty was sure sooner or later to follow.

The most important and successful treaty with which Seward's name will always remain associated, was that for the purchase of Alaska. To many people it seemed a wild and visionary scheme to annex, at the cost of more than seven millions of dollars, this frozen region of the north; but Mr. Sumner was induced to see both its political and pecuniary value, and he made these so clear to the Senate that the treaty was easily ratified. Subsequent events have justified its wisdom; Alaska has returned to the treasury of the United States many fold the original purchase money.

Another treaty to which Seward attached great importance, that for the purchase from Denmark of the island of St. Thomas in the West Indies, failed in the Senate, partly, one cannot but think, because of the bitter enmity of that body and its leaders to the President. We had suffered exceedingly during the whole civil war from the want of a foothold and a harbor of our own in the West Indies, which might serve as a coaling and naval station; and the great importance of a possession of this sort to us, in any war in which we might be either neutrals or belligerents, had been recognized by our military and naval commanders. St. Thomas fulfilled exactly the desired conditions. A small island, with a limited population, its purchase would give rise to no embarrassing questions as to how its people should be governed, or as to their participation in the public affairs of this country. It is poor in agricultural products and resources, but has a magnificent land-locked harbor; it was at that time the great commercial entrepôt for trade with Venezuela, Porto Rico, San Domingo, and Hayti, and the principal rendezvous for the steam packets of various important West India lines; it had a population two thirds Protestant, with a language almost exclusively English. The facts that its agricultural products were few, and that it suffered from time to time, like other tropical islands, from the violent disturbances of the elements, rendered it no less valuable or important to us for the purposes for which we required it.

This treaty had been much valued by Seward, and was vigorously championed by him, though it was not finally disposed of until after his term of office had expired. "It became a part of the great controversy between the Executive and Congress. The President and the State Department had negotiated this treaty, and therefore, if for no other reason, the Senate would not consent to it." [1] There were questions as to the price to be paid, and other financial considerations, which might have led to its rejection; but the judgment of practical experts like Secretary Fox and Admiral Porter, that the island would be of the greatest value and importance to us for naval purposes, is certainly entitled to far more weight than the opinions, however emphatic and decided, of those persons who had no such special knowledge or

[1] Dawes's *Sumner*, 282.

qualifications. The admiral and the secretary were both strenuous advocates of this treaty.

At the close of President Johnson's administration Seward resigned his office, and left Washington. "I never saw him," wrote a friend at this time, "more happy than he is now; so different (without his stilts) from what he has been the last ten years."

With short intervals of rest at home, the next two years and a half were spent by him in travel. He visited the western coast of America from Alaska to Lower California, crossed Mexico and returned by the West Indies, and later made a journey round the world, of which an account has been published, taken from his journals and dictation. After his return he passed the remainder of his days, either in his homestead at Auburn, or in his son's cottage on Owasco Lake. Here, with his strength gradually failing, his temper always serene and cheerful, his mind clear and untouched, he waited the slow approach of Death. At work in the morning with his adopted daughter on his notes of travel, he lay down to rest, and the end came. He died on the 10th of October, 1872.

It may not be entirely amiss here to say a word of Seward as a man. In all the relations of private life he was most admirable: a devoted husband, a kind and sympathetic father, a firm and loyal friend, an excellent neighbor and citizen. The bitter disappointment of the people of Auburn at his failure to receive the presidential nomination in 1860 showed the love they bore him. His optimism in politics and in life generally was not merely the result of a disposition naturally cheerful and buoyant, but of a firm faith in an overruling Providence. His industry was tireless, his capacity for work enormous. He often wrote far into the night, and during the years of his active practice as a lawyer the young men in his office would frequently find in the morning the floor of his room strewn with papers which he had written while they were asleep.

His political life stretched over a period of nearly forty years, occupied with the discussion and settlement of the most vital and exciting questions both by legislation and war. He has been charged with having no political convictions, but an examination of his public career seems to prove exactly the contrary. From first to last he was a consistent Whig. He believed in and advocated a protective tariff, internal improvements, and all the doctrines which formed the policy of that party. His hostility to slavery began with his life in Georgia, and what he saw there, while he was yet a mere lad. His opposition to it never ceased so long as slavery in any form was a political question; and he had the satisfaction, as secretary of state, of signing his name not merely to the Proclamation of Emancipation, but to both the constitutional amendments which secured to the colored people of this country complete civil equality

with the whites.   He was never, however, an abolitionist.   He was a steady and persistent advocate
of gradual and compensated emancipation.   From
his short life at the South he realized more fully
perhaps than any other Northern statesman the
enormous difficulties and embarrassments which
the sudden and violent freeing of the slaves would
bring about at the South, — the destruction of
property and the temporary ruin of all industries
which such an emancipation would be likely to
cause; and he had therefore a compassion for the
people of that region, rebels though they had been,
which people at the North could hardly understand.

He not only had convictions, but he had the
courage of his convictions, and did not hesitate to
separate himself from his friends, to oppose his
party, or to risk his own popularity in support of
these convictions.   His defense of the poor negro
Freeman is a striking example of this.   His political life is full of illustrations of the same quality.
His persistent support of what he regarded as
the rights of the Roman Catholics in the public
schools, and his opposition to the Know-nothing
party, which cost him his nomination at Chicago,
are marked instances of it.   His political contro-
versies never degenerated into personalities.   He
gave to his opponents the same credit for honesty
of conviction which he expected them to accord
to him, and numbered among his friends many of
those who in public life were his political opponents.   He was not a shrewd political manager;

he trusted to others to manage for him. Perfectly clean-handed himself, by the admission of those who had the least confidence in him, he may have permitted his political managers and friends to do what they thought was for his interest; but he knew very little about this; he surrendered himself entirely into their hands, and had to bear the consequences of their mistakes, as well as receive the benefit of their successes. The severest judgments on him came from members of his own party, from whom he happened to differ as to a particular measure or policy, who were not clear-sighted enough to see, as he did, that "one half the effort of the anti-slavery men was lost, because it consisted of the incrimination of other anti-slavery men for shades of difference of opinion; and that the field was broad enough for all."

He was most severely attacked, however, by the leaders of his own party for remaining in Johnson's cabinet; and they spoke of him and treated him as a traitor. It would have been easier and pleasanter for him to have resigned, but to abandon Johnson under the actual circumstances would have seemed to Seward like desertion, and he had to bring himself to bear, with such equanimity as he was master of, his old friends' avoidance of him. The cordial welcome he received and the honors paid him in all parts of the world during the next two years must have served to efface the recollection of this coldness and neglect. Though he never recovered his vigor of body after his injuries in 1865, the activity of his mind was inexhaustible. He planned his travels, lest "rest should mean rust," and with the thought that the study of mankind would be the most interesting and least fatiguing pursuit for him. He might have expected a kindly welcome in California, for whose admission as a free State he had labored in the Senate, and in Alaska, which he had made a part of our country. He might have looked for a friendly reception from the republican president of Mexico, who was largely indebted to him as secretary of state; but he could hardly have thought that from the day of his arrival until the day of his departure from that country he was to be, at every stage of his journey and at every resting place, not merely the government's, but the people's guest. There was apparently no hamlet so small that his name and fame had not preceded him there. Not the least grateful token of recognition that he received was in a village of cane huts, where the tall, swarthy headman handed into the carriage, with a profound bow, a scroll on which was written, "To the great statesman of the great Republic of the North. Techaluta is poor, but she is not ungrateful."

In the East he was everywhere received with the highest honors. The Mikado of Japan unveiled his face to him in a friendly audience, an honor said to have been never before bestowed on a foreigner; he also desired his ministers to converse with him on affairs of state, and it must have been gratifying to Seward to have been asked by them to observe that, in dealing with the vanquished party in a late rebellion, "the government of Japan had copied the example of toleration given them by the United States."

Throughout the entire East his reception was the same. His reputation had everywhere preceded him. The prince-regent of China rose from a sick-bed to visit him. The ministers of the various countries were eager to see and to talk with the distinguished statesman of the West, of whom they had heard so much; the European governors and native princes of India vied with each other in their attentions to him.

Seward's observation was quick and his perceptions acute, and he returned home with his mind stored with the results and experience of travel, and with new and healthful interests and occupations for the remainder of his days. In spite of his great sorrows and of his increasing infirmities, his last years were happy ones. Even in the busiest period of his life his own hearthstone had been always the place dearest to him, and now the companionship and affection of his children and grandchildren and the society of his lifelong friends and neighbors were the solace and enjoyment of his serene old age.

INDEX

INDEX

provements in, 22, 23; education in, 23; spoils system in, 24–26; McLeod case in, 28–31; controversy with United States, 30, 31; defeat of Whigs in, 39; decides election of 1844, 45, 47; decides election of 1848, 50, 55; campaign of Seward in, 50–52; elects Seward senator, 55; Fillmore and Seward factions in, 96; campaign of 1854 in, 138–140; carried by Know-Nothings, 142.

Nicaragua, treaty with, concerning canal, 391.

North, its intention in 1825 to work for emancipation stated by Seward, 10; its interpretation of squatter sovereignty, 64; reasons for its opposition to slavery extension, 71, 72; disappointed at Webster's 7th of March speech, 80; enraged at Fugitive Slave Law, 98, 99, 100; meetings in, to uphold law, 100; resistance in, to law, 101; weary of slavery agitation in 1852, 114; alarmed at Kansas-Nebraska bill, 127, 128; becomes consolidated in Congress of 1856, 149, 150; determines to save Kansas for freedom, 152; affected by Kansas outrages, 162; enraged by assault on Sumner, 164; its economic situation described by Seward, 190, 191; wishes to stop secession by concessions, 209; expects European sympathy in war with South, 271; its slowness leads Europe to consider disunion successful, 273, 274; tour of Seward in, to urge a fresh call for troops, 327.

North Carolina, reconstruction in, 377.

Nott, Dr. Eliphalet, his relations with Seward while at Union College, 3.

Ohio, Seward's tour in, during campaign of 1848, 51.

Palmerston, Lord, threatens war in case McLeod is executed, 28, 29; refuses an apology for Caroline case, 33; disapproves Russell's proposal to intervene with France between North and South, 321; agrees in 1862 to intervene, 324.

Peace Congress of 1861, 217.

Pickens, Francis W., interview of Lamon with, 247; expects Sumter to be evacuated, 247; asks commissioners for information, 247; promised a warning by Lincoln, 247, 248, 250.

Pickens, Fort, its successful relief, 234, 236.

Pierce, Franklin, nominated for president, 112; elected, 113, 114; his first message, 115; persuaded to favor Kansas-Nebraska bill, 118; appoints Reeder governor of Kansas, 153; replaces him by Shannon, 155; calls free-state organization treasonable, 156; replaces Shannon by Geary, 157; his policy condemned, 157, 158; denounced by Seward, 160, 161, 166.

Polk, James K., nominated for president in 1844, 44; orders Taylor to invade Mexico, 61; urges Congress to organize Territories, 62.

Popular sovereignty in Territories, doctrine of, announced by Cass, 64; different interpretations of, 64.

Porter, Admiral David D., on annexation of St. Thomas, 394.

Postage, cheap, efforts of Seward to secure, 104.

Protection, attempt of Whigs to make a party question in 1832, 18.

Prussia, naturalization treaty with, 391.

Pugh, George E., votes against Davis's resolutions on slavery, 189.

Raymond, Henry J., defeats Greeley for Whig nomination for governor, 140.

Reconstruction, Lincoln's plan of, 366–368, 371; first congressional bill for, passed, 368, 369; Lincoln's veto, 369, 370; controversy between Congress and Lincoln over, 369, 370; possibility of success of Lincoln's plan, 371–373; Johnson's plan of, 374–377, 381–384; carried out by Johnson, 377; congressional theory of, 380; controversy between Johnson and Congress over, 384–388; passage of freedman's bureau act over veto, 385; passage of civil rights

www.ingramcontent.com/pod-product-compliance
Lightning Source LLC
Chambersburg PA
CBHW030944110726
47900CB00004B/1116